P9-CPV-154

THE
CAMELOT
CONSPIRACY

A NOVEL

THE CAMELOT CONSPIRACY

DIANE / DAVID
MUNSON

FaithWalk
PUBLISHING
Grand Haven, Michigan

©2008 Diane Munson and David Munson
Published by FaithWalk Publishing
Grand Haven, Michigan 49417

All rights reserved. No part of this book may be reproduced or transmitted in any form by any means, electronic or mechanical, including photocopying and recording, or by any information storage and retrieval system, except as may be expressly permitted by the 1976 Copyright Act or by the publisher. Requests for permission should be made in writing to: FaithWalk Publishing, 101 Washington, PMB #305, Grand Haven, Michigan, 49417.

Scripture quotations, unless otherwise indicated, are taken from the HOLY BIBLE, NEW INTERNATIONAL VERSION®. NIV®. Copyright ©1973, 1978, 1984 by International Bible Society. Used by permission of Zondervan. All rights reserved.

This is a work of fiction. Names, characters, places, and incidents either are the product of the authors' imaginations or are used fictitiously. The authors and publishers intend that all persons, organizations, events and locales portrayed in the work be considered as fictitious.

Printed in the United States of America
13 12 11 10 09 08   7 6 5 4 3 2 1

Library of Congress Cataloging-in-Publication Data

Munson, Diane.
    The Camelot conspiracy / Diane and David Munson.
       p. cm.
    ISBN-13: 978-1-932902-74-7 (pbk. : alk. paper)
    ISBN-10: 1-932902-74-0
    1. Kowicki, Kat (Fictitious character)—Fiction. 2. Montanna, Eva (Fictitious character)—Fiction. 3. Topping, Griff (Fictitious character)—Fiction. 4. Women television journalists—Fiction. 5. United States. Federal Bureau of Investigation—Officials and employees—Fiction. 6. Kennedy, John F. (John Fitzgerald), 1917–1963—Assassination—Fiction. 7. Conspiracies—Fiction. 8. Presidents—Assassination—Fiction. I. Munson, David. II. Title.
    PS3613.U693C36 2007
    813'.6—dc22
                          2007025273

DEDICATION

To our family, whom we love.

"There is a time for everything,
and a season for every activity under heaven:
A time to weep and a time to laugh,
A time to tear and a time to mend,
A time to be silent and a time to speak,
A time to love and a time to hate,
A time for war and a time for peace.

He has made everything beautiful in its time.
He has also set eternity in the hearts of men,
Yet they can not fathom what God
Has done from beginning to end.
For God will bring every deed into judgment,
Including every hidden thing,
Whether it is good or evil."

Ecclesiasties 3:1, 4, 7–8, 11, 12:14 (NIV)

ACKNOWLEDGMENTS

Vital scenes from *The Camelot Conspiracy* take place in Pentwater, Michigan, which is a real and wonderful place. One of the great delights in writing this book was spending time there and meeting so many nice folks, including Police Chief Mike Schuitema, Karen Way from The Abbey B&B, Linda Watson from The Cottage Garden Cafe, Marilyn Cluchey from Pentwater Library, and MaryJo Neidow from the Candlewyk B&B. Your graciousness to us, plus all those special things that make Pentwater what it is, will be remembered.

Regarding the Kennedy assassination, we say thanks to Dennis Carlson, a JFK assassination aficionado and Roger Clouse, our expert on the Italian Mannlicher-Carcano rifle. The time you both took to listen to our theories and provide feedback was instrumental in developing the storyline.

Our deep appreciation goes to M.D. VanDeMae, M.D., who assisted in the medical aspects of the story. Thank you for your expertise and encouragement. May God continue to bless the work of your hands.

Sergeant John Hamilton, deserves thanks, not only for his help, but also for what he does everyday to further justice. To LTJG Jeremy Loeb, U.S. Coast Guard and Mel Marcus, Coast Guard Auxiliary, thank you and your colleagues for all you to do perform search and rescue on the Great Lakes. Thanks to Dave Helmholdt, our car doctor, for all your help. Lisa LaPlante, you were kind to answer our questions about what life and work were like for "Kat," our fictional television reporter. Thank you for your insights. To those of you who wanted "plausible deniability," your contributions helped us fashion certain aspects of the story, for which we are grateful.

To the FaithWalk Publishing crew, you are the best.

ONE

Summer, that longed-for season of kite flying, wave jumping, and building sandcastles on the beach, was scarcely eight hours old when the strange call came. The man's plea, and the suspicion it aroused in Eva Montanna's mind, eclipsed all thoughts of how best to keep three children occupied on a 12-hour car trip the next day. Her vacation with family on the shores of Lake Michigan could not come soon enough for Eva, but for the moment, she forgot all about it.

Before she could react, he repeated the extraordinary words, "Free me, *please.*"

His voice was a mere whisper, with a strong Spanish accent, and she had to press the receiver hard against her ear to hear the rest. Her mental calculations were quick. Might be a hoax or, more likely, the call was prompted by information leaked to the *Washington Star*, which appeared in that morning's edition, about how the FBI had infiltrated a mosque near Seattle.

Eva was a federal ICE agent, on loan to the Senate for a special assignment. Just two days before, the FBI briefed the Senate Committee on Intelligence, where she would work for the balance of the summer, about the secret operation. For the *Star* to now casually mention carefully guarded intelligence as if it were some accident report was more than alarming; it made her distrust everyone she worked with.

To decipher the caller's true intent, Eva tried flushing him out, a bird dog after a pheasant in the brush. "I want to help, but I can hardly hear you. What do you think I can do?"

She waited, and when a scratching sound was all she heard, she was tempted to hang up, telling herself that he was simply planting bogus information with the Committee. So far, he had claimed to be an 80-year-old prisoner who desperately wanted out. Well, so did thousands of others in jails across the country, and releasing convicts was not the job of the Senate.

As part of her Congressional Fellowship, Eva was helping the Senate on intelligence matters, her specialty, and though the call perplexed her, the receptionist *had* transferred the man to her. He insisted it was a matter of life and death. It was her job to see what she could do to aid him. Still, time was limited. In fourteen minutes, she had a hearing to attend.

Impatient, Eva said, "Sir, you must tell me more."

Static smothered some of his words, but then she barely made out, "I need a doctor who is not trying to kill me."

Was this nonsense or real? Never had she seen a case where the government tried to kill a prisoner. Eva was torn. It made sense to refer him to a human rights group and hang up; however, not one to let go of a mystery so quickly, she asked a question, hoping to clinch if he was legitimate. "How can you call from prison without dialing collect?"

"Nurse smuggled in a cell phone. They will find it, and take it away. God kept me alive to tell what I know." The effort to talk seemed to diminish his strength.

"*What* do you know?"

Breathing more heavily now, he gasped, "Not over the phone."

Eva stifled a sigh. Prisoners who claimed they had evidence of abuse, and who wanted to come to Washington to talk in person, were not rare. After all, cooperating with the government was a sure way to escape the confines of prison. Her reply was simply, "Why not?"

"Please, I am across the border from Guantanamo Bay."

He was in a *Cuban* prison? And using a cell phone to call her in Washington, D.C.? "Sir, if you can, tell me your name."

"Perhaps the U.S. Navy—" He faded away.

Eva stalled, still hoping for a name, anything to go on. "Can you call back at one o'clock?"

Again, he rallied. "My Abuela came to me in a dream. She told me children, hundreds, maybe thousands, would die if I do nothing. Can you get me out?"

That clinched it for Eva. A mother of three, she could dismiss him no longer. She had plenty of experience with life-changing dreams, the kind that shook her awake at night, where every fiber strained to know if it was hokum or a warning. Even if her caller was a quack, she had to take a chance that his story held a tiny grain of truth.

Because of the leaked article and today's hearing on national security, where Cuba was on the agenda, she should not move too quickly on the call, which might be a ruse to influence policy against the Communist dictator. That jolted her to reality. In minutes, Eva was due in the hearing room to give Senator Hernandez a list of questions.

A sigh, a stutter, "My name, I am, General Raul San Felipe, political prisoner of the regime—"

The connection cut off, she clicked her receiver. "Hello?"

No small tidbit of information, the General's call, if true, was even more astonishing than the leak about the FBI's case. Eva quickly gathered a sheaf of papers from her desk drawer, and was careful to close and lock it. As she grabbed her jacket and headed for her office door, she recalled an article in a Pentagon paper about General Raul San Felipe once being a confidant of Fidel Castro. In the 1970s the Cuban government jailed him as an enemy of the State. No doubt, he *was* real and Eva, now picturing a frail man in a weakened condition fighting for his life, felt enormous compassion.

But not quite belief, not yet. With dozens of questions and few answers, she reckoned it was probably nothing. After all, anyone could surf the Internet, make a phony call to the Senate. As she was about to leave the Sensitive Compartmented Information Facility, a supersecret office sealed against electronic signal penetration, she passed CIA agent Bo Ryder, who had recently returned from a foreign assignment that no one talked about openly.

Committee rumor had it that Bo's cover was blown in a world hot spot, so he flew home for his own protection. The sight of him, hair curling over his ears, head bent over a sudoku puzzle reminded her how sensitive her staff position was: She had the nation's classified operations at her fingertips and she had to be careful, for her sake, and her family's.

Eva hated to interrupt him. "Bo, if you're here later, someone claiming to be the Cuban General Raul San Felipe is calling back at one. I want you to talk to him."

Bo raised his eyebrows, gave her thumbs up. "It may seem like I'm goofing off, but actually, this is a new type of code."

It mattered not what he was doing, her mind was appraising how a Cuban political prisoner might change the dynamics of the National Threat Assessment hearing, to which she now hurried. She dug a Dutch peppermint from her pocket, calculating how, if it came to it, she would convince the CIA agent that General San Felipe was begging for freedom from a Cuban jail.

Her appetite for intrigue stoked, if the caller was for real Eva was inclined to launch a full-scale effort to smuggle the General out of Cuba. Her last undercover assignment—with FBI Agent Griff Topping and British MI-5 agent Brewster Miles—leaped into her mind. They had posed as scientists studying frankincense trees on a small island in the Indian Ocean to apprehend the vicious leader of a terror cell. A sudden feeling of excitement caught Eva off guard.

Outside the hearing room, Eva forced herself to stop and focus her thoughts. After the birth of their youngest son Martin, she and her husband Scott had agreed that such dangerous assignments were in the past. She dearly loved Scott and the kids—Andy, Kaley, and the baby they called Marty. While she had accepted the fact of working behind a desk, Eva now faced her season of discontent.

Another four months of simply giving technical advice to politicians, who hoped to convince the electorate they knew much about everything, would be an awful grind. The sooner she left the Senate and returned to her old job, where she could at least *supervise* challenging cases, the better.

She yanked open the door to the Senate hearing room where photographers were snapping pictures of Senators shaking hands with Wilt Kangas, the CIA's Deputy Director for Intelligence, who was about to testify. Her next thought gave Eva even more pause than her personal situation, as stagnant as that might be.

If the call from General San Felipe was real, could the American government smuggle him out without creating an international incident? Eva could not know that, before the onset of winter, her quest for this answer and others would lead her to question not only her life's work, but also the government she worked for.

MARY KATHERINE KOWICKI, known as Kat to those who saw her reports on network television, knew nothing about General San Felipe or his desperate call to escape from a Cuban prison. If she did, she certainly would not have been sitting in the crowded Senate hearing room, bored to the point of doodling on a pad, as a lone CIA witness made a rare public appearance to testify about the threat to America from worldwide terrorism.

What Kat did realize was that Wilt Kangas kept a wealth of secrets hidden behind words carefully chosen, the genuine facts locked in his mind or classified documents she could never access. Her gut told her the parade before her eyes was not the whole truth; it was not even close.

She clicked out lead on her mechanical pencil, chasing a story that did not exist. If only she could uncover the backstory, the one that certain men and women in power clawed to keep hidden, and which others leaked for political advantage. An hour before, at 8:30 a.m., cameras began broadcasting the Congressional hearing, allowing

Senator Lars Zorn to grab a megaphone and sound off to the outside world. This morning he was in rare form as he postured not just for constituents back home, but for the electorate at large, hoping to convince them that he had the stuff to be President.

Two things made it hard for Kat to report objectively about the Senator from California. Besides disgusting her with nearly everything he said or did, Zorn was waging a behind-the-scenes smear campaign against all potential candidates, while appearing to the public as the answer to their problems. His political expediency offended her; while lives were being lost to terrorism around the globe, here was Zorn, the Chairman of the Senate Intelligence Committee, lobbing one softball after another to Kangas, Deputy Director at the CIA.

"Mr. Kangas, Latin American drug cartels rise in power, but the current Administration does not have an effective plan to address it. What more can be done?"

The mundane question sealed her opinion. With Zorn at the helm, the country would be in ruins within one week. Unconcealed irritation darted over her pretty features. Many people told Kat that, because of her diminutive stature and soft brown eyes, she did not come across as a world-class reporter. Such unvarnished criticism irked her, made her even more hard-charging and determined.

Some things worked in her favor. Viewers flooded her station with emails saying they found her "refreshingly honest," and the colorful sneakers that matched her outfits were "a special touch." Today, clad in bright pink suit and shoes, a fragment of an idea formed in the recesses of her mind. Maybe this once she'd find a way to use her attributes to her advantage.

Kangas's reply, "When we meet in closed session, I will provide more details," was nothing but a smokescreen. Worse, toying with a pen on the green tablecloth, he looked tired of his job, or something. Kat wished she knew what the "something" was; perhaps then, she would get the explosive story she craved.

She had to admit, charts showing funds flowing to various countries deadened her senses, too. Still, Kat reasoned, Kangas should at least fake like he was on the ball, to secure his reputation for being a straight shooter.

The trick was to expose Senator Zorn, and most other Senators for that matter, for being out of touch with the people they represented. Against her desires—after all, the nation's security *was* important to her viewers—Kat stayed for the entire hearing, which had been postponed until today because of a silly disagreement between the Senate Majority Leader and Zorn that had spilled over into the headlines.

Kat could use that angle, if nothing more interesting surfaced. Save a few quotes in shorthand and etchings of seagulls, her pad was empty, so it looked like it was going to be unlikely she could scoop other reporters. Mostly, she froze the images in her mind, a camera snapping one photo after another of Zorn peering over half-glasses, making it appear if he was smart—only he read all his questions, so he must not be.

A long five minutes later, Zorn yielded the microphone to the junior Senator from Florida, Olivia Hernandez. "Director Kangas, Americans believe you and your colleagues are not connecting the right dots. Does the current government in Venezuela pose a threat?"

To Kat, that question had substance, and she wondered how Kangas, tapping a pen against the finger of one hand, would answer it. "While attacks continue abroad, Americans should feel safe, because we have strengthened our ability to protect the homeland, especially with laws such as the Patriot Act."

As usual, his answer was dry as dust, and didn't even address the question. No fodder for the evening news here. It was all Kat could do not to walk out. After graduating from Medill School of Journalism at Northwestern University, she had reported from Chicago for a couple years before network boss Elliot Tucker elevated her to the Washington bureau, where initially she covered Homeland Security. Kat's latest assignment was to give the national audience an inside look at Congress, so for the past few months she'd been busy acquiring and cultivating sources among Congressional staff members.

Kat noticed a blonde woman sitting behind Senator Hernandez and wondered when Eva Montanna snuck in. An agent who had solved many terror cases for her agency, Immigration Customs Enforcement, Eva had quickly become a key resource for Kat. Their relationship was spotty, though, mostly because Kat pushed and Eva, not eager to say much beyond the official line, pulled back. Still, Kat respected her and thought Eva wise enough to realize Kat was doing her job.

The agent leaned forward, whispering in the Senator's ear and, oh, how Kat wished she could hear what Montanna was saying to Hernandez. Perhaps there was a way to find out. The week before Kat had run into Eva at the Hart Office Building, and Eva had been talkative, mentioning her fellowship on the Hill, before dashing off to a meeting.

Easily ignoring Kangas, Kat decided to catch up with Eva after the hearing and ask to have coffee at the Senate cafeteria. Kat preferred to establish a friendly relationship before she began drilling for information. With Eva, Kat had well deserved resistance to overcome; in one case that Eva had tried to keep out of the media, Kat pushed much too hard.

Another doodle, another question from Senator Hernandez; the answer to this one perhaps proving more interesting than the last. "To your knowledge, is the CIA or other agency monitoring, without court order, domestic telephone conversations of American citizens?"

Kangas slumped in his seat, drew his hands together as though weary of that particular question. "The CIA is not monitoring domestic phone traffic. To my knowledge, no other U.S. agency is, either."

"Does that go for calls to Cuba as well? There are reports otherwise."

Kangas just shrugged that one off, and Kat wrote his denials in her notes. This constant mantra from special interest groups about domestic spying was a bit tiresome. It seemed to her the government had better things to do than listen to people arranging for babysitters, or asking their spouses to buy bread.

Senator Hernandez suddenly sliced in a fastball Kat nearly missed. "Mr. Kangas, who leaked classified information about our efforts to infiltrate a mosque in Seattle? Whoever did so threatens our national security."

From a side-view, Kangas seemed stoic, not moving finger or pen. Kat had glimpsed a five-sentence article about the leak in that morning's *Star* but hadn't been able to follow up before the hearing, so it was all news to her, too. A peculiar look on Agent Montanna's face suggested to Kat there was something to this. Scorn or outrage, either way, Kat had her story and Eva would play a major role.

The entire Senate panel was arguing at once. Zorn called for order. When none came, he banged the gavel again.

Kat saw Eva hurry from her seat and rushed to catch up with her. "Eva, great to see you again. Can we have coffee sometime in the next few days?"

"Sorry, Kat, but I'm leaving for vacation tomorrow and I'm snowed under."

"Then maybe when you get back. Eva, was Senator Hernandez in the briefing about the FBI's case she just said was leaked?"

Eva recoiled. "Five Senators attended," was all she said.

Kat pressed on. "Was Senator Zorn one of the five?"

"It's classified, but do call," and Eva was gone. Watching Eva dash away, Kat had a brainstorm. The Hart Building's brightly lit hall was a perfect place to execute her plan. The public had a right to know that in time of trouble Lars Zorn was letting America down. Besides having to field a few barbs from a pompous Senator, what did she have to fear from the "distinguished" Senator from California and man who would be President? On her side, Kat had not only the freedom of the press, but also the support of her news director and the eyes and ears of millions of viewers.

Seemingly defeated, Zorn gaveled an end to the hearing until a closed-door session after lunch. Kat scooted from the hearing room, out to the hallway, motioning for the photographer to come with her.

"Deet," she pointed to the end of the hall. "Wait in the crowd that assembles by the elevator. When you see me talking with Zorn, shoot us wide, then come in close. I want his reaction to what I ask, but do not intimidate him with your lens. Got it?"

The two were a team. For the past year, Deet filmed her stories, and they got on well. He shook his curly head, a masterpiece of black cornrows, and popped a smile. "You're the man, Kat."

When she flashed back her trademark glare, he became defensive. "I know you're not the man, but you are THE MAN!"

He had coined the phrase earlier that year when she broke a major exposé. Hearing it again today, made her believe the scheme to get Zorn on camera, when he least expected it, could work. She hummed inwardly, centering energy in her compact frame, contracting core muscles she kept strong lifting weights while watching television.

Kat peeked through the open door. Yes! Zorn was heading straight for her. With the C-Span camera shooting inside, he would not dare backtrack to get away from her. He was cornered, and Kat got ready for the kill. The one-time FBI agent swaggered toward the door, exuding a confidence built upon fame he acquired first as a movie star and then Governor of California, before becoming a U.S. Senator, all part of his carefully crafted plan to arrive at the Oval Office. Zorn possessed one trait Kat would use against him, inexhaustible pride in his record. Kat hoped the old adage, pride goes before a fall, was about to come true.

One foot outside the room, she plunged in, pencil and pad in hand. "Senator Zorn, critics charge you always vote against measures to keep our country safe. What do *you* know about this leak of secret efforts by the FBI to infiltrate a radical Muslim group using a mosque in Seattle as their headquarters?"

Zorn, caught off guard, jerked his head away from her, almost violently. The two stood in the hallway, as close as two boxers in the ring. He sneered at her small notebook. Kat guessed he was thinking, *no camera. This is a nobody.* It would be her word against his. She aimed to goad him into saying something provocative.

The former actor, named by a woman's magazine as the sexiest man on the Hill, stared into Kat's eyes. With no fanfare, he flashed a single finger, a lurid gesture of ill will, and said, "Drop dead," before stalking away.

Giddy, Kat ran over to Deet. "Did you see what he did?"

Deet's smile was wide. "Yup. Got it all on tape."

She could hardly contain her excitement. "Take care of that tape. Finally, we captured the real Senator Zorn. I'm calling the network, to make sure Elliot Tucker watches tonight. This is going to be huge, I know it."

TWO

That same morning, a blustery one in Chicago, the start of summer heralded a season not of tranquility and rest for Terry, a graduate student at Northwestern University, but a time to plot how to morph into the militant extremist he dreamed of becoming. Though his bag was X-rayed, his body scanned for explosives, all the terror-detecting devices at O'Hare Airport were inadequate to stop him, and hours later, thirty thousand feet in the air en route to Venezuela, Terry still carried the weapon he concealed—a desire and plan to kill people.

He pushed back his seat, closed the windowshade and thought about how, if his fellow students knew the mission he embarked upon, one of them would surely turn him in to the police. Therefore, at home in Evanston, he was careful to tell no one about his scheme to kill as many as humanly possible. After his trip to South America, others would find out, but only a select few.

Born near Detroit, Terry grew up in a cocoon of privilege and received the finest education money could buy. After graduating from prep school, he spent four years at Oxford University, graduating with a degree in political science and economics. As part of his studies, Terry learned how, during WWII and the Cold War, whispered lies, the stuff of spies, lit all-consuming fires that changed kingdoms overnight. Four years abroad taught him something else. Post 9/11, well placed deception could transform public opinion into panic in an instant.

As he soared far above the earth in seat 12A, he held this truth close to his heart, along with another secret—his real name. As a precautionary measure, he did not register at Oxford or at Northwestern under Abu Tarim. Compliments of a friend at the county clerk's office, his birth certificate was changed to Terry Tarim. His U.S. passport carried that name, too. A Western sounding name made it easier for people to see only what was on the surface—a grad student working on a master's degree in economics.

Terry had not always been willing to sacrifice such vain pursuits as education and money for greater glory. But, two summers before, an internship at a London bank changed his life forever. There he met Reni Jubayl, the bank's manager. When she asked about his family, Terry told her that his Saudi Arabian father was the director of international operations for a bank in Michigan. While his answer seemed simple, Ms. Jubayl was so kind afterwards. She invited him to a meeting of other Middle Eastern nationals, where he learned all about how Hezbollah filled medical and social needs of the poor.

He quickly agreed to attend a series of lectures in the Bekaa Valley, that fertile part of Lebanon where cannabis and poppy crops supplied Hezbollah with money to spread its brand of help throughout the world. It was there that Terry met Luis San Felipe, a Cuban convert to Islam, who lived in Venezuela. Hezbollah's most trusted operative in the South American frontier, Luis inflamed Terry with his rhetoric about global power and convinced him, an American by birth, that changing the world had to start in the U.S.

Now Terry turned to his seatmate, an old man who was snoring. *Good*, he thought, he wanted to speak to no one. He was a long way from the land of his father, a tiny dot in the desert of Saudi Arabia once visited by Lawrence of Arabia nearly one hundred years ago. Terry snapped off the overhead light and closed his eyes, eyes that were more golden than brown. If Luis sanctioned the mission and it succeeded, Terry was poised to become a leader of thousands, or tens of thousands, like Luis. His homeland would be proud to claim him as their fortunate son. Soon enough, he would know.

Warm breezes welcomed him to Caracas. Terry met Luis at the airport curb, and holding his backpack, he bent his six-foot frame and folded himself into the front seat of a black Mercedes. A commanding presence, Luis wasted no time calling him Abu, his Arabic name, and admonishing in English, "Do not forget, your cover is a student impressed by important changes made by the Venezuelan government. Were you followed?"

"No." Terry swallowed, choosing not to tell him that, back at O'Hare, a Chicago police officer had entered the men's washroom at the same time he did and made him nervous. Nothing happened, but he was certain that Luis, a serious man who never smiled, did not like weakness. Terry glanced sideways at Hezbollah's director for the entire Western Hemisphere, and felt a stab of pride. It was an honor to travel alongside him, even if it was dark and Luis said little.

Born to an influential Cuban general who dealt with the Soviet military, Luis received the best schooling Cuba had to offer. Besides English, he spoke Spanish and Russian. At the training camp in Lebanon, Luis confided to Terry, almost as if a badge of honor, that in the seventies the Cuban government accused his father of funneling information to the American CIA. Luis's father was smart and, before going to prison, he got Luis and his mother aboard a flight to Caracas, where he had friends and funds.

Terry concluded that Luis hated America because of what happened to his father. Tonight, eager to tell him about his research for ways to bring Israel's most avid supporters to their knees, Terry waited for a chance to speak. Many Americans felt a kinship with Israel, sending millions of dollars in military and economic aid to that blight in the midst of the sacred land of Islam.

Luis drove the Mercedes into a garage beneath a large building encircled by high chain-link fences. He used a passkey to open doors and, after relocking them, ushered Terry into a spacious room that reminded him of his parents' home in Dearborn, Michigan. A television screen covered one wall, and Persian rugs stretched across the floor.

If Terry expected warm hospitality—an offer of rest and a meal—it was not forthcoming. Luis handed Terry a bottle of water, which he gratefully accepted. Although he was hungry as well as thirsty, Terry did not dare ask for anything more. Luis seemed tense—he even looked different from how Terry remembered him. In Lebanon, he boasted a full beard rather than the goatee he now wore. When Luis sat suddenly, Terry copied his every move.

Luis's next words startled him. "Plans changed. You will not stay here tonight, but at the Commodore Hotel downtown. Tomorrow, you meet with the professor as arranged, to discuss import-export law and then leave the country. Now, I want to hear again the inspiration for your plan."

Said like that, his tone accusatory, Terry wondered if Luis believed him. "I first thought of it when I was invited to an international student banquet in the Chicago suburbs. Even though I am an American citizen, I am Saudi, so they asked me to come."

Arms folded, Luis looked skeptical. "If you associate too much with infidels, you could easily be trapped in a wrong lifestyle."

Certain that Luis already knew he was not corrupted, Terry explained, "I met students from all over—the Philippines, Jordan, and France. Over dinner, I probed how they think. Repelled by the American way of life, the students at my table told me they want education, but remain loyal to their own countries. All of a sudden, the idea exploded in my mind."

Terry noticed a hostile frown cross his commander's face. Luis pulled away from him, narrowed his black eyes. "You disappoint me, Abu. What you say is all about you."

No! He had made a terrible mistake. Terry leaned forward in his seat, gripped the arms of his chair so hard his knuckles hurt. "Please, hear the rest. The students seemed genuinely interested in learning about Islam."

Luis's glare never wavered. "You told them about the true faith?"

As Terry sat here in a foreign country, face to face with this man who was so influential in the international Islamic movement, he again felt the intense sensation that overpowered him at that student event months before, as if a thousand needles pricked his arms, legs, and back. Even the top of his head was on fire. He struggled to convey what he believed—no, what he *knew*—to Luis. There was a time and place to be emotional—like at a soccer game, which he loved—but not with Luis. Such displays were at odds with his calculating methods.

Terry grasped the water bottle as if it contained the substance of life. "Yes, I encouraged them to read our holy book."

Luis nodded for him to continue; his arms, which had been folded across his chest like a barrier, dropped to his sides. Terry was drained from the trip, but he drank some water, amazed at how this simple act helped him think. More importantly, it cooled the burning desire to succeed where others before him had failed. Calmly, he gathered his thoughts. He recalled Al Qaeda's first attack on the World Trade Center—the one in 1993; where an explosives-laden van destroyed only six infidels—and the foiled Al Qaeda shoe bomb plot.

His mission was not dependent on men. Terry was convinced he would be victorious. "One student treated me to lunch, invited me to regular meetings of their group." Irritated at even a passing reference to himself, Terry added, "Americans are lax about security, especially at large venues where many people gather. There is no security at the doors. I attended a play and ballet without being searched."

"This is when you got your idea?"

Terry nodded so vigorously, his insides shook. "Yes! They care only to let everyone participate. Things are not about to change soon."

Focused now, he told Luis in detail the scheme he spent the last month formulating in his mind, making no notes of any kind, when he should have been studying for exams. If he did not pass, so be it. This undertaking was the most important part of his life now, and Luis the key to his future. Whatever he told Terry to do, he would do. Terry finished talking and looked at Luis, who was silent for a long time. The waiting was terrible. At last, Luis rose to his feet. So did Terry, wondering if his plan was acceptable. Then Luis gripped Terry's arms, kissed him lightly on both cheeks, and said, "This vision was truly sent from above." Terry felt relief surge through him.

From his front shirt pocket, Luis took out a folded piece of paper and gave it to Terry. "Memorize this list of names and text message codes. Destroy it by shredding it and flushing it down the toilet."

Did Luis realize how much Terry looked up to him, wanted to be him? Of course, he planned to follow every instruction completely. Luis used his key card to open the front door, and stepped aside for Terry to exit first. "In America, you will recruit allies in other cities for a coordinated assault. This will take time, but we have plenty of that. Consumed by visions of peace, Americans are sure we are not a threat. Peace they will have,"—Luis forced a smile that Terry thought looked strange on his rugged face—"until we strike again."

THREE

K at's plan to unmask Zorn's political hypocrisy backfired in a humiliating way. Instead of the kudos she had hoped for, she received a terse e-mail from the man upon whom she always relied, which tore her life to shreds. Because she told the truth, live on air, Elliot Tucker sent her packing back to Chicago.

Devastated, at the first opportunity Kat sought refuge at her mother's cottage near Pentwater, on the shore of Lake Michigan. Tonight, tired from the emotional roller coaster of the past four weeks, after watching the fireball of a sun slide into the water she skipped the Thursday night concert on the green and fell into bed.

Pulling the sheet up to her chin, sleep—of sorts—came quickly, but it was the disturbed kind, filled with dreams of her car flying off the Skyway Bridge. She woke, drank some water, and finally fell into a deep sleep. Without warning, she awoke to a loud "Bang!"

Kat's heart lurched. Her eyes sprang open to a very dark room. She lay there, listening to her own rapid breathing, nothing else. It was unnerving. She strained to hear, uncertain what woke her. Seconds later, a terrible sound filled the room—the low, sad blast of a foghorn.

Sleep-drugged, she tried to remember where she was. This wasn't the bed at her townhouse in Washington, D.C. Another blare from the foghorn brought back the lonely feeling in the pit of her stomach. Kat had fled from Chicago to Pentwater to console herself, get a grip on her life. As objects took shape in the guest bedroom, she heard a drumming noise.

Thump, thump! Was somebody pounding on the back door? Oh, how Kat wished she were back in the condominium in Chicago—where city lights filtered through the window all night and everything was familiar—and not alone in the pitch-black night in the wilds of Michigan. She groped for the lamp and, fingers trembling, turned it on. Everything in the room looked the same as when she fell into bed. Kat slipped into her robe and cautiously made her way out of the bedroom and down the stairs to the living room. Braver now, she went to the front door, which faced Pentwater Lake.

She found the door secure, locks bolted. No broken glass littered the floor. Kat hit the wall switch. Outside floodlights lit only a thick blanket of fog, enveloping the house in a white curtain. Maybe she was dreaming.

The foghorn her constant companion, Kat passed through the house, heading for the rear entrance, which led to the driveway and the street. The microwave clock gave enough light for her to see that the back door was fine. She grasped the doorknob, rattled it, and gazed out a small window into the fog. Something or someone was moving down the driveway.

Kat switched on the rear flood light, only to be greeted by another sheet of fog. She killed the floodlight, grabbed a flashlight from its holder next to the door and trained the beam down the driveway.

A metal garbage can lay on its side, no doubt the cause of the loud noise that nearly gave her a heart attack. The lid was off and garbage was strewn about—probably from raccoons. Relief washed over her, and then she remembered how her mother had lectured her to close the gate across the front of the bin to keep the annoying creatures from digging in the garbage. Kat smiled. She could hear Mom saying, "I told you so" as if she were standing next to her right now.

Well, Kat had ignored that warning, along with plenty of others in her life, and now she had another mess to clean up. The lighted digital clock said it was only five o'clock. Banana peels and eggshells could stay on the driveway until later. She needed sleep.

Back in the guest room, sleep eluded her. The reasons Kat had come to Pentwater less than two weeks before swamped her mind. At this moment, she despised Elliot. No, that was not strong enough, and what she had penned in her journal last night, she now voiced aloud, "Elliot Tucker, I hate you!"

In the loneliness of this place, the harsh words echoed around her like the foghorn outside. Kat turned on the lamp, and then off again, willing her brain to rest. But her thoughts kept returning to how unfair Elliot was to demote her.

In typical fashion, she had reacted swiftly to the setback by packing up and leaving D.C. and settling into her new digs in downtown Chicago. Kat reported back to her old station and stepped into her former job as if nothing had happened, oblivious to the stares and whispers of her coworkers. She stayed in Chicago long enough to satisfy the new station manager and then escaped on the pretense that she had a lead to check out, but really to get away from her caustic coworkers, especially Randy. The minute her old boyfriend saw her on the set, he started calling again.

No room in Kat's life or heart for an old flame, she'd been right to come to Pentwater, where Elliot's octopus-like reach could not snag her. At her mom's summer home, she was far from his ever-increasing demands on her. Seclusion was what she wanted. Then, why allow Elliot's control to twist her stomach into knots?

If she were not free from his clutches here, hidden by the massive Lake Michigan and the rolling sand dunes of its shores, where would she be free from them? Maybe she should do something bold and break his hold—something besides changing her residence for a couple of weeks.

Kat tossed on the brass bed, which once belonged to her grandmother, until her angst toward Elliot propelled her to throw back the sheet and get up, splash water on her face, and get dressed. There was one thing she could do to take her mind off her troubles, which she started after yesterday's storm. She grabbed her digital camera and headed for the channel walkway, which led to the beach.

Kat loved photography and, if her television career was over, she might as well launch into a new one. With no idea how her life was about to change, Kat unlocked the front door and stepped into the fog.

AT THE SAME MOMENT that Kat was threading her way to the beach, her boss and mentor, Elliot Tucker, was flying away from Chicago, his jet gaining altitude over the western shore of Lake Michigan. A man who never quit until he got what he wanted, for the past 365 days Elliot had cajoled, bargained, and strained nonstop to buy six television stations across the country.

On this bright July morning, he was not off chasing new acquisitions. His corporate jet rose from the Palwaukee Municipal airport northwest of Chicago and headed for Washington D.C. to finalize the deal with the FCC. Instead of being elated because his dream was nearly realized, Elliot felt more like a prisoner buckled in the leather seat.

He glanced at his watch, and it took him a second to understand he was restless because he needed to go somewhere else first. It was his airplane, and the pilot, Mark Young, worked for him. Elliot wrapped the headset over his generous head of white hair. "Mark, I want to change course and stop in Pentwater, Michigan. Muskegon is the nearest instrument airport."

"Roger that, boss."

Their left wing dipped, the jet banking to fly a northerly route. El-liot yanked off the headset and stuffed back into his computer case the broadcast agreement that he would sign in Washington tomorrow. This agreement was everything to him, up until two weeks ago, when life crashed down around him.

As Chicago's north shore faded and they crossed the calm waters of the big lake's western shore, the memory of the fiasco Kat brought upon him provoked a hurt that swelled to anger. Elliot switched on his cell phone, trying once more to reach her. It nagged at his con-science that he had to discipline her. Still, it was either that or lose his precious TV stations.

What stymied him was how Kat refused to return his calls. Her stubbornness was the sole reason for his abrupt decision to fly to Pentwater. Until he was airborne, he had refused to feel the pain of their estrangement.

Since she was two years old and her father died, Kat was like a daughter to Elliott, the child he never had. This rift between them was absurd. Elliot ground his teeth as he remembered the tongue-lashing he endured from Senator Zorn after Kat did a story suggest-ing that Zorn was to blame for a leak of classified intelligence.

Worse, when Zorn refused to respond to her allegation, Kat taunt-ed him. Imagine the nation's shock when his ungentlemanly gesture flashed over the evening news. The zinger of a story turned into a disaster for Elliot and the company he had worked a lifetime to build, Tucker World Wide.

Senator Zorn's huffing and puffing did not faze him. No, it was his not-so-veiled threat to sink his broadcast deal that got Elliot's atten-tion. What stung was Kat's failure to see that he was preserving her from political enemies, saving her career. Elliot did not admit to Kat or even to himself that, in Chicago, he could keep better track of her.

He arranged for her to stay in a condo owned by his Vice-President, who was currently on assignment in China. The condo was one floor below his penthouse on Lake Shore Drive. It was wrong, he supposed, to assume she'd be grateful that he hired a housekeeper to clean and cook—*and* give him a constant flow of information about Kat.

Why couldn't she see that her new assignment was a plum? Politi-cal corruption in Chicago was as old as the city itself, and Elliot knew under which rocks to look. If Kat handled it right, she'd ascend even higher in broadcast news, maybe even achieve her mother's superstar status.

Again, he called Kat's cell. It went right to voicemail, so he left another message. "Kat, you work for me, not the other way around. You
are abusing your position. I never said there would be trouble if you
don't call me back, but are you *sure* you want to test me like this?"

He cleared his throat. That sounded unkind. The wisp of a girl was
everything to him, and here he was bullying her again. Elliot knew by
now that she shared his determination and drive, especially when it
came to outwitting an opponent. He sucked in a long breath, "If we
could just talk, I can make you see things my way."

Oh bother, that was not what he meant to say. Where were these
words coming from? Elliot softened his tone, became conciliatory:
"*Please* call me right away."

He ended the call, his nerves on fire. How dare she treat him like
dirt? Life always went according to his plan; Elliot had amassed the
power and money to ensure that it did. Of everyone in his universe,
Kat was the only one who didn't dance to his tune. After she returned
to Chicago and did one piece on shoddy workmanship in a city sewer
project, she told her news director she had a story to check out and
disappeared.

The housekeeper informed Elliot that Kat went to Pentwater. At
first, he was okay with it—let her stew a few days, then return to his
good graces. However, this morning, his insomnia in full roar, he had
had enough, especially when he discovered she closed her Washington bank account and disconnected her phone at the townhouse he
bought for her close to the U.S. Capitol.

Elliot had ways to investigate people. Before now, he never used
them against Kat, or her mother, Laurel Eastland, who also worked
for him. Kat believed the money for her townhouse and the condo
rental came from her mother, which was the way Elliot wanted it.

About to make another call, he realized he fostered their mother-
daughter relationship, partly for her good and partly due to his own
guilt. Mike Kowicki was covering the Soviet invasion of Afghanistan
for Elliot's network when his helicopter was shot down, killing him
instantly. Kat was barely two years old and Elliot still blamed himself
that she had lost her father.

Soon after, Laurel Kowicki returned to her journalism career, using her maiden name of Eastland. Her life became her work, and it
paid off. Based in Elliot's London Bureau, Laurel Eastland became
more famous than the heads of state she interviewed.

As he thought of all he had done for Laurel and her daughter, he grew madder by the minute. He punched Laurel's speed-dial number and, when she failed to answer, he felt no remorse leaving a blast she would not soon forget. "I am sick of your daughter's insolence. Tell her, unless she calls me within the hour, she is through at Tucker World Wide. I am a patient man, but there is a limit. Do not bother trying to smooth things over. Kat calls or else."

Elliot rang up Thomas Marshall, his long-time lawyer in one of Chicago's oldest firms on LaSalle Street. "What about my lawsuit against the pipsqueak professor who smeared my name?"

A faint moan on the other end, then Thomas, the only person on the planet who spoke forcefully to Elliot, wasted no time correcting him. "Professor Dudley has the Free Speech Legal Clinic representing him. They are reaping a harvest of donations to stop media moguls like you. I hope you have not forgotten your deposition is next Monday at nine. We're going over your testimony tomorrow."

Elliot wanted to rip Dudley's head right off for daring to write that he, Elliot Tucker, funneled money to terrorists in Chechnya to ensure they did not harm his reporters. "The man libeled me. At least his book never sold."

Thomas reminded him, "No, not until your lawsuit gave it a boost. Now, every internet blog lights up the night bashing you. I told you to ignore the man, the book, everything. But then," Thomas's voice grew stern, "why I think you'd start taking my advice after all these years is beyond me."

"Forget that. I want to change my trust."

Thomas grunted. "I don't believe it. What has the girl done now to rile you?"

Elliot pulled the phone away from his right ear. It sounded like the drone of the aircraft's twin engines had gone quiet. He shrugged, unconcerned. A former pilot in the U.S. Air Force, Mark handled the Lear with expertise.

"Thomas, if something happens to me, I want Kat to wait until she is thirty-five to begin drawing her funds. The way it is now, she is eligible at age thirty, which she turns in August. Do you know she has not had the courage to take any of my phone calls?"

This time, Thomas did not disguise his sigh. "We can discuss it tomorrow."

Elliot gave final instructions to his lawyer to call him in Washington, and hung up, when a strange sound reached his ears. The engine starter was rotating. Elliot put on his head set. The words he heard startled him.

Calmly, Mark was saying to Chicago Center at O'Hare airport, "We lost an engine and request permission to return to Palwaukee." Immediately, the door to the cockpit opened. Mark turned and looked back. Seconds later, Elliot heard him say in his head set, "One of our engines cut out. While I try to restart it, we are returning to Palwaukee. Should be no big deal."

Not a pilot, Elliot knew one thing about planes. One engine's problems could affect the other. He no more than thought this when the remaining engine shut off. Both engines were gone! The plane banked hard left. Before Elliot could put on his seatbelt or shout at Mark to refire, the jet descended through the air in overwhelming silence, interrupted by the futile cranking of the starters.

"May Day! May Day!" Mark gave their exact location to Chicago Center. Elliot heard Mark's voice in his ears, "Boss, get on your life vest. Prepare for a water landing. I'll try to make it smooth. The emergency locator beacon is on."

Elliot had read about how, before you died, your life flashed before your eyes. His did now, and what he saw shook him to the bone, some horror movie at the speed of light. In less than one minute, his real estate and media empire would be blotted out. Never mind the stations, or the hundreds of people who worked for him. His life was about to end!

What stuck in his mind was a horrifying picture of no one coming to his funeral, not even Kat. Mark would be dead, along with him. Only, Mark would have a grieving widow. Elliot balled his fists, squeezed shut his eyes. The plane dropped. So did his stomach.

He lived a rough-and-tumble life, but always got his way. None of that mattered now. Elliot steeled his body, his mind, to hit the water at full force. He cried inside, *No! It can't end this way!*

His heart pumping, Elliot looked toward the cockpit. While gliding in a descent toward the water, Mark struggled to put on his life vest. His vest on, Elliot was not prepared to die, to face a God he heard of all his life, but never would live under. Elliot Tucker, self-made man, buckled to no one, not a single person.

He squeezed his eyes shut again and then opened them, only to see in the far distance the shadowy outline of Chicago's north shore, his favorite city in the world. The beauty was beyond him. The jet was almost upon the glassy surface.

His fingers dug into the leather arms. A strange pain welled in his throat. This was where he would breathe his last. Elliot ducked his head between his knees. From somewhere deep inside, words ruptured that were foreign to his whole way of thinking, and everyone who knew Elliot would be surprised at his final act of submission.

"God, if you're there, protect Mark! He's got a fam—"

The plane's nose lifted in a flare onto the water, hitting tail first. The powerful impact caused the plane to porpoise, driving the nose and left wing tip crashing into the water. For Elliot, everything went black. He could not see the plane turning somersaults on the lake. He could not see the jet breaking in two.

A bright light absorbed him. The shimmering white light hovered, glowed all around. He felt no pain, was floating on air. Was he in heaven?

FOUR

Lieutenant Junior Grade Carson Wade was enjoying his coffee and caramel roll at the U.S. Coast Guard complex at Waukegan Regional Airport, north of Chicago. Each summer, Lieutenant Wade's team—an HH-65-C Dolphin helicopter and crew of five—moved from the air facility in Traverse City, Michigan, to the suburbs of Chicago. While they provided search-and-rescue protection for boating activities on Lake Michigan's southwestern shore, rescues here were uncommon compared to busier seaports such as Boston.

In fact, many days were plain routine. Just as Carson decided that July 19th was just another one of them, the loudspeaker above his head squawked to life. Coast Guard District 9 Headquarters in Cleveland was forwarding a distress message from Chicago Center. He listened intently to the message and the codes and was surprised to learn a private jet lost both engines and ditched in Lake Michigan.

Without wasting a second, he ran to his locker, grabbed his flight gear, and joined the other Coast Guard petty officers in the staging area. Helmet in hand, he and the crew headed for the Dolphin.

After several minutes of pre-flight checks, the Dolphin lifted off, Lt. Wade at the controls, hoping they found the plane in time to rescue anyone. If the pilot and passengers were still alive, could they survive in the water? That was a big *if*. Being summer, the water was warm, but with waves and drift, it might be hard to find them.

Not everyone survived a crash into the water, Carson knew. As the shore disappeared behind the Dolphin, his copilot received coordinates from HQ, based on the jet's position at the time of the crash. A computer-generated search zone compensated for the direction and speed of wind in the area. Carson checked the instrument panel and saw the crashed jet's emergency transponder was transmitting a locator signal on channel 99. He adjusted his course to head for the jet's exact location.

Out the chopper's window, toward the south, two 25-foot RBS rescue boats were streaking from the Coast Guard station at Wilmette Harbor to the beacon to assist in the search for survivors. Fifteen minutes after liftoff, ten miles from shore, the copilot was the first to see it. "One o'clock, at about a half mile, there's something in the water!"

Lt. Wade descended, circled the chopper above a lone survivor floating in the water, supported by a flotation device. He assumed a stable hover twenty-five feet above the surface and ordered the rescue swimmer, who stood in the open doorway attached to a hoist, into the water. Wade, thankful the wind was almost still, received directions from the flight mechanic as he conned the craft into a hold position.

His swimmer descended on the hoist, slipped into the water next to an older man who seemed lifeless, but who was being held afloat by his vest. In seconds, the rescuer radioed up to the chopper for a litter with the words, "Man alive."

While the chopper hovered, waiting for the rescue litter to go down, the two rescue boats arrived on scene and began searching for any other survivors. The litter aboard, the hoist then went back down to retrieve the swimmer. After advising the rescue boats to continue searching and learning everything was secure in the rear, Lieutenant Wade increased power, set a course for Cook County Hospital.

As he flew the copter toward shore, the team at the crash area radioed, "No trace of the plane or any survivor found."

Once his passenger was unloaded at the hospital, Wade would return to help his colleagues search for others missing off the shore of Glencoe. As each second passed, he lost any hope that they would find more survivors.

AT A FRIENDLY PORT along the eastern shore of Lake Michigan, a man who never heard of Elliot Tucker woke from a tortured sleep to sounds of a cell phone ringing. He had turned off all means to communicate with the outside world, except that one. Dazed, he flipped open the phone as the foghorn outside his boat released a mournful blast.

"Jack," the caller said in a hushed voice, "What are you doing?"

The foghorn had interrupted his sleep all night. Grouchy, Jack McKenna let a few choice words rumble from his throat, like a motor sputtering from lack of oil. "Who is this?"

"Whad'ya mean? It's Pablo. Remember you asked me to set up a deal with—"

"You crazy? Don't mention his name on a cell phone." Jack tried to clear his head. He ought to have recognized Pablo's Mexican accent.

Pablo shot back, "Right. What's that noise? Where are you?"

A lousy way to start his day, one that was supposed to be carefree. Jack needed time away, to think about his future. A month ago, a heartless woman who professed to love him wrecked his plans, and it seemed to Jack that life was slipping into an abyss. He sat up in his berth, rubbed his blue Irish eyes. At that, Winston raised his enormous head and let out a big *woof,* adding another discordant noise to Jack's misery. He kicked the dog off the bed.

"None of your business. What do you mean calling so early?"

"Right, I just hung up from our, ah, people . . . down south. They said I got to meet them at Norman's Cay. Want us there tonight."

"Norman's Cay?" As if repeating it gave Jack a clue where that was.

"Small island in the Bahamas. They have a resort there, and control much of it. You're gonna pay for my flight, right?"

If Pablo said "right" one more time, Jack would hang up. Instead, he felt for his watch, caught by the ultimate irony—he and Melissa had planned to honeymoon in the Bahamas. Only their marriage never happened. The island chain, a well known haunt of drug cartels, was a fine place to meet and confer about shipments of cocaine from Colombia through Mexico destined for the streets of Chicago.

Used to dictating the timing of these operations, Jack did not like Manuel Ochoa, the Mexican drug lord, ordering him to appear on the spot. "I've got other business."

Pablo said again, "Right."

"Look, knock it off. I know I'm right."

"Ri—I mean, he doesn't know you own the company. You insisted on coming. If you don't go, I am. I sorta like eating and breathing. So does my wife."

Okay for Pablo, but Jack had no wife. He should have, but agonizing over Melissa did no one any good, especially not Jack. On June 2, she had left him standing with the preacher, white orchid on his suit, and flew home to Oregon without even a note. He learned later, that on the way to the airport, she had stuffed her gown in a dumpster, leaving Jack to face hundreds of guests and figure out what he had done to mess up his own wedding.

While he nursed his injured ego, nasty reporters from coast-to-coast speculated which runaway bride had abandoned her dress. Finally, last week, he got a letter, a few short sentences where Melissa complained about his risky lifestyle. How those words echoed in his mind now.

The stay on his boat in Pentwater these last few days soothed part of the rejection, until Mexican drug smugglers edged in their greedy noses. There was no way to beg off, ask for more time. That was not how this business worked. You moved when there was product, money, and buyers, in that order.

Jack peered out a porthole; saw only shadows shrouded in fog, as if he was living in a cloud. It was perfect weather to run on the beach, and Jack was obsessive about staying fit. Was there time? His passport was at home, and he had to get Winston back before he could fly to the Bahamas. His feet hit the floor.

"I'll be in Chicago in four hours. You check on flights through Miami and call me back."

Without saying another word, Pablo hung up. Jack changed into running gear. So much for edging away from the abyss—he was heading straight for it. Up on deck, there sat Winston looking at him, leash in his mouth. He and the dog, they liked to run.

Yesterday, they spent the day together, doing what visitors did in this charming town along the western Michigan shore. Fortunately, the storm that moved in early had blown itself out by noon, so, on the stern of his 28-foot Sea Ray cruiser, *Day Dreamer,* they kicked back and watched boaters motor out of the channel connecting Pentwater Lake to enormous Lake Michigan.

With Winston at his side the whole day, Jack played his harmonica. He knew a handful of tunes, gave his mouth organ a good workout. Friends mocked his choice of instruments, but Grandpa Jack had taught him and, for Jack, that was the end of it.

Last night, he skipped the concert, made Winston stay on the boat. Alone, he walked up the hill to the historic Nickerson Inn for a steak with mushrooms. Shock rippled through him when all he found was an empty hilltop. The place was gone. That was a bad sign, gone like his marriage. Sour thoughts plagued him on the way back to the boat. When he passed a man in a baseball uniform Jack decided to ask, "Hey! Do you know what happened to the Nickerson Inn? I heard they had great steaks."

Without stopping, the guy said over his shoulder, "Burned to the ground May 21. Where have you been?"

Planning a gigantic wedding that never happened, he wanted to say. In fact, Jack didn't find Pentwater until after May 21, when Melissa took off with her friends for one last shindig before the wedding. He once kept his boat in South Haven, less than three hours from his home in southwest Chicago, but moved the extra hour-and-a-half north to escape a Chicago cop whose houseboat was next to Jack's slip, and with whom he had a run-in.

To prevent further problems, Jack pulled *Day Dreamer* out and headed north to Pentwater, which he stumbled on while driving up the lakeshore in his restored MG. It took finagling to get his boat and car here, but he leased a slip and was glad he did. Maybe he would move here, after he reached his monetary goal. Then he'd leave Chicago, the city where his life was in constant danger, just as Melissa said.

Winston sniffed his leg, started licking it. "Aw, cut it out fella."

Jack grabbed the leash and they started out on their run. This quiet town suited his need for a slower pace. Green lawns, white gazebos in the municipal park separated one major street of restaurants and kite shops from the waterfront. Jack had not counted on the town's one shortcoming: The police chief was a friendly sort who kept crime down by talking to everyone.

This morning, steering clear from the shops, with large strides his feet connected with the pavement and he turned over the problem Pablo presented. The truth was he *had* ordered Pablo to include him in all planning sessions, so it would be awkward, if not stupid, to back out now.

Jack would run two miles, then pack up and head out for one of the biggest and most dangerous ventures of his entire life, one he asked for. Foghorn pulsing in his ears, he had to question if he was ready for it.

FIVE

If Kat had any inkling of Elliot's plane crash, she never would have allowed the disagreement to blossom into hate. Alone on the channel, the foghorn drove her dislike for Elliot in deep, far deeper than the pain of a distant mother who traveled the globe to find a story. Kat stopped expecting much from Laurel years ago.

She blinked her eyes, unable to stop Elliot's email from rushing back at her, bruising her ego afresh. *Kat, I am sending you back to Chicago, where I have a special plan for you. Will call.*

Tired of waiting along the channel for the fog to lift, she fairly flew down the sidewalk at the State Park, almost slipping on piles of fine sand on the cement. Camera around her neck, jeans rolled to her knees, Kat ran to the lake, thrust her bare feet into the cool water, which did nothing to temper her boiling anger. Yesterday, she snapped photos of gigantic waves, a perfect match to her strong feelings. Now, it was as if the heavens swooped down from above, surrounding her body and soul.

Things were calm, eerily so. Still, inwardly she felt electrified, like the lightning that had arced in the storm, sky to ground, nearly thirty times. Kat had done smarter things in life besides standing in a violent storm, but she watched nature's majestic display yesterday until the storm raged past.

With no one on the beach to hear—at least she couldn't *see* anyone the fog was so thick—she kicked the calm waters of Lake Michigan, splashing her hands, her arms and yelled, "Elliot, quit ruining my life!"

With her foot, she struck the water harder this time, a light spray landing on her face. It was wonderful! For the first time since she soared away from Washington, a city she loved, Kat toyed with severing ties to Tucker World Wide for good.

In seconds, reality oppressed her like the dense fog. It was insane to think she could secure a new position. She was the talk of the media, which only recently had forecast she was a rising star. Her star had fallen, and it perplexed Kat how to make it rise again.

Restless, she left the water and aimlessly walked north on the beach, only to stub her toe against a log. Tired and hungry, Kat plopped on it, and rubbed out the sting. Even though her head felt light from no breakfast, an idea began to take shape. Before long, Kat had devised a full-fledged plan to stick out her punishment, make a name in Chicago, and then blaze back to Washington.

How long would that take? The unknown never sat well with Kat; she poked and prodded until she found an answer. Only, she had no idea from where this answer would come. Hoping it wouldn't be too long before she flew back to her life in Washington, she fingered the camera around her neck, vowing to deal swiftly with Randy, her ex-beau who already pestered her to go out, followed her around the station, watched from behind doors. His whole persona was creepy. Why she dated him in the first place was a mystery.

Kat pulled the clip from her hair, shook light-brown tresses around her shoulders, and contemplated the cost of giving Elliot the silent treatment for a month, maybe a whole year. Just blowing him off these last few days was empowering. Angry and hurt at her demotion, Kat had tossed suits and jeans into a suitcase, flew to Chicago, and paid for a rental car.

At WEWW, she reported to Bud Long, senior manager of the television station. A veteran broadcaster who had covered Vietnam on the ground, Bud was pleasant enough, introduced her around, tried to pump her up about an interview he had set up for her. She spent two weeks in Chicago at a condo that her mother had somehow arranged for her—from India.

Kat managed to snag an interview with Mayor Sullivan, who tried to convince her all was well at the Public Works Department and she should ignore allegations of corruption. After her piece aired on the early news, along with a live shot of her in front of City Hall, she became a fugitive from the city, driving down Lake Shore Drive, out Stony Island Avenue, and accelerating over the Skyway Bridge. Her breakneck speed got her to the cottage in four hours.

The best thing about her time in Pentwater, besides an ever-evolving landscape to photograph, was her new friend, Sydney, a native of Australia. The two women shopped for funny hats, ran on the beach and ate in every restaurant in town. Meantime, she ignored Elliot's messages and emails. Her mother called once to see how she was getting along.

With the foghorn still playing in the background, she stirred from the log and crunched down the top layer of the sand, crusty from yesterday's rain. Kat made a game of pretending to squish down Elliot each time her foot broke through. Maybe her idea of staying alone at the family retreat was not so brilliant. Her mind was stagnating, like the air around her. A few more steps, then the sun broke through from the east. Her spirits lifted.

In the diffused light, Kat focused the lens where she stepped, an astronaut walking on the moon. A figure rose out of the swirling mist, running straight toward her. She quelled a crazy urge to shout, "Elliot, leave me alone."

Her mind chided her. It was probably some local out for a morning run. A dark shape kept pace with the figure. Kat moved back toward the sand dune, took a wide-angle shot. A little shaky from lack of breakfast, Kat clutched her camera with both hands. The man stopped directly in front of her, turned to stare.

Kat's heart skipped a beat. He was tall and blond, with a hint of gray at his temples. His lips parted. A thin space between his two front teeth dazzled her. In the blink of an eye, it seemed the incident happened before, only she could not place the date or time. She nearly blurted, "Have we met somewhere?"

To prove he was in charge, a huge dog at his side barked once, loud and strong. Was the beast on a leash? Unsure what to do, Kat withdrew.

The man edged closer. "Why are you taking my picture?"

Challenged, Kat stood her ground, lifted her pert chin. "It's legal to take pictures of fog."

The man snapped the leash. "Yeah? You need to get a life!"

His rude comments burst her magic moment. Man and dog ran down the beach, side-by-side, melting into the diminishing fog. Kat was left alone, wanting to shout back, "And you're a jerk!"

Agitated, she wondered if that was an offhand comment or if somehow he knew about her life, and a disturbing thought came to her. She was the subject of gossip here, too. Kat told only Sydney Chadwick what Elliot had done, except Kat considered her friend a woman of character, who would never breach a confidence.

As for the rest of the town, Kat was the daughter of famous reporter, Laurel Eastland, end of story. No television star yet, but she *was* similar to her mom in one way—neither woman sought close relationships. Kat preferred a good book to a night on the town. It was fun hanging out occasionally in Georgetown with colleagues. But Kat was convinced she was on the verge of a major breakthrough—and people interfered with her ambitions.

Kat started for the cottage, tossing around ideas about an appropriate payback for Elliot. Nothing seemed right. She recalled the time he had invited her as his guest to a State Dinner at the White House. He had been as proud of her as her own father would have been—even regaling the First Lady with the story of how Kat got an exclusive interview with the new Supreme Court Justice. Uncustomary tears filled her eyes; she could count on both hands the times she cried.

A darker picture loomed. The breach with the man she considered a father was the fault of Lars Zorn. Even if he was a U.S. Senator with high ambition, he was an imposter; and Kat became more convinced she had to expose him. Back on her porch, Kat felt foolish for acting like a spoiled child, avoiding Elliot.

He had left her a zillion messages, well maybe ten, and she erased every one without listening. If she called him now, would he even speak to her? She felt for her cell phone. It was not on her waistband. Her zest for hurting him gone, she hurried inside to give him a chance to explain his stupid decision. She dialed his number and when no voice mail clicked on, she nestled her phone into her leather carrier and left to find Sydney.

A world traveler and single like Kat, Sydney, for some unfathomable reason, had settled in Pentwater the year before. With her sheep dog and Aussie accent, she stood out like a daisy in a mown lawn. Kat laughed at Sydney's stories of lost Indian gold in the neighboring hills. On this morning, Kat burned with a question for her friend, one that had nothing to do with Elliot or buried treasure, and everything to do with the man running on the beach.

FIVE MINUTES LATER, Kat got no answer to her knock at the Chadwick House, Sydney's B & B, convincing her once again she'd have to face her problems alone. Out front, she tried Elliot on his cell phone. Still no answer. Kat got into her car and jammed it into reverse.

It was impossible to call his office; Mrs. Ingersol, Elliot's secretary for more years than Kat's age, acted like his private detective. She would wiggle it out of Kat that she was hiding in Pentwater, and that she did not want Elliot to know, not yet.

Unsure where to go, or where to turn, she thought of going for breakfast at a local restaurant. The car drifting backwards, she hit the brakes and put it in park. She would leave her friend a note to join her. In her purse, Kat found a pen, but no paper. Then she remembered Sydney kept a pad just outside the front door for visitors.

Over one hundred years old, the bed and breakfast was popular with vacationing couples in the summer. It was close to Kat's cottage, and Sydney issued an open invitation to Kat to share breakfast. She reciprocated by taking Sydney out to dinner. After posting her note, Kat headed down the porch stairs, trying Elliot one more time.

No longer mad at him, Kat felt strange being unable to reach him, and it dawned on her that maybe he felt the same way. This time, a hollow sound pulsed against her right ear. Probably Elliot was teaching her a lesson right back, changed his cell number, or worse, had fired her for insubordination. Kat ended the call, scrolled for his office phone.

A strange cry reached her ears, a kind of whimpering, as a lost kitten would make. Kat once had a kitty, a black cat named Ink Spot. Her feet moved toward the sound. It was no cat, but a girl sitting on the picnic table at the side of the house. Wet strands of dyed red and black hair fell across her face, which was buried in her hands as she sobbed. Though Kat came up beside her, she was oblivious to Kat's presence.

"Are you all right?"

The girl lifted swollen eyes to Kat. She looked scared. Before Kat could help it, her investigative-reporter instincts took over. "Can I call your family to come help?"

The girl's eyes grew wide. She jumped from the table. "Don't. Please."

Kat guessed the girl was about fourteen. She might be waiting for some rowdy kid she had met on the Internet and didn't want her parents to know. Kat remembered her own troubles and ended her questioning; she was the last person to snoop around in someone else's personal problems.

She hit speed dial. "Sydney, I'm out front, trying to get in. Call back on my cell."

A hand gripped her shoulder. Kat whirled around to face the girl gaping at her, her lips quivering. "You know my Aunt Sydney? I have to find her right away."

When Kat was this girl's age, she *never* gave her mom trouble. She didn't dare. On the rare occasion that Laurel was home, instead of out covering a world crisis like the war in Kosovo, Kat played nice.

"I don't recall Sydney mentioning she had a niece. What's so tragic?"

The whole mess tumbled out. Sydney's brother, this girl's father, died when Nikki was a little girl. Kat could relate to that. Her father died when she was two. Although Nikki rarely saw her aunt, Sydney had always stayed in touch with her from Australia. What Nikki confided next, if true, convinced Kat she needed to get help for the girl, even without Sydney.

She touched Nikki's arm. "Let's walk to the police station. Chief Able will know what to do."

At that moment, Sydney came running around the corner of the Chadwick House. When she saw her niece, she gasped. "Nikki, how did you get here? What's wrong?"

The girl started weeping again, so Kat spoke for her. "It's Nikki's stepdad. He hit her last night, so she ran away. She came looking for you. I have a way to check up on him, see if he has a criminal record, only I need my laptop back at the cottage. Be back in a jiffy."

With her hand, Sydney stopped her, "Wait," and then wrapped her arms around Nikki. A moment later she released her niece. "Love, we'll face it together. Go inside and I'll be right there."

Kat watched Nikki trudge up the steps and waited until the door closed behind her before saying, "Sydney, she is not safe with that man. When she came home from school, she caught him smoking marijuana and threatened to tell her school counselor."

Sydney creased her freckled face. "Is that when he hit her?"

Kat pulled the car keys from her pocket. "It gets worse. Last night, Nikki pitched a fit with her mother and this morning, Mr. Jetson made your sister-in-law choose, him or Nikki. So Nikki ran away."

With both palms, Sydney wiped her face, but could not erase the obvious pain etched between her green eyes. "Now you know why I moved here."

Kat was even more determined to find out all she could on Nathan Jetson. "I'll do what I can, but need my computer." Thanks to Elliot, Kat could investigate people by accessing a special website. She was eager to try it out now.

She gave a little wave, started for her car, but Sydney ran after her. "I'll care for Nikki. You have a bigger problem. It's all over the news. I just heard it in the car."

Kat's thoughts leapt to her mother. Laurel was in India. "Is it my mom? Has something happened?"

Sydney shook her head. "Not your mother. Elliot Tucker's plane crashed in Lake Michigan!"

FEAR HAD LODGED IN HER THROAT from the moment she heard the news, and she felt like it was suffocating her. Kat stowed her computer and overnight bag in the trunk of the rental car. She had called Elliot's office as soon as Sydney told her about the crash. An intern who answered the phone said the Coast Guard found the crash site and recovered him. He was in the trauma unit at Cook County Hospital. That was all she knew, but it was something.

On the outskirts of town, she noticed her gas tank hovering near empty. Kat swerved into the gas station by the highway. Her tank full, she ran inside to grab something to eat.

A man wearing shades held the door open for her, but Kat brushed by him as if he did not exist. From a refrigerated case, she pulled a couple liters of water and pieces of fruit. Her hand reached for an ice cream bar. She never ate sweets, but dark chocolate usually eased her nerves. She took it.

On the road to the highway, Kat had passed by without seeing the red barn built by Charles Mears, for whom the State Park was named. Any other day, she might have stopped to take a picture of a piece of history; today her mind was filled with regret and too many questions, none of which she had answers to. Mostly, she agonized over Elliot. Was he still alive? Wouldn't she know if he wasn't?

Their lives were so connected; he was more than the CEO of Tucker World Wide, more than the owner of the company where she worked. Elliot had been there for her ever since she first learned to ride a bike. He even bought her first bike—a purple one that she loved—and, standing in for her father, held on and ran behind it until she could make it stop wobbling and ride it on her own. She felt like she was wobbling again now.

Kat pounded the wheel with the palm of her hand and uttered an urgent plea, more like a stifled sob. She had so much to redeem. If only she could get there to tell him before it was too late.

SIX

That afternoon in the Miami airport, Pablo told Jack McKenna that Manuel Ochoa, the drug kingpin from Mexico they were supposed to meet, called while Jack was at a kiosk buying a snack. Fast as swallows diving for bugs, Pablo's tiny black eyes darted around the gate area, looking for someone or something, Jack did not know who or what.

He did figure Pablo was nervous for some reason when he said, "Manuel is not coming. We're meeting Ochoa's new customer, an even bigger runner from down south."

Jack peeled off a stick of red licorice and chewed it quickly. Sudden change meant one thing: trouble. Retreat was not an option, so he boarded the plane for Nassau, and from there the men caught an island hopper bound for the Cay. On the brink of evening, as the sun lost its searing heat, Jack's deal remained tenuous. Ochoa's customer was late.

Under a thatched-roof cabana along a beach, Jack sipped a cold drink, wondering if he lost his mind. On the surface, he appeared to be a legitimate Chicago businessman looking for serious money. In reality, he was about to make a pact with the devil, his soon-to-be partner.

In a paradise like Norman's Cay, drugs and money were a strange combination, evoking an era long gone, where pirates once counted gold on the backs and blood of wealthy British and Dutch colonists. The tiny Bahamian island, a jewel in the aquamarine waters, now attracted drug runners, with only the occasional angler. Impatience mounting, Jack glanced around and counted eight security goons roaming the perimeter carrying heavy weapons. While he expected *some* guns, he now saw how outgunned he was.

From contacts in Chicago's underworld, Jack knew Manuel Ochoa was a dangerous leader of a fierce drug gang based in central Mexico. A man at war with rival cartel leaders in his home state of Michoacan, he was the reason that dozens had lost their lives. Jack shuddered to think—some, even their heads. Yet, Pablo had been dealing with Ochoa and nothing bad had happened.

A voice inside his head warned him that calm dealings were about to end. Anxious to meet Ochoa's connection, all Jack could pry from Pablo was a first name—Luis. Jack swiped at his blowing hair, and finished his drink. Unused to doing business standing blindfolded in a shooting gallery, he was aware that the unknown—this man named Luis—could be more deadly than Manuel, or even a U.S. undercover agent. The devil you know is usually preferable to the one you don't.

Though the resort was exactly how he pictured it in his mind, this was no vacation even though that's what he told his dad to get him to watch Winston. Big John implied it was time Jack got over Melissa, grabbed Winston's leash and took the dog for a walk. Jack left before they returned, to avoid grilling about where he was going.

If Luis failed to show, there was no way to escape the island before tomorrow, when the charter was scheduled to pick them up. Pablo sucked a gin fizz through a straw, the sound grating on Jack's nerves. A small bird dove onto the outdoor café table, helping itself to a treat from the jam jar. Maybe the bird that had perched on a bush for a while waiting for his chance, was smarter than he was. Jack hated to wait, but south of the border, that was how things were. Slow.

Pablo shoved his glass away, sat on his hands, eyes closed. What a character to have along at a time like this. Sunlight reflecting on something at the far end of the island startled him. Jack knew planes, and he watched a Beech King Air silently touch down on the runway. It taxied to a stop within a hundred yards of the resort.

As three muscular men in tropical shirts descended the short flight of steps, Jack focused on automatic weapons hanging from their shoulders. His brain shifted into over-drive as he tried to guess which one was Luis. Seconds later, a Latin male, who carried no visible weapon, stepped down onto the runway. This man's head was large and powerful looking, and his features were sharp, as if carved from granite.

Before Jack could wrap his mind around what might happen next, Pablo darted out of his chair so quickly it took Jack a moment to realize he was gone. He hurried to the landing strip and immediately became engaged in a discussion with the men. The four turned back toward the plane, but not before Pablo motioned Jack over. Were he and Pablo being made to fly somewhere else? With eyes that saw everything about a person in three seconds, Jack scrutinized the men and the plane, trying to divine what came next.

Caution overcame a fascination with aircraft that was lifelong, ever since Uncle Chuck, who flew fighter jets in Nam, took him to Midway airport to watch planes take off and land. Jack followed Pablo from a distance. Then, as if the Chicago duo was not present, the contingent from the King Air disappeared into a villa, leaving Jack, Pablo at his side, to stare at the closed door. When the door stayed closed, he felt it in the air; something was seriously wrong.

He studied the plane, but his mind refused to grasp what bothered him about it. Far from Jack's thoughts, Pablo wormed back in, "I don't like Manuel not coming."

Jack snapped his eyes from the tail numbers, sized up his traveling companion. Pablo was holding back the identity of the man on the King Air, and he wanted to throttle him. Better wait though, until there were no guns around. "Let's walk to our table and you can tell me what you've been hiding."

At Pablo's sudden compliance, Jack tensed inwardly. What did he expect, grilled shrimp on the barbie? Even in paradise, if you put yourself smack-dab in an illegal scheme, you had to be ready for danger. He was, or so he convinced himself, except there was one problem. Well, two.

Ten armed men guarded the north end of the resort, and Jack had no weapon. Searched when he stepped off the charter plane from Nassau, his only way to protect himself was with a cell phone one of the guards miraculously let him keep. Of course, a phone was no match for the firepower these smugglers had, but it might be useful. From somewhere beyond his eyesight, Jack felt a carbine trained at him. In his line of work, you sensed when someone wanted to blow your head off.

Jack pointed a finger at Pablo. "Who was on the plane?"

Pablo stuttered, "I-uh-wish I knew."

Before Jack could goad Pablo into saying more, the Latino, protected by three guards, emerged from the villa and walked over, settling at a nearby table. Waiters materialized with drinks and hovered over the men. Jack hissed, "Is the man in the middle Luis?"

Pablo simply shrugged and looked worried. A guard approached the Latino, who immediately backhanded him in the face. The man looked stunned, but shook it off. He walked over to Pablo, speaking in Spanish so fast all Jack made out was "Luis."

One question answered, others buzzed like angry wasps in his head. Luis's scraggly goatee covered a sloping jaw, and flowered shirt hung over his trousers, a sure sign he wore a gun. More than a dangerous appearance gave him an evil air. Contempt for anyone who got in his way exuded from cold eyes, permeated the breath he exhaled.

Jack forced himself to swallow. Pablo did not look too confident, either. Why Manuel Ochoa decided to forgo the meeting ate at Jack's stomach, which was a mess to begin with. He left Chicago with no antacid tablets to placate gnawing pains. Last week at breakfast, his dad pointed a finger, "Careful, son. You'll end up with an ulcer like me."

He laughed off Big John's admonition, but sitting here with Luis staring at them as if he could destroy them with his eyes, it was not so funny. For the last year, Pablo had altered large motor homes for Manuel, to hold nearly a half-ton of illegal drugs that were smuggled into the U.S. through tunnels beneath the border. With their cargo hidden in secret compartments, druggies drove the RVs to major cities knowing that their loads were safe from discovery by police. And there the drugs were sold for millions of dollars of profit.

Most likely, Manuel had told Luis what he thought to be true, that Interstate Van Conversions was *Pablo's* company, not Jack's, so Jack's presence caused alarm. Then again, maybe the exorbitant prices Jack was charging caused the change. Jack kicked Pablo under the table. "What did Ochoa tell you about Luis?"

Pablo scolded him with his eyes, flashing a message to keep quiet. Jack steadied hands around his glass, feeling like he was in a war zone, sensing the guards were growing edgy. Without warning, Luis moved to an empty chair on the other side of Pablo, his bodyguard a whisper away from Luis's right ear, and grabbed Pablo's colorful shirt, upbraiding him in Spanish.

"I don't like this Gringo. You should not have brought him."

Oh-oh, Jack winced inwardly. Outwardly, he pretended not to understand Spanish, even though he had studied it in school. Pablo pulled back, smoothed the front of his shirt. Jack struggled to keep up with his rapid-fire reply in his native tongue.

"Jack does not speak our language, but he *does* own the company. He is not willing to risk his business without being here. Besides, he knows we use his vans to run reefer."

Luis shot back in Spanish, words Jack would never have spoken in front of his mother or even Big John for that matter. While Jack kept his mouth shut, Luis flexed his right hand, preparing to slug Pablo this time. At this precarious moment, Jack's cell phone vibrated. What terrible timing! Who could be calling now? He hated to answer it and risk that the moment he had waited for, planned for, would drop like the sun over the horizon. He decided to ignore it.

His eyes roved across the sand, the water, lingering on a green fishing boat bobbing in the bay. Was that black thing on its bow a pelican looking for lunch or a guard with a gun? Too far away for Jack to be certain, he prepared himself for just about anything.

In his staccato sales pitch, Pablo explained that, when he doubled the price on the RV conversions, per Jack's instructions, Manuel ordered this meeting. "Jack lets me convert vans because to him, marijuana smuggling is no big deal."

Jack kept his head from nodding so as not to spoil the ruse that he spoke no Spanish. Perched on his wicker chair, Pablo, whose eyes danced from Jack to Luis, started speaking a mix of Spanish and English. "Señor Luis, once the order came for smaller RVs with smaller hiding places, Señor Jack figured you wanted to haul a drug shipped in smaller loads, maybe cocaine."

Luis's expression darkened, but Pablo kept talking. "Señor Jack realized your people switched to coke, meaning greater risk and profits. If he was going to lose his company and face jail time, he wanted more money, so you pay more, even if it is nearly twice as much."

Jack could tell Luis was furious. While he might accept Jack's reason for showing up uninvited, the money thing was different. The way Pablo moved his hands so fast, it was as if he suddenly realized he had said too much to a man carrying a gun. He motioned to Jack, indicating he was part of the fiasco, too. "In our shop, we will keep customizing the smaller vans with hidden compartments to hold your dope."

Luis held up a manicured hand, turned his stormy eyes to Jack. What he said shocked Jack, not for the exact words, but because they were spoken in perfect English, with an American accent, as if he'd lived there all his life. "Why do you think I move cocaine?"

At last, Pablo had accomplished what Jack demanded—Luis was dealing with *him*, not Pablo. Without exposing any concern, Jack chose his words carefully. "When you go from large hidden compartments to smaller ones it's obvious to me that you want to move coke. I only hope it isn't obvious to the police."

Luis drew black-brown brows into a straight line, silently motioned to a burly guard, who came over. He whispered in the guard's ear, the guard turned and went inside the villa. Jack saw a gun butt moving under his shirt, and determined to get out of there alive, said, "You want to carry *two* twenty-pound propane tanks. I figure you intend to hide cocaine inside them. It is smart, but, because most small RVs have one twenty-pound tank, two tanks will alert police if the vans are stopped."

His face a strange mix of anger and respect, Luis nodded for Jack to continue, so he went on. "Instead, we will build a compartment to hold one tank so it is next to shelves for camping supplies."

Jack used his hands to illustrate what he meant. "When you haul your drug of choice, the shelves can be removed to insert another tank for the trips." Managing a tight smile, he assured his host, "You will like the results."

The guard returned with fruit for Luis, plus a knife with a long, thin blade, and adrenaline rushed through Jack's body. The drug boss sliced off some nectarine and dropped it into his mouth, savoring it. He pointed the blade at Jack's eyes. "You convinced me. The deal is on. You and your company will order five vans and convert them as you described for our special use."

As Luis dropped the blade to cut another piece of the orange fruit, Jack exhaled. "Because Manuel vouches for you, we'll do what we do for him—no cash up front. How soon do we deliver the vans?"

Luis flicked the knife in front of him, as if deciding whether to carve something else, like Jack's hand. Jack was relieved when he finally told him, "My people will arrive in Chicago to pick up the first two vans. You will get cash for those, two hundred grand, and a fifty-percent deposit for the other three."

The negotiations apparently about to end, Luis rose, still clutching the knife. "I want the first delivery in three weeks."

Jack flinched at the quick deadline, but stood his full six-foot-two inches, hovering slightly above the kingpin. "When do I get the balance?"

Luis smiled, revealing white teeth. "You deliver the final three, we pay the rest." With that, he took his knife and one bodyguard with him into the lobby.

Jack dipped his head to check his cell phone. The call came from the 312 area code, Chicago, but he didn't recognize the number. His phone gave a short stutter, alerting him there was a voicemail message. He pressed the phone snugly to his ear, listened to Irish-accented words that were too horrible to comprehend.

"Come to Christ Hospital quick as you can, me boy. Big John's had a stroke and may be at death's door."

A shudder tearing through him, Jack felt heavy, as if floundering in wet cement. This had to be some mistake, but he couldn't just ring up Tooey, his Dad's former partner, to confirm what he'd heard. Jack hurriedly erased the message so no one could get hold of it. Thankfully, Tooey mentioned no names to link back to him.

Back in his room and careful not to reveal the reason for leaving sooner than planned—in case Luis had security covering the phones—Jack spent an hour trying to get off the blasted island. If he admitted to his so-called host that his father was in the hospital, no doubt Luis would offer him a way off, for a price. It was one thing doing business with a man like Luis, but being in his debt was dangerous. Even Big John did not have to tell him that.

Pablo watched a Western on a small TV with a DVD connection, and was no help. The chartered flight that was supposed to pick them up tomorrow morning could not leave sooner. Today's flight to the Cay was long gone. Jack tried to secure a flight from a nearby island but learned that the pilot was too drunk to fly.

He needed to get to Chicago, but every force in the universe conspired to thwart him. Determined to get to the hospital before morning, he struggled with the obstacles in his path. As he stared out the open window, not seeing the glistening water, his eyes locked onto a boat speeding by.

"That's it!" He jerked the telephone receiver from its stand and asked the front desk to connect him with any charter fishing company. In less than a minute, he negotiated his way home.

Jack grabbed his bag, threw open the door. "Pablo, I hope you don't get seasick. We're outta here on a boat and I have no idea how long it will take us to get to Nassau."

Pablo looked at him as if about to be sick already. "I'm not getting on any boat like some refugee from Cuba."

With his foot, Jack shut off the TV. "I say you are."

Pablo got to his feet like it was the hardest thing he ever did. "You owe me big time."

Jack pushed him out of the room. "When we get back to the windy city, we'll see who owes who." For the benefit of any surreptitious listeners, Jack added, "I want to get this deal moving so Luis knows we mean business. If he thinks otherwise, your life is not worth much. Remember, *you* set this up with his people."

Glad he was leaving the island alive; Jack was not so sure about his dad. On the boat to Nassau, what was weird about that King Air finally hit him. The letters "YV" preceded the tail numbers. All U.S. registered aircraft had the letter "N" in front of the tail numbers. Pablo had said Luis was from "down south." Well, that was no American airplane, and he thought long and hard about where the plane and Luis were really from.

SEVEN

K at's trip back to Chicago was fraught with challenges. First, she dodged a runaway tire, then a wandering semi. She fared no better at the hospital. In the last parking spot for miles it seemed, Kat wedged her rental in beside a pickup truck with dual rear-wheels and ran to the information desk, where a volunteer directed her to the third-floor critical-care unit.

She raced off the elevator to Elliot's room, scarcely daring to breathe, only to have the floor nurse stop her with a curt, "No visitors until tomorrow. Doctor's orders."

Stunned, Kat fretted over her disappointment and then decided to retrieve her laptop from the trunk. A short time later, she tried again to get into Elliot's room. This time, two security guards outside refused her entry. Not on the approved list, they said. No matter how she cajoled the cute one, he stood frozen, telling her nothing about Elliot's condition.

Unwilling to accept defeat Kat marched to the nurse's station, where she tried in vain to get someone's attention. The lone nurse talked on the phone, never looking up. She marched back to the chair in the hallway, flopped into the seat, and, called her mother, who was trying to get a flight from India. Some terrorist plot had shut down the airport.

On the phone, Laurel's voice was reassuring. "Elliot will pull through. I have it on good authority."

"You talked with the doctor? What did he tell you?"

Laurel was silent, then said, "Not the doctor, I've been praying for Elliot. Wait—" her mother stopped talking, then "I'm being paged. I have to go. Remember I love you."

She did? It was ages since Laurel had said those words. The call ended before Kat could tell her she loved her back. To hear that Laurel had turned to prayer was astonishing. Kat could not remember a time when her mother had gone to church or talked of God. Once, in a letter to Laurel, who was in Kuwait covering the first Gulf War, Kat had written that a seventh-grade friend invited her to a Sunday school. The letter prompted a call from her mother to discourage the idea, so she never went.

In a high school Lit course, Kat read some of the Bible for homework, some poems. Back then, Laurel was reporting from the Balkans War. Kat worried that her mother would not make it out alive, and she was comforted when she read about a Jewish King named David who relied on a higher power when he was at war.

Kat put away the phone. It was so long ago, she recalled none of the poems, even though she wished she could. In Washington, Kat had found yoga. Her instructor encouraged her to meditate with positive thoughts. She tried that now, and an image surfaced from one of those Psalms, an image of walking through the valley of the shadow of death, and fearing no evil. The thought made her shudder; she opened her eyes.

A different nurse in a purple jacket hurried by, and Kat jumped up. "Excuse me. I have been trying to visit Elliot Tucker, but his guards won't let me in. I know he wants to see me. Before the crash, he called me."

The nurse looked down at Kat above slate-blue glasses. "Are you family?"

She was, she guessed. "In a way."

The nurse was unconvinced. "Haven't I seen you on TV? The hospital posted security at his room to keep out reporters who pretend to be family to get a story. Come with me to the desk. I will check the list of permitted visitors, but I doubt you are on it."

Kat knew she was not, the room guards said as much. She gave her name anyway, and a strange thing happened, which she wondered about later. There, at the top of the typed page, was her name in red ink, Kat Kowicki, as if someone had just written it in for her.

The nurse whisked off her glasses and scowled. "Mr. Tucker is under sedation for twenty-four hours, to allow his body to heal. Because you don't appear to be family, I am not permitted to tell you any more about his condition. I will inform the guards you may go in, but only for a very short period of time, and I mean short."

Anxious to see Elliot before her name disappeared from the list, she kept her distance, a tentative smile on her face, as the nurse showed the guards Kat's name in red. The nice guard rolled back the glass door, letting Kat inside.

She drew close, shocked to see Elliot's head and left arm covered in bandages.

She had spent little time in sick rooms and was clueless how to react, how to feel. Her emotions locked away, Kat stared at the IV running to his right hand, feeling numb, until her brain uncorked words,
tender words bottled up inside on the drive down. *Elliot, how could
I think so ill of you?*

At his bedside, her heart ached at the sight of purple bruises under
his eyes, and a clear tube coming out of his mouth. His cheeks, chalk-
white, and the sound of his breathing, slow and even, made her want
to flee. About two weeks ago she ran away from Elliot to find solace at
her mom's cottage. As she looked back on it now, she realized she had
found no peace in Pentwater. In his hospital room, with Elliot badly
damaged and relying on tubes to breathe, she felt lonely, as if she was
apart even from herself. How peculiar it all seemed.

Elliott was a strong man who used power to build his empire, but
the plane crash had robbed him of his former might and influence.
Kat touched his right hand, which was spotted with purple bruises
from the IV. Memories of her life with Elliot replayed in her mind one
by one, and she saw all his goodness to her.

At thirteen, when she won an award for making a video about
Colonel Robert R. McCormick, long-time publisher and editor of the
Chicago Tribune, Elliot took her on a shopping trip at Water Tower
Place on Michigan Avenue. It was Christmastime, she wore a black
beret, snowflakes fell softly on their cheeks, and at Marshall Field's
he bought her a slim watch with diamonds.

That night over Chicago-style deep dish at Pizzeria Due, he talked to her about his childhood, something he had never done before.
He recounted how he had plowed fields with his father in Nebraska,
churning clumps of soil to plant winter wheat. He liked to grow things,
he said, until the eighth grade when he saw a TV broadcast at his
friend's house and fell in love with television. Now, rather than grain,
he grew reporters into media stars.

His passion for broadcasting, more so even than the example of
her mother's stellar career, was the reason Kat became a reporter. Elliot arranged for her first internship at the Chicago Tribune, the first
step in exposing her to all facets of the profession.

Tonight, the long drive, nerve-fraying wait, and the shock of seeing Elliot incapacitated overwhelmed her. Her emotions alive at last,
she felt tears prick her eyes. As desperate as she had been to see
him, and as grateful as she was to find him still alive, now she wanted
to be anywhere but that hospital room, watching him breathe with

a machine. Warm chai tea was what she needed. She remained for a moment of silence by Elliot's bed, wondering what it was like to pray as Laurel did. With no idea, Kat walked quietly from the room.

Her computer slung over her shoulder, she rode the elevator to the first floor and in the coffee shop ordered a tall cup of tea. The liquid soothing her from the inside out, Kat opened her laptop to investigate Nikki's stepdad. Kat figured if she occupied her mind with something useful, the time until Elliot regained consciousness would go faster.

While the laptop booted up, she slid from her wallet a special credit card. Once, she took it out of her wallet by mistake and tried to pay for dinner with it. The waiter hustled to her table with a whispered apology, "Miss Kowicki, this card is rejected."

Of course it was. Designed to look like other credit cards, right down to the hologram, it really was her secret account number to a special website. Elliot arranged for her to have exclusive access to sources of information on *CamelotConnection.com.*

As she typed the account number from the embossed card, Elliot's earlier warning jostled her mind: "Kat, this source is sensitive and unlike any you used before. It gives you entrée to all types of information, provided you pay for it. But, you must be an invited subscriber."

For a moment, Kat fought to keep from imagining the worst—life without him. *Elliot, please live!* How could she have been so wrong about him, and what could she possibly say when he awoke to make up for the pain she caused him?

She owed him so much. After he nominated her to receive an invitation to *Camelot*, in the mail came a letter on plain white paper asking her to join. Nothing fancy, but Kat felt like a celebrity. She was, in a way, because fewer than five hundred people, mostly from government agencies and large corporations, had account numbers for *Camelot*.

After she typed her access code, the next screen displayed cautions and instructions. She scrolled to a field and selected from a drop-down menu, indicating she wanted, "All information available." On the drive from Pentwater, she called Sydney for data and by the time she reached Michigan City, her friend called back with the info Kat needed.

After typing in name, address, and date of birth, she waited to enter the most crucial piece of information. The first time she used *Camelot,* checking a license number of a person who parked in her assigned spot, Kat neglected to say how much she would pay. Along with the woman's name and address, Kat got her credit report, marriage license application, and complaints and judgments for three divorces, one from London. The total tab was a whopping $5,400.00.

Kat complained to Elliot, who laughed. "I warned you that the cost was deducted from your bank account, which you put on your application. Next time, be more careful."

The next day, Elliot told her the company adjusted her bill, crediting half of the charge back into her bank. She was certainly more careful after that. Tonight, she specified the cost should not exceed $500, hoping that would get her whatever information the data brokers had on Jetson.

Her request on its way to *Camelot,* she'd have to wait for the plain brown parcel to arrive via the brown truck. Kat hated to wait for anything, but if she stayed at the hospital, time should pass quickly. She shut off the computer, unsure what to do next with her life.

A SMOOTH BOAT RIDE to Nassau eased only a fraction of Jack's frustration at not reaching Tooey. Their charter flight got them in Miami too late for the last flight to Chicago, so he and Pablo spent the night in the airport. Each time he called Tooey, voice mail clicked on. Jack finally talked to a night nurse at Christ Hospital, who told him only that Big John had stabilized. On the first morning flight out, Jack kept an eye on Pablo from a few rows behind, but his mind was on his dad's condition.

Father and son had grown extremely close after Jack's mom passed away when Jack was a boy. He could taste, even now, Dad's special beans and sausages served over mashed potatoes. Jack flipped through a mental photo album, seeing his father correcting his homework, in the stands watching Jack play baseball in high school. Big John never missed a game.

Without Jack's realizing it, the jet had landed at O'Hare. The second the door opened, Pablo sprang from his seat and was out of the plane and racing down the jetway, apparently not wanting to be seen with Jack. Once clear of the gate area and certain none of Luis's men followed him from the Cay, Jack stepped into a bookstore and flipped open his cell phone.

The male voice that answered was all business. "Chicago Police Airport Group."

Jack kept his voice low. "This is Sergeant Jack McKenna, from the Joint Terrorism Task Force. I parked in your area on my outbound flight and was told if I called your office someone would pick me up."

"Yes, sir. An officer will be right over with your car. Which airline were you on?"

Concern for Big John eclipsed any relief Jack felt that one thing was coming together. "I'll be at the curb in the United Airlines arrival area."

Jack shut his phone, aware he was home where he commanded respect and had influence. When you worked undercover with criminals, you had to believe you were the person you pretended to be and, at all costs, could not slip up.

While Jack waited for the officer to bring his unmarked Chevy Impala, he left messages for Tooey, all unanswered. A good ten minutes later, after taking the patrolman back to the airport office, Jack swung south on the Tri-State Tollway, heading for Christ Hospital in Evergreen Park, one of Chicago's southwest suburbs. Like so many other Irishmen in Chicago, Jack followed in his dad's footsteps, right to the Chicago Police Department.

After earning a degree in criminal justice and starting classes at John Marshall Law School, he moved swiftly through assignments. Happy being a Detective Sergeant, Jack liked the task force, except for his boss, who seemed unsure of himself.

As he passed through the tollbooth and onto the road, events of the past few days filled his thoughts. Because of Pablo's phone call, Jack flew to Norman's Cay and was infiltrating a drug-smuggling cartel instead of being with his father when he had a stroke. While he had no way of knowing if he could have made a difference, he wished he had been by his dad's side.

Too late to rewrite history, Jack considered when to brief his team about Luis's order for five vans. At the FBI's Joint Terrorism Task Force, he supervised several Chicago police officers on loan to the FBI, and worked closely with other federal agents, whose expertise in tax law and criminal procedure sure expanded his knowledge.

A month ago his group supervisor, FBI agent Gordon Paige called Jack into his office. On the phone with FBI Headquarters in Washington, Gordon asked Jack what he knew about a business on Chicago's south side.

Jack had toyed with the licorice stick he always ate on duty. "I've been in Chicago my entire life and never heard of Interstate Van Conversions."

"That's what I guessed." Cowlick sticking up behind his head, Gordon returned to the caller. "The local coppers in my group will look into these people."

After hanging up, he told Jack, "Headquarters has information that Interstate Vans is transitioning from customizing large RVs to small half-ton vans. You know, the ones whose tops are extended for camping or to accommodate quadriplegics."

Jack had asked a simple question, "Why are they of interest to us?" As he approached another toll, Jack reflected how Gordon worked it out. "Simple. The vans are customized with hidden compartments, our guys call traps, to transport drugs."

He stopped Gordon right there, hating to sound like a bureaucrat but trying to understand his role at the task force. "DEA or ICE has the mission to stop drugs. We identify and neutralize threats of terrorism in the U.S."

After paying the toll, Jack accelerated up to speed, sensing Gordon knew more about Interstate Vans than he let on. When Jack probed to find out who the source was, Gordon simply plastered his hair back, and said, "The source hints Interstate's real intent is to support terrorism, but Headquarters is not disclosing the identity. I want you to conduct surveillance on the company and its owner, Pablo Rodriquez."

Only after watching Pablo for a week did Jack learn the FBI wanted him to catch Pablo aiding drug smugglers and then flip him. Instead of assigning the case to an officer with drug experience, Jack pursued it himself.

Along with two CPD officers and three IRS agents, he spent three weeks surveilling Pablo and his company, making late night visits to the trash dumpster, where Jack pieced together the scraps of a torn pencil sketch of hidden compartments. The next day, he and his team observed known drug smugglers take delivery of vans at the company's garage.

At the hospital, Jack turned off 95th Street into the parking lot, feeling good about the case. Pablo had convinced Luis that Jack owned Interstate, placing him in a position to learn if terrorism was involved. Still, he had to find out more about Luis's plans.

As Jack shut off the motor, reality finally hit him. Somewhere in that hospital, Dad was in a life-and-death struggle. In the parking garage, in the quiet of his mind, he shoved aside his guilt at not praying sooner, and sought the presence of Almighty God, letting flow a prayer for healing.

Long ago, he learned to talk with God as easily as he did his own father. Countless times his faith helped him at his work. Recently, his dad advised him to memorize Psalms and other verses, to bring them to mind when he needed them most.

Jack locked the Chevy, shoved the keys in his pocket. Rain started to fall, so he quickened his pace and, fighting back worry Dad might die, called on Jesus to help get Big John through. One whiff of fear, and his father would sense it. Signs directed him to the hospital entrance. With heart pounding and stomach churning from airport food and too much coffee, he took the elevator to the sixth floor and went straight to the critical-care unit.

No one stopped him from going in. Big John was connected to so many machines, Jack felt like he was in a science fiction movie. A mechanical ventilator helped his father breathe. Maybe God heard his meager prayer, because he was alive, if barely.

A nurse walked in to check the machines. Jack noticed she was a pretty woman, who smiled but said, "He should not have visitors."

"I'm his son. I just flew in from Florida."

Her smile never wavered. "It looks worse than it is." She held a clipboard, shuffled some papers. "There's a note in the chart. A friend, Mr. Tooey, said your father prepared a power of attorney giving you authority to make his medical decisions. Do you have it?"

Surprised to hear he had power of attorney, Jack shook his head.

She whispered, "Do you think you could find it, bring it to the hospital? He was unable to speak when he arrived." She held the door open. "It is imperative he have complete quiet. After the doctor visits him, you can check back."

Jack's hand lingered on his dad's arm. "Love you, big guy."

The nurse shut the door behind him. Alone, Jack went down the elevator, and drove, not focusing on what he was doing, or where he was going. Somewhere in the far reaches of his mind, he felt comforted that a hand was guiding the things over which he had no control.

Ten minutes later, his car idled in front of his childhood home, the place his dad urged Jack and Winston to move back to after Melissa dumped him, claiming he liked their company. To Jack, at first it was like being in high school all over again, but he adjusted. Last week he put his condo up for sale. Once inside, Winston's whining reminded Jack to let him out, fast.

He flipped on the hall light, opened the crate, and Winston made a dash for the back door. Jack hustled to open it so the dog could run in the fenced-in back yard. Next, he got his gun from the safe, jammed the Beretta into his waistband, just in case, and went out to sit on the back step. Somehow, he felt more normal, having his gun nearby.

Its weight ushered in the panoply of dangers he faced hours earlier at Norman's Cay. Winston raced around the fence, and Jack went over in his mind how IRS agents found enough financial records detailing purchases of vans and equipment to extrapolate Pablo's income, which was a lot more than he declared on his income tax return.

One morning while Pablo was driving one of his newly converted vans, the task force struck. They were prepared to get a search warrant, but Pablo must have thought his work was so good they'd never find the hidden trap because he gave consent for a search. Pablo's error was the team's gain.

At the JTTF warehouse, southwest of Chicago, it took only two hours for Jack's team to find the compartment. Cold handcuffs were barely on before Pablo became a fountain of intelligence. Jack laughed as IRS agents primed the pump, mentioning the dozen undocumented aliens working for Pablo and his failure to withhold Federal income taxes from their pay.

Pablo's confession was complete, and he fully identified the Mexicans who paid him for the vans. In exchange for less prison time, Pablo told his Mexican customers he was not the owner of Interstate Van Conversions, and introduced them to the silent owner of the company, Jack McKenna. Yesterday's meeting with Luis was the result.

Jack should have been supervising the Op behind a desk, and not risking his life on Norman's Cay. He refused to take the Lieutenant's exam, preferring rewards of street work, and then finagled his way onto the task force, where he made a reputation for seeking out undercover assignments.

Winston's cold nose on Jack's hand was welcome, but licks to his hands and face were warded off. Jack scratched Winston behind the ears, and they stayed on the back step—a man with a gun and a badge, finding solace from the warm breath of his dog.

Strange how Melissa wanted the dog in the first place, then left Winston and Jack behind after the gangland-style shooting Jack was in a week before his wedding. No bullets touched or even grazed him, but Melissa went berserk, ragging on him about his future. He shrugged off her fear as natural, never thinking of it again, until it was too late.

"Okay, buddy. Let's get your chow."

Winston barked once, nudged Jack's arm with his round head. The poor animal was probably starving. Jack might be hungry, too, but desire to eat had evaporated. His knees stiff, Jack pulled himself up on the porch rail and walked inside with his dog, determined to forget

Melissa. Matters more important demanded his attention. Big John for one, the best Chicago cop who ever lived. Jack grew up in his shadow and owed so much to the father whose love and care filled the void after his mother died.

After giving Winston an extra cup of dog food, he took his time walking to the small room off the kitchen. The sight of Big John's old desk, his pride and joy, brought a painful lump to his throat. Jack had to keep believing that Dad would live.

The chair squeaked as Jack sat down in it. He ran his hands over the oak beauty. It had been found in the Chicago garage where the 1929 St. Valentine's massacre occurred. Big John maintained an avid fascination with the era when Al Capone ran roughshod over Chicago. Like so many unsolved murders, it was never proved that Capone was behind the killing of Bugs Moran's boys.

Jack wheeled the chair closer, pulled a brass knob on the drawer where Dad kept his bills and other papers. Jack might be a cop, but still he didn't feel right snooping in his father's things. He flipped up the roll top, where all appeared in order, each cubicle filled with pens, envelopes, and stamps. He rifled through neatly filed papers until he found an envelope with a rotted rubber band around it, his name printed on the outside in black ink.

The rubber band snapped in his hands. Jack pulled a sheaf of papers from the large, heavy envelope. He scanned the top one expecting it to be the power of attorney. Instead, what he read rocked him, and challenged his detective instincts. How had this been allowed to happen?

Not until later that afternoon, still pondering the revelation while watching the local news on the television in the hospital waiting room, did he figure out how to handle it. When he got home, the first thing he did was to fire up his computer and type in the website address for Chicago's WEWW-TV.

EIGHT

E arly Friday morning in sumptuous offices on Fourteenth Street in Washington D.C., Philip Harding, leaned back in an expensive leather chair and contemplated the bust of John F. Kennedy on the corner of his mahogany desk. For the umpteenth time he read the words engraved on the bronze faceplate: "Ich bin ein Berliner."

Kennedy had proclaimed those famous words in 1963, conveying his sympathy with West Berliners divided from East Berlin by a wall built by the Soviets. Philip turned his chair to face the framed photograph that hung above his credenza, of President Kennedy speaking to a cheering German crowd on that June day when he confronted the very idea of Communism.

Philip sighed. JFK's challenge on that day probably led to his death and the end of the era known as Camelot. With his company, Harding & Associates, Philip was doing his utmost to stop modern threats to freedom by giving information and advice to the corporate world, recently adding the U.S. government to his elite clientele. Yes, things were going well for him and, in another minute, he would have a chance to turn the tables on an old adversary.

Already he had kept Wilt Kangas, the DDI for the CIA, waiting in the lobby a full five minutes. That fact made him smile, which raised the right side of his face higher than the left. His lopsided grin drove his wife crazy. She had not wanted him to start his own consulting business, but he did anyway. The strength of his convictions in creating the company in the first place swelled within his not-so-powerful chest. What was right then was more right now.

His resumé boasted more than twenty-five years of loyal service to the CIA, or the Agency, as he affectionately still called it. He began his career when the Cold War was going full tilt, which was why JFK's speech in Berlin still resonated with him. At the Agency, Philip rose from low-level analyst to Deputy Assistant Director of Intelligence. He was well known in high circles because he had been able to compromise, and then flip, one of Libya's most senior intelligence officers.

True to his reputation for total discretion, Philip never told a living soul how he did it.

In the chaotic aftermath of 9/11, Philip retired and started Harding & Associates, leveraging his experience and thousands of contacts from his spy days. International businesses needed help surviving in the age of exploding terrorism, kidnappings, and subterfuge, and getting crucial information to protect their operations, especially in certain dangerous foreign countries.

He hired some of the most experienced retired federal agents and spies, luring many too young to retire with high wages to work overseas. The fact that Kangas took the time to dial and ask to meet with him told Philip the Agency had positive reports on him and his work. It must have taken a lot for the Deputy Director of Intelligence to acknowledge that Philip, called Flip by insiders, was a valuable asset to the CIA.

He checked his watch, thirty seconds to go. It was silly engaging in this countdown, but he had to make the point that whatever game Kangas was playing, it would be run by Flip's rules. At the Agency he and Wilt had spectacular run-ins, the last one when his boss failed to agree with Flip that they needed sophisticated technical equipment.

When the terrorists struck on 9/11 and Congress blamed the CIA, Flip bailed out big time. A bitter taste on his tongue, he recalled how Kangas transferred the heat he got to Flip. That stung, because he was the one who tried to warn his boss about the dangers from radical jihadism. And in those dark days immediately following the worst attack on American shores, Kangas made Flip wait in the reception area of his CIA office, where he spent hours in meetings. For Flip, inaction was worse than half-hearted measures. So he left the Agency and never looked back.

This July morning, he managed a chuckle at how things had "flipped" to his favor. Not only was he raking in lots of money helping corporate America keep employees safe in hostile countries, Flip even assisted the media to obtain release of some British reporters held hostage. On the phone, Wilt hinted that he heard about Flip's most recent coup. Harding & Associates had provided information to the FBI that led to a massive criminal investigation and indictments for price fixing against three oil company executives in New Jersey.

Revenge is sweet, but Flip never sought it. The DDI, always punctual, must have been doing a slow burn at having to wait. As he announced himself on the intercom a second time, he sounded aggravated. The receptionist had not arrived, so Flip escorted him in. Flip only let her make coffee and type innocuous reports anyway. Secret stuff he kept to himself, like this 6:00 a.m. meeting with Wilt.

As the only person with an overview of the entire company, sometimes even Flip was astonished by the breadth of information and influence the company could wield. His three directors operated their divisions,with no crossover. Wilt stepped into his inner sanctum, and Flip extended a thin but strong hand, which the DDI grasped firmly. An imposing man, he had a reputation for integrity, and Flip was all for that.

"Wilt, I've looked forward to seeing you." This was true, to a point.

Kangas dropped his arm. "Based on what I hear, Harding, this new operation is doing all right by you." He looked around, "I see you still have all your trappings of Kennedy and his three-year-reign in Camelot."

Flip shrugged off the sarcasm. The DDI hadn't changed much in six years. He still dressed impeccably and called people by their last name. The only physical change was a little more gray in his hair. Flip had lost most of his on top. Worry could do that to a man. Besides, Flip never cared for fashion. For this meeting, though, he selected a red and blue striped tie. Wilt was big on patriotic symbols. Sure enough, he wore a little flag pin on his lapel.

Flip ushered his former boss into a special conference room reserved for meeting with clients. A laptop computer sat open on a glass-topped table, flanked by two chairs. They each took a chair, and Flip could not resist saying, "Odd seeing you here. I thought you never left your fortress at Langley."

Wilt ignored the barb, got right to his point. "Several of our station chiefs observed retired Agency and FBI types in their countries and tell me these guys work for Harding and Associates. I assumed you mostly consulted with companies engaged overseas."

Kangas tapped the glass table lightly with his fingertips, crossed long legs. "Then recently word got out—you know how Washington is, gossip is like smoke, it sure moves around—that the FBI got a little domestic help from you."

Flip tried to disguise how eager he was to find out what Kangas wanted. He was not kept waiting long.

"Even though the war on terror multiplied the Agency's budget, there still isn't enough money to hire the number of people we need for HUMINT."

Ah. There was a huge need for human intelligence, which was the most expensive and difficult aspect of covert operations. Flip opened his hands, palms up to let Kangas know he was receptive. Where business was concerned, it was easy to bury the past. "President Reagan swung the federal government to privatization. Everyone thought he was trying to help his corporate base."

By force of habit, Flip lowered his voice. "By hiring the best retired CIA, FBI, DEA, and IRS agents, as well as retired local cops, we provide the same expertise you do." He shot Kangas a lopsided grin. "And we can do it for lower cost."

To prove his company's efficiency, he ran through graphs and charts on the computer. At the end, Kangas twisted his large frame, looked uneasy in the small chair.

At last he cleared his throat and said, "There *might* be ways we can work together. Of course, we'd need certain assurances from you."

Flip interrupted, "Obviously. You mentioned our helping the FBI, but you did not hear it from me. Even now, I won't confirm or deny it. *We* never do."

He shut the computer with a click, ready to divulge part of a plan he had turned over in his mind ever since Kangas reached out to him. "You pay us as consultants on certain projects. In others, let's say more sensitive ones, we provide you with actionable information, and you pay us from your confidential source funds."

Kangas opened his lips to reply, but Flip was not finished. "Don't forget, we're not constrained by the same boneheaded ideas placed on you by some of our less illustrious members of Congress."

When Kangas visibly stiffened, Flip sensed he had touched a sore point. Back in the 1970s, Senator Frank Church had added amendments to a CIA appropriations bill, which had seriously hamstrung the CIA in the ways it gathered information from valuable but unsavory sources. Flip was convinced these and other restrictions made it harder for federal agents to find out about the 9/11 attacks in advance.

Ready to find out what Kangas wanted, Flip broke the silence. "We take privatization to a level even Reagan didn't envision. Both government and the private sector benefit by not knowing where we get our information. You get something you want and need, plausible deniability."

A seasoned Cold-War era spy, Flip had a doctorate in psychology and over the years he had developed a profile of his former boss.

Right now, judging by the DDI's tense expression, he guessed Kangas was at war within himself whether to go with Harding or walk out. Flip knew that Wilt shared his deep desire to protect the nation from all foreign enemies. The two men were patriots above everything else. He could afford to be patient. If Kangas didn't bite today, he might come around tomorrow or next week.

Wilt rapped the table again. "Can you help us in Venezuela? Next week, I testify again before the Senate Intelligence Committee. With the ill will between our countries, we're thin there right now."

Caught off guard by such a personal request, Flip's reply was swift. "One of my most reliable operatives is in country right now, on a project I am not at liberty to reveal. What do you need?"

Tension eased around Kangas's mouth, but his eyes remained slightly narrowed. "Eyes and ears on the ground. President Upata's braggadocio and meddling in the region will bring who knows what. He's all over the map, wheeling oil deals with our enemies. I need to know what threat he poses in drugs and terror specifically."

Flip took no notes, keeping it all in his mega-RAM brain. Inwardly he relaxed. This was going to be easier than he thought. Once Kangas was on the hook, the possibilities of working together were limitless. "I will have up-to-date information for you by seven tomorrow. My sources are highly placed."

Kangas then shocked Harding. "I need to retrieve a general from prison in Cuba."

Flip got up, began to pace. He never dreamed Kangas would dare tinker in Cuba. Not now, not after all that happened. He turned to face Kangas. "Cuba surprises me."

Wilt massaged his chin. "You're the last person I need to remind about the Bay of Pigs disaster. That chapter of American history will never be repeated, and I mean *never.*"

At the Bay of Pigs, when President Kennedy pulled back the air cover, many patriotic Cubans who sought to topple Fidel Castro died. Even today, that act and what came after had serious ramifications for U.S. policy with the tiny island nation.

Flip sat again and scowled at Kangas. "Which general?"

Kangas pushed back his chair, moisture breaking out on his forehead. This was a new Kangas, a man almost trapped by something. "Raul San Felipe."

Flip whistled softly. "That old geezer is still alive? I haven't thought about him in years. Why get him out now?"

"Can't and won't tell you, except to say it has national security written all over it. Everything we've thought of to extract him won't work."

Kangas started for the conference room door, stopped and turned. "Cuba is more pressing than Venezuela. I need a contact by tonight or it may be too late."

He then told Flip the name of the nurse helping the general and his location. In return, Flip made a promise, "A good source left the region after the Kennedy assassination, and I haven't heard from him in awhile. Let me try to find him."

Kangas wiped sweat from his brow. "Don't forget, by tonight." He disappeared out the door.

On his laptop, Flip activated his encrypted e-mail. Five minutes later, he sent a request to Harding's Miami office, and then left a phone message for the medical doctor and friend there who fled Cuba as a young man. The doctor's contacts in Cuba were legion; he had extended family in the country. Flip sent an encrypted email to his office in Caracas for the Venezuelan Intel, certain he and his staff would have Kangas's answer in hours rather than days.

MEANWHILE, IN TAMPA, FLORIDA, the Hezbollah cell leader named Terry relished his future. Since Luis handed him the names of other Hezbollah members attending universities in the U.S., he had contacted five cell members waiting to be told their mission and willing to die for their cause. All the pieces were moving into place.

While waiting for Luis's final "go" signal, Terry's conversations with him had been few, each message scripted according to the codes Luis had him memorize in Venezuela. Recently, he stocked up on items essential to their plot—prepaid telephones and cards from stores throughout Illinois, Wisconsin, and Indiana. After meeting with the last recruit, where he gave her a phone and instructions how to use it, Terry left the parking lot at Tampa's Airport and drove over to the International Mall.

There he used a prepaid phone and his call was answered by a woman who spoke in Spanish. "Buenos dias."

Terry replied in English, along with precise code words, "I have six stores and need six additional shipments of red roses."

"Un minuto," was her reply. Music playing in his ear, Terry waited patiently. He was good at waiting, following orders.

A click, then a different woman said in English, "The addresses are not on file."

Unprepared, Terry almost hung up. He had addresses, but no code to send them. Was he even speaking to the correct number? Everything had gone according to plan up until now. Was it a test, was the operation compromised? "Excuse please. I did not hear the last sentence."

The woman simply said, "Hold on." For at least a minute he waited. He heard no music, nothing, on the other end, and worried that the connection had been broken. He was sweating profusely by the time a voice he recognized told him, "Provide the addresses by other means."

After giving these instructions, Luis San Felipe hung up. Terry must have misunderstood Luis's original instructions, and that was a terrible thing. Now, Luis wanted to know the cities where the attacks would take place, attacks to carry out Mission Red Moon, the term Terry chose after a second dream he had in which the moon ran blood red.

On his cell phone, he typed an IM to Luis's cell phone listing Boston, Chicago, Dallas, Nashville, Tampa, and Washington, D.C., hoping it was untraceable, or his life was over. Done, he disabled the cell phone battery, and began the long drive to Chicago, stopping only for fuel. Late Saturday night he reached his apartment, where he smashed both sections of the phone with a hammer.

He put each mangled piece in plastic bags from the grocery store. The next morning, a new cell phone clipped to his belt, he tossed the bags one at a time in different trash receptacles around campus. He returned to his apartment. It was time to pray, and Terry never missed his prayers.

NINE

The thirty hours since Kat Kowicki had rushed to the hospital to see Elliot passed in a blur for her. Despite her regular calls to Bud Long, her station manager, she felt out of touch with the rest of the world. Then, last night she received a positive report from the nurse, who told her that Elliot's vital signs were improving. That good news eliminated much of the stress she felt, and allowed her to doze off in her own bed for a couple of hours.

By 7:00 a.m., Kat had showered, finished a blueberry muffin, and opened her emails. She planned to make a brief appearance at the station and then spend the rest of the day with Elliot at the hospital. A call to the nurses' station brought even better news—he was out of the ICU but still weak. A cup of chai tea at her elbow, she read an email from Sydney, who was seeking guardianship of her niece. Surprisingly, Nikki's mother objected.

Kat closed Sydney's message without reply. Later, she'd check the mailroom to see if her package on Mr. Jetson had arrived from *CamelotConnection.com*. The information might help determine whether Nikki would have a loving guardian to raise her.

A second message was peculiar. Forwarded from WEWW-TV's website, Kat stared at the cryptic words, *Nice to see you're back on Chicago news. When I saw you in Pentwater, you didn't seem to remember me. My father, John McKenna, retired Chicago Police detective, has undisclosed evidence on the JFK assassination. Email me right back. It seems important. Jack McKenna.*

She met no Jack McKenna in Pentwater. Maybe, it was a fan email. It seemed unlikely a Chicago viewer would know she had been in Pentwater. Could Randy have mentioned it on air? The thought of him violating her privacy was infuriating.

With all she was juggling, Kat did not want to be roped into another Kennedy conspiracy theory. She emailed back, *Thanks for the suggestion, but am too busy to chase something that "seems" important. Kat Kowicki.*

Her message sent into cyberspace, Kat took a second look at the words in Jack McKenna's email. This time the truth hit her as strong as straight-line winds. Could Jack be the man on the beach, the one with the beautiful smile? She *had* thought he looked familiar.

Kat returned to her keyboard. Neither his snarling dog nor his surly "Get a life" mattered. He was the handsomest man she had ever seen. Now that she knew his name, she conjured up a profile of him. McKenna sounded Irish. Jack ran, so he liked to stay in shape, was kind to animals, and drank dark beer. She was guessing on the beer part, but it fit.

She checked her watch; it was too early to leave, so she replied to Sydney's missive. *Who is Jack McKenna? I met a tall blond man on the beach in Pentwater the day I left. He runs with a dog. I have good reason for wanting to know, but don't ask.*

Kat sent it, remembering she took Jack's photo, and ran for her camera to send Sydney a copy. The sight of Jack smiling at her in the display screen caused her to regret her impulsive dismissal of him. On a favorite search engine, she requested information about John McKenna, the retired Chicago detective, and sure enough, found a nice article in the Tribune about his career. The story from his son, Jack, just might give her something positive to speed Elliot's recovery. Kat sent another, more receptive email, leaving Jack her cell number if he wanted to call.

MEANWHILE, OTHER THINGS occupied Jack's mind. Pablo had just called him at home with bad news about Luis's order for five conversion vans. Their primary mechanic needed surgery on a broken foot, and Luis wanted a sixth van. Pablo was afraid to do anything without Jack's approval, and Jack wanted to keep it that way.

Winston shoved his nose under his hand, interrupting Jack's thoughts of what Luis was up to with the extra van. When Jack's boss Gordon suggested Interstate Vans might be connected to terrorism, Jack figured Gordon had found an excuse for their terrorism task force to get another case. Then, meeting Luis, now coupled with this new order, Jack wasn't so sure. To infiltrate the drug cartel further, he had to deliver on his end, meaning no delays.

Before going to the office, he quickly checked his emails, deleting a bunch of spam. An email from Kat Kowicki was nothing more than a blip, blowing him off. His dealings with women certainly needed a tune-up.

Debating how to interest Kat in Big John's assertion that more than one person had shot President Kennedy, Jack clicked on the third message, his eyes reading without absorbing its contents. It took a long moment to realize Kat was asking him to call her after all.

He did, hoping she would answer a call that said "private" on her cell phone's screen. He'd worried for naught; she answered on the first ring.

"This is Detective Jack McKenna, Chicago police. I think you're expecting my call.

"Jack, it's you! Sorry about my first email. I do recall seeing you in Pentwater. Want my help?"

Thrilled, Jack replied, "I sure do."

"Can you call me at home? My cell is about to die."

Jack wrote down the number, called back, wasting no time with small talk. "My dad worked on the Kennedy assassination the night of November 22, 1963, when he found new evidence. He's just had a stroke. I'd like to read you a letter I recently found, which gives you a sense of what I'm talking about."

"I leave for the station in a few minutes."

Jack slid the note from the file and read to her, "Son, too much time has gone by to prove who was behind the St. Valentine's massacre, and it probably is the same with Kennedy. I never discussed with you the things in here because I was hoping it would come to light publicly. I pushed the FBI hard, but hit a brick wall. I think they and the CIA are still covering up for mistakes they made. My conscience has never been easy because of it, but I am tired and giving it up."

Jack drew breath, and continued. "If you have found this, it means I am no longer here. I wanted you to have this so you, and maybe your children someday, will know I tried. The night of Kennedy's assassination, I found records at Klein's Sporting Goods of a second rifle that was also shipped to Dallas, where Oswald's rifle was sent. In the years I spent studying the crime, I talked on the phone to a researcher interested in my find, but he was killed in a car accident before we ever met. Son, I have always been proud to be your Dad."

Just saying his dad's words to Kat connected Jack in a strange way to her, and he wondered if she felt it, too. Silent at first, her reply—"If I got a note like that, I would want to follow up"—made him think he was right to contact her.

Before hanging up, Kat assured him she could not wait to find out more. With Kat on board, Jack felt he could now assure his father he *was* following up on the evidence and imagined telling him, *Dad, be-*

cause of you, the President ordered a new commission to review Jack Kennedy's assassination.

That was more or less a pipe dream. He rang the hospital and got marvelous news. Big John now breathed without a ventilator. Jack hoped to spend the afternoon at the hospital. He called Tooey, who was on his way to visit Big John, and gladly gave him the update. Next, he called their neighbor, a feisty lady everyone called Miss Lizzie, who agreed to look after Winston *if* he was a nice dog. Recently retired from a job as supervisor at the Post Office, she needed something to do besides knit caps for newborns.

He and Dad had always enjoyed the fried greens, ham hocks, and macaroni and cheese dishes she brought over, recipes handed down from her great-grandmother, a slave freed after the Civil War. Now Miss Lizzy came over to get acquainted with Winston. It took only a minute for Winston to charm her with his sweet ways and friendly tongue. They headed out the door together, Miss Lizzie with Winston on his leash in one hand, and his food bowls and rope-bone in the other. "Tell Big John I'm prayin' for him," she called back over her shoulder.

Out on the front step, Jack watched them pile into her car, and what he saw gave him a much-needed laugh. Miss Lizzie, head smothered in tiny white curls, black shades covering her small face, sped off in her pumpkin-orange PT Cruiser, with Winston looking out the back window, tongue hanging out. What a pair they made. He locked up, got into his Chevy and headed for the office.

The trip to the JTTF gave him time to review the facts so that he could synopsize them for Kat without burdening her. Two investigations tried and failed to find the truth about the murder of the thirty-fifth President. The first was the 1964 Warren Commission, so called for its Chairman, Earl Warren, Chief Justice of the U.S. Supreme Court.

By now, Jack had skimmed Big John's massive file and learned the FBI interviewed 25,000 people, the Secret Service another 1,500. Those two agencies submitted more than 3,000 reports to the Warren Commission, which decided not to hire its own investigators other than legal staff, including a young lawyer—who was now Senator— Arlen Specter.

It took the Commission ten months to conclude that Lee Harvey Oswald, acting alone, killed the President from the Texas School Depository with a World War II vintage Italian rifle, a Mannlicher-Carcano.

Since the report's release in September 1964, countless researchers poked holes in that theory, revealing important eyewitnesses never interviewed who saw smoke from the grassy knoll, which was in front of the President and not behind him, as was the Depository.

New theories and evidence prompted another review of Kennedy's death in the late seventies, when the House Assassinations Committee concluded that another unnamed shooter was involved and four shots, not three, were fired. Of course, official records made no mention of the evidence Big John found. That was because some in power stymied him, claiming what he found was inconsequential.

At his office, Jack quickly typed Kat an email. With his dad so ill, he would love to give him good news, and soon. This he also wrote, along with how, Big John always spoke of President Kennedy with awe. His affinity for him was partly because he was Irish and Catholic, same as Big John.

Like many generations before him, Jack McKenna attended Catholic grade schools, but he never paid much attention to spiritual things until the summer he turned thirteen. That was when the friend next door asked Jack to go with him to Bible camp, and Jack's religious training became something more. He left the woods on the last day believing God was real and cared for him. When Jack returned from camp, he asked his father to let him attend church with his friend. At first, Dad said no, but later changed his mind. Jack never knew the reasons for his father's initial objection, nor the subsequent change of mind. Jack still attended the same church. For the past three years, Big John had been going with him, too.

He left religion out of his email, but did tell Kat a little more about his father. A man who rejected most conspiracy theories, Big John was as sure as the sun rose each morning that there was more to Kennedy's death than the government admitted officially. Since Jack saw the evidence, the burden passed to him, and he now believed Dad's records proved there was more to the lone assassin theory.

Jack unlocked his desk drawer, where he had put the important papers, and pulled out pages of blue type made by old-style carbon paper, along with some fading microfilm copies of documents. These he put with his Dad's letter, the one he had been carrying and had read to Kat over the phone. Jack resolved to stop at a copy place and make extras just in case.

Theories abounded of who really was behind it. The Cubans did it to avenge the Bay of Pigs. The Russians killed him to stop his involvement in Vietnam. The Mob hated John F. Kennedy because his brother Bobby, the Attorney General, tried to shut them down. All had means and motive.

The strange thing was, after Big John discovered evidence of a second shooter, those in authority refused to consider the possibility. Through the years, he worked on his own theory, studying official reports, exhibits, and reading books on bullet trajectory, head wounds, and Lee Harvey Oswald.

Jack checked his watch—he wanted to leave in ten minutes for Christ Hospital—so he ended his email to Kat with two questions. Would she meet him and look at the evidence herself? What Big John knew could blow the historical mystery wide open, but would it ever solve the murder?

KAT DISCOVERED THAT, because of Elliot's crash, things were not business as usual at the station. Everyone, including Bud, was focused on whether Elliott would recover and anxious about the pilot who had been lost. The staff took up a collection for the pilot's wife and two college-age daughters. Kat contributed and, now inside Bud's glassed-in office, she waited while he talked to the U.S. Coast Guard in Cleveland. She gleaned from his end of the conversation that the plane was located; and so was Mark's body.

Sadness coursed through her and she made a mental note to send flowers or a condolence letter to the family. Still on the call, Bud thrust a sheet of paper into her hands. It listed a woman's name, number, and a note to call him at three o'clock about the public works corruption case.

Mouthing, "I will," Kat left to check her mail slot. Nothing but the usual office memos, which she threw in the trash.

"Guess you're not big on corporate communications. I'm independent, too."

Kat whirled around. A lanky guy with smiling, coal-black eyes and wavy black hair stared back at her. Caught off guard, she managed a grin. "Please don't tell on me. It's only my third week here and I've been on assignment for the last two. We haven't met yet," she said, extending her hand. "I'm Kat."

"Your secret's safe with me."

"Thanks, but who are you?"

"Ian Dobson, your photographer."

The two spent a minute going over their day, agreeing to connect after she called the woman and visited Elliot in the hospital. Ian left her alone to make her call.

Over the phone, Kat introduced herself to her contact, Sheila Wagner, who whispered, "Last night, my husband flew off in a helicopter with two million dollars in payoffs."

Stunned to silence by this kind of lead, she let Sheila talk. "He runs the department that handles towed vehicles. Can you meet me by cosmetics at the old Marshall Fields on State Street?"

"Sure. Does noon work?"

It did, so Kat gathered her things, and on the cab ride to the hospital decided *not* to bring up the pain Elliot caused her, at least not until he was out of danger. The nurse said he was weak, which gave Kat a bigger dilemma. Would it be fair to use this chance to cajole him to send her back to Washington?

Shame welled within her and she dismissed the thought. Kat drew in a sharp breath, certain that Elliot had no idea everyone considered his survival a miracle. She did not want to be the one to tell him that Mark did not survive.

At the information desk she found out Elliot had been moved to a private room. Kat went straight there, breezing past the guard posted outside the door. As she entered the room, she took in all the details in an instant: Elliott breathed without a machine, his eyes were open, but Kat was concerned how his head slumped down, chin on chest. A doctor in a white coat leaned over him, listening through a stethoscope. The sight made Kat stop suddenly, and her sneakers squeaked against the tile floor.

Today, she wore bright green ones that matched the lime-green jacket she had thrown over jeans, hoping the colors would cheer him. With great effort, Elliott raised his head and his eyes met hers. It was as if the sun burst through a bank of clouds, erasing the gray cast to his face.

He smiled wanly. "My dear, come in. Aren't we finished, Doctor?"

The wiry doctor straightened. "Almost."

She gave Elliot a little wave. "I'll get some tea."

The way Elliot's head flopped from side to side scared her a little. Barely above the level of whisper, he implored, "Don't leave. I want you to hear what Doctor Van Halsma tells me."

The irritated look flashing across the doctor's face told Kat he was used to calling the shots. He pulled the stethoscope from his ears. "Elliot, before the crash you were in good shape, otherwise, you would not have survived. Your blood pressure has dropped dangerously low. Your right leg is broken along with three ribs. We may have to remove your spleen. I've seen your X-rays, but I want an MRI of your head.

You have a nasty swelling that is not going down as I would like. In the next hour, the technician will wheel you down."

Elliot pursed his lips. "I have never been operated on in my entire life and am not about to start now. Do you read me, Doctor VanHalsma?"

Kat suppressed a smile. Nothing kept the Elliot she knew down for long, not even falling from the sky into Lake Michigan. The doctor uttered a noncommittal, "We'll see," and left.

Her stomach fluttering, Kat approached the bed. She had not rehearsed what to say. She set the computer case on a chair, and stood stiffly, hands gripping the side rails. Words slipped out before she could consider them. "I was so afraid you were dead."

That sounded so cold, so final. What if he *had* died? Thoughts of separation from him made her heart contract. How Elliot had aged since she saw him last. His hair, which had been salt-and-pepper then, was now completely white. Fine lines feathered away from his lips. Somehow, Kat thought he would go on living forever.

Beneath heavy lids, Elliot gazed at her. "I would have been one sorry fellow to leave before I was ready."

Tears crept to her eyes. She leaned over, kissed his cheek, and whisker stubble pricked her lips. With effort, he lifted his free hand, patted hers. Was it possible Kat could make it up to him for treating him so abominably? Surely life was more than a series of grudge matches only to end when everything went black.

Kat said something like this to Elliot, yet later when she tried to recall the conversation, her mind was a void. All she remembered was Elliot saying, "I saw him. He was surrounded by a great light," and then his head collapsed on the pillow.

For an awful moment, Kat thought he died right in front of her, only she heard his breathing and realized he drifted to sleep. She held his hand, and stayed with him like that for a while. Whom had he seen? Her father? When he woke up, she would ask.

His cold hand in her warm one, Kat vowed to succeed in Chicago. After a time she stood up, placed his hand carefully on his chest, and brushed his cheeks again with her lips. She whispered, "I'll be back."

At the coffee shop, Kat drank tea and munched a toasted bagel, worrying about Elliot but wanting to take a few minutes to call Mayor Sullivan's office. Yesterday, he claimed to be tracking those in his administration who used their authority to commit abuses. She wanted a quote on what progress he had made. After setting an appointment to interview him later by phone, Kat wondered if Jack sent a followup email about the Kennedy assassination. She enjoyed talking to him, even if the story he wanted her to cover turned out to be nothing.

With no time now, she decided to check on Elliot before his MRI and her trip to Marshall Fields. Sheila Wagner's tale just might shake up the city's political machine. Without finishing her tea, she dashed back upstairs.

The guard outside Elliot's room gave her a slight nod. Inside, the privacy curtain was drawn. Low voices made her slow her steps. She peeked around the curtain and saw a doctor in a white coat bending over him. When he straightened up she saw he was a good four inches taller than Dr. Van Halsma and actually looked friendly.

Was it right to listen in? Maybe she should leave, come back tonight. Her curiosity got the better of her, and Kat strained to hear what this doctor told Elliot. He spoke in soft, almost melodic tones. She thought it was a great voice for television.

"Elliot, you survived the crash for a reason. Do you recall what I said, what you promised?"

Eyes closed, Elliot's head bobbled on the skimpy pillow, but he seemed to rally his strength. Two words escaped from cracked lips. "Always remember."

The doctor seemed pleased, and tucked a blanket around Elliot's chest. As the doctor started backing up, Kat felt caught. She hurried toward the door, to give the appearance she just came in. Before she made it, the doctor was right beside her.

His bluer than blue eyes were kind, and his presence was soothing—unlike Van Halsma, who had seemed perturbed by her presence. He gazed directly into Kat's face, and when he spoke she felt calmer than she had for days. In fact, she was mesmerized.

"Kat, I am so glad you are here. You will be happy to know your mother's prayers are answered. Please call and tell her that Elliot has no need for more tests or surgery, and his bones will heal. Laurel can remain in India, where we have much need of her."

Kat was speechless. This doctor knew her name and her mother's. How did he know Laurel worked in India? His nametag said he was Dr. Semeion. Before she had a chance to ask a single question, he was gone.

Well, she could ask him later. Kat tiptoed to Elliot's bedside, where he was sleeping peacefully, Maybe it was better to wait to tell him how hard she was working on the story Bud gave her. As Kat walked out of the room, she nearly smacked into a technician wheeling a gurney. She asked, "What are you doing?"

"Not that it's your business, but Mr. Tucker has to go for his MRI."

Kat held out her arm. "No, Dr. Semeion said he was fine. There is no need for tests."

The tech looked confused. "Who?"

"Doctor Semeion, he just left. You wait here. I'm going to get the head nurse."

Kat was perplexed when she learned that the head nurse never heard of Dr. Semeion, either. No such doctor worked at the hospital. The nurse checked Elliot's blood pressure. Sure enough, it was back to normal, so she paged Dr. Van Halsma and told the technician to come back later.

When Kat kissed Elliot's forehead, his skin felt much warmer.

Eager to call Laurel and tell her what happened, she quietly put the computer over her shoulder, and left his room. Outside the hospital, she hailed a cab. On the taxi ride to the former Marshall Field's, now Macy's, Kat telephoned Laurel and left a message on her voicemail, telling her Elliot was much improved and a little bit about the mysterious Dr. Semeion, who insisted she remain in India.

The cabbie lurched to a sudden stop by the store. Kat quickly paid her fare, all the while wondering if what she witnessed in Elliot's room was evidence of a second miracle.

TEN

For Jack, between juggling demands at work and carving out time to visit with Big John at the hospital, the next five days roared by. He ate little, slept even less, but prayed much until his dad slowly opened one eye and moved his lips. From those first jerky movements, Big John progressed rapidly to sitting up in a chair, swallowing gelatin that Jack fed him, and starting to talk.

Yesterday, Jack arranged for his dad to go to rehab. Miss Lizzy was fantastic, watching Winston and at the same time packing the fridge with potato salad, ham, buns, and fruit. Jack and Kat traded emails and, when he found out she might go to Pentwater to help her friend Sydney, he decided it was a good idea to head north. He and Winston needed a break.

As he sped toward the Chicago FBI office, Jack got a call from Pablo.

"Jack, thought you'd wanna know, I ordered the sixth van and all the parts we need for the hidden traps."

"Good. Means we're right on target."

"Right," Pablo said and hung up.

Jack sure hoped his case was coming together. When he first joined the task force, he worked in the Loop, at Jackson and Dearborn Streets, but the FBI moved to an office near Roosevelt and Ogden on the southwest side, about three miles away. This morning, he passed through security gates designed to keep bombers away from the perimeter.

Since the Oklahoma City bombing, most federal law enforcement agencies moved out of buildings housing U.S. Courts and Senate and Congressional offices and into more secure locations. Some said the Bureau didn't choose to move the Chicago office, but judges and politicians refused to share space with agencies that might attract a violent fringe. Jack figured everyone in the system, including him, was a target.

As Jack unlocked his desk, Gordon stuck his head around the corner. "McKenna, in five minutes I leave for the U.S. Attorney's press conference. We're announcing an indictment against the terrorists who were planning to blow up Wrigley Field at the last Cubs game of the year."

Others on the team foiled that terror plot, so this was one press conference Jack could skip. He followed Gordon to his office, where he gave an abbreviated briefing on his undercover meeting in the Bahamas. Gordon had been in D.C. at Bureau Headquarters since Jack's return.

Jack voiced aloud a concern that had been gnawing at him. "I wonder if these vans are being made to carry drugs, or something much worse."

Gordon seemed thoughtful as he played with hair sticking up at the back of his head, but he didn't answer. "I need to brief the Special Agent in Charge, so keep me posted as you move the case along. Check with the Bureau's aviation division about the Beech King Air."

Unsatisfied, Jack fired off another question. "How did the Bureau learn of Interstate Van Conversions? You simply mentioned there was an informant."

Suddenly his boss grew circumspect. "Sometimes information comes from the CIA or NSA, and we guess about their source. I got the info on Interstate Van Conversions from someone high in the Bureau who told me to authorize a large informant payment. We don't know yet if the source has value. It *is* strange," he admitted, "I was not given the usual informant identification number."

Rather than press his boss about the original informant, Jack asked Gordon to approve his request for an Hispanic officer from JTTF to work undercover at Interstate. That way, Jack would have inside eyes to ensure Pablo was not doing unapproved work for Luis or other criminals. Gordon signed off on it, tossed the pen on his desk and headed out the door. Jack stopped him. "I also need FBI technicians to enter the plant at night and install tracking devices in the vans."

Gordon stared, obviously calculating the cost, but agreed. Back at his cubicle, Jack called the Aviation Division and, expecting to get voice mail, was pleasantly surprised when Sean Malone answered on the third ring.

"It's Jack McKenna, JTTF in Chicago. I need to know about an aircraft that brought suspected drug smugglers to an undercover meeting in the Bahamas."

"We aim to please. Give me the specifics."

Jack gave Sean the tail number for the Beech King Air. "Can you tell me the country of origin?"

"What you have is a Venezuelan tail number. Were Venezuelans at the meeting?" Without waiting for Jack's answer, Malone grumbled, "We get little cooperation from that government, but we'll try to get the registered owner's name. Good chance it's a rental or charter. I'll get back."

Jack thanked the agent for his help and they traded a couple of interesting stories about their dads, both Irish cops. The law enforcement community was a large fraternity. Jack suppressed an urge to tell Malone about his father's evidence, or that someone at Bureau Headquarters impeded Big John, rightly suspecting FBI ties were tighter. He ended the call and started thinking: Besides Venezuela, where else would his case lead?

FEDERAL AGENT EVA MONTANNA, sitting behind Senator Hernandez at a televised hearing of the Senate Intelligence Committee, had her own questions, ones not easily answered. She struggled to maintain her composure, keep her lips closed in a straight line, in case the C-Span camera panned over her face. Eva did not want viewers to think federal agents were not dedicated to catching those using money from the drug trade to finance terrorism, the subject of the hearing.

It was just that Senator Lars Zorn was turning this hearing into a circus again, which was not what Eva had bargained for when she accepted her assignment on Capitol Hill. The end of her fellowship in September seemed eons away. At least she had enjoyed the vacation with her family at a beautiful beach in Holland, Michigan, where for one blissful week she was able to forget about Congress.

But now that she was back, the antics she was witnessing told her that many politicians were more interested in scoring political points than making America a safer place. With her years of experience in financial investigations, Eva had expected to give the Senate fresh ideas for dealing with terrorism. But Lars Zorn was one Senator who only seemed interested in hearing *himself* talk.

Her husband Scott reminded Eva that she was a woman of action, always would be. As press secretary to the Secretary of Defense, he was used to a hectic pace, too. Before she left on vacation, she drew up a list of tough questions for Senator Hernandez to ask Wilt Kangas, who today was concluding his public testimony about the National Threat Assessment.

Senator Hernandez had yet to ask these, or even get a word in edgewise. There was Zorn, finger pointing at Kangas, engaging in a one-man filibuster for benefit of the cameras. His antics appalled Eva. It was easy to see that he had no clue what kept the nation safe, nor did he even appear to know that Mexico and Venezuela were two of nine countries designated by the President as giving refuge to Drug Transit Organizations.

Eva became lost in reverie about dinner with her family the night before in the backyard. Scott grilled steaks and corn on the cob. She set the picnic table while Andy and Kaley played on swings. The baby on her lap, Eva shared her frustration with Scott. "The election next year has made political infighting so intense, everyone seems to be taking their eyes off our security."

As he flipped the steaks, smoke rose up around his face. When he closed the lid, he reached to hug her. "Never mind them. What you are doing is important."

Eva had argued with him, "After Zorn accused Hernandez of leaking classified information they refuse to be seen in public together."

Scott sat beside her, pulled her close, and kissed the top of her head. "Your fellowship is up soon."

That had not assuaged Eva's sense of injustice. "The constant leaks worry me, leaks of our intelligence for political advantage."

Scott released her and went back to check the meat. "I did think it was convenient that Zorn accused Hernandez *after* Channel 14 ran that story by Kat Kowicki accusing him of the leak."

Back in real time, Eva glanced at Lars Zorn. In her near-fifteen year career, she steered away from politics, rebuffing calls to run for Congress after she made a major bust a few years back. She looked in the audience for Kat, who had asked her to have coffee the last time they had run into each other, before her vacation. So far, Eva had heard nothing from her.

Laughter among the spectators brought Eva back to the proceedings. Wilt Kangas was taking a sip of his water. The long-time spook seemed a bit rattled. Eva had never met Director Kangas but, judging from his past performance, he seemed dedicated to finding the truth. She found herself approving of him as a public servant.

Zorn repeated the question. "Director Kangas, are you telling this body you cannot reveal what the CIA is doing to protect Americans from Hezbollah and Hamas? Both are setting up strongholds in Latin America, including Venezuela."

Eva was amazed that the Senator asked such an improper question in a public setting. Others must share her opinion, judging by the uncomfortable laughter.

Kangas pressed his hands together in front of him. "Senator, you know I am not permitted to discuss classified intelligence in open session. Be assured, my Agency has assets in place in the region. The Drug Enforcement Administration is working closely with us to capture Middle Eastern terrorists who fund their murderous activities with drug profits. The war is brutal, with many South American judges, lawyers, and police officers losing their lives in the brave fight."

Eva thought his answer unusually long. She was more surprised when Kangas added, "I predict that before the year ends, we will give a major announcement, but that is all I will say at present."

What a bold statement to utter over television. Still, Eva liked his courage and felt a burning desire to be right in the middle of whatever operation that was. Senator Zorn gaveled for a break, and Eva jumped from her seat, tempted to ask Director Kangas more about his prediction. As she worked her way around the Senators, the CIA agent assigned to the Committee came up behind her.

In her ear, he said, "He's not out, but will be by tonight. Don't ask me anymore."

Eva turned to Bo Ryder. "You mean the—?" She caught herself before saying General San Felipe's name. Eva was intrigued! How would the CIA get an ailing 80-year-old man out of a Cuban prison hospital?

Bo looked beyond her. "How is your fellowship going?"

The way he dodged her question, Eva sensed someone was behind her, so instead of asking anything else she played along. "Fine, let's grab lunch and talk about it."

Bo nodded, and hurried off. Breath on the back of her neck, Eva pivoted to face Ingrid Swanson, Senator Zorn's assistant, who narrowed her eyes at her. "What were you and Bo talking about? It sounds classified."

Oh great, now Zorn's staffer was going to accuse Eva of being behind the leaks. In reply, she shook her head at Ingrid. "Nothing you need be concerned with."

ELEVEN

After chasing Mayor Sullivan from one meeting to the next most of the day, Kat gave up trying to interview him and went home. In the front hall, she tossed a stack of mail on the hall table and double bolted the door. A woman had been attacked in the parking garage of a building down the street, and Kat was being extra careful. After kicking off her yellow sneakers, she padded on stocking feet to the kitchen, which was much too large for a single person.

In the commercial-sized fridge, her selection for dinner was meager: two apples, mozzarella cheese sticks, and a few liters of water. The housekeeper had the day off, so she would have to make dinner on her own. If she ordered a pizza that meant going to the lobby and forgoing the safety she felt behind locked doors. From the cupboard, Kat took a granola bar and devoured it while she sat at the counter reading her emails.

The one from Jack McKenna, marked "Urgent," she quickly read, *Will you have time to meet me at Abbey's Roost in Pentwater on Saturday? Let me know ASAP. I will bring the file with me if you are able to get together. Jack*

A chance to spend time in Pentwater with Jack McKenna was tempting. Plus, Kat did want to get her hands on the supposed "undisclosed" evidence, which she had yet to see. She had hinted to Sydney she just might drive up. The problem was she still didn't have the data she requested about Mr. Jetson from *CamelotConnection*. Besides, she wondered if it was wise to leave Elliot when he was still recovering and distraught over Mark's death. She typed a reply to Jack, only to erase it.

She pulled a bottle of water from the fridge and took a sip. The more she thought about it, she realized Elliot would want her to chase a story about JFK's assassination. Besides, her big tip about the helicopter flight and briefcases of cash was disintegrating. Now Sheila Wagner was claiming she and her husband had just had a spat.

Kat put off answering Jack, for now. Bored with the other emails, Kat closed the computer and caught up on her mail. There was a healthy stack to wade through, mostly bills and junk, except for a blue card notifying her that a package was waiting for her in the building office, which closed at six.

Only four minutes to make it, Kat grabbed her key, wedged her feet into her shoes and unlocked the door. Three minutes and some change remained. She pressed the down button. It seemed an eternity, but finally the elevator arrived to take her down. Two stops later, she bolted out the narrow door and tapped on the glass window to the office. It was already closed, but a light was still on and Kat could see a thick package on the desk. Kat knocked louder, got no response. She tried the door. Strangely enough, it was open.

The package was addressed to her. Kat called out. When no one answered, she picked up the package that was marked Urgent. The return address told her it was the info she'd sent for on Jetson, which meant she could drive to Pentwater to help Sydney *and* get the new lead from Jack.

Safely back upstairs, Kat tore open the package, anxious to learn about Nikki's stepfather. A court date in two weeks would decide the guardianship. Meanwhile, Nikki was safe with Sydney at the Chadwick House.

At first, what Kat found inside the envelope left her confused. There was a copy of her driver's license and driving record, a copy of her credit report and copies of three charge card bills. Her eyes quickly scrolled down her list of purchases, including one she had just made at the lingerie department at Macy's.

Was it possible that *CamelotConnection* provided such complimentary info to all its newer clientele? She didn't think so.

The next pages shocked her to bone and marrow. She consumed one page after another, her hands shaking, until she could stand it no longer. This was an invasion of privacy of the worst kind! What she held was a word-for-word transcript of her phone conversations, including the one where Jack read John McKenna's letter.

However, compared to the others, that call was innocuous. Words danced before her eyes and Kat felt sick at heart as she recalled curling up in a leather chair in her living room, talking to Sydney about her enemies and a lot of other things that were now mocking her from the pages in her hands! The typed black letters, fragments of her life, were more than embarrassing; they were devastating.

The transcripts in her hands did not lie. Not only was her choice of words poor, she realized that she had discussed subjects she should have kept to herself. Elliot had already transferred her back to Chicago for suggesting the Senator leaked classified intelligence. Who knew what he would do if he read what she told her friend about Zorn?

When Kat returned from Pentwater, she had telephoned Sydney, sharing how Elliot survived the plane crash. The two women got to talking about other things and Kat confided how she blamed Zorn for her transfer. *Sydney, the day I left Washington for Chicago, I was so low. And, guess who was at the airport to taunt me? There was Zorn getting out of a stretch limousine with a man with, long blond wavy hair.*

Sydney had advised Kat not to let him have power over her mind, but Kat did not listen. What she told Sydney two days later was not just flippant, it was dangerous. She read those words, and a cold chill ran down her spine to the roots of her hair. *I was in the newsroom. Remember the man I saw with Senator Zorn, the one with the long blond hair, well, he was just arrested for allegedly shooting a Russian spy. I think that's one Senator who is in deep with the Russian mafia.*

All around the world, critics of the Russian regime were being shot, poisoned—in a word—killed. Kat shuddered to think she might be the next target or that she had put Sydney in danger. A deeper question riveted her to the expensive oak floor. Who had been listening? Who transcribed her conversations?

Kat could not figure out why *Camelot* sent them to her instead of the information she requested about Nikki's stepfather. She expected his rap sheet but, instead, what lay before her was her most personal information. To answer the why and how, Kat first had to know what she said. She dug further into the transcripts.

Besides the call with Jack, one conversation was with the Mayor's assistant to set up an interview, another with her producer about the Russian ambassador visiting Chicago, and a third call with Sydney about her niece, where Kat got a little excited about Mr. Jetson's harsh treatment of Nikki, calling him a moron. Seeing the black-and-white evidence of her impetuous nature was a real wake-up call.

Now, she picked up the phone to call Sydney, but dropped it. The condo phone had to be tapped! The thought of someone spying on her made Kat want to find her mother. She felt violated body and soul.

Who would do such a thing? Restless, like a cat on the prowl, thoughts darted through her mind. This began with her request for information about Mr. Jetson. Did he have the power to do this? It could be his way of sending her the message, "Don't mess with me." Kat closed the drapes, deciding it was unlikely that Jetson had an account with *Camelot;* it was too exclusive.

In the past, when she ordered information from the website, packages came with a return address of Almaty, Kazakhstan, and invoices showed the sums withdrawn from her bank account, not the website or business name. Her name as requester of information never appeared, just her account number.

Then it dawned on Kat to check the invoice. She tore through the pages and, as before, the return address was from the former Soviet republic of Kazakhstan. The invoice revealed the cost for her personal data and transcripts was $7,000.00, but the account number was not hers. There was no doubt, *CamelotConnection.com*, the same website she used for sensitive information, sent the parcel. The realization was crushing.

Nearly breathless, Kat balled her fists. Her mom was in India, and Elliot was still in the hospital. There was no one else, not a single person besides Sydney whom she could trust.

The truth sunk in as deep as a bitterly cold day in winter. When she gave her account number for information about Mr. Jetson, someone requested information about her, using his or her account number. Logic collided with emotion, leaving her with a provocative question.

Was Elliot so angry that he would stoop to listening to Kat's calls, and then send her the transcripts to let her know he was in charge of her life? Indeed, Elliot had the power and means to do this. At the hospital, he seemed so vulnerable. While she felt guilty for suspecting such a thing, she wondered again if he was trying to control her.

Kat felt foolish. Well, she could beat him at his game. She didn't even care if she had to work as a production assistant in Kalamazoo, Michigan—anything was better than being Elliot's pawn. So what if it was a shipping error? The proof was before her eyes and she would confront Elliot, now!

WITH NO DOCTORS or nurses to shield him, Elliott was a sitting duck for Kat's rage, and she let him have it with both barrels despite the fact he was still hooked up to an IV and looked weak. "You hounded me, tricked me. Why did you do it? I will never forgive you as long as I live!"

Kat shook from head to toe, her insides burning. One look at Elliot's face told her that he was shocked at her behavior. Had she been so malleable all these years that he actually thought he could get away with tapping her phones? Well, she had saved a little something, and his silence drove her to reveal it now.

"When I leave here, I'm going to meet with the U.S. Attorney. I know bugging people without their permission is a crime, Elliott, a federal crime. You'll go to prison."

A wicked thought caught in her throat and she swallowed down the words, *It would have been better for him not to have survived the crash.* She looked at him, his face was growing red, and he was choking, gasping for air. Kat's heart contracted. She could not just leave him like that.

"I'll call the nurse." Kat pressed the button, but with a vice-like grip, Elliot stopped her, pointed to the water cup. She reached across the tray and handed it to him.

He took a long sip as Kat fumed. Then he licked his lips and said. "Kat, sit down."

She shook her head, firmly. No, he was not going to worm out of this one.

He sipped more water. "Please."

"No." Kat stepped toward the door.

He opened his mouth, and she fully expected him to offer her any-thing just to appease her—her old job back in Washington, maybe a nightly anchor position. She would not bend. This time, Elliot Tucker had gone too far.

He coughed, "Must talk."

Just then, an aide dressed in aqua scrubs walked in with a tray of food.

"Hello," she intoned brightly. "Your dinner has arrived, Mr. Elliot, just as you ordered it. Homemade chicken soup, lime gelatin, and applesauce." She lifted up the lid. "I even sneaked you a piece of cherry pie, your favorite." She pressed a finger to her lips, "Don't tell your doctor."

Kat was furious. Elliot was even cajoling the aide to get his way. He was hopeless. She strode to the door, put her hand on the jamb. "You don't need me. I'm going."

The nurse's aide hustled to her, whispering, "He's not strong, you know. If you could help him eat the soup, it would help. At lunch he didn't touch a thing."

Kat eyed the woman, wondering if she was on the level. She smiled so sweetly, Kat believed her. Elliot fumbled with something on his lap. His face was now beet-red, yet he appeared tired and worn. She knew he had it in him to be a terrible person, but he really did look sick, probably at the thought of spending years behind bars.

"Okay." She'd think of it as his last meal.

The aide left them alone. Kat said not a word as she tore open a plastic spoon and napkin, which she spread on his chest. Elliot caught her wrist. "I don't care to eat until you tell me what you are talking about. What has upset you?"

His hand dropped to the bed.

"You're kidding right? You think because you are so powerful, you can hide behind Camelot and they won't answer a subpoena? They'll pretend it was someone else who tapped my phone calls?"

Her eyes felt sore, almost as if etched by sand from the beach. When Elliot moved his head from side to side, it made a funny noise. "Never, have I asked anyone to listen into your phone calls. Did I call you many times? Yes. Did you call back? Not once."

Elliot sounded hurt. "Was I beside myself with worry that something happened to you? Yes. Did I ask your mother to arrange for a condo in a nice neighborhood? I admit that. Did I hire a housekeeper and ask her to make your life comfortable? Yes, but, did I compromise my ethics and do anything illegal to harass you? Never."

Elliot licked his lips again, closed his eyes. When he opened them, he said forcefully, "I was on my way to see you in Pentwater when the plane went down."

Astonished by the admission, Kat sunk to the chair. "You were? How did you know I was there?"

Elliot sighed. "I figured you had sought refuge at the place you loved. Your mother told me she talked with you once, but never revealed where you were. She honored your privacy."

Kat's insides felt ripped apart. She was close to tears for the second time in recent days. "I don't know what to believe. This afternoon when I opened my mail, I had a package, which I thought contained information I ordered to help out a friend."

She wiped her eyes, her face. "Instead, I found my private information and transcripts of my calls with the mayor's office, my friends, and others. Elliot, it was the same unmarked envelope Camelot uses, from Kazakhstan." Kat stopped, thinking about the tough things she told Sydney about Senator Zorn. Her cheeks flamed hot, fearing Elliot might ask to see them.

Thankfully, he did not. Instead, what he said next convinced her that his denials were genuine. "Kat, when I get out of here, I will help you track down whoever did such a loathsome thing. You are right, it is illegal, and whoever would do it to you, would do it to me. Maybe even has."

Kat thought about what Elliot had said and decided she had, once again, jumped to a conclusion—a wrong conclusion. When would she learn? Elliot's offer of help told her he was gaining strength. A quick trip to Pentwater wouldn't hurt. After all, he was laid up in the hospital, where he couldn't do much. And, there would be someone in Pentwater who could.

She patted his hand and smiled. "I'm sorry I accused you Elliott. Please don't worry, just get better. I'm going back to Pentwater for a few days. There's something I have to do there."

Elliot rested his head against the pillow. "You will be careful and come see me when you get back?"

Kat assured him that she would. She said good night, with a plan firmly implanted in her mind. Detective McKenna needed her help. Why not ask for his? As soon as she got back home, it did not take her long to send him a brief email. *Jack, Saturday at nine sounds great. Am looking forward to seeing you again. Kat Kowicki*

TWELVE

U p earlier than on most Saturdays, Kat checked her reflection in the floor-length mirror. This morning, unlike other days at the beach when she threw on a tee shirt and shorts, and pulled her hair under a ball cap, she spent more time on her appearance. Satisfied that she looked just right to meet Jack McKenna—in pink blouse, beige skirt, and sandals—she applied shiny lip-gloss and left the house, walking along the lakeshore.

Sun warming her cheeks, Kat was excited at the prospect of seeing the intriguing Jack McKenna again. After a flurry of emails, he had given her the number to his Chicago office and, when the man who answered said she had reached the FBI's Terrorism Task Force, Kat did a double take. What else didn't she know about Jack, her stunning man on the beach?

Another thing was odd. When Sydney emailed back to say she never heard of him, Kat recalled how upset he was when she took his picture. By meeting him today, Kat hoped to unravel part of the mysterious Jack.

Inside the dining room at Abbey's Roost, she saw some empty tables, and others occupied by couples and women only. One table in the rear had a lone male, but he was not her admirer from the beach. She thought of checking the porch, which overlooked Pentwater Lake, but those tables were empty. With the sun still behind the restaurant, it was a bit cool for porch dining.

Instead, Kat asked for a table up front where she could see through the porch to the water and spot Jack when he arrived. Barely seated, Kat watched in horror as the man from the rear approached, like so many who recognized her from television. This guy was definitely better looking than most, but not as handsome as Jack McKenna.

Before Kat could think what to do, he stuck out his hand. "Hi, Kat. I see you don't recognize me."

Kat felt like rolling her eyes at that old line, dearly hoping Jack did not choose this moment to walk through the door. She had planned it all in her mind. She would sit quietly, sip her tea, and watch him come to her. Kat recoiled her fingers, dropped her arm. "You're right. I have no idea who you are. If you don't mind, I am expecting someone."

In reply, the man stared. What was she going to have to do, get the manager? She started up from her chair, when he shocked her. "I'm Jack McKenna. I think you are expecting *me.*"

Kat stared back, her brain muddled. He couldn't be Jack McKenna, the man on the beach, the one in her picture. The interloper pulled out a chair and sat across from her while Kat struggled to make sense of what was happening.

"Did I see you running on the beach with your dog?" That sounded so lame.

"You may have. I run on the beach, but don't remember seeing you there."

"Do you mind showing me your business card?" Such strange things happened to her lately; it seemed prudent to see identification. Jack reached into his wallet, and Kat glimpsed his gold badge. She snatched the card he offered. Sure enough, it had his name, Detective Jack McKenna, and a gold seal saying he worked for the FBI Terrorism Task Force.

Her hopes deflated, Kat sunk back into the chair, disappointed Jack wasn't Jack, the man she saw running on the beach. She gathered her wits, suppressing the urge to leave. "In your email, you claimed you saw me once in Pentwater. Where exactly?"

They were interrupted by a server, who brought them coffee before Kat had a chance to ask for tea. Jack took his cup. "I ordered coffee for both of us. Breakfast is on me, by the way. Do you know what you want?"

When Kat shook her head, the server went away, and Jack sipped his coffee. "To answer your question, a few weeks ago, I was coming out of the gas station and you were going in. I held the door for you. I recognized you and smiled, but you didn't appear to know me. Guess I've changed more than you since high school."

Maybe she knew Jack after all. "You went to Lake Forest Academy?"

He flashed an enormous smile, as though he was enjoying the riddle that was unfolding. "No, I didn't. That's where we first met, though. Fact is, we danced together."

Now Kat was beyond puzzled. She honestly did not remember this man. She noticed a slim space between his front teeth, just like the guy she ran into on the beach the last time she was in Pentwater. If twelve years ago Jack looked like he did today, she should have remembered him. His eyes were so incredibly blue; they reminded her of Lake Michigan. So far, he had put her at ease with his good humor.

Not touching her coffee, she asked, "Where did we dance?"

Jack's eyes twinkled at her. "I first met you at a homecoming dance at Lake Forest and again later when Valerie begged me to escort her to your prom at the Chicago Hilton Hotel ball room, which is where we danced."

Kat's mind flew back in time. She always envied Val, her friend at school. Her life seemed so together. They both boarded at the Academy. "Impossible! I remember dancing with Val's date. His name was John."

She scrutinized his face, as if he was trying to deceive her. "That was you?"

Jack grinned. "My family always called me Johnnie, but at the dance, I insisted Valerie call me John. Only I was not really her date, I'm her cousin."

Tickled by that, Kat laughed. "Val never admitted you were her cousin. At the time, I remember thinking she made a great catch because you seemed so normal."

Jack's face turned funny just then, and Kat wished she could retrieve her words. For some reason, it was the wrong thing to say. The server returned and Jack ordered a hearty breakfast of eggs and pancakes. Kat's stomach felt squeamish, so she asked for something safe, a toasted bagel and peppermint tea.

When the server left, Jack seemed to have recovered. They shared stories of growing up in Chicago, with Jack telling how after his mom died, he grew close to his dad who raised him, and he graduated from Morgan Park High School four years before Kat graduated from Lake Forest. His family was hard-working, middle-class, but his mother's sister, Maud, married a wealthy man, owner of a Chicago printing company. "Maud's daughter is Valerie, classmate to another privileged socialite, Kat Kowicki."

Jack seemed to watch closely for her reaction. Kat found it strange to hear him describe her as privileged. He had no idea how lonely she was growing up with neither mother nor father in her life. She ventured a new topic. "You were Johnnie, then John. How did you become Jack?"

His gracious smile hinted he'd known Kat all these years. "At the police academy, there were too many Johns in my class. An instructor called me Jack and it stuck."

Her tea arrived, so she drank some to settle her nerves. Kat had interviewed a Chicago police captain or two, but knew no police officers on a personal level. Jack could give background for crime stories, or be a terrific source for new stories.

"What do you do at the terrorism task force?"

"I work out of the FBI office, mostly with federal agents. We identify and eliminate threats to our country. It's enjoyable and rewarding work."

To Kat's reply, "It sounds dangerous," Jack dug his fork into the fried eggs that had just been set in front of him. The breakfast crowd dwindled, but their conversation was just getting going. They talked about the years since the dance, the Pentwater scene, ending with Kat's career and her mom. Their server kept them supplied with coffee and tea. For someone who portrayed himself as less fortunate than Kat, Jack appeared to enjoy talking with her, and showed no lasting scars of a deprived youth.

Kat found the conversation stimulating, though she wanted to take it a level deeper. "You haven't mentioned the rest of your family. Are you married?"

Jack brought his coffee cup to his lips, as though to camouflage the stricken look that swept over his face. When he said nothing, Kat was sorry she brought it up.

She shoved aside her plate and returned to their reason for meeting. "You promised I could see your dad's evidence of the JFK assassination. I'm ready."

Jack looked around the room. Most tables empty, he still spoke quietly, "In November 1963, he was a detective assigned to the First District." Kat moved her head forward to show she was interested, prompting him to lean toward her. "On the night of November 22, my dad was contacted after business hours by an FBI agent."

He glanced over his shoulder. "That's the day President Kennedy was shot and killed in Dallas. The FBI agent asked my dad to locate for him the owner of Klein's Sporting Goods. He and the owner met the FBI there."

As Jack lowered his voice a notch, Kat strained to hear. "It turned out the gun used to kill Kennedy was purchased through the mail from Klein's, but Lee Harvey Oswald used a fake name."

Kat wanted to see the evidence herself, but she had already said things that bothered Jack and didn't want to appear too pushy, so she simply nodded. Jack drained his coffee cup. "Anyway, Dad helped search microfilm records. The FBI agent found the record of Oswald's purchase of the six-point-five-millimeter Italian Mannlicher-Carcano rifle, using the alias A. Hidell. Kat, but I assume you know all that. Here's the kicker. My father found another record for an identical weapon, plus ammunition, that Oswald-Hidell did not order. A different person purchased these, and Klein's shipped the second order to Dallas a few days later."

Kat took it to the next, logical step. "Why didn't the FBI follow up? It doesn't make any sense to ignore such important evidence."

When Jack blinked, light reflected off his beautiful eyes. Oblivious to her interest in him, he stuck to the case at hand. "Dad showed the record to the FBI, but they never pursued it. He copied everything, which he's kept all these years. I'll show you a letter in the file from the FBI."

Revved up by the intrigue of it all, Kat asked, "Can we look at it now?"

Jack held his hands up, palms out. "Stay with me a minute longer. Some years later, he sent copies of what he found to FBI headquarters, but they continued to ignore that second purchase. It's as though they don't want to consider any conclusion other than the Warren Commission's, that Lee Harvey Oswald was the lone assassin."

Kat felt drawn to Jack. "How can I help? I wasn't even born in 1963."

When he set down his cup, their server refilled it with hot coffee. "After Big John's stroke, I found records and research, along with the note I read you. Now I'd like to pursue what he is convinced is a coverup of a failed investigation. My dilemma is I work on the FBI task force, and don't want to bite the hand that feeds me."

His smile was magnetic. "You are, on the other hand, a respected investigative journalist. I turn Dad's files over to you. If you find them credible, you reveal the coverup. Dad's theory gets a thorough review and you get credit for a major story."

Her instincts said to grab and run with it. Yet, she had thought the stranger on the beach was Jack. Jack McKenna may be her friend's cousin, and she danced with him a decade ago, but who was he really? After all, he turned green when she asked if he was married.

Kat took money from her purse to pay for her meal. "Okay, I am interested. When do I see the documents?"

Jack slapped the table. "Right now. They're on my boat."

"You live on a boat?"

He grabbed the check. "Yeah, and the meal is on me. I have a 28-foot Sea Ray, called *Day Dreamer.* Winston might be there, too."

Winston sounded like a guy's name. Was that why he didn't want to talk about being married? Kat gave him a quizzical look, and then plunged ahead. Maybe Winston was his brother. "And Winston is —?"

Jack grinned at her. "A real sweetie, even if he has an ugly face."

Kat was shocked at that. Good thing she decided to check him out.

His grin got wider, as if he was having fun at her expense. "He's a boxer."

"Middle or heavy weight?"

Jack took her elbow. "Come on, you'll like him. He's especially friendly to women."

Kat stopped in her tracks. "Jack, I don't want to go to your boat just now. Maybe later. You tell Winston about me first."

"Naw, it'll just take a few minutes. You can sit on the aft deck, watch the water and read my dad's documents."

JACK UNLOCKED HIS BICYCLE and wheeled it alongside him as they walked together to the marina. Kat was uneasy about going and vowed to herself to leave his boat as soon as she saw the evidence. At the marina, an idyllic scene softened her stance. Men cleaned fish at a stand; speedboats and sailboats bobbed at the moorings. Chief Able was striding toward them. She started to feel safer.

When he spotted Kat, he waved and closed in. Jack, she noticed, made a beeline for his boat. Kat wanted to talk with the Chief, who had phoned her a few days ago about Mr. Jetson's assault on Nikki. "Chief Able, I want to ask you something. Will you be at the police station? I've got something to finish here first."

He seemed to know what she wanted. "Sydney and her niece are doing all right, but Mrs. Jetson is giving them fits. I have a bit of news to share with you, too. At the station, pick up the phone by the door and dispatch will reach me."

Kat promised to come see him, wishing she had received Mr. Jetson's criminal record that she ordered on *CamelotConnection*. Just thinking about that website brought the pain of being listened to rushing over her, making her more determined to seek Jack's help. Since he worked with the FBI, he was the perfect person to guide her.

And she needed his help now, finding his boat. She tried hard to remember the name of it. Two large boats looked nearly identical, both with sterns backed in. Her eyes went from one, *Day Tripper*, to the other, *Day Dreamer*. Besides the weird coincidence, Jack was nowhere in sight.

He never mentioned that the boat next to his had a similar name; he was a man with secrets, and that bothered her. Well, his was "Day" something. She shrugged, stepped on board the nearest one, and called loudly, "Jack."

From the cabin, she heard a man's voice say "Just a minute." He sounded like Jack. Kat shielded her eyes from the blinding sunlight and, before she could see it coming, a muscular brown dog with a black muzzle and jowls was licking her hands, her arms, and wagging its entire hind end.

Jack bounded from below deck. "Kat, I told you that Winston would like you."

She was dumbstruck. Winston was a dog. "You own a boxer."

"What did you think I meant?"

Oh, never mind Jack, she wanted to say, but held her tongue. He tricked her and he knew it. Kat laughed at his joke and, she laughed to herself, too, because the man on the beach had a vicious dog, and the real Jack had a sweet one. A little voice told her that this was something to remember about him.

She patted the dog's head. Kat didn't mind animals; she just had not been around them much. "Jack, I saw the police chief and have to talk with him about something else before he leaves for the day."

Jack held out an accordion envelope. "It's all here. At this point, this is strictly confidential. If you decline, what's in there stays there, right?"

Hurt by his need to caution her, Kat felt defensive. "Of course."

"Don't say anything to the Chief about me or this case."

She understood his reluctance, but wondered if concealing things was an essential part of Jack's nature. When she had asked about his family, he certainly clammed up.

"I won't tell, but dare I ask why?"

"Sometimes I work undercover and never know who I'll run into. Once people in town know I'm a cop, my cover is blown."

That made sense. Kat let it go. She settled into a captain's chair, her feet propped on a footrest. File spread on her lap, she began reading through different documents, some handwritten, and some typed. What caught her interest was the microfilm copy of a Klein's Sporting Goods handwritten order form. On it, someone requested that a Mannlicher-Carcano rifle *and* ammunition be mailed to a Dallas P.O. box. She made a note to check that one against Oswald's box number.

His evidence, just as scintillating as Jack said in his email, seemed to link another person to the assassination of President Kennedy. For a fleeting moment, Kat envisioned receiving a Pulitzer Prize for solving a mystery that captivated Americans since the day Jack Ruby, who was born in Chicago, had gunned down Lee Harvey Oswald.

She turned a page. Winston licked her hand, and looked at her with enormous brown eyes. Kat rubbed his head. This caused more licking up her arm. She could not help squealing, which brought Jack up from the cabin.

"Winston," he scolded, "No licking."

The dog whined and wagged his back half. Jack did not give in. "I said no. Leave the lady alone. Go to your bed."

Winston dropped his head, and padded off, but not before sneaking in another lick, catching the fingers of her left hand.

"I don't mind Jack, really."

"He has to learn manners. I am gone all day, and he is lonely, even though my dad used to take him for walks every morning and afternoon."

Kat set down the papers. "How is he, Jack?"

Jack put his bare foot on the boat seat. "Not back to normal speech, but he's walking better. I really want to let him know his efforts on JFK have been worth it."

As he talked, he glanced across the water, overpowering Kat with what a forceful man he was. Elliot Tucker was rich, wielded influence all across the country, but he had none of Jack's magnetism. She blinked her eyes. *No,* her brain warned, *get your eyes off him and onto the papers.*

She left him to his private thoughts and went back to reading Big John's memo. To him, Oswald was more than an ex-Marine who turned sour. It seemed the alleged assassin might have been a spy. Dallas detectives reported finding a Minox, a special kind of camera loaded with film in Oswald's Marine sea bag. According to Big John, it was the size of a five-stick pack of gum. His notes said that, in World War II, spies on both sides allegedly used the same type of German-made camera. However, it was not readily available to the public in 1963. How did Oswald get one?

His military occupation specialty was "Aviation Electronics Operator." Assigned to Atsugi Air Base, the same place the CIA operated from in the Far East, with a confidential security clearance, Oswald worked with radar codes. These signal codes, the ones by which military planes in flight identified each other, were changed after he defected to Russia.

Besides taking photographs in Japan with an Imperial Reflex 35-millimeter camera, Oswald was seen in the company of a woman from the Queen Bee, a Tokyo nightclub and known espionage location. Allegedly, he admitted to George De Mohrenschildt, his friend in Dallas, this was where the Communists first contacted him.

There was so much here, Kat's head was spinning from the sheer volume. There was no way she could read it all at once. She skipped to the letter Big John wrote when he forwarded the second gun order to FBI headquarters. Music floated to her ears and Kat turned to see Jack playing a harmonica down on the dock. The tune was wistful; Kat reflected that this Chicago detective had more layers to his personality than she imagined.

She went on reading, seconds later, gasping, "Oh, no!" Her hand flew to cover her mouth.

Jack was on board in an instant. "What's wrong?"

Her heart thumping, she rustled the paper. "Did you read this letter the FBI sent your Dad back in the early eighties when they rejected the idea of a second gun order?"

Harmonica in one hand, Jack nodded. "I did, why?"

Obviously, he did not realize the importance of it, what it meant to Kat. How could he? She had not mentioned it until now. "What we have is a smoking gun. I had a run-in with the very person who denied your dad a hearing on his evidence."

Jack took a seat. "I don't understand."

Kat could not keep her lips from parting in a wide smile. "Senator Lars Zorn from California is to blame for my being transferred back to Chicago." She tapped the letter with her petite fingers. "But, that has nothing to do with what's in here. Before he was a Senator, Zorn was Governor of California. Before that, an actor, and before that, the 'pretty boy' was an FBI agent assigned to FBI headquarters."

"Wow." Winston started to whine, so Jack retrieved the boxer from below, gripping his collar to keep the dog from wandering over to Kat. "I heard something about him. Sorry to admit it, but he's not high on my radar screen."

Kat kept her hands away from Winston's tongue. "When I was assigned to Congress, I covered hearings he presided over. He loves to be on air. This letter from the FBI, telling your dad there is nothing to the records he found was signed by—"

Jack interrupted, "Zorn."

Kat could not believe it. Maybe she'd get double justice for America, shed light on who killed Kennedy, and wipe Zorn off the Presidential map. "Seems he kept your dad's microfilm copies and never returned them with the letter."

Jack seemed interested, but not as enthused as Kat. It was almost as if he was suddenly preoccupied. He did ask if she wanted to read the rest.

Arms wrapped around the accordion file, Kat clutched it to her chest. "You couldn't snatch this baby from me, even with Winston's help."

She more fully understood Jack's desire to help his father. "After your email, I read up on the assassination. I never saw any mention of this other six-point-five-millimeter Mannlicher-Carcano purchase. Is it possible officials like Zorn have known the truth and kept it from the American public all these years? Jack, your dad's material will keep me awake tonight."

"Does that mean you'll pursue the whole idea, wherever it takes you?"

Kat rose, feeling it was time to leave. "More than you'll ever know. Peculiar things are happening to me that might involve the Senator. I'd like to get your opinion, but should see Chief Able first. Could you stop over to my cottage later?"

She pointed beneath low hanging trees along the waterfront. "That house with teal shutters, around the curve of the shore as the channel wall begins, is my Mom's cottage."

Jack agreed to come by, so Kat took a chance and offered to do something she rarely did—cook. "Stop over at one o'clock and I'll feed us soup and sandwiches."

She walked to the rear starboard side of the boat, and tickled Winston's ears. "Bring your friend if you want."

Jack laughed. "We'd like that."

Kat headed toward shore, accordion file tucked safely in her arms, a smile on her face, and many questions in her heart.

THIRTEEN

From the Chief, Kat learned Nikki's stepfather had been caught driving on a suspended license. Jetson's parole was vacated and Chief Able gave him a free ride to the county jail to wait for his trip back to state prison. It looked like Nikki would be spared testifying against him for assault. With the good news, Kat headed to the deli, where she ordered chicken sandwiches and minestrone soup for lunch with Jack.

Kat hurried inside the cottage to set the table. As she put out mugs for tea, she glanced out the front window and her heart leapt at what she saw there.

Jack sat on the bench overlooking the lake, Winston at his side. She felt butterflies in her stomach, and wondered why. Nothing about Jack's manner should make her nervous. Kat tore her eyes away, plugged in the teapot to boil. Whatever was churning her stomach was also destroying her appetite.

Well, she would sip tea while Jack ate his lunch. She mentally told her stomach to get over it, having found what she willed with the mind, her body usually followed. It was not that Kat felt she had special powers, she simply believed in positive thinking.

She stuck her head out of the cottage's lakeside door and called to her guests. Just breathing in the fresh air she felt better. Winston came bounding up and, with his fat, pink tongue he gave her hand a tremendous lick before Jack could stop him.

Jack tugged the leash on Winston's collar. "He's still a puppy, but I'm working with him. I'll secure him to the bench in the shade. Maybe you could run water in an old bowl."

They saw to the dog, and once in Jack's company, Kat's spirits soared. Jack, on the other hand, seemed uninspired by her company and absorbed by his surroundings. He took it all in—the large dining room table, chandelier, and Picasso painting hanging above the sideboard.

"Please sit," Kat invited.

Kat sampled her tea, as Jack bowed his head. When he looked up, she could not help asking, "Don't you like the sandwich? I was not sure what you liked." She smiled, hoping to put him at ease, "Except pancakes and fried eggs."

Jack took a bite and chewed. "Yes, it's good. I was saying thanks for our meal."

"Oh." Kat stirred her soup, never having given thanks for lunch in her entire life. Whenever food appeared, she ate it.

Before Jack could take another bite of his sandwich, Winston began to bark. "Sorry. No doubt he wants to chase a squirrel."

He jumped up and soon the dog was quiet. Jack returned, slipped into his chair without missing a beat. Kat surmised he was used to grabbing a hot dog on the run. They ate in silence for some moments, Kat trying the soup. Finding it tasty, she finished the bowl.

Jack's bowl was empty, too. "What you call a cottage is a mansion to me."

Kat considered the cathedral ceilings, stone fireplace, and high windows built to display the lake view. Maybe it was a bad idea to bring him here. He seemed more at home on his boat.

She shrugged. "It's my Mom's home. She sees so much war and despair on her travels and comes here to unwind. It is big, I guess, but to me, it's a safe haven." Jack put down his sandwich. "You had something to ask. If you don't mind, I should get Winston back pretty soon."

Kat hurried to clear the uneaten food. "Let's sit on the porch. I love that part of the house."

Settled on a lounge chair, she confided in him about how receiving the charge bills, credit report and the transcripts blew her life apart. "Except for Elliot, I told no one. He was so fired up, I am afraid he will have a setback. If there's a bug on my phone, is the device actually located in my condo or at the phone company?"

Jack leaned forward on his wrought iron chair, laced his fingers together before answering. "In criminal cases, I have obtained court-ordered wiretaps."

The direct gaze he leveled at her almost made Kat feel trapped. She lifted her chin. "I am not involved in crime, except for reporting it, if that is what you mean."

Jack did not lessen his stare. "Left a trail of scorned lovers in your wake, have you?"

His caustic tone was unexpected. Kat was unsure what made his kind nature disappear like a vapor. "None that I know of," she snapped back. "Please wait a moment. I'll be right back."

She bounced from the chair, stalked upstairs to her room, wondering if he would be gone when she returned. It was hard to imagine what had gotten into him, but she intended to show him that she was not making it up. From her suitcase, Kat threw her sweaters, socks, and shorts on the bed, until she found what she was looking for.

As she flew back down the stairs, her heart questioned what she was about to do. Still, he had started it and Kat was not a woman to back down, not even to a Chicago cop. She had nothing to hide.

Jack stood by the porch window, looking out over the lake. As she approached, he turned. Unable to decipher the look on his face, she shoved the transcript toward him, daring him to take it.

He did, but before opening it, he tossed her a grin. "I didn't mean to hurt your feelings by suggesting you did anything wrong. The detective in me looks at everything with a jaundiced eye. Every day I work with disguise and deceit. Forgive me?"

Kat stood rooted to the floor. Never had a person asked for her forgiveness. It was such a foreign idea she was speechless. Well, almost. "There's nothing to forgive."

The hope in his face returned her good opinion of him, and her composure. "When you read this, you'll understand my concern."

This time, Jack selected a comfy chair to leaf through the pages. Soon, it was his turn to gasp. "This is me talking to you, reading my dad's letter."

Kat bounced off the wrought-iron chair. "I tried to tell you, but I guess it's hard to appreciate the shock until you see it yourself. Jack, what can we do? I'm in the middle of trying to root out a political corruption scandal." She wanted his opinion. "Do you think it's related to that?"

Face grim, his lips barely moved. "Tell me again when and how you got this."

Kat handed him the *CamelotConnection* account card, explaining how she used it to order legitimate information about Nikki's stepdad. "It came from Kazakhstan in a brown envelope. For seven thousand dollars, someone got my five hundred dollars worth of data on Mr. Jetson, and for five hundred dollars, which Camelot took from my account, I got seven thousand dollars worth of my own private information. The only way I found to contact the company is via the website, so I sent an email asking about my request. I was careful not to mention anything else."

He inspected the card, before giving it and the transcripts back to her. "That was smart. I've never heard of Camelot Connection, but I do understand your concern. I don't like the idea of someone listening to me talking to you. A friend of mine is retired from the phone company. Let me look into it."

That is just what Kat hoped he would say. "Thanks Jack. Your concern helps me to get a grip on this."

Jack stood, so did Kat, reminding him that he had both her phone numbers. A hand on the doorknob, Jack said, "I'm not about to call and have your ex-boyfriends coming after me."

Her eyes narrowed. Was he joking or for real? It was not easy figuring out this detective. She pursed her lips. "Really, Jack, don't worry about that."

Jack flashed a warm smile. "I was kidding. Please be careful what you say on the phone, especially about me or my dad's accordion file."

Kat promised she would be cautious. Despite Jack's offer to help, as he and Winston walked back to the boat, she felt lonely and a little afraid of the future.

MONDAY MORNING, JACK ARRIVED at his office later than usual. He had enjoyed boating in yesterday's sun, but while it gave him a healthy glow, it sapped his energy. On top of that, the long drive from Pentwater left him mentally weary; he spent the four hours trying to pinpoint the gaps in the case against Luis and how best to hunt down the Venezuelan plane. FBI agent Malone was checking, but so far Jack heard nothing.

In between, Jack found his mind wandering to Kat. Was it his imagination, or was he starting to see her as more than an acquaintance? Obviously, discovering someone was listening to her personal conversations really shook her. He suggested they keep their phone calls to a minimum, and now he was sorry he did. Even if Kat didn't share his dry sense of humor, he respected her professionalism.

Besides, he sensed she was alone in the world. His mind told him to forget her, get back to work. Cut from different cloth than she, Jack feared their differences might tear at a relationship, just as the Bible cautioned not to sew a new, unshrunk patch to an old garment; the unshrunk patch would break away from the garment when washed. If he had seen those differences in Melissa, Jack would have saved himself from a world of hurt. Still, Kat needed a friend to look after her, and he could do that much.

The office was abuzz with agents and officers making phone calls, arranging their week's activities; Jack filled his coffee cup. Enrique "Ricky" Vazquez waved the phone at him. "Sean Malone for you."

Jack hurried to his desk, picked up the receiver and made small talk, asking Malone about his weekend.

Malone usually talked like a machine gun, but this morning he sounded as tired as Jack was. "The usual honeydew kind, you know, 'Honey do this, honey do that'."

Jack's coffee was over by the pot. "I'm not married, and my dog doesn't say much. I spent time on my boat in Michigan."

The agent's voice held a note of envy. "No boats, but I did improve my son's batting stance for t-ball. The Venezuelan intelligence service, DISIP, is closed tighter than a drum. We can't get anything from them, though we have good relations with other nations who are on better terms."

While Jack listened intently, Ricky walked over to Jack's desk with the cup he had left on the coffee counter to take Malone's call. He mouthed, "Thanks."

Sean Malone was not finished. "The King Air is owned by a corrupt charter outfit in Caracas. They reportedly fly missions for Hezbollah. You can bet Venezuelan Intelligence will keep an eye on both the charter company and terror group, even if the government is cozy with some Middle Eastern countries."

Jack was due to meet with Gordon in thirty seconds. "Thanks Malone. If you ever get up this way, you've got a ticket to ride on my boat."

"McKenna, I just may take you up on that. D.C. is a regular sauna this summer, and I melt in the heat. Just between you and me, I'm hoping to get back to the Midwest."

A good Irishman, Malone had a gift of gab, but Jack had to run. "Catch ya later."

He jammed down the receiver and hustled to Gordon's office, minus his coffee. Gordon was on the phone and pointed to a chair, "Sir, I brief you on the Mexican cartel at ten."

Jack checked his watch. He had about six minutes.

Over the weekend, Gordon cut his hair military style, shaved so close Jack saw a vein throbbing by his ear. "That was my top boss, the SAC. Jack, there is something going on with this Luis San Felipe thing I don't understand."

Jack sucked in a breath, ready to tell what he knew, which wasn't much. "Pablo finished the first of six vans Luis ordered. The second one should be done by tonight. The conversions don't take too long, so if Pablo receives the other vans he ordered, they should be converted and ready for pick up soon."

His boss fumbled with a file on his desk. Unsure Gordon was listening, Jack asked, "Ever heard of a web group called Camelot Connection? It provides legal and technical resources."

Gordon's silence told volumes. So did his probing eyes. "How did you hear of it?"

To Jack, his boss sounded miffed. Perhaps it would be wiser to keep mum about Kat's phone tap. Jack grew evasive. "Some media types nosing around. They let it slip about the web site where they get extraordinary information about people, like criminal records, phone records, and surveillance reports."

Gordon's reply seemed carefully couched. "It's a company of retired Agency, Bureau, and local police officers, who conduct minor investigations and provide security for private industry. They are selective about the companies they work with. I must say McKenna," file under his arm, Gordon was out of his seat and edging toward the door, "I am surprised they do anything for the media. We're all adverse to that kind of scrutiny."

As Jack stood eye-to-eye with Gordon, he got the impression his supervisor knew more. Jack sought to draw him out. "At least you knew about it. It was a surprise to me."

Gordon glanced at the open door. "Camelot shouldn't be dealing with the media. The people there may, and I stress *may*, furnish information to Federal investigative agencies, the kind of info that is shared at the top, then trickles down to us. I won't discuss it. At the Bureau, it's treated like a confidential informant."

Jack realized his blunder in asking about *Camelot*. Gordon left the room, leaving Jack standing alone, trying to grasp how Kat got involved with a source that furnished information to the highest levels of the FBI.

Back at his desk, Jack phoned Lenny Moses to help him check out Kat's phones. One thing was clear; he would not mention *Camelot* to Gordon again. When Lenny's phone rang busy, Jack looked between the blinds on the window toward Pablo's shop.

In these new digs, Jack had the distinction of being within spitting distance of auto body and repair shops along Ogden Avenue. Here, among privately owned tool shops, Jack's informant appeared to eke out a living altering recreational vehicles. Jack got busy on his report, explaining how Pablo made reams of money helping dopers like Manuel Ochoa, Mexican Cartel kingpin, outfitting RVs with hidden compartments, until the task force caught him with a vehicle he converted. Now an informant, Pablo hoped to stay out of prison by snaring those higher up in the criminal chain.

Before he finished the last paragraph, Jack's cell phone rang. Kat was cryptic. "Jack," she whispered, "I am using someone else's phone. Can we meet tonight?"

"Nope. I'll be out late." Other plans prevented him from asking her to lunch.

"I see," was all she said, sounding deflated.

Jack struggled to regain a footing. "I'm free tomorrow morning."

Kat sighed. "That doesn't work. I am off to Dallas to cover a story, and I want to see your father today before I leave. You said he is home. Could you arrange it?"

"Sure."

Her voice dropped. "To reach me on my cell, touch star 67 so it won't display your phone number. Just identify yourself as Winston. I'll call you from another phone."

Her call jogged his mind to try Lenny again. This time he reached the man he worked with off and on for years. Happy to do this favor, Lenny told Jack he had no other jobs to interfere tomorrow and he'd get to it then. After a quick call to Big John, Jack reached Kat and gave her directions.

"Have a safe trip," he said before hanging up. Kat's enthusiasm for life seemed to match his, and it had been easy to apologize to Kat and ask her forgiveness. Yet, Jack still held tremendous animosity in his heart toward Melissa. He should reconcile that, hand it over to God, and ask for *his* forgiveness.

Big John told him it was better to find out what kind of person Melissa was before the wedding, not after. If faith meant anything to him, Jack had to follow what Christ taught; he would receive God's forgiveness in the same measure as he gave it.

Forgiveness aside, he never answered her letter, and did not intend to. At the keyboard, he tucked away personal feelings to finish his report. The task force allowed Pablo to continue making traps for smugglers, with one catch. Jack installed Ricky as a full-time employee in Pablo's shop. As far as the other workers knew, Ricky was tight with Pablo, so he came and went as he pleased.

In reality, because he was a Chicago Police Officer on the task force, Ricky did little work at Interstate Vans. However, he did have his own keys to the place, so on some nights Jack and Ricky entered without Pablo's knowledge. That way, if Pablo planned something sneaky after hours, the task force would find out.

As his meeting at Norman's Cay made clear, they had to reach further into the cartel before shutting down Interstate Vans. Not knowing how or if that would happen, Jack routed his report for Gordon's approval before it was sent to Headquarters.

In fifteen minutes, he and Ricky were meeting to plan tonight's op, but there were some kinks to work out. The FBI agent who assisted them on technical aspects, had transferred to Washington, and Jack wanted to check out the agent recommended to replace him. He ordered two deluxe pizzas for their lunch, and as he waited for the delivery, his thoughts strayed again to Melissa.

They met four years ago at a class on criminal behavior, where they both spoke. She was a therapist who worked with repeat offenders. It seemed to Jack they shared the same values. For some unknown reason, God had a different plan for his life. He stood, stared out the blinds again, not thinking of the van, but wondering how he failed to see heartache coming. The excuse Melissa offered in the letter bothered him. It was unlikely the dangers he faced really upset her; she worked with criminals every day.

Jack shook off the question to which he might never find an answer. He should learn from it, not remain stuck in the past. He looked to Dad for inspiration, who taught him the bee stings of life helped you build up immunity. Not a man to hold a grudge, Jack touched the pain Melissa brought him, and did one of the most difficult things he'd ever done. In his mind and heart, he forgave.

On the way to pay for the pizzas, he reminded himself though, that he didn't have to be a chump. If Melissa ever tried to make up with him, he would run, not walk away.

FOURTEEN

Kat set the fruit she'd brought for Big John McKenna on the table next to his recliner chair. His feet were propped up and Winston was by his side, looking as if he were ready to help if necessary.

"I hope you like sweet cherries and peaches. Are you up to talking?"

Big John's fingers stroked the animal's head. "Best talk today. Don't know how long I've got. My life is in the Almighty's hands now."

Instead of responding to something she knew nothing about, Kat opened her notebook and began questioning the man who spent thousands of hours of his life trying to explain who killed Kennedy and why. She listened to overlooked and forgotten evidence. His insights razor sharp, he filled many gaps in her knowledge. From him she learned that Klein's Sporting Goods was no longer in business, so she crossed that off her list.

The high points she noted, with half an idea of where to go next. "I leave for Dallas tomorrow, where I have developed one or two leads."

John McKenna raised an eyebrow and in that moment, his skeptical expression reminded Kat of Jack when she first told him about the transcripts of her phone conversations.

Kat clicked the cap onto her pen. "I don't want to get your hopes up. Besides touring the Sixth Floor Museum, I am meeting a private researcher as well as a man who was an intern at the hospital where the President received treatment. He is retired from medicine now and has a few thoughts to share about the pristine bullet. I don't believe one bullet did all that damage." She watched his face as she asked, "Do you?"

"I don't believe the moon is made of cheese or that our government blew up the World Trade Center, either." John closed his eyes.

Kat put down her pad, ready to run any errand he needed. "Can I get you anything?"

He pointed to the kitchen. "Glass of water."

Winston trotted beside her to the sink. She forced herself to resist looking around the house where Jack was born. After John took his medicine, she asked, "What do you think of Oswald marrying Marina in Russia after they knew each other for only a few weeks?"

He set down his glass. "Her uncle, Ilya Prusakov, was a Lieutenant Colonel in the MVD, the military arm of Soviet Intelligence. All we know of what Oswald did in Minsk was what he wrote in his supposed diary, but there are many timing errors in it. I read it all and, believe me; it resembles an intelligence brief about a place where we had little information."

Kat gathered her thoughts. "It is troubling, with all the evidence pointing to Oswald, why the paraffin test on his cheek came up negative. I mean, if he fired that rifle from the Depository, shouldn't it have been positive?"

Big John talked to her with his eyes closed. "That's a real interesting question. Could be Oswald was a patsy like he said. Plenty of witnesses saw other people on the sixth floor before the shooting. Be sure to ask your Dallas researcher about the President's limo going to Detroit forty-eight hours afterwards and being torn apart. If there were more bullets, blood, what have you, it was gone."

Kat asked his thoughts on the Warren Commission. "Was it a rubber stamp for J. Edgar Hoover and President Johnson?"

He opened his eyes, set down his glass. "One Commission member did pretty well for himself, going on to become the only unelected President this country ever had."

Kat agreed it was something. "With President Ford's death, there are no Commission members still living."

With that, the big man seemed to sag. He quit petting the dog, which was snoring by his feet. They made quite a picture, reminding her of what she meant to ask Jack's father. "Before I leave, mind if I ask a final question?"

A faint smile lit his manly face, and then vanished, much like a rainbow does when a cloud masks the sun. "You reporters always have one more question."

Kat could not argue there. "Your son is intelligent and a great cop. Does he agree with your theories about JFK?"

A shadow of sadness passed over his face. "I've never shared this with Jack. Like you, he wasn't born when Kennedy was killed. Because my wife died when Jack was still a boy, he never had a mother-son relationship. I was both, so I didn't fill his mind with my idle time projects. I thought once I was gone, he might just want to know.

That's all. I sometimes think the absence of his mom's affection is why he has never married."

Kat noticed that the house was clean and tidy as a showroom, every lamp and table in its functional place. Still, it lacked the feminine touch of pictures or flowers. There was something more Kat hoped to learn about Jack. She closed her notebook and put away her pen. "Jack told me he almost married. I believe he thinks his dangerous work isn't compatible with a family."

John stirred in his chair, seemingly no more comfortable with personal revelations than his son was. "That's probably where I failed him. A child needs two parents."

Something about his openness gave Kat the freedom to say, "My father died when I was two. I have no memories of him. My mother went to work, and I guess she's not to blame that her career skyrocketed, took her away from me."

Unsure from where her painfully honest feelings came, Kat continued, "It must have been hard on you, caring for a small son, working the hours police officers have to."

John leaned over, petted Winston's head. "Yeah it was, but my Jack is bright. He learned to cook burgers, do the wash, and still get As in school."

"He thinks the world of you, sir, and was devastated by your stroke. He told me that much."

Big John sipped some water, smacked his lips. "Told ya that, did he? Well, we're close. Always have been. I never missed any of his ball games. His Grandma, my mother, rest her soul, taught him things I couldn't, like how to dance for his school prom."

Kat smiled inwardly at pleasant memories of dancing with him. A more vivid memory eclipsed the dance—how Jack looked at her on the porch in Pentwater. Strong feelings for Jack overpowered her just then and she wished she was not leaving him behind for a trip to Dallas.

"My name is John."

What did he say? "Excuse me, sir?"

"Call me John. Sir is someone the Queen taps on the shoulder with a sword. I'm no knight and my son is no saint."

Rather than ask what he meant, she told him more about herself. "With my mom gone a lot, school was everything to me. I boarded at Lake Forest Academy and that's where I met Jack once, long ago, at a school dance. He was an *excellent* dancer. He was there with his cousin Valerie—she was my friend."

John was nodding his head as though he remembered. "Now, Jack finally knows all about my pet project, and has you working on it. I appreciate it, Ms. Kowicki."

Kat lifted her petite chin. "What's fair is fair, John. I am Kat, and you are welcome. To be honest, I'm searching for a story, one that will take me back to Washington."

John grunted. "So, you don't like languishing in Chicago, not big enough news for you. Want to go to glamour parties and be seen. Well, *she* was like that and it didn't stick."

She? Was he talking of Jack's mother? "You mean, Mrs. McKenna?"

John shook his head. "No, supposed to be, but fortunately she left before the vows were said. She never even showed up at the church to get married."

Kat was confused. "You were never married to Jack's mother?"

John boomed, as if unbeaten by the stroke, "Say what? You're confusing our generations. Course we were married. Eight years before Jack ever came along. I am talking about Jack's engagement to Melissa Horner."

His voice grew even louder, "On the second of June, she left my boy, my Jack, standing at the altar, left all of us in shock, but I was glad. She was too independent for her own good, liked to travel the world. Before the wedding, she got it in her head she wanted to see some crater in Oregon. Jack had to work and she—" John snapped his fingers— "Missy, that's what I called her, went off with friends, just like that. No good for a union, if one is selfish, always thinking of her own needs first."

Kat was stunned. Jack was supposed to have been married in June, just weeks before she met him. Here it was not quite two months later. No wonder he was secretive. He must still be in shock. A terrible thought lingered; Jack still loved his bride-to-be.

"Where is Melissa now?" Kat asked as if she knew all about it.

"Gone back to Oregon. Good riddance I say. Jack is better off without her. He—"

Kat's cell phone rang and she looked down at the display. Elliot was calling, but he could wait. She did not want to interrupt John.

Too late, John slapped his knee. "Well, that's enough about us. I don't want to keep you from your research and I could use a cat nap. Don't mean to take your name in vain." Big John's grin lit up the room.

Hoping she had not taxed him with the interview, Kat was satisfied that she had gleaned all she could about Jack, for the moment.

She planned to consult with Big John again when she got back from Dallas.

On a piece of paper, she wrote her number, handed it to him. "Here's my number, please call if you think of anything else I should know."

Big John stood along with her, a gentleman like his son. Winston woke up too, and trailed behind the older man, all the way to the door. "Kat, please call me any time you have a question, or just want to talk for that matter."

She treated him to a smile. "John, of that you can be sure."

Before leaving, she took a quick look around. Although she had learned nothing from the surroundings, she had learned *a lot* from Jack's father. Stood up at the altar! Well, at least Jack had thought marriage was a good idea. No one ever asked Kat to marry. They each had their own kind of pain.

DOWNTOWN CHICAGO DAZZLED at night. However, this night, Jack was miles from the glitzy part of town, where the lighted spires of the Sears Tower and John Hancock Center pierced the black sky. He was following Ricky, in his city-owned Camaro, down Ogden Avenue, which was certainly no destination point, its Mom-and-Pop businesses shuttered after dark. Cup of coffee in the holder next to his knee, more importantly, Jack dove into dinner—from the bag on the passenger's seat.

Just the thought of the sack of "sliders," those greasy little square-hamburgers eaten by generations of Chicago cops before him, made this late-night expedition worthwhile. It was going to be a long night; he might as well fill his stomach before the hard work began.

Several blocks past Pulaski Avenue, Ricky slowed. So did Jack, his mind engaged on the job ahead. When his partner reached Interstate Van's overhead door, Jack eased his Chevy to the curb, waiting for Ricky to open up and drive inside. The last of the sliders was about to go down his throat when his FBI radio crackled.

In a faint Spanish accent, Ricky said, "The party begins."

As Jack pulled away from the curb, headlights bursting on behind him did not disturb—and for good reason. He simply drove under the open overhead door, wheeled his car around stacks of tires and tool chests. The source of the lights, the FBI tech van, followed closely behind. Ricky quickly lowered the door. Their secret work—away from prying eyes of Pablo and his crew—was about to begin.

Stink of solvents heavy in the air, Jack was glad he finished off his burgers before coming inside. Ricky motioned him and two FBI tech agents to come over and inspect the two Dodge Sprinter vans. "Pablo has outfitted these perfectly. Look what he made for the propane tank."

Ricky opened an exterior door revealing a compact area big enough for just one twenty-pound propane tank. Jack ducked his head, peered inside. "That tank looks exactly like the one on my grill at home."

He moved aside for the tech agents. In no time, they disconnected the hose leading to the camper stove, lifted out the tank, and placed it on the garage floor. Ricky stepped in front of the others and rubbed his hands together. "Watch closely, amigos."

He turned his open palms toward them, as if about to perform a magic trick, then leaned into the void. After some pulling and banging, he removed the sidewall of the compartment. "Voila," he pointed to a hidden compartment with an identical tank.

"That's crazy," interrupted Art, the FBI tech Jack met over pizza, "the stove in this van can't use that much gas in a person's lifetime."

Jack agreed. "Remember why you're here. While Luis allowed me to believe he is hauling cocaine in these tanks, we now suspect they might be used to haul a bomb."

At the very idea, Jack tensed. Bombs meant people could die. They died from drugs, too, but bombs killed innocent mothers, fathers, and children who never dabbled in illegal narcotics. He and Ricky had devised a way for the vans to be under constant surveillance, but even perfect setups went awry.

Earlier this afternoon, Art and Herb, the other FBI agent who was a technical expert, briefed Jack and Ricky on how the vans were to be equipped with technology so sensitive it would alert them when drugs or a bomb were loaded into the vans. More familiar with the criminal mind than the ins and outs of a computer, Jack wanted to believe these two agents knew what they were talking about.

Amidst smells of rubber, Jack and Ricky drank coffee while the technical wizards put in and tested two of their super-devices. His burgers a distant memory, Jack read every old magazine in Interstate's office before Art and Herb said they were done.

Then the techies explained how it all worked, and Jack listened carefully. First, they wired a tracking device into the tachometer for each of the two vans. This would send a GPS signal to a satellite. Once either van reached road speed, the FBI would know *exactly* where it was. If Luis or another terrorist examined it for emitting electronic tracking signals, even with the engine idling, they would not find it. That was because there would be *no* signal unless, and until, the van reached a certain speed.

They hid a second device under the floor of the propane tank compartment, which would notify the same satellite if any weight greater than that of a single gas tank was placed in the compartment. Jack was amazed; it was truly a masterful job.

The agents had one more thing to do to prove it worked. The four of them put scrap steel in the compartments to add weight, and then Art and Herb each drove a van down the Eisenhower Expressway for a test.

They were gone such a long time Jack consulted his watch every few minutes. "We have got to get out of here before the regulars show up for work."

Normally laid back, Ricky looked as wired as Jack felt. "I hear you partner."

Their stomachs rumbling from too much coffee, they checked the time again. Jack's mind wandered to Kat. She was an enigma to him, strong yet vulnerable. He wondered if Ricky was married, had kids. Strange he never asked, so he took the time now.

Ricky jerked his eyes from a car magazine. "Twelve years, before I even went to the Academy. Theresa lived in my village, Guadalupe. Our parents moved to America at the same time, to give us a better life."

Jack figured that was quite a story how a Mexican immigrant's son became a Chicago Police Officer. Just now, he had a more pressing question. "You're happy?"

Ricky cracked a smile, erasing the worn look on his face. "She's the best."

Before Jack could ask more questions, Art, Herb, and the vans wheeled into the garage. Art was not even out of the van when Jack pressed, "Well?"

As if disappointed, the FBI tech hung his head, then laughed. "It was sweet. FBI's Virginia logistic center got me on the cell, could tell my van carried more than just propane and monitored my exact location right back to the front of the Interstate building." Art yelled over to Herb, "Same with you, right?"

Herb confirmed the same results. Operation Vantastic was a go! Jack and Ricky traded high fives, while the techs looked on amused. Confident the FBI would always know where the vans were located;

Jack stretched his arms over his head. "Let's pack up. If our techs agree, I say these first two vans are ready for pickup."

They did. After removing tools, tape, and coffee cups, the entire group left. Back out on Ogden Avenue, Jack let Ricky lock up, and he started his Chevy, certain Pablo would never be the wiser. It was right to let Pablo keep building the vans. Now, they just had to notify Luis the first two were ready. Jack doubted Luis would come in person. Tomorrow, he would have Pablo see to those details.

From what Gordon told him, and what Jack gleaned from higher ups at the Bureau, Luis had some connection to Hezbollah. As a result, this case now had priority over everything else he was working on, including Kat's bugging episode. He just wished that, at Norman's Cay, he had learned more about Luis and his true motives.

FIFTEEN

Kat gazed out the sixth-floor window of the Dallas museum at Dealey Plaza, mesmerized by the most famous street in the country. It might look like any other road, but its cement curbs, trees, and grassy knoll held a forty-year-old mystery that cried out for justice. While its name, Elm Street, evoked family gatherings and children playing, on November 22, 1963, this was no picnic scene but the sight of a ghastly murder.

Millions of Americans felt Kennedy's death was unsolved. To help discover the truth, this morning she combed through newspaper archives. Now, on the same floor of the old Texas School Book Depository from where Oswald allegedly shot Kennedy, Kat focused her eyes and feelings as she might a camera lens. Not born until 1977, Kat had not paid any attention to JFK's assassination when it was covered in school.

Anxious to learn more, Kat left the window to examine other exhibits of the Sixth Floor Museum. As she read about civil unrest at the time, and ads taken out in the Dallas paper warning the President, she tried to imagine what it would have been like to witness such a cold-blooded act. She had covered gang killings that had devastated communities in Chicago, but John Kennedy's death traumatized a whole nation.

In October 1962, the Cuban Missile Crisis caused the Cold War to get colder. U-2 spy planes discovered the Soviets were building missile sites in Cuba. Kennedy ordered a sea blockade against ships streaming to Cuba, which forced Soviet Premier Nikita Khrushchev to dismantle the bases, but the U.S. paid a price. Kennedy had to pledge not to invade Cuba, by then a Communist stronghold. The crisis ended, but did not erase fears of World War III starting ninety miles off the Florida Coast.

Her tour complete, Kat returned to stare at the corner of Houston and Elm, where the open Presidential limousine had slowly turned at less than five miles per hour, escorting the thirty-fifth President of the United States to his violent death. The sight of the large white X marking the death-spot in the road made her shudder.

Speculation about who really was behind it ranged from Vice-President Lyndon Johnson ordering the killing to be President, the mob, anti-Castro Cubans in league with rogue government types, to the Soviets. Kat felt the enormity of bringing out the truth. Perhaps the most she could hope for was to shed some light on those dark days.

Kat drank in the scene below at Dealey Plaza. No weapons expert, she had a nose for detail. So did Big John apparently. Kat prepped herself to ask enough questions of Elaine Greenburg, a private researcher, but also to make sure that she didn't let on to her what John McKenna shared in strict confidence about the second gun.

At a quiet coffee shop, two cups of tea and a bowl of soup later, Kat flipped to her museum notes. Already Elaine had given her ideas for further study, and several books on Oswald's life in Russia, Dallas, and New Orleans. So far, Kat could tell Elaine's mind retained everything she ever learned about the assassination.

Pen poised, Kat asked, "Do you believe the House Committee's conclusion that a shooter fired from the grassy knoll?"

Elaine removed pearl-rimmed glasses, made large for her ailing eyesight and daily close work. "Miss Kowicki, I trust this is not repeated." She tapped her eyeglasses to her thin, bottom lip.

Kat plunked down her pen, folded her hands. "Okay, it's off the record."

When Elaine smiled, Kat imagined her skin, nearly as translucent as parchment paper, actually crackled. "I worked for the government, the Agency." She paused for effect, Kat thought.

"By that you mean the CIA."

Kat's host inclined her head. "In the late fifties, all through the sixties, my husband and I both were CIA, mostly in Western Europe."

She shoved her glasses back on. "I don't appreciate that movie made by Oliver Stone with its ridiculous conclusion the CIA was involved. Hundreds of good people work for our government and would not allow a stealth conspiracy to bring down our country. We wouldn't stand for it."

"Is that why you write so many articles on the assassination, to dispel the notion?"

"We all have our causes. I'm sure you have yours." Elaine wagged a crooked finger at Kat. "To answer your question, no, that is not why. I am passionate about history, for history's sake. Like the eternal flame on Kennedy's grave, we have to keep the light alive. My family fled Germany in the late thirties, thanks to dear patriots in the Netherlands."

A grave shadow flickered across craggy features that once masked the secrets of a nation. "We got out, but so many others didn't."

Kat ached to pick up her pen to begin writing this down. "Elaine, your story is fascinating. My network is always looking for human interest stories."

"Not today, dear. You asked about the grassy knoll."

Kat interjected, "The House Committee found an open mike on a police motorcycle next to the limo. Those acoustics helped it conclude a second gunman fired from behind the fence on the knoll and missed the President."

Elaine reset her glasses. "You'll want to examine the photo that shows a dark shape up there. Some assassination experts refer to it as the 'black-dog theory'."

From memory, she gave Kat names of several witnesses on or near the knoll who talked with researchers through the years, and Kat made a note of them. "Are you aware of a second rifle or ammunition ever being found?"

In a fast motion, Elaine started twisting a lock of hair, as Kat used to do in school. It was uncanny how this simple act provided a bond between two women separated by two generations. "Acoustic evidence, photos, bullet trajectories, all point to another shooter, but I don't know of forensic evidence identifying another rifle."

Kat searched through her pad. "Okay. It says at 1:12 p.m., about thirty minutes after JFK was shot, Deputy Sheriff Luke Mooney searched the sixth floor. In a cubbyhole made from stacked boxes, he found three spent rifle cartridges on the floor. The police also found up there what they later identified as finger and palm prints of Oswald's and a large paper bag he used to carry the rifle into the building."

Without consulting any notes, Elaine added, "That was in the southeast corner, facing Dealey Plaza. Ten minutes later, after the cartridges were located, Dallas County Sheriff's Deputy Eugene Boone found a rifle in the northwest corner, shoved between some boxes—a 1940 Mannlicher-Carcano rifle from Italy—and a cartridge clip. You did write down that the Dallas police later discovered part of a palm print on the rifle barrel under the stock, which they identified as Oswald's, right?"

Kat needed clarification. "How is the barrel of the rifle different from the stock?"

"The barrel is the metal part the bullet travels through, while the stock is the wooden portion where you rest the rifle in your hand.

What's unusual is Oswald's print was found on a section not normally handled by a shooter."

Kat had read about this controversy. "Some say Oswald left the print when he had the rifle disassembled. Up on the knoll, they found no cartridges."

Elaine stopped twisting her hair, and Kat wondered if she was ready to leave. However, she still had much to say, "They found foot-prints, cigarette butts, hobos from the nearby railroad cars, but no direct evidence traced to the shooting."

Kat found the spot she wanted in her notes. "Oswald ordered the Mannlicher-Carcano from Klein's Sporting Goods in Chicago, but no ammunition. Yet, six-point-five-millimeter shell casings were found by the sixth floor window. Where did he get the ammo?"

"Experts claim he could have bought the ammunition in any gun shop."

Kat formed her next question carefully. "Hypothetically, if an ac-complice right here in Dallas also purchased an identical rifle and am-munition from Klein's and then shared that ammunition with Oswald, wouldn't it be a significant piece of evidence in the whole mystery?"

Elaine's eyes grew large. "That would be earth shattering. As you know, there were more investigations of Kennedy's killing than in most other cases. Such evidence simply does not exist. So, I would be careful making such a claim."

Excitement welled within Kat; however, she suppressed it in front of the researcher. She shut her notebook, grateful that Elaine had not pressed *her* for any answers. "Elaine thanks for your advice and time with me today. I want to walk the streets outside the museum one more time, to fix it in my mind."

JACK'S FRIEND LENNY MOSES parked his Ford in a circle drive in front of Kat's condo building in the heart of Chicago's Gold Coast, miles from the Cabrini-Green projects where Lenny grew up. A mag-netic sign on the Explorer's side identified it as a telephone company vehicle. It really wasn't. However, Lenny was retired from the phone company and still did contract work for them, so his signage and em-ployee identification badge were legitimate. Today he was doing a favor for Jack, which was no big deal. Lenny only hoped it would be quick; he wanted to see the Cubs play.

At the rear of the vehicle, he strapped on a tool belt, put on his hard hat, and headed for the building's bowels. When Jack asked him to check phone lines for him, he agreed, because he liked Jack. Work brought them together; when Jack's task force had court-ordered wiretaps to install, Lenny was trusted to help the agents.

Of course the FBI checked him out good before they let him work for them. That Lenny was an ordained part-time minister, and a married father of three with no police record sure helped. He and Jack shared a love of baseball besides. A diehard White Sox fan, Jack gave Lenny lots of ribbing for favoring the Cubbies.

In the basement wire room, where the company's lines were dispersed to individual condos, Lenny opened the cabinet, pushed up thick black-rimmed glasses to get a good look. Sure enough, row after row of small wires ran from the main bundle to individual posts. From his tool belt, he got out his butt set, used it to find the number Jack gave him. He touched the wires attached to Kat's posts, and then saw a second pair going to another row.

Something was strange. He thought Jack said there was no court-approved tap on the lady's phone. These wires disappeared behind the rack on the wall. Lenny leaned closer. With nimble fingers used to such intricate work, he followed the wires behind the rack, and when he pulled the rack away from its mount to follow the wires, he saw the intruder, recognized it immediately.

Kat's phone wires were attached to a diverter, an electronic device that grabbed her phone calls and transferred them, so they also rang at an extension somewhere else. Secured to that line was a repair order tag, which told Lenny that a repair technician was working on Kat's line. It served as a warning not to interfere with the wires.

Wait a minute—this was no typical installation. Lenny took his butt set and connected it to the leads coming from the diverter. He knew how to tell if this was legitimate. A small recorder from his tool belt ready, he dialed the lady's phone number with his cell phone.

Instantly, tones emitting from the diverter were recorded. After a few rings, a female voice on an answering device told Lenny to leave a message. Instead, he hung up, disconnected his butt set and secured the diverter behind the rack. Jack had said this request was urgent, so he retraced his steps.

An extension was receiving her calls all right, but Lenny did not know where. Could be a monitoring room operated by the feds, or local police. Could be Jack's research failed to find a record sealed by the court. Lenny's eyes got big. *Could be something more sinister.*

When he agreed to help Jack, they both assumed he'd do a quick check, come back, and say everything was cool. But he had stumbled onto that diverter. He had one thing left to do. After closing the phone service cabinet, he went back to his Explorer, took a pen and pad, and turned his recorder to slow mode.

Lenny played back the ring tones from the lady's line and wrote down the numbers. Funny, there were more tones than he usually heard. Unprepared for that puzzle, he called a service rep, and what he found out, worried him greatly.

The whole thing spooked him, and he'd seen some weird stuff in his life. On Jack's voice mail, he left a message, but not his name. "Jack, we have to talk in person. Soon!" He drove out of there, but for a long time after he left Lake Shore Drive and the sparkling waters of Lake Michigan, his eyes stayed glued to the rearview mirror.

JACK'S DAY WAS FILLED with constant interruptions. He and Ricky were in the middle of a meeting about Pablo's strange behavior—he disappeared during the day only to return hours later, looking winded—when the FBI called from Missouri. The cell connection was mostly static, but before it cut out entirely, Jack found out the agents tracking the two vans picked up by Luis's people this morning were now heading for the border. Jack figured they would watch them go into Mexico and then get back to him.

When he hung up, his cell alerted him that he had a voice message. It was from Lenny, who sure sounded in a panic. Jack got right back to him, and promised to meet at Barney's hot dog stand for an early supper. Now, he spotted his friend, horn-rimmed glasses bigger than life, walking from the take-out window, heading for his Ford and gripping a brown paper bag.

He swung his Chevy next to Lenny in the lot, sauntered over to his open window, and leaned on it. "Got here as quick as I could. What gives?"

Lenny spread his paper sack on his lap. The rustling noise it made and blasting car radio prevented Jack from hearing what he said, so he shouted, "Say again!"

Lenny popped a french fry in his mouth. "Oh, that's hot!" He guzzled some cola, turned off the radio. "Jack, you won't believe what I found when I checked your friend's phone. Grab a dog and enter my conference room."

Sounded good to Jack. As he headed toward the hot dog stand, he caught a glimpse of Lenny's head bowed over the open sack. He knew Lenny wasn't smelling the hot dog. Good to see other men thought the way he did about offering thanks for their food.

At the window, Jack was in no hurry to order. He had been coming for years to Barney's, a regular Chicago institution, but he always loved to watch the owner's production line. Barney looked up from his work, white paper hat on his head and apron tied behind his back. "Hey Jack. Where you been? Ain't seen you in a while."

Jack ordered his usual combo. "They've got me assigned to a special deal, so I don't get around the District much."

Barney looked up from the dogs he was assembling, "What? You don't want two today?"

Jack put his thumbs in the waste band of his slacks, pretending he couldn't pull them out. "Nah, I can't do that anymore."

Barney lifted the basket from the deep fryer, hung it on a bracket, and Jack watched grease pour from the fries. Barney returned to the counter underneath the serving window where he displayed his artistic flair in building the most delicious Chicago hot dog on earth. With his trademark wooden board, its dividers making individual stalls for four buns, he dropped buns in the holders and filled each with a steaming hot dog.

Barney slathered them with generous portions of mustard, tomatoes, onions, and sweet pickle relish, all topped with dill pickle spears. Using a giant saltshaker, he rained celery salt across all four. In four paper bags, he dropped a fistful of greasy, salted fries to the bottom, and wrapped each dog in tissue before placing it on top of the fries.

He handed three of the bags to the customer who had been waiting ahead of Jack, and the fourth he gave to Jack. When Jack saw the grease spot on the bottom of his bag, he began to salivate. Back at Lenny's Explorer, he slid into the passenger seat and set the bag on the floor between his feet. Once he put one of Barney's bags on the seat of his commander's car. He never made that mistake again.

Lenny looked at Jack, nodded toward the bag on the floor. "These dogs can kill, you know. You'd best bless it before you eat. I can wait."

Jack bowed his head for a silent prayer, and started in on his fries while Lenny finished off his. "She's right, Jack. There is a tap on her phone. But it's sorta different from what we usually see."

Hot dog hovering near his lips, Jack grimaced. "I was afraid something was wrong."

Lenny licked salt from his fingers, wiped his mouth. "Someone put a device in the wire room of the condo. They took trouble disguising it with a repair tag, so anyone looking would think it's supposed to be there."

Jack bit into his dog totally enjoying it, and let Lenny continue. "What someone did is create a slave."

"What?" Jack mumbled around a mouthful of hot dog.

"Someone, I have no idea who, put wires on the lady's pair and attached a slave. It's like an extension inside the wire closet. It leads to a diverter, which picks up every incoming and outgoing call, then sends it someplace else where her conversations are monitored."

"Where's it going?"

Through thick glasses, Lenny stared at Jack. "It's diverting to a zero-one-one number."

Puzzled, Jack drank some cola. "What do you mean a zero-one-one number?"

With a paper napkin, Lenny wiped off his entire face from the grease bath. "I looked it up. Her calls are forwarded to a place I never heard of—Almaty, Kazakhstan."

Jack knew the country, not the city. "Part of the former Soviet Union wedged in between China and Russia. Maybe the woman," he did not say Kat's name, "is working on a foreign story and Russians are bugging her place."

Not mentioning Kat's local corruption case, Jack thought it unlikely locals would transfer calls to Kazakhstan. He polished off his hot dog, enjoying it less.

"There's no court-ordered tap and no federal agency would perform an illegal one." Jack wadded up his bag, put a hand out for Lenny's bag. "Sounds like a foreign government."

Jack reached for the door handle to get out, but Lenny grabbed his arm. "What do you want me to do here? I might have a hard time explaining how I discovered this device, but I should report it."

Jack reached into his pocket and pulled out a piece of red licorice. "You did tell someone." He twisted off a piece. "Me. I'll investigate, and try not to get either of us in any trouble."

As he said the words, Jack sincerely hoped they were true.

SIXTEEN

It was late Saturday afternoon when Kat jumped off the shuttle at O'Hare airport and began to search for her rental, which was not where she thought she parked it. Before panic could set in, her cell rang. Kat snatched it from the side of her purse, and said hi to Jack. Did she simply imagine he sounded happy she was back?

"I hoped to catch you before I head to court. How was your trip?"

The sound of the shuttle bus leaving diverted Kat's attention. She looked around, startled to find she was alone among hundreds of cars. Thinking fast, she pushed the alarm button on her remote and followed the sound of the beeping horn to her car, a row away. She quickly got in.

"Kat, you there?"

After pressing the locks, she told him, "I'm in my car now." Her stomach muscles started to relax. "The trip was successful."

Jack's tone implied he was in a hurry. "I have to get going, but I wanted you to know you have a problem. Are you free later?"

They agreed to meet at nine o'clock at her news station. A hectic drive to the Loop only intensified anxiety about her "problem." Hands gripping the wheel, she dodged maniac drivers on the Kennedy, all the while fighting her emotions.

Jack's warning convinced her not to use her condo phone. Her eyes continually checked her rearview mirror. As she neared her exit, Kat was positive someone was following her. It was a white van, and the driver, a young male with dark glasses, changed lanes when she did and stayed a couple of inches from her bumper.

To avoid walking two blocks alone, she parked in the garage closest to the station, paying a fortune. Kat's mind was spinning; she needed to decide where next to go with the proof of the second rifle purchased from Klein's. Maybe she could interview some local FBI agents from the era.

Safely at the office, she waved to Ian, then sought refuge in her cubicle. She tried to concentrate on her stories, but all she could think of was that there *was* a tap on her phones. It felt like the bottom had dropped out of her stomach. Perplexed, Kat felt uneasy waiting until tonight to talk it over with Jack. All she wanted now was to air a story about how a U. S. Senator was messing up her life. Remarkably, her thoughts of revenge against Lars Zorn led her to a possible idea of who might help her.

Kat went to Bud's office, but he was gone. Unperturbed, she borrowed his phone to dial Washington. In moments, she reached the Senate Intelligence Committee. The secretary put her on hold. When no prompts came on for what seemed like minutes, Kat nearly hung up.

"Eva Montanna."

Startled by the abrupt greeting, Kat fumbled for a reply. "Hi Eva, it's me, Kat Kowicki. We spoke after the hearing in June. I have something important to discuss with you. Can you call me back from a secure phone?"

That is when Eva laughed. "This phone is more secure than the one you're on."

Relieved not to have burned that bridge, Kat told the agent why she called. "I have sensitive information of a scandal involving the highest levels of our nation's security. To say more on the phone is dangerous. Can we meet in Washington next weekend?"

Eva voiced a concern. "I need to make sure it won't be a conflict of interest."

That made sense. "It does not involve ICE directly, but does touch Congress and Homeland Security. I am desperate and there aren't too many people I can confide in."

"Does your boss know?"

Kat sighed. "Not my immediate supervisor. I told Mr. Tucker some, but he is still recovering from the plane crash. I will keep him in the loop if you think I should. Otherwise, another person knows but I won't say his name on the phone."

The plea in Kat's voice must have swayed Eva because she agreed to meet her in the west wing of the National Art Museum two weeks from Sunday. Kat hung up, satisfied that she'd locked in an important part of what she hoped to accomplish in Washington. She had kept the true nature of her trip from Eva but planned to reveal it to the next person she called, who just might be harder to convince.

As it turned out, she was unable to reach Mary Conrad, her former classmate at Lake Forest Academy, who now worked at the National Archives. When Kat lived in D.C., the two women often had dinner together. This afternoon, dialing the 202-phone number, she caught a recorded message giving a 703-number. When Kat tried it, Mary's new roommate answered. She told Kat that Mary was at an appointment and would return in an hour.

Stymied on this aspect of her plan, Kat began to doubt it was such a great idea. From Bud's office, she next rang Elliot, now at a rehab facility and doing well by his account. "That's great to hear Elliot. I flew to Dallas on Tuesday and just got back. When can I come see you?"

He chuckled. "The physical therapist will have me racing down the hall in no time. He's a regular drill sergeant with bad breath to boot. I go home tomorrow, Kitten."

Kitten? Was he getting senile? Maybe just lonely. With all her travels and developing stories to occupy her time, she had neglected him. "For your last night, let's celebrate. I can order whatever you like—egg rolls, pizza—and bring it by in an hour."

"Bring what you want," he said, and hung up.

My, he was volatile—one minute chuckling, the next minute snapping. When had he ever called her "Kitten?" Had something happened? Kat concluded that Elliott's meds must be out of balance.

She found the facility with no problems, even though traffic had her chewing on her lips. Their visit was actually pleasant. Face to face, he didn't seem confused. They ate fried rice, chicken and pea pods right out of the paper cartons with chopsticks, which was a good sign he was mending. Kat enjoyed reminiscing about their ride years ago to top of the Sears Tower to admire the Chicago skyline.

Suddenly, Elliot tossed down his chopsticks, and shifted gears. "You said you were in Dallas. I called Bud at home after you phoned and he was hush-hush. Is your trip connected to that corruption case?"

While Kat busied herself cleaning up the mess, tossing paper cartons in the wastebasket, she debated how much to tell him. He would probably find out anyway, but Jack had asked her to keep it quiet until the proper moment.

She fluffed a pillow behind his head, and then sat in the chair by his bed. "I'd rather tell you once you're settled at home. I have a few leads, which I promised to keep confidential."

"Not from me you didn't."

Technically, that was true. He was her boss and, if she was working on a story for his network, he had a right to know. "It's about the Kennedy assassination."

"Tell me something, anything. I'm going crazy in here."

Elliot looked tired, as if he needed to get back to his life. She drew in breath and let it out slowly. "A new source has evidence of another shooter. The FBI is involved, so I sent a request to see if they have the documents buried in their files."

"Bah, a Freedom of Information request will produce nothing substantial."

Kat knew that. Should she admit to Elliott that she wanted to see if the Bureau would turn over Zorn's letter to John McKenna rejecting the second gun evidence? A voice in her head urged, *not yet!*

She downplayed the case. "You know how these conspiracy people are—they see spooks around every corner." Kat kissed his forehead. "What time tomorrow? I want to be here when you escape."

Elliot grabbed her hand. "I'd like to know what you consider important in life. What are you after really?"

She opened her lips to speak, but he stopped her. "Not tonight. You give it some thought and, when I get home, you can come for tea."

His questions about life, after the crash, seemed plausible. But tea? Elliot hated the stuff. He was getting weird again. "Of course, Elliot, whatever you say."

With that, she slid back her hand, gave him a short wave. Reluctant to leave him like this, she had other calls to make before meeting Jack. In the visitor's lounge, Kat used the phone to call Virginia. This time Mary was home.

After chitchat about Mary's move and new roommate, Kat checked her watch. She was due at WEWW in thirty minutes to make sure Jack could get past security. "I need a favor. I would like to meet with you at Union Station, for a story. Does two weeks from today, Saturday the eighteenth work for you?"

Before she left for Dallas, Jack helped her figure out how long it would take for someone bugging her phone to get the call transcribed and into the hands of the requester. She hoped Mary was going to help her set up a trap.

Kat's friend giggled. "Will I be on television?"

"No. Nothing like that."

"Oh, all right. Too much fame might get *me* sent to Chicago."

"In that case, I need to send you a script."

Mary shrieked, "What? I thought you said I wouldn't be on television."

Ear throbbing, Kat said, "Someone is eavesdropping on my phone calls. When you get the script, call me at home, and we will read it aloud, like in a play, only this is my real life. Mary, please, do not tell *anyone,* not even your roomie. If anyone else shows up to our meet-ing, my suspicions of who is involved will be confirmed."

"Kat, it sounds risky. Are you dragging me into a dangerous situa-tion?"

She tried to ease her friend's concern. "I truly need your help. It's not as perilous as some of the silly things we did at Lake Forest."

Tension gone from her voice, Mary laughed. "Send me the script. Let's save time to catch up."

Evening became night and, in her luxurious, borrowed condo, door double-bolted, Kat closed the curtains tightly, her heart in turmoil. Jack had stopped by the studio and told her flat out that her condo phones were tapped. Unfortunately, neither he, nor his technician who checked the line, could say the tap wasn't on the line before she moved in. Jack asked if she was working on anything foreign, since her calls were routed to Kazakhstan.

She told him no, her intuition wanting to yell, *Zorn is the one!* Fortunately, before she made a fool of herself, Jack had to leave, but he did convince her to allow him to keep the tap in place until he could find out its origin. Otherwise, whoever put it there might real-ize the listening device was gone and leads would dry up.

Now, no matter how secure her door locks were, she regretted that decision, feeling like a prisoner. Unable to talk on her home phone, she did not trust her cell. For all she knew, it was bugged, too.

THE FOLLOWING FRIDAY, which allowed Mary plenty of time to get and become familiar with the overnight parcel, Kat answered her home phone at exactly 7:45 p.m. "Hello?"

Mary had a flair for the theatrical—some at Lake Forest Academy had dubbed her "the drama queen"—but Kat hoped her friend would not giggle at the wrong time or give away the fact that the two women were reading a script.

"Is this Kat Kowicki?" Mary was pitch perfect.

"Who is this?"

Mary adopted a stern tone. "My name is not important, but what I have to tell you is. Since you left television in D.C. I've been look-ing for you. I figured your last report that embarrassed a certain U.S. Senator got you canned. I guess you don't have a lot of respect for him and wouldn't mind seeing him brought down."

Kat's eyes followed the script. "Miss, whatever your name is, you assume a great deal. Tell me why you are calling, or I'll simply hang up."

A sigh from the other end almost blew Kat's cover—she clamped a hand over her mouth to keep from laughing. What Mary stage-whispered next convinced Kat her friend should be an actress. "I have a videotape, which the Senator I referred to would not want you or anyone else to see. I want you to have it."

"Most everything about people in Congress is already known, so I don't see why I or the Senator would be interested."

Mary lowered her voice. "You are so wrong. This tape was made by one of the Senator's trusted staff members without his knowledge. What it reveals could result in criminal charges and the end of his political career."

Kat loved Mary's sincerity and wished Jack was here to witness her handiwork. But she hadn't told him anything about her plan, for fear he'd talk her out of it. "You won't give me your name, yet you want to give me this tape. Why?"

Mary said unflinchingly, "Because I trust you to expose these misdeeds, or turn the tape over to the proper authorities. If you meet me Saturday in the coffee shop at Union Station, you can have it."

"Well," Kat began, as if thinking how to reply. "It so happens I'll be back in Washington that day, so we can meet. But I can't make any promises I will use your evidence."

Mary laughed. "I promise that when you see it you'll find a way. It'll be the top news story for a long time. Justice is long overdue. See you in the coffee shop Saturday at two o'clock."

A click, the line went dead. Kat's cheeks burned. At the kitchen sink, she ran some water on a paper towel, pressed it to her cheeks to cool her face. She wished she could fast-forward to Saturday and discover Senator Zorn's next move. He had messed with the wrong reporter and Kat hoped this time he would be the one demoted—right out of the public eye for good.

SEVENTEEN

It took days of cajoling from Kat, before Jack agreed to go with her to Washington. At first, he begged off because one of his cases was heating up, but then that must have resolved itself, because he finally said okay. It was obvious he thought she was swimming in dangerous waters, and it was up to him to save her. Let him think what he wanted. While she was glad he would be at Union Station with her, in her heart, Kat knew she had to orchestrate this meeting. Jack might have taken too long to do anything and the waiting was killing her.

At least, this trip got her away from the constant feeling that someone was watching her. She now ate all of her meals out and had started looking for a new place. It wasn't an easy task; her rent was so inexpensive that, to find something comparable, she would have to live in the suburbs, which meant an extra hour commute each way.

Before the sun broke night's hold on the dawn, Jack picked her up at her building's front door. On the way to the airport she showed him the small video camera she wanted him to use at Union Station. His face pulled into a frown, Jack said, "I'm afraid you are wasting your time and mine.

In hopes of lightening his mood, she teased, "But you promised."

"I've kicked myself ever since."

Kat set the camera on the seat between them, pulled down the visor and checked the mirror, fluffing her hair.

"Now you're trying to divert me with your beauty."

This was something new. Kat didn't want him to know her heart was pounding, so she cast a sidelong glance, only to see a big grin on his face. She couldn't tell if he was kidding, so she changed the subject. "From a distance, you film our meeting; see if anyone is watching. Mary will approach me and hand me a brown envelope."

Jack exited onto Mannheim Road. "We'll park at the Chicago Police airport office and get driven to the airport."

"Sounds like a great plan." Kat wanted him to know she respected his professional skills, even if he didn't think as much of hers. She was just trying to make conversation, but when silence greeted her, she told him about her trip to Dallas.

"Jack, your dad is really onto something with the second rifle being shipped to Dallas. As soon as I get back from D.C., I want to have a long talk with him about where to go next."

He shot her a quick glance. "He has asked me nearly every day since you left what you found out." Jack cleared his throat. "I told him you got stuck investigating a major story."

Kat felt a stab of guilt at neglecting Big John; she should remedy that right away. "Does he know you and I are traveling together?" She held her breath. His answer would reveal more about how his mind worked.

For the first time that morning, he smiled, "Yeah, I mentioned I was helping you."

She smiled back. "Since you're in such a helping mood, how about you meet with your dad and me, but first I have a few more leads to track down."

He wheeled into a parking place reserved for Chicago police. "I'm happy to, just keep in mind I want to keep a low profile."

They both got out of the Chevy and Jack took her bag from the trunk. "You really think that whoever is listening will come to your meeting?"

Kat nodded, watching Jack sling a computer bag over his shoulder, then slam the trunk. "Where's your suitcase?"

He smiled, slapped the side of his bag. "We're staying at the Willard, right?"

Kat thought about this and stopped. Maybe this time he was not kidding. "You said you would sleep on Mary's couch. I have the guest bedroom, but we can switch."

Jack smiled, "Oh yeah, I forgot this investigation is being paid for out of your pocket."

IT WAS A BLISTERING AFTERNOON in the nation's capital when Jack left Kat two blocks from Union Station. The taxi would take her to the corner of E Street and North Capitol, while he walked to the station. Best he arrived ahead, to avoid their walking in together. Warm humid air clung to his skin and the smell of hot pavement stung his nostrils. Already, sweat dripped down his arms.

Inside the air-conditioned Union Station, he found relief from the heat. He sauntered to a newsstand and picked up the morning edition of the Washington Star. Feigning interest in the headlines, his eyes furtively searched the hall filled with people hurrying in and out of shops or heading for their trains. He noticed a group of school children being herded by a woman holding an umbrella in the air. The woman kept shouting, "Class, stay together."

They seemed harmless enough. He folded the paper and tucked it under his arm, then sauntered among the crowds, looking for anyone suspicious. He enjoyed watching people, tried to imagine their lives, what kind of dog they had. A lanky fellow dressed in a light gray suit strode by and Jack pictured him with a Greyhound on a leash.

It was getting close to two o'clock, so he made his way to the coffee shop. Kat should arrive any moment. Jack put the video camera up to his eyes, adjusted the focus and lighting. Wow, he thought, the telephoto was incredible, bringing the tables much closer than they were. He sat across from the place and hid the camera under his newspaper.

Suddenly he saw her, the woman he was starting to admire. In jeans, bright purple sneakers and top, Kat might be a Washingtonian having coffee before heading to an appointment at the Capitol or taking in an exhibit at the National Gallery of Art. Watching her stand in line, Jack guessed she ordered a chai tea, which she loved. He wondered if she was thinking of him, if he was in position with his camera. Would she turn to look?

Some tourists studying a map walked by. Kat did not turn. Rather, acting her part, she paid for her tea and took a seat at the front of the shop, across from the escalators that disappeared to the Metro trains below.

They had not rehearsed this part, and he was impressed—Kat's instincts were perfect. He could film her from two different sides. Jack noticed her lips tremble in a slight smile and figured now she saw him. Unlike working with Ricky and other agents on cases, Jack sensed this investigation with Kat was trouble, and it bothered him.

For one thing, he had no jurisdiction in D.C., and if things turned sour, they had no backup. Of course there were D.C. police at strategic points on the main floor, and Metro police below. But none of them were tuned into this plan to catch an eavesdropper.

He fingered his earlobe, the prearranged signal that he was ready. Something else was eating at him. While he found Kat intriguing, her stubborn streak verged on being reckless. It was not that Jack wanted to control her, this was her situation to make right, but he had vast experience working cases. If only she would listen to his advice, he'd be more confident in success.

He brushed aside, like an old cobweb, thoughts that, if he got too close to Kat, he'd end up being sorry. He had to stop thinking every woman was like Melissa. His eyes inspected patrons reading, sipping from large cups, or talking with friends, a real microcosm of America. Two tables away sat a young man dressed all in black, a perfect match to his spiked-hair standing straight on end. Some wanna-be rock star, Jack figured, with all that silver jewelry hanging from his brows, his nose.

In seconds, Jack's probing eyes took in the rest of the shop. At the table adjoining Kat's, two men wearing suits were deep in conversation. They could be involved, but Jack was not sure. From the corner of his eye, he caught sight of a tall, lanky blonde woman walking from the counter, holding a cup with a lid.

Jack found her every bit as pretty as Kat, only in a different way. She snagged a seat a few tables away from Kat. Beneath the newspaper, Jack touched the on-button and kept his finger there, ready for what came next.

It did not take him long to find out what that was. A petite brunette who matched Kat's description of Mary walked up and shook Kat's hand. Casually, Jack raised the camera and shot footage, as a tourist might. Mary took a seat next to Kat and, in slow motion, placed a manila envelope in front of her. As Kat put her hand on top of it, Jack was relieved to see others using cameras. The historic Union Station was a grand subject to photograph.

He noticed that the tall blonde had stood up next to her table and was snapping photos with a camera. Jack reflected on how likely it was that they were filming each other. Moving his eye away from the viewer, he saw Kat and Mary leaning close together, obviously trying to muffle their conversation. At the adjoining table, one of the young men in suits turned his head as if listening. Dressed in a collared-shirt, he reminded Jack of a government-type waiting for a train to the suburbs.

Aside from him and the guy he talked with, Jack thought Kat's whole ruse was about to fizzle. He panned to a wider angle, half-admiring the blonde woman and half watching Kat in the same frame. He kept both in his sight for a few seconds, until the spike-haired gothic kid walked to stand by the trash container, totally blocking his view of Kat.

Jack pressed the telephoto, wanting to shout or wave, anything to make him move. He forced himself to play his part, film what he could. Rather than throwing away his cup and leave the shop, the same kid sauntered back into the frame, past Kat's table.

With one hasty swipe, he snatched the manila envelope right from Kat's hands and bolted for the exit to the train station. Kat stood, Mary shrieked, and the others in the shop looked up with interest, but no one made a move to help. Jack was conflicted. His instinct was to chase after the thief, but he reminded himself he was here to keep gathering evidence. So he filmed it all, focusing his lens on Kat while his eyes followed the blonde.

She seemed uneasy as she left her cup on the table and walked out of the coffee shop. Pretty sure there would be no more drama, Jack turned off the camera and left, too, intending to meet Kat as agreed. Some street punk taking the tape but leaving Mary's and Kat's purses alone proved that Kat was right—and he intended to tell her so.

There was one problem. It meant whoever was listening might realize they blew it by making a public spectacle, and things could get dicey for Kat. If only he could convince her to leave the eavesdropping matter to him and the professionals. In his gut, Jack sensed that was unlikely; his mind got busy planning his next move.

EIGHTEEN

L ater that evening at Mary's, Jack praised both women for their poise under fire. Kat bought two deluxe pizzas, which they ate while watching the video he took. When it finished, Jack told Kat he wanted to meet tomorrow with Eva Montanna by himself. And that is when Kat not only rejected his idea, she flashed him a dark look and snapped, "You forget, I set this plan in motion and I intend to see it through."

Jack ran a hand through his hair and found a ball game on TV in the living room. Kat failed to understand he was worried about her. From the kitchen, she raised her voice, "If you keep this up Jack, I will meet with Eva alone."

He could see how worked up she was, so he shut his mouth and watched his Chicago White Sox lose to the Detroit Tigers. The rest of the night was no easier. Jack tossed and turned on Mary's small, lumpy sofa. Saving money had cost him a night's sleep.

Sunday morning he rose very early and went to St. John's church near the White House, thinking he might see the President. He did not, but the minister posed a challenge Jack found worth mulling over. In times of trouble, Jesus Christ, who conquered death by rising from the grave, had power to rescue you from despair like no one else. Jack could draw strength from a truth like that. Outside, he shook hands with the preacher and told him, "Thanks for the spiritual check-up."

Jack escaped the oppressive heat at a nearby hotel, where he ate an expensive breakfast, lingering over coffee. He took his time because Kat and Mary were out shopping in Georgetown. Washington might be a fine place to visit, but he was glad he lived in Chicago. He paid his bill and, back outside by the church, he got to thinking about how his faith had been challenged that summer.

On the day of his would-be wedding, when he realized Melissa was not walking down the aisle, Jack never felt so abandoned—not just by Melissa, but by God, too. He had to admit, though, that today, close to three months later, he felt more hopeful about his future. Maybe that had something to do with Kat. He shrugged off deep thoughts for the time being and hailed a taxi for a quick tour of the monuments.

As the cabbie drove past the south lawn of the White House, it finally hit Jack why his dad was obsessed with finding President Kennedy's killer. When he was called out that night to find the murder weapon, he became a part of the biggest criminal investigation of the century, during a pivotal moment in the nation's history. And he was the one who found evidence that was never officially acknowledged. For those reasons, and also because he identified so strongly with President Kennedy, Big John took the questions swirling around JFK's assassination even more personally than most.

Jack owed a lot to Kat for taking this on, and he started to think that maybe his meeting this afternoon would provide a way around the FBI. Jack realized something else, too. His faith began to mend when Big John suffered his stroke and he began to talk to God again, on his father's behalf. Credit belonged in part to Dad who, on the day he came home from rehab, told Jack how comforting it was to know Jack was praying for him.

At the Capitol, he tapped the driver's shoulder. "Skip the Jefferson, and take me to the Marine Memorial."

The driver, who spoke little English, nodded his head, covered in a knitted cap, looped around "the People's House," and swung back onto Constitution Avenue. They crossed the Potomac River and drove straight to the Iwo Jima Memorial, where Jack told the driver to keep the motor running. "I'll be back in a few minutes."

Engulfed by a blast of heat when he opened the door, Jack approached the memorial honoring all U.S. Marines who lost their lives defending America. He admired the sculpture of four Marines and one Navy corpsman lifting the American flag on the island of Iwo Jima, site of one of the bloodiest battles of World War II. By controlling the airfields on that tiny island, U.S. troops prevented Japanese Kamikaze pilots from launching attacks, thus saving many Navy ships.

If only he and the FBI could find such a strategic way to stop terrorists. Jack shoved his hands in his pockets, and gazed across the river at the Lincoln Memorial. The whole of Washington spread before his eyes, and the sight thrilled him. He loved his country, loved being a Chicago cop. Sometimes he forgot that what he did every day helped keep Americans free.

Jack took one long last look at the monument, white marble against a cloudless blue sky, and headed back to the cab, now even more resolute that the task force would root out Luis, a new breed of terrorist who colluded with drug lords to achieve his evil agenda. Luis might be free to operate in Venezuela, but Jack intended to bar the door to the United States.

Jack McKenna was part of that core of insiders who saw what others didn't. Beneath the political grandstanding, the media-managed sound bites and slogans, Jack knew without a doubt that these extremists would not relinquish violence until the entire world was subjugated by their religion. He felt a kinship with every soldier, sailor, and U.S. Marine who held that door firmly closed and said, "You are not coming in on my watch."

Some of them paid with their lives. If Jack lost his, with God's help, it would not be in vain. He would give his life, if in so doing he stopped one terrorist from wiping out innocent lives.

Maybe there was a reason he and Melissa were not married. Maybe Jack was going to be single until the end. Opening the taxi door and climbing back in, Jack realized he was ready for the ultimate goal, no matter the cost.

WITH RENEWED VIGOR, Jack got out at the National Gallery of Art, where he and Kat were to meet an ICE agent named Eva Montanna. The ICE agents Jack knew in Chicago were some of the best investigators he ever worked with. Would Eva measure up?

Inside the Gallery he strolled to the café, where he spotted Kat and another woman sitting at a table, their heads inclined together as they engaged in what appeared to be an intense conversation. Jack walked up, put aside feelings of being an outsider, and introduced himself.

Eva's grip was firm, but not too strong, as if she had something to prove. She was attractive, and Jack's eyes traveled to her left hand, where he spied a thin, gold band. Thankfully, he was now past the point of envying those with the good fortune to be married.

Before Jack got in another word, Kat exclaimed, "Jack, I just found out that Agent Montanna and I have something in common. She vacations at Lake Michigan, too."

"In Pentwater?" Jack asked.

Eva shook her head. "My grandfather, Marty VanderGoes, grew up in Zeeland, close to Holland. My family and I try to spend time there every summer."

Jack picked the chair near Kat. "The Big Lake is fickle. Storms can blow up with little warning, so I've got my boat rigged with radar, GPS, and a sea anchor."

They settled down to small talk and it didn't take long for Jack and Eva to find out they both knew the same ICE agent in Chicago.

After that, Kat smiled at him. "Jack is a second generation Chicago police officer."

Eva seemed genuinely interested. Her sincere questions got him talking about his father. "My dad retired from police work after many years. Something that happened long ago in his career, which I just learned about, reconnected me with Kat after—what—twelve years?" He glanced over at Kat, who nodded in agreement. "For the past few years, I've worked with the FBI's Joint Terrorism Task Force."

When Eva commented, "Terrorism cases seem to be my specialty lately," Jack felt instant camaraderie, as though they were members of the same family, and that put him more at ease.

After a waiter took their orders, Eva unfolded a napkin on her lap. "When Kat and I first met, my group was closing up a townhouse where we executed a search warrant on terrorists. We left by the rear door. Imagine my shock to see Kat and her photographer at eight in the morning, demanding to interview us."

A smile played on Eva's lips. "Kat, you always made me nervous because you had an uncanny knack for showing up precisely when we didn't want any publicity."

Jack fully expected Kat to frown, lash out. Instead, while her cheeks were rosy, her eyes twinkled. Good, she was growing a sense of humor. He felt free to share his own story. "My memories of Kat go back to high school, where she and my cousin were classmates. Recently, when I discovered my father was sitting on evidence important to a national case, I called on Kat, because I respect her ethical reporting."

Kat looked at him and said, "Thanks." His eyes held hers for a long moment, which ended only when a waiter brought their drinks.

Jack sipped his cola. "Now, she is targeted and we don't know by whom. We'd like your opinion," he leaned in, dropped his voice, "whether Kat stumbled onto local corruption or something bigger."

Kat showed Eva the transcripts. "Have you heard of the web site, Camelot Connection? Instead of what I asked for, I got these. I was sent to Chicago after a run-in with Senator Zorn, which makes me think he's behind the eavesdropping."

Eva held up a hand. "Senator Zorn is a member of the Senate Intelligence Committee, where I will serve for another few weeks."

Jack noticed Eva said nothing about *CamelotConnection,* she just looked through the transcripts until their food came. After saying grace, Jack dove into his burger, which turned out to be a dry and tasteless meal. Kat told Eva how she and Mary read a script over the tapped telephone, where they referred to an "incriminating" tape of a certain Senator. "We did not use Zorn's name, but it was implied. I wanted to test if he ordered the phone tap."

Eva studied Kat before asking, "What happened at Union Station?"

Kat flashed Jack her bright smile, and suddenly he didn't mind that his hamburger was overcooked. "Show Eva the video you shot."

Jack wiped his mouth and fingers with a napkin, but he gazed at her until he opened the screen on the video camera to show Eva. "I filmed Kat's meeting with Mary, hoping it would answer Kat's questions." He shrugged, "See what you think."

He pushed play and Eva studied the screen, squinting suddenly, then gasping, "That kid stole your package. Did anyone catch him?"

"A theft of a junk tape does not equal destroying evidence." Jack decided to get Eva's reaction to something he saw as soon as the kid stole the video. "Both of their purses were on the table, but the kid stole the envelope."

Eva stared at Kat and Jack, eventually handing the camera back to him. "I don't know what to say. I may have recognized someone on the tape."

Immediately, Jack figured Eva knew more than she was willing to say, trusting neither him nor Kat. He reached for his wallet, ready to pay the bill.

Kat touched Jack's arm. "Wait. Eva, who is it?"

Eva's long silence hinted at an inner struggle. "I hesitate to tell you, Kat, for fear what you will do with it. We don't know the person committed a crime. You must promise to be careful how you proceed."

Her hard stare at Kat reminded Jack what she'd said about Kat pushing into Eva's search warrant. His mind replayed Kat's severe look last night when he challenged her. A kernel of doubt sprung in his mind; was he right to trust her with Big John's evidence?

Eva was not backing down. "Can you do that?"

Kat responded without missing a beat. "My life is the one in turmoil. Eva, please tell me who you recognized."

Caught between two independent women, the last place Jack wanted to be, he was curious how Eva would handle Kat. Maybe he could learn from her.

Not at all ruffled, Eva graced Kat with a sympathetic look. "It's a person who works on the Hill, somewhere in the House or the Senate."

Kat's face changed from sunny to cloudy and then downright thunderous. Jack was beginning to get used to this—after all, he'd motored out into Lake Michigan in some pretty rough seas. So, at first he didn't react when she jumped up from her chair and exclaimed, "I knew it! Zorn's the one trying to ruin me. It's time for paybacks. I'll expose his shenanigans and I don't care what Elliott does to me."

Others nearby turned to stare. Now Jack put a hand on Kat's arm, pulled her toward her seat. Once she calmed down, Jack turned to Eva. "At Union Station, we were two blocks from Capitol Hill. Isn't it possible whoever you saw was on a coffee break?"

Kat's voice rang with pure sarcasm. "Yesterday was Saturday, their day off."

At that, Eva smiled, "It's Sunday and I'm working, meeting with you."

Determined to get back on course, Jack asked Eva, "Stolen tape aside, is there anything you can do about the intercept on Kat's phone?"

As Eva flipped through the transcript, her faced stoic, Jack knew she'd be great undercover. She finally looked up and said, "Illegal eavesdropping in Chicago. Normally, we would refer that to the State's Attorney."

Kat interjected, "What about the theft of evidence that could incriminate a U.S. Senator?"

Eva drew her hands together in front of her, kept her voice low. "It could be a total coincidence. Congress created the office of Inspector General to investigate wrongful conduct in the Executive Branch, but there is *none* to watch over Congress, which is how our representatives want it. If they do wrong, people vote them out."

"If people find out about it," Jack couldn't keep from adding.

"*That* would be my job," Kat piped right back.

Jack had an idea. "The FBI got involved in Abscam and other investigations of Congress. I've developed close relationships; we could refer the case to them."

Then, he remembered Senator Zorn once was an FBI agent and wished he'd kept his mouth shut. Things were getting stickier, especially with Kat's probing the Kennedy assassination at the same time.

Eva glanced around the room. "The Bureau was criticized for those, too. After all, the FBI's funding comes from Congress. Now, even when they find their marked money in a congressman's freezer, they still are slow to act."

Kat looked like she was at a tennis match, her head going back and forth between Jack and Eva, with an occasional nod, up and down, but, surprisingly, this time she remained quiet.

Jack kept at it, determined to find a solution. "If the FBI or even the CIA is involved, what do you suggest?"

Eva puffed her cheeks, blew out the air slowly. "Let me talk to a few people; see who has jurisdiction. Kat, if we mess up the front end, we risk tarnishing your case."

Jack could see Eva was dead serious, and his confidence in her grew. Kat's brown eyes narrowed to dark slits, but instead of erupting, she simply stood to go. "Okay, Eva, stay in touch with Jack. Calls to me are suspect and we don't want to tip our hand. He has ways of reaching me."

With Kat's sudden compliance, Jack sensed she was already working on another scheme in her mind. He rose, thrust a business card in Eva's hand, and put a thumb near his ear, small finger by his lips, silently mouthing, "Call me."

Eva blinked back, to indicate she got the message. "I am due back at ICE in about a month. Maybe my boss will agree it must be sooner, so I can personally work on what may have national security implications."

Kat whirled around, grabbed Eva's hand. "I knew I could count on you!"

NINETEEN

Glad to be back in Chicago at his desk where he felt some semblance of control, Jack finished off his second cup of coffee. Try as he might, he could not allay strong suspicions that escalated on the flight home with Kat, suspicions she *was* finagling how to beat Eva to the punch and bring down Senator Zorn singlehandedly. Throughout the flight, her sunny self concealed by clouds again, she simply stared out the window.

When they landed at O'Hare, she finally turned to him and spoke, her eyes boring through him. "Who enforces eavesdropping laws in Illinois?"

Jack had tried to stall her. "Kat, I know this is driving you crazy. I feel the same way. Let me at least hear back from Eva, or we could end up with egg on our faces, or worse, reveal too much too soon. I've seen that happen, and then the culprits are never convicted."

Kat closed her eyes, as if debating with herself. She opened them again and, undeterred, asked again, "Who exactly, Jack? I want his name."

"As Eva said, it's the State's Attorney for Cook County, but I promised her the courtesy of waiting."

This morning, drinking cup after cup of coffee could not obliterate the withering glare Kat bestowed on him after he said that. The memory of it made him wonder how easy it was to contain a fireball. In the recesses of his mind, he couldn't stop himself from saying, *Thanks Dad, for getting me into this.* He decided to blot out Kat for a while, at least until she called about the meeting with his dad. Instead, he'd see how Pablo was coming on the remaining four vans. Something was amiss there, too.

Before flying to D.C., Jack had stopped by Interstate and found it closed tight. He'd immediately called Ricky, who assured him the parts had not come in, so they left early. Ready now to dial Pablo, Jack's phone rang instead.

He almost barked, "McKenna, here."

"It's Eva, at my headquarters office on a secure phone. Am I right, you wanted to tell me more?"

Jack was gratified. He'd been right about Eva, she was a good investigator. "I would hate to see this exposed on TV just because we're not moving fast enough for Kat. What I'm about to say I have not told her."

Eva agreed. "We need to keep a lid on it 'til we figure out what's going on."

Jack told her about using Lenny to check Kat's line. "He found a tap diverting her home phone calls to Almaty, Kazakhstan. One of those recorded was with me, on a confidential matter."

Jack could relate to Eva's, "Oh no!" That was exactly how he felt. "Eva, the stuff she orders from CamelotConnection.com gets shipped to her in brown envelopes from Kazakhstan. Do you think some foreign government is interested in what Kat's reporting?"

"When you hear what I say next, you'll know why I came to headquarters to call."

Jack was intrigued. "I thought you held something back."

Eva laughed. "All agents like to lead, so we make poor dance partners."

Jack's mind flashed to the dance with Kat all those years ago. Had she let him lead? He thought so—but Eva brought him back to the present. "There was more I could have said, but Kat is too emotional, and rightly so, considering what's happening to her. You saw the tall blonde on your video?"

"The one taking pictures."

Eva whispered, "It's Ingrid Swanson, Senator Zorn's Chief of Staff."

Jack could hardly contain himself. "I guess it proves she's right."

"I concede nothing, at this point. Though Zorn holds a sensitive position on the Senate Intelligence Committee, and might have powerful connections, eavesdropping is definitely unlawful. I intend to talk to somebody here in D.C. on where to go next."

With Eva following up, Jack did not have to mention anything to Gordon and get things started from his end. "Give me a shout when you know something. Meanwhile, I'll placate Kat." He hung up realizing that might be more difficult than trying to dock his boat in heavy seas.

LIFE HAS A WAY of moving in circles, sometimes overlapping, sometimes never connecting. On this Monday, three federal agents gathered for the first time at a favorite lunch spot. To a stranger who happened to overhear, they might simply be talking about their lives and careers. In reality, Eva asked two old friends—and fellow FBI agents—Griff Topping and Sal Domingo for their take on what Kat and Jack had dumped in her lap Sunday.

At a Tex-Mex place in Vienna, Virginia, where Sal brought his wife every Friday night, Eva confided, "I need advice from agents with no connection to anyone on the Hill."

That prompted a low whistle from Sal. Over enchiladas, Eva briefly sketched details about Kat's transcripts, and the mix-up with Kat's request for other data, leaving out any reference to Senator Zorn. Griff motioned the server for more coffee and twirled his fork in gobs of melted cheese. Eva gave up coffee, too much acid in her stomach. Tea was her choice and she drank some.

Griff set down his cup. "Who can forget that reporter, Kat Kowicki? She's been a thorn in my side, so I'm not surprised she's made a bunch of enemies along the way."

His harsh tone amazed Eva. "You're not suggesting she deserved to be spied on?"

"No, just comes with the territory she's carved for herself. Earlier, this summer, she zinged one Senator, only I can't remember who. Ambushed him, on air, I heard."

Too anxious to eat, Eva's appetite always dwindled when confronted by a thorny problem. "It *was* Senator Zorn. With his presidential aspirations, I can imagine he didn't appreciate being caught on camera making an obscene gesture."

Sal put in his three cents. "Yeah. I liked what she did, asking him straight out if he was behind the leaks. I don't trust that former actor, even if he was one of us, once. Now he wants to have his finger on our nuclear arsenal. That's one scary thought."

Eva waved a hand over her uneaten food. "We can talk about Zorn later." She leaned forward, "Kat is convinced there is a link between CamelotConnection.com, Senator Zorn, and the wiretap on her phone. Do either of you know anything about this Camelot web site?"

Sal quipped, "Sure, some agents use it to advance their investigations. It's a members-only search engine that does some of your leg work, for a hefty fee of course."

Griff shook his head, plate empty, except for a pile of rice. "Never heard of it. That's because I make my cases the old-fashioned way, plain hard work." He stared at Eva's plate. "Are you going to eat those chips?"

She shook her head, and he grabbed a handful. About to crunch one, he stopped, mouth open. "Wait. A retired agent talked to me awhile back, wanted me to leave the Bureau, join a private firm. It's hazy, but I think they were looking for someone in Kazakhstan, which didn't interest me."

Sal grimaced. "Yeah, Russians are getting shot at, poisoned across the globe. Leave me in the good ol' U.S.A."

Eva saw a vital connection. "Griff, can you find out more about that agent and his offer?"

Griff ate his chips before answering. "Eva, I know you well enough to believe you already sorted this out. What do you want me and Sal to do?"

A laugh escaped her throat. "Caught. I want to tell the Attorney General directly. First, I thought of going to the Inspector General, but, no, I can't. He reports to Congress, and this may involve criminal conduct by a Senator. I hope when shown the evidence thus far, Alexia Kyros will authorize an investigation. You both know what a straight arrow she is." The Attorney General was Eva's long-time friend and mentor.

Griff arched his heavy brows. "And?"

Eva popped a Dutch peppermint in her mouth to settle her stomach. "If I can convince her to authorize a task force, I want you both on it."

Sal rapped the table with his knuckles. "Count me in. I have one big case, but it's hit a lull. I'm growing old at my desk."

Griff wiped his palm over his moustache. "If you're going to the Attorney General, you must know something more than what you told us."

Sal signaled for more coffee and, when it was poured, took a long sip. "I was out late last night at church. Say, remember Wally, the young man from Sudan who Griff helped to get a scholarship?"

Eva did. "He's in college, right Griff? How's he doing?"

Griff ate the last chip. "Wally's got a lot of grit, with all he's been through. He's about to start his second year, majoring in business. I drive up next week to see him."

Sal nodded. "Yeah, meeting Wally got Maria started in a church group mentoring international students. Makes it seem like they have family here. The church puts on a banquet for them, but this year the students are bringing foods from their homelands. That's where I was last night—a meeting to plan it all."

Eva brightened. "Sal, Scott and I would be interested in coming. Since our trip to Africa, we enjoy learning about other countries."

Griff's partner rapped the table again. "Okay, we'll get tickets. Griff, you like to eat. Want to join us?"

Not big on socializing, Griff had accepted Eva's invitations to church services and dinner afterwards from time to time, but not often. "Remind me later, I'll check my calendar."

They paid their checks, and Eva said, "I meet with the Deputy Attorney General at three. I'll call you tomorrow morning, eight sharp."

Eva hoped to get Griff to meet the *Camelot* people in Almaty, only she had discovered it worked better when he came up with such ideas himself. In the parking lot, the three stopped at Sal's Bureau car, or bucar, a Ford Mustang, and Eva suddenly grabbed Griff's arm. "Rack your brain about that Kazakhstan offer. Let me know as soon as you come up with anything."

EVERY NOW AND THEN, the wheels of government do turn quickly. Sometimes it is due to the strength of evidence and sometimes the strength of relationships forged over time. When Eva asked the Attorney General to create a task force, Alexia Kyrios didn't need long to consider Eva's arguments before giving her approval.

Eager to empty her desk at the Senate Intelligence Committee and get back to the work she really loved, Eva wasted no time processing the paperwork to add Griff, Sal, and IRS agent, Earl Simmons, a computer whiz, to the task force. This seasoned foursome had worked together before, with excellent results.

Sonya Haddad, another agent who had teamed up with some of them on other cases completed the team. Each agent was on loan for the special project; but their agencies were not told its true purpose. Her team complete, Eva moved them into a far corner of Main Justice on Pennsylvania Avenue. For the three small adjoining rooms, she requisitioned as many desks as could fit, hoping to get at least five, and prepared to share desks if necessary.

When only four desks showed up, Griff—ever the gentleman— came up with a temporary solution: "About the job offer in Kazakhstan, the retired agent I know is in South America for awhile. I'd like to go to Chicago, look into the wiretap. Some of my contacts are still around from when I was assigned there."

With her plan coming together, Eva did not hesitate to sign his travel authorization.

TWENTY

G riff wasn't surprised how quickly Eva arranged his travel. Because of his expertise with electronics—his previous duty had been on an FBI Technical Support Group—Griff could likely move things forward if he got an eye on that tap.

About to land at O'Hare, Griff thought how his life changed since he left Chicago. His wife, Sue, had died and now he was firmly entrenched in northern Virginia. Since tracking down international drug smugglers last year, things were seeming too tame for Griff. One who thrived on risk, he was eager to discover whatever adventures Chicago might bring.

For one thing, he had no idea where the new FBI office was. Normally Griff would go straight there, but that wasn't an option this time around—his presence might raise too many questions. He had called Jack McKenna and they agreed to meet elsewhere.

Griff's seatmate, a man of about eighty, nudged his elbow. When Griff turned, the man put a finger to his lips and nodded his head across the aisle. "That young fella, the one with the black hair and beard, went to the lavatory at least six times since we left Reagan National. Mighty strange, I'd say."

As much as he did not want to look, Griff's eyes drifted over to seat 12A. He supposed the old man's fear was natural, but had he really counted the times he went to the bathroom? "Maybe he's sick, some people don't fly well." Griff tried to change the subject, "Me, I love to fly. I even have a pilot's license."

The man shook his head. "Those terrorists did a terrible thing, hijacking airplanes on 9/11, killing so many people. I flew in World War Two, fighter planes, and I worry about my grandkids' future."

Griff sighed. Threats of terrorism would probably never end, not in his lifetime anyway, not unless God intervened in some miraculous way. Hatred among people had festered for thousands of years. As he fastened his seatbelt, his gaze went once again to the man in seat 12A, and he wondered if there was anything to the old man's observations. After the 2005 London bombings, Al Qaeda had broadcast a warning to the West: convert to Islam or be killed.

The plane turned abruptly, and Griff readied for action in case of attack. The pilot came on overhead, said they were making another pass at landing because a plane was on their runway. His seatmate nudged him again, but this time Griff shut his eyes, thinking he'd now been a widower for eight years. Last year, while working a case in Florida, he met a special woman in Panama City. Dawn Ahern's husband had died, and it would be a few years before her teenage son enrolled in college.

Meanwhile, they talked on the phone, traded emails and cards. For her birthday, he sent a dozen pink roses. So far, Dawn had not replied, which irked him. He didn't like not knowing where things stood. Maybe she was tired of their friendship carried on from a distance. Maybe she had found someone else.

Griff stared out the window, not enjoying another jerky landing attempt. As a pilot, he wanted to get her down. Ten minutes later, the jet eased onto the runway and Griff wasted no time getting off the plane and down to baggage claim. After grabbing his suitcase and tools from the carousel, he walked out to the arrival area and stood at the curb looking for Jack McKenna. He saw a Chevy Impala approaching, weaving through congestion as if driven by a cop. It came to a sudden stop in front of him. The passenger window lowered, the driver leaned over and asked, "You Topping?"

Griff nodded. "You McKenna?"

Jack laughed, "Sure am."

The trunk lid opened and Griff threw in his suitcase. In the front seat, the men shook hands, then Jack pulled from the curb, dodging cars that were double parked. Griff mused that any second Jack would probably start driving with his knees—because that is just what Griff would do. As the Chicago detective swung into the exit lane, Griff checked out the window. "You sure you know where you're going?"

Jack darted in and out of traffic. "Yup, it's a shortcut."

"When I was assigned to an FBI Tech Group here, guess where we ate?"

One hand on the wheel, Jack smiled. "Barney's?"

Griff wet his lips. "I cannot wait to bite into one of those Chicago dogs again."

Jack slammed on his brakes. "Welcome back to Chicago gridlock." He started the slow tap, tap on the brakes as traffic inched along. He caught Griff up on his end of the investigation: "Lenny's meeting us at Barney's—he's the guy who discovered the wiretap for me."

At the sight of Griff's hopeful smile, Jack added, "Don't get your hopes up. The way Lenny eats, by the time we get there, there might not be any left."

By four o'clock, the trio had finished three hot dogs apiece. Now it was time to inspect what Griff flew to Chicago to see. At Kat's condo building, Jack circled the block searching for a place to park.

Expensive autos lined up bumper to bumper along every curb. Griff remarked, "Never spent much time with the upper-crust. I lived in Naperville, and the cases I worked kept me in high-crime areas." He pointed, "There's a spot. Grab it."

Already past the space, Jack floored the brakes, threw the Chevy in reverse, and started backing up. "Better jump out. Curbs are high in this part of town, and you may not be able to open the door."

Out on the sidewalk, Griff breathed in the scent of Lake Michigan, less than a quarter mile across the street. Waves of homesickness assailed him; one taste of Barney's hot dog had done it. He had no idea how much he missed the Midwest and its simpler life far from Washington's culture of distrust.

Griff pulled his leather toolcase out of the trunk. "You may have to send me a case of dogs. They are the best."

Jack locked the car. "Kat has never even tried one. She's lived most of her life here, but," his tone grew serious, "she's not happy being back, with her phones tapped and all."

Lenny whizzed by and pulled his Explorer in a block ahead. As they waited, Griff thought to lower his voice. "Who do you think is targeting Kat?"

His face unsmiling, Jack waved at Lenny. "I hope you can help us find out."

Hardhat on his head, telephone company identification around his neck, Lenny led them into the lobby and signed in with the doorman. "We have to inspect the phone wires in the basement."

The elderly doorman, watching a soap opera on a tiny TV, couldn't have cared less what they did. Eager to see the device that sent Kat's calls to Kazakhstan, Griff was careful not to mention to Jack or Lenny he might travel there soon. He hadn't even told Eva yet about his plan.

In the wire room, Lenny showed the installation to Griff, who'd seen hundreds of bugs like it in training and on the job. He pulled Jack aside, told him what he thought they should do. "Whoever installed it might have been careless enough not to wear latex gloves. If we take it now and find no prints, we could lose other evidence. I say leave it and see where it leads. Do you trust Kat not to reveal this?"

Jack scratched his head. "I do, but for how long is the question. You know Kat."

Griff left that alone, and instead told Lenny that he was done. Ready to return the diverter to its hidden spot behind the wire rack, Lenny looked at the two men, his eyes huge behind thick glasses. "I sure am glad Jack brought in the FBI. This whole thing makes me nervous."

Jack thanked Lenny for his help. "Griff and I have other stops to make, but I'll call if we need you further. Let's keep this among us for now."

Lenny was more than agreeable. "Believe me, Jack, I won't breathe a word. I *already* forgot what I saw and where I saw it. Good day, gentlemen." He tipped his hard hat and went up the stairs.

Griff was putting away his tools when Jack sprung a surprise. "I know it sounds unusual, but Kat is really upset. I'm a little worried about what she may decide to do on her own. Maybe if you talked with her, it might set her mind at ease, slow her down."

Oh great. He had no appetite for another confrontation with Kat, who had impeded a past search, and showed up with cameras outside the courtroom where Griff was testifying, badgering him when he walked out. "That's not a good idea. She and I, well, our goals differ dramatically."

Jack slapped him on the back. "I read you loud and clear. We cops don't like the media breathing down our necks."

Griff put away the digital camera he used to photograph the diverter, and Jack persisted. "Five minutes and you are out of there. Eva raved about your electronics savvy, and I happened to mention it to Kat."

"So you already told her I'd come. Why didn't you say so?"

Relief spread across Jack's face, giving Griff the idea that Jack's interest in Kat's dilemma went beyond the professional.

KAT BUZZED THEM UP and opened the door. Standing there in the foyer, Jack thought she looked uncharacteristically subdued in black jeans, sweater and sneakers. He was used to her wearing brighter colors. Tension sizzled in the air, and Jack was at a loss for words.

Griff broke the ice by shaking her hand. "I don't have fond memories of your microphone," he smiled, "but it is nice to see you again, Ms. Kowicki."

Kat dropped her hand, and quickly bolted the door. "If I was aggressive, Agent Topping, it is because I want my viewers to have the truth. Now, in retaliation for showing them what kind of man he is, Senator Zorn and his secret source are out to get me."

Stiffly, she offered them a seat in a room overlooking Lake Michigan. Griff declined, kept his feet planted on the tile floor. It was the first time Jack had been to Kat's place, so he walked straight into the living room. Thankfully, they followed.

Griff got right to the point. "Ms. Kowicki, I saw the tap. I question why a U.S. Senator would risk his career coming after you, doing something illegal. More likely, some local hoodlum you're trying to expose is behind this."

Kat picked up a brass letter opener from a corner table, turned it over in her hands. Jack felt an absurd desire to hold them, tell her everything would be all right. She seemed cold as ice.

"Agent Topping, you think me insignificant, a reporter shunted back to the Midwest. That occurred because a story I did tore the mask of civility from Zorn. He may be a U. S. Senator, but he is a man who stops at nothing to get his way."

Griff shifted from one foot to another. "That begs the question—why stoop to illegality when he has legitimate power at his fingertips."

Kat tapped the letter opener on her palm, her voice rising, "You agents need to find out why. Meanwhile, how long do I have to live in a fishbowl, worrying my every move is being watched, where I can't talk on my own phone? I fear my cell phone is tapped, too. If you don't resolve this soon, I go public, with *all* of it."

With no authority over Griff or any right to tell Kat what to do, Jack felt an odd twinge, not as dangerous as jealousy, nor as simple as curiosity. Was there something more beneath their disagreement? He watched closely, waiting for Griff's response.

The agent's nostrils flared, but he answered calmly, "Far be it from me to stand in the way of a free press; however, let me caution if you do that, you could keep the person behind this from ever being discovered."

Kat folded her arms across her chest. "I told you. It's Zorn."

Griff held up a hand. "I heard what you think. Frankly, I want to see more evidence and to get it, we have to dance on the head of a pin, very carefully. Think for a moment about the story you ran about the Senator. I know all about his flipping a finger at you. I saw your newscast. What did you get for your trouble?"

Kat flinched, dropped her arms. "Go on."

Griff gripped Jack by the shoulder. "We keep ourselves alive by staying one step ahead of our adversary."

Kat rolled her eyes. "I know, but this is *my* life."

Griff lowered his arm, softened his tone. "Granted. Let those of us who wear a badge handle it. We'll get to the truth, won't we Jack?"

At last, Jack had his chance. Resisting the urge to take her hands, instead, he looked into her brown eyes, filled with concern. "Kat, you have my promise that I will do everything I can to protect you, but if you run with this, there is no guarantee anyone will ever be charged."

As quick as Jack got the stage, Griff snatched it back. "Remember while you report our successes for thirty seconds on TV, in most cases you find out about them only after we've put in hundreds of hours of intricate investigative work. This time, you learn right along with us how hard it is to achieve positive results."

Once again, Kat folded her arms across her chest, as if steeling herself against Griff, her new adversary.

Jack wanted to jump in, save the situation, but Griff got there ahead of him. "Consider the victims whose lives are split open when you reporters rummage around in their suffering. Will the public see your pain?"

Griff's words were true. Jack hoped they sunk in, yet Kat looked so skeptical, he suspected they might have the opposite effect. If she persisted, Jack would go to Elliot Tucker, the one person with control over her.

Kat's letter opener fell to the floor. She swept it aside with her foot. "I'm good at compromise. I'll give you one week."

As Griff thrust his hands in his jean pockets, Jack felt his frustration. Kat was a ticking time bomb, her own worst enemy. Griff had an idea, however, and, surprisingly, she heard him out and approved his plan.

Thirty minutes later, Griff finished sweeping her place with an electronic device. "I am happy to report there are no transmitters."

Before leaving, Griff had one more request to make of Kat. When Jack heard it, he told Kat he was all for it. However, this time, it took more convincing. In the end—the two men went to the FBI office to get supplies and Griff worked for several more hours in Kat's condo. Kat begrudgingly admitted it was workable, and agreed to another few weeks for them to figure out who was listening to her calls.

Griff threw his leather work-belt and tool pouch over his shoulder and after a quick goodbye was out the door. Jack took a moment to say good night to Kat, then followed. On the elevator down to the lobby, neither man spoke. Jack wondered what else the FBI agent knew about the phone tap.

Secrecy was logical. After all, Jack had not told Griff anything about the vans he and Pablo were building for Luis. Sure, Griff could be trusted with the information, but he had no need to know. Neither did Jack about the tap, at least not yet.

Outside, it was pitch black. The closest street light was dark. Before he saw it coming, a crashing blow landed on the side of his head. As he went down, he saw a figure rush into Griff. Jack landed on the asphalt and intense pain rocked his body.

Seeing Griff on the ground, Jack scrambled to his knees, dove at their attacker, whose leg slid right through Jack's grip. Griff was up, chasing after their assailant. Jack followed him through the best part of Chicago, where crimes like this were not supposed to happen, forcing his legs to vault the high curbs, doing his best to keep up.

He almost caught up to Griff when their prey came under a street light. Their attacker wore a stocking over his face and was dressed in black. This looked like a professional job, but if it was, why didn't the guy shoot? Maybe it was a warning. The man in black ran across Lake Shore Drive.

Jack wove and darted to get across one lane, when a car came straight at him. Horns blared. Out of breath, he finally made it to the other side. Griff was already on the beach, but the man vanished into the night. With all the rocks, it was useless to try to chase him down there. Jack scrambled over them anyway, called out to Griff, "It's dangerous here this time of night! Be careful." If only the moon was full to give some natural light.

Griff jogged back, wiping down his face. "He's gone. Are you okay?"

"Sore. And you?"

"Same. The worst of it is, he got my leather pack, grabbed it right off my shoulder. Probably thought it contained credit cards or money. Instead, he got hundreds of dollars worth of my electronic tools."

Jack exhaled. "That's a shame. In the department, if we lose equipment we reimburse the city. What does the Bureau say when you're a victim of a crime?"

Griff shrugged. "There's a first time for everything."

They crossed both directions of traffic and, back at his car, Jack thought of a way to make it up to Griff. "Want some Due's pizza?"

Griff perked up. "A chance at Chicago's famous pizza, try and stop me. Oh and Jack, I don't want to file a report with Chicago P.D. Too much to explain."

Jack started the car. "I'm with you all the way on that one."

TWENTY ONE

On Monday, one of those September days where the sun seared the pavement soon after peering above the eastern horizon, Jack was out for a stroll with Winston on the leash trying to decide if he should call Kat. He loved early morning, when he usually did some of his best thinking before the chaos of the day's urgent tasks set in.

Just about home, he was no closer to an answer. The only thing he did know was that, dressed in jeans and short-sleeved cotton shirt, he was hot. In the kitchen, the sight of his dad cooking at the stove, surprised him. Smells of bacon frying made him hungry. Winston dashed over to Big John and licked the back of his hand.

Jack was firm. "Steady boy, we have our breakfast first. Then you eat. Go in your bed." The dog obeyed, but not before letting out a short whine in protest.

The table set with two plates and cups, Jack asked his dad, "Are you up to cooking the eggs or should I?"

His father lifted a cover off a pan. "They're all ready, son. You sit and eat a nourishing meal for a change."

Jack patted his stomach, unwilling to admit he had gained two pounds from gorging on Barney's hot dogs last week. Still, it was wonderful to see Dad almost back to his old self, save for a slight lag in his left leg.

Gingerly, as if trying not to stumble, Big John stepped to the table and scooped out perfectly scrambled eggs. A few bits landed on the floor, and Winston was on the specks in a second, lapping them up.

Jack shooed him back to the corner. "I mean it, Winston."

He moved the plates from the edge of the table. If only he had time to take Winston to obedience school, but there were no extra hours to go around. He was even wondering if he would make it back to Pentwater before summer officially ended. It was not too early to think of winterizing the boat; with the Interstate Van case revving up, he doubted he could spend much more time at the marina. Answers did not come easy these days, especially since Gordon sprung on him the sudden trip to the border.

Big John forked bacon on their plates and sat down still holding the pan, his breathing labored. Jack did not ask if he was all right, for the simple reason, like his dad, he hated nagging about his health. "Dad, it looks great. Shall I say grace?"

Father and son bowed their heads and Jack gave thanks for the food. "And Lord, thanks for healing Dad and for what he means to me. Guide and protect us, Amen."

Jack found his father staring at him, rubbing the stubble on his chin. "I forgot to shave. You didn't say, but do you have special need of protection, son?"

Perhaps he did. When Jack prayed for it, he was thinking of Big John, but now an internal debate waged within over how much to tell. Even though Dad was a retired cop and could be trusted, Jack's rule was never to reveal what he was working on undercover. It was safer for him and his father that way.

He ate his eggs. "One case has me baffled. You know I cannot say much, but I leave tonight to drive a southerly route. They're predicting a hurricane for the Gulf States and I would like to get out of there before it hits."

Big John nodded. "Saw the forecast. They're saying Mexico will get hit."

Jack smiled. "That's my dad, ace investigator."

Big John ate a slice of bacon, wiped his mouth on a napkin. "You've never concerned yourself over weather. What is troubling you? I see on your face the mark of a man's fist. Did not want to mention it, but your safety is on my mind."

"It involves possible terrorism and," Jack put down his fork, searching for a way to tell the truth without revealing too much. "People might be in danger if I am not smart enough, not fast enough. Saturday night I let my guard down and was sucker punched by a mugger."

He might be wrong, but Jack had concluded the attack was random, unrelated to what he was doing for Luis or Kat.

Big John sipped his coffee. "You and I sought out a perilous job. You knew that going in, from pampering my bruises, watching my broken arm heal many years ago. However, this sounds more serious than a petty car thief who busted my arm. The only thing I can say is you are not alone. I pray for you every single night, each morning. There is nothing more I can do and neither can you, except your best."

Jack wiped his forehead with a napkin. It sure was hot. "I tell myself I am not a team of one, but sometimes it feels that way. My boss never worked in a covert capacity and he's—well," he got up and checked the setting on the AC, "green is the kindest way to put it. Loves reports and computers, but as for understanding the dangers, forget it."

Dad suddenly changed the subject, or so Jack thought. "It's hard on wives, too."

Jack swallowed a mouthful of coffee. "You mean Melissa, don't you?"

"Can't say I meant her specifically. I think you've dealt with that heartache and can now see it was best you two did not marry. No, I was thinking of a pretty woman who came to see *me* recently."

Speechless for a moment, Jack was surprised his Dad was thinking about getting married again after being on his own for decades. "You didn't tell me there was someone you were interested in."

Big John thumped down his cup, waved around his big hand as if swatting a fly. "Don't speak nonsense. I am talking about you."

"Someone came to see you about me?"

"Don't play games. You have seen a lot of Mary Katherine Kowicki."

Jack chomped the last of his bacon, hoping to divert his dad's attention. "You of all people know that's business; she is helping you ferret out the Kennedy assassination."

His father raised his eyebrows, now tinged with white since his stroke. "Is she now? Seems Kat admires you a great deal. She called recently, told me how awful she felt staring at the white spot where Kennedy was killed. Son, she's working hard on my evidence, wants the three of us to meet soon. Just for the record, I like her, but she has a strong mind of her own. A calculating one, I'd say."

Hmm. Unsure how he felt about Kat and Big John talking about him behind his back, Jack knew one thing. He could not very well discuss his relationship with Kat when he had not defined it for himself. Jack lived in the present with an eye always to the future, logically planning each move. This "thing" with Kat—if it was anything at all—was like taking his boat on a river with no charts to steer him around the underwater hazards.

"I am not going to get involved so soon after Melissa. Kat won't be staying long in Chicago anyway."

Big John did not utter another word. He was like that. Said his peace, and let the words sink in or disappear on their own. Dad just picked up his cup, drank his coffee, giving Jack something to chew on.

Jack got up, walked over and put a hand on his father's shoulder. "I should be back Thursday, late. I called Tooey and he's coming over tomorrow to challenge you in checkers."

Big John just nodded. Jack squeezed his shoulder. "I hope you win. Miss Lizzy will look in on you every day. I'd like to buy her a gift certificate. While I'm gone, try to find out where she likes to eat."

His father grabbed his hand and Jack felt fortunate to be his son. "And Dad, I'll be careful."

At the JTTF office an hour later, Jack did ring Kat, partly to prove what he told his dad was true. He reached her on her supervisor's phone, identified himself as Jack. She sounded friendly, but distant.

"Kat, I wanted you to know if anything comes up, I'll be out of town a few days. You can get me on my cell. Big John appreciated your phone call. If you still want to go over things on Dad's research, count me in. Just let us know when." There. That should let her know it *was* business.

She sounded all business, too. "I can stop by Sunday, if that's okay. I found out Lee Harvey Oswald went to both the Soviet and Cuban Embassies in Mexico City before the assassination. He probably met with KGB agents."

Jack was reluctant to discuss the details over the phone. "Come about four. You can tell us more then. Now, I should get going."

Kat's reply was off the mark. "Have a nice vacation. I wish I could go to Pentwater, but am stuck covering a search warrant on a nursing home owned by the Public Works Director."

"Kat, I'm not going to Pentwater, and this is no vacation."

"Are you going to see Melissa?"

Jack was stunned. First Dad, now Kat. He never told her of his broken engagement. "How did—"

She interrupted, "Don't ask. A good reporter never reveals her sources."

Jack felt his temper rise, and he began to see why Griff was irritated with her. "For your information, she's in Oregon. I am heading to Texas."

"You sound grouchy. I'm tempted to ask if you're checking up on my work in Dallas, but that would be ridiculous. It must be something you don't want me to know."

"Very perceptive." Jack thought better of that remark, cautioning himself not to tempt her to nose into his case. Perhaps it was time to remove the mystery in her mind about Melissa. "I was engaged, thought I found a woman who I would cherish forever, but she did not feel the same about me. It's over, end of story."

Kat's usual hard-charging tone grew tender. "Listen, Jack, I'm not trying to pry into your private life. You have not asked me one personal question since we had breakfast in Pentwater, except about Elliot's health. Forget I mentioned it."

Jack had not meant to sound so prickly. "No harm done. It's just that," he paused, "to hear you say her name, well, it was unexpected." What he confided next amazed him even more. "She did not call off the wedding, just left me to face our families, our guests. There are movies and stories about runaway brides, well I ..."

His voice trailed off. Kat was quick to say she was sorry. "Have you spoken?"

This was going where he did not want to go. Still, hadn't he read somewhere that it helped to talk about your pain? Maybe, but Jack was uncomfortable divulging too much; must be his cop instincts shut down for a second. Now, they became a sturdy wall. "Not one word, which is fine with me. She wrote me a letter, which I threw away."

He hoped Kat took the hint and quit asking questions. He should ask about Elliot, but before he got the words out, again she probed, "You didn't call or write her back?"

It was better to keep his trap shut, so he did.

Kat came back at him. "I get it. Your pride is too hurt to acknowledge her existence. I have not been where you were, but I was in Melissa's shoes, only not close to marriage. A man I worked with, Randy, was head over heels about me. We dated, but I never felt the same. When I moved to Washington, and told him I wanted to be friends, I never heard from him again—not even a Christmas card. I would have preferred knowing he accepted things, especially now since we're working together again."

Wow, that shot a jolt of jealousy through Jack's veins. He sat up straighter in his chair. Kat had not mentioned an old flame in her office. He tried to sound matter-of-fact. "You mean Randy is assigned to WEWW, your Chicago station?"

Kat sounded cagey when all she said was, "Yes."

Jack had to know more. "Is he a reporter, cameraman, or what?"

She chuckled. "They detest that term you know, cameraman. We call them videographers or photographers."

"So Randy is one of those people who puts you on air."

Another chuckle, "Since you finally confided *one* fact of your life, I will tell you one back, then we're even. No, you have it wrong. Randy is on air, like me."

Jack couldn't help it, he asked one more question. "Do you and he travel together for your news stories?"

"No, he is the evening anchor. Maybe you've seen him."

Oh, *that* Randy. He slumped in his chair. Not that Jack watched the news very often, but now he pictured the all-American type, straight white teeth, smooth tan, and too-perfect hairstyle. Before he could pretend this revelation did not bother him, his cell phone rang. He checked the LED screen.

"Kat, I have to take this. I'll ring you in a couple days." To his ears, that sounded flat, but he really did have to hang up.

She ended with, "Not on my cell."

Jack answered before his caller went to voicemail. It was Gordon, and why he did not walk the thirty feet from his office to Jack's desk was unclear.

"McKenna," Gordon was his usual curt self, "The Bureau authorized payment of your airfare back to Chicago. Draw out cash from the imprest fund. We don't want credit card records of the flights. Have the FBI group at the airport get your tickets so you won't pick up a profile tail by paying cash."

Jack had given his boss regular updates about the conversions done by Pablo, who still thought they were for drug smuggling. The way things were coming together, Jack, Gordon, and the Bureau were convinced the vans were to be used to move bombs. The first two vans had gone into Mexico. This time, FBI higher-ups wanted Jack, Ricky, and Pablo to deliver the next two completed ones to Luis near the border so that agents would not have to follow them all the way down there.

Jack voiced doubts about delivering the vans in stages. "What if they put a bomb in one of their first two vans and kill someone before we arrest them?"

Gordon sounded more sure of himself than usual. "We are certain they will make a big statement by setting off six bombs simultaneously. We want to track where they go from Texas, it might help us identify who is directing Luis."

Jack was not looking forward to driving anywhere with Pablo let alone all the way to McAllen, Texas, an outpost near the Mexican border. He was with him at Norman's Cay, when his dad had a stroke. Not that Jack believed in bad luck, he prayed for safety, he simply did not trust Pablo. Pablo gave off vibes that he was always working some side deal Jack couldn't put his finger on.

He never did find out why Pablo left for hours for three days in a row. On the third day, Jack told Ricky to follow Pablo and he did, all the way to the dentist. After that, Pablo stayed around but Jack was uneasy.

With no choice, he agreed to what his boss wanted. "After we deliver these two and get back, we'll convert the final two vans. They are already at the shop."

Gordon waxed positive. "If they place bombs or drugs in the compartments, we'll know from the sensors that feed to the satellite. Then we'll have to take action."

Jack hung up, feeling no better about his excursion south. Then he recalled what the minister in Washington said. If God was for him, who could be against him?

TWENTY TWO

E va squeezed into the small third room where they monitored a court-ordered wiretap on *CamelotConnection's* web site. Sonya Haddad's thin finger pointed to a computer monitor, "Eva, I have accessed the requests from their subscribers, internal emails, and accounting entries. This order is from a labor union that requested records of credit card purchases made by a company's CEO."

Astonished by the amount of information legally ordered through cyberspace, Eva asked about a second monitor filled with numbers. "I suppose these are the accounting transactions."

Sonya always looked serious, and today was no exception. "Yes. Interestingly enough, they are reflected as debits in the requestors' bank accounts."

Eva jumped on that connection. "Tell Earl, he's IRS. It might have tax implications. I see you are tracking emails. Find anything substantive?"

Agent Haddad gazed at Eva with large, dark eyes, as if troubled by something. "Early this morning an email from their D.C. office to their Kazakhstan office mentioned Agent Topping."

That, Eva could not absorb. "Our Griff?"

While Sonya continued tapping keys, Eva voiced her fears. "If Griff showed up on an email, that could mean Camelot got wind of our investigation."

She leaned over the monitor to watch Sonya try to locate the email with Griff's name, but it seemed to have disappeared.

A voice behind Eva startled her. "I can tell you why."

She pivoted, came face-to-face with Griff. "You better tell me."

He wore a solemn expression. "Eva, you better sit down."

Oh no, it was as she feared, word *was* leaked before their group could uncover any illegal activities of the data brokers. "Are we dead in the water?"

A smile played underneath his moustache. "Hardly. I have arranged to go to Kazakhstan. That's probably why my name surfaced on the Camelot email. I wanted to go sooner, but my buddy at Harding and

Associates said they want me in two weeks. They still have an opening there and have arranged for me to see the whole operation. I said nothing to him about Camelot Connection, so I may not find anything, but it's a start."

Relieved, Eva wanted to slug Griff in the arm for pulling a stunt like that, and she would have if Sonya were not in the room. She got even by ordering him to write up an undercover travel request.

It was her turn to smile. "Give it to me in the next half-hour Griff. We're flying under the radar of everyone except the Attorney General, but if Congress gets a bug in their ear, I want everything documented."

Griff dipped his head, "I'm not sure of the dates yet, but thought I'd put in for vacation time."

Eva twisted her wedding ring. "We have to let Harding pay your travel expenses so it will seem like you're really considering their job offer. Submit an annual leave request, so it appears that way, even to people at the Bureau. After the case is complete and public, we'll reverse it, and show your absence as undercover hours."

Consumed by her monitor, Sonya seemed oblivious to their banter. Seconds later, she gasped, "Look at this, it's unbelievable."

Eva and Griff wheeled around at the same time, and nearly collided. On the screen was an email from Flip Harding to Wilt Kangas at the CIA. At least Eva thought it was for Kangas. The recipient's email was DDICIA. It read: *Stop by in twenty-four hours. You have your package from Havana, but we have not been paid. Flip*

Agent Haddad shook her head. "It looks like a classified document."

Eva's thoughts pulsed at the speed of sound. "Sonya, print that out for me. I may have personal knowledge of what this is about."

The agent handed a sheet to Eva, and then stretched her back. "I need a break. Will Earl or Sal be in anytime soon? I've been on the computer since six this morning."

Eva rolled the chair away from the computer. "Go home, get some sleep. I can watch the monitors for now."

Alone with Griff, who seemed to be bursting with questions, Eva tried not to show how shook up she was by that email, which meant *Camelot Connection* was helping the CIA. Moreover, it most likely referred to General San Felipe, who wanted to flee the Cuban prison. The CIA agent, Bo Ryder, had mentioned to Eva he was getting out. She wanted to call Bo right away and ask for an update, but that was not a smart thing to do with Griff standing there, staring at the computer, looking as if he wanted a whack now at probing the secrets of *Camelot*, before he even got to Kazakhstan.

For now Eva folded the email and stuffed it into the pocket of her suit jacket. "Griff, forget what you saw. If there is follow up, I will do it. For right now, write up what you learned about Harding—and I mean every word your friend there told you."

"If anything, my going to Kazakhstan to see Harding's operations is more important to unraveling what is going on." He hesitated, then asked, "You haven't had visions about my trip have you?"

Eva understood the question. The year before, when Griff was working on a case involving a Cabinet member's son, Eva told him of her dream, where someone shot him in the woods. She was very upset, but he shrugged it off, until something happened almost exactly as she had described it beforehand. Ever since, Griff had been curious about her dreams.

"No." She shooed him out the door. "Be cautious in Kazakhstan. Do *not* use your official passport; it will raise too many questions. Everything about this case is as strange as that email we just saw. My instincts tell me these people are smarter at using technology to their advantage than we suspect."

Griff gave her a salute and left Eva in the tech room pondering Flip Harding's email to Kangas and debating whether to call Bo, who remained on loan to the Senate Intelligence Committee until September's end. He might blow her off, claiming she no longer had a "need to know." Besides, she had her own reasons for not wanting Bo to ask why she left the Committee prior to her fellowship expiring.

KAT EASILY DECIPHERED the cryptic text message on her cell. *Betsy Ross* meant ICE agent Eva Montanna was calling, and Kat was to call back from a safe phone. It took only seconds, thanks to a prepaid cell phone she had bought for calling Jack and Eva. When her minutes were up, she planned to throw it away and buy a new one.

As she punched in Eva's number, Kat shuddered as she thought about terrorists using these types of phones to avoid detection. She wanted nothing to do with monsters like that, except to report their activities on television. "Agent Montanna, here. Is this Kat?"

Kat stood on the Civic Center plaza, under the Picasso sculpture. While it was a perfect late-summer day, Kat did not see the blue sky or feel the gentle breeze from Lake Michigan. In fact, she counted none of her blessings—she was on a mission dear to her heart, to stop whoever was after her, and hoped Eva had a part in it. Woman-to-woman, she trusted her almost completely.

"Please say you caught whoever is tapping my phone. It's making me crazy, and I'm starting to feel as if I'm the one in the wrong."

Eva's reply did not illuminate. "A team of agents is working on that as we speak. Can you do— "

A gust of wind muffled her words. Kat spoke, as she walked, "I can't hear you. I'm going inside the Civic Center." Kat heard static. She quickly turned her back to the wind. "Hello, Agent Montanna?"

"I'm here."

Good, she had not lost the connection. Kat made it through the revolving door, into the calm of the lobby, and asked Eva to repeat what she wanted. When she found out what it was, Kat promised to get to her computer right away.

"Oh, and Kat, call me Eva."

Kat found herself smiling. "Okay and Eva, I'll rush your request. Do you think it's safe? I mean, if they find out I'm on to them, I wonder what they'll do."

Eva was firm. "Use the code system we arranged for talking on the phone. Try to carry on with life as normally as you can. I know it is difficult. Every day we're working against the clock, trying to stop those who would harm our country, avoid our laws; I have to watch my back, too. After a while, we agents take it for granted. Some are better than others are at living with it. You met Griff Topping."

Kat answered guardedly, "Yes." Where was Eva going with this? Griff seemed capable, but his confidence bordered on arrogance.

Eva's opinion shed new light. "I've known Griff for years. He's one of the fearless types, whereas I have my family to consider, so I analyze everything carefully.

Kat had not thought much about how people in Eva's position confronted danger on a daily basis, how they dealt with having a job that could result in their being killed. When Griff and Jack visited her condo, they both acted so casual about her quandary. Eva was helping her to see why; they lived with danger up close and personal every day.

She said so to Eva, and added, "I think Jack McKenna is a mix of you and Griff. I thought he didn't want to tell me things because I'm a reporter, but maybe he's the more cautious type."

To herself, Kat thought, *Griff goes to the limit, like me.*

Eva was chuckling. "My husband is not in law enforcement, either, except he flew fighter jets. From the moment we met, we had an instant understanding of our values and dreams. It's not always easy, especially when I go overseas on a case and we can't talk to each other. No matter whom you marry, or even if you never marry, without a strong faith in God, life can be rocky and shallow."

Kat wondered what Eva meant, but something more serious was bothering her, and she brought it up now. "Did you learn anything more about the person in the video you recognized?" She heard a clicking noise. "What's that?"

"A call for me. I did find out, but I'll have to tell you later."

Before Kat could ask anymore, Eva was gone; leaving Kat to stare at the prepaid phone, wanting to believe Eva was keeping her word. Then, she remembered her promise to Eva to get on her computer right away. Kat hurried through the revolving doors to head for the station and ran right into a man with oily hair, a scraggly beard, and bad odor. Kat caught her breath. Was he a street person or a fake one following her? Without waiting to find out, she fled to the office, keeping one eye behind her the entire time.

Back at the station, trying to catch her breath, Kat's hands froze above her keyboard. What Eva requested sounded simple enough, though she had a hard time deciding what to ask for. She typed in something innocuous, and then deleted it.

Her mind searched for the right subject to get the blood boiling of whoever was behind the move to ruin her. A war of wills raged within, and she tried to recall Eva's exact words, *"Kat, go on CamelotConnection.com, use your account as you would normally. I'd like you to ask for information on some story you are working on."* Did she add, *so as not to ring any alarm bells*, or was it Kat's imagination?

Eva assured Kat the federal government would reimburse her for the cost, so long as it was not exorbitant. Her slim fingers flew over the keys, first to the web site, then her account number. Mark Young, Elliot's pilot who died, had two college-age daughters. It might be nice for Kat to get in touch with them and see how they were surviving. They shared a common bond, all losing their fathers. Besides, it was a human-interest story that should not raise eyebrows.

Kat did not know their names, so she called Matt Larsen, the reporter who covered the original story. If her "watchers" recorded it, they should be convinced she was going on as usual.

Matt gave her both names, but not before prying, "What are you working on?"

She snickered, "I'm not horning in on your story if that's what you think. I had a few minutes to spare and thought I'd search the web to see what kind of coverage you got across the country. I'll be sure to tell you what I find."

Matt sounded gleeful, "Thanks, Kat. I appreciate it."

Kat hung up before he had a chance to meddle any further. He wanted to go places, so Matt kept his distance, in case her star truly had fallen. She drew herself together, said under her breath, "Matt baby, watch and learn."

About to enter the field for biographical data, a voice over her shoulder intoned, "What are you doing, Kat?"

She turned in her swivel chair and immediately stood up gasping. A light shone in Elliot's eyes, which she had not seen before. "Elliott—" then catching herself, realizing they were at work—"Sir, you look terrific! It's great to see you here." She held out a hand, which Elliot gently grasped.

"I'm cleared for take-off, Kat, and want to hear about your assignments." As he gazed around the station, Kat noticed he seemed to soak in the cacophony of voices and the other sounds of a busy television station like a classical music fan would soak in a symphony. This was Elliott's element.

Elliot checked his watch. "How about lunch?"

Kat leaned over to click the mouse. "Let me finish this request."

On the way to the elevator, a few heads, including Matt's, turned to stare. Kat walked on by smiling. It wasn't everyday a reporter left with the owner of the station. Some might even hope he was escorting her out for good. Not that Kat made enemies; she just did not have many friends, except for Ian. He was great. Maybe Randy, her ex-boyfriend had poisoned the others toward her.

"I am supposed to walk a mile a day," Elliot pushed the elevator button, "are you up for something at the Lantern on Lower Wacker?"

They crossed Wacker Drive, descended the stairs to Lower Wacker, a street that ran beneath Wacker Drive and was frequented mostly by the locals. As drivers took the underground shortcut from the Eisenhower Expressway to North Michigan Avenue, it always felt creepy to Kat the way the headlights and light coming in from the open area along the Chicago River illuminated cars whizzing along in the darkness.

Kat thought it was an unlikely location for a restaurant, and was surprised by how crowded Mrs. O'Leary's Lantern was for lunch. Elliot pushed past everyone waiting for a table, telling the host he had a reservation. In moments, they took their seats on the patio, where Kat tried to relax, shrug off fears someone was watching them.

A glorious day on the Chicago River, its dark surface sparkling like a silver ribbon winding through a canyon whose walls were skyscrapers, Kat sipped iced tea through a straw. Elliot ordered water. "I turned over a new leaf, no more caffeine."

They ate chicken salad topped with fresh pineapple, content to make small talk while other diners were nearby. She asked about his health.

"I feel terrific, Kitten. And we are celebrating."

Kat raised her eyebrows a fraction. "Oh? Have you completed physical therapy?"

He lifted his water glass. "The FCC approved my acquisition of the television stations."

After what he survived, Kat was happy for him and told him so. She pressed a white cloth napkin to her lips. "Elliot, you asked about my stories. When you came in, I was seeking info on Camelot Connection about Mark's two daughters. Do you think they will be back in college in the fall?"

Elliot seemed not to have heard. Maybe it was difficult to talk about Mark's death. She tried again, "Elliot thanks for asking me to lunch. The crash made me realize how hard it would be if I lost you."

There was much more she wanted to tell him, but it was as if Elliot was in a far-away place. His coloring looked grayer than it had earlier. Kat grew concerned that the doctors were wrong to release Elliott back to work already.

"Elliot, did I say something to offend you?"

Hands cradling his mug of coffee, his eyes drifted to hers. "No, my dear. I was thinking what you said about Mark's daughters. I want to pay for their college. I asked my lawyer to look into it, as well as some other things."

"That is admirable, Elliot."

His eyes never wavered from hers. "I made a promise, and want to stick with it."

Elliot was not making any sense, at least not to her. "Sorry, but what promise?" She drank the last of her tea, waiting for him to explain.

He folded his hands on the table, and leaned over to her. "Remember when you brought me Chinese food the night before I left rehab? I asked you to think about what you were living for—awards, fame, money—or something else."

She pulled her hair back from her face and looked away, sensing where this was heading. He was getting ready to send her to Texas—or somewhere even farther away, like Arizona. "The stories I am working on have priority in my life."

"Do they really?"

What did he want her to say, she was ready to go anywhere to work on a story? Kat searched her mind and her heart, and suddenly a feeling of emptiness overwhelmed her, not unlike what she felt when she first stood by Elliot in the hospital bed.

Kat dropped her arms to her lap. "A minute ago, I said I would be lost without you, and it's true. Since your accident, I realize my relationship with you is the most important thing in my life; I love my mother, but I hardly ever see or hear from her. You're the one who's there for me, Elliott."

Her emotions surged, and tears threatened her eyes. "You are a father to me."

His eyes were already glistening. "If you only knew how, for so many years, I hoped you would feel this way. I never wanted to replace your dad, but I felt that, losing him when you were only two, you would never know him. I tried to be there for you day in, day out, in times of trouble and success."

It was true, and Kat thanked Elliot for all he had done for her.

That sparked a twinkle in his eye. "I assume that includes being back in Chicago?"

She flashed a smile, but then thinking of the taps on her phone, it was gone. "There is something I need to tell you."

"Well, that makes two of us."

Kat insisted Elliott speak first. Before she knew it, he veered away from their relationship to something mysterious. The way he whispered, yet sounded strong, drew her into his story and she scarcely breathed.

"As my plane was going down, all I could think to do was to ask God to save Mark. In my life, I never talked to or sought a higher power. A brilliant white light beckoned me to come, and there was beauty all around me. As I grew nearer to it, a holy presence said, 'I am the way, the truth, the life.' Next thing, I have no idea how much time passed,

I awoke in the hospital, amazed I was alive. Before I ever found out Mark had died—" Elliot closed his eyes for a moment, cleared his throat.

Kat patted his hand, asked if he was sure he could go on. "I must tell you of an extraordinary change in my life. You know part of it because you were in my room when Dr. Van Halsma said my head troubled him and I needed an MRI."

She recalled the grouchy doctor but did not interrupt Elliot, whose face had taken on a glow. "Later, an angel appeared to me, who told me God spared my life to give me a chance to know him. I made a promise to live the rest of my life trying to do that."

Kat had heard of angels, but was astonished to think they were real. She remembered all too clearly the second doctor who told her Elliot was healed. Dr. Semeion also told her to tell Laurel to stay in India. Kat had done what he advised. When her Mom called back, she was relieved she didn't need to travel because she had urgent business there and should not leave. Laurel also thought the whole thing was evidence of a miracle. With her investigations, travels, and meeting Jack, Kat had somehow put the occurrence out of her mind.

Now, she found the words to tell Elliot about the strange encounter with Dr. Semeion, what he told her, and how she followed up.

Elliot nodded gravely, but he wasn't surprised. "Kat, I only know the angel that came to me was some kind of spiritual being from God, because he knew all about my prayers for Mark."

She shook her head, tried to think more clearly. "I know you never had an MRI. Your blood pressure went back to normal and stayed there, and everyone thinks it is miraculous."

A waiter bringing the check abruptly ended the special moment they shared. Elliot gave him a credit card. When he left, Kat laughingly said, "I hope you did not give him your Camelot Connection card like I once did."

Elliot switched gears as if he was driving an old Triumph Spitfire on a two-lane country road. "Camelot Connection you say? Is someone still listening to your phone calls? Tell me everything. My mind has been in a fog lately. Must be all the painkillers I was on, which I'm off for good."

Kat was relieved. The old Elliot was back, it seemed. Her voice low, she told him about Jack McKenna, her Chicago detective. "He and his team found something suspicious," Kat purposely did not mention Eva, Griff, or the feds being involved, "and are tracking down the source."

She pushed back the chair. "We should head back. I need to call my source about the Kennedy assassination. I may have found a way to access records from the Mexican Embassy about Oswald's trips there in the fall of 1963."

Elliot signed the credit slip. "Soon, I want you to tell me everything you dug up on Kennedy. I smell a big story. I can see it in your eyes."

He noticed that did he? Kat only smiled. "Now that you are back to full speed, please fit me in your schedule."

Apparently, Elliot did not hear. "Please think about what I said."

Kat stared back, hoping it was true that he had stopped taking the painkillers. "I just said pick a time, any time."

His voice was kind, his tone tender. "No, no. I want you to consider the purpose of your life. I cannot rest easy until I have your answer."

Kat sat back, wondering how to tell him that with phone taps, pre-paid phones, flying to Washington and Dallas, running down stories of corruption at City Hall, and driving back and forth between a condo in Chicago and the cottage in Pentwater, neither of which was really home, she just wanted her life back, no matter what its purpose.

But, rather than burden him with the chaos her life had become, she was gentle in return. "I promise to think about it, Elliot." Inwardly, she promised that would come later, much later.

TWENTY THREE

The ringing in Jack's ears would not stop. An alarm! A train was coming at full speed! He couldn't drive the van off the tracks, something heavy was on his legs. He breathed fast, trying to move them but something was tying his legs down.

His mind tumbled, and without knowing why, he suddenly realized he was not on any train tracks. Jack kicked his feet, and groggy, rolled over to shut off the alarm clock. A brown ball of fur thumped to the floor, let out a whimper. Jack sat up and rubbed his eyes. He was in his own bed.

While he had driven the van straight through to McAllen, Texas and passed plenty of trains, he was never stuck on the tracks. Yet that dream seemed so real. Storms on the outer edge of a hurricane bore down on the eastern coast of Mexico, threatening his flight to Chicago. Finally making it home at two that morning, Jack had fallen into a tormented sleep, like someone drugged.

Now, he hurried to take Winston out. Back inside, he showered, careful to be quiet; Big John was asleep. Jack told Winston to get in his bed and locked the back door as he left. By nine o'clock, he was at his desk and had already downed three cups of black coffee and two doughnuts Gordon bought to celebrate his one-year anniversary of running the task force.

About to grab another, Jack's boss called, "How did it go in McAllen?"

Jack flopped in a chair across from Gordon's desk, forced his sluggish mind to tell about the trip. He was on sugar overload and nothing clicked.

Gordon fiddled with his pen, seemed anxious. "Bureau bigwigs are coming unglued about who these people are. That bomb scare at LAX did not help my sleep last night. Have we confirmed the connections with terrorism yet?"

His legs cramping, Jack talked and flexed his calf muscles simultaneously. "Luis now has four vans. Maybe we should delay final delivery until we learn what they're doing with the two that Pablo and I delivered."

Gordon stopped writing. "Did Luis personally accept them or someone else?"

"Ricky rode with Pablo to monitor who he talked to, what he said. I followed in the other van. I am told that the GPS device we installed transmitted the vans' location directly to the satellite."

His boss objected, "Whoa Jack, these guys aren't dumb. They'll have their technicians sweep the vans to see if they're emitting a GPS signal."

Hair fell in Jack's eyes; he pushed it back off his forehead. "We anticipated that. The tracking signal begins *only* when the van is moving, like when your car gets to a certain speed and the doors lock. If the van is parked, even with the engine running, Luis can sweep it and won't find a thing."

"Who took delivery of the vans in Texas?"

"While Pablo and Ricky met two mutts sent up by Luis, I did surveillance; got the meet on film. The one I recognized from Norman's Cay paid Pablo with hundred-dollar bills and took delivery. ICE's drug dog at the border smelled the money and didn't alert."

"So?"

To Jack, the implications should have been obvious to the least experienced investigator. "Big drug deals are paid for with U.S. hundred-dollar bills. Same hands that touch the drugs also handle the currency. Most drug money gets a positive hit from the drug dog. This stuff didn't."

At Gordon's shrug and perplexed look, Jack stifled a sigh. "The money Luis's guys used to pay for these vans is probably *not* from drug trafficking. They're getting their currency someplace else." He tried to disguise the sarcasm he felt. "Like maybe from where terrorists get their money. *So,* these vans are meant, not for smuggling drugs, but terror." There, Jack laid out his worst fears.

Gordon scowled, as if deep in thought. "Where are the two vans you drove now?"

Jack explained how Luis's people left McAllen in the two vans, crossed the border into Mexico at Reynosa. "The FBI tech center reported they drove to Monterrey, Mexico, where the transmitters stopped transmitting."

Gordon's reaction tossed cold water on Jack's sense of support from his boss. "Great. I predicted they would quit working."

Jack exploded, "Not quit working! Gordon, I told you the transmitter does *not* transmit when the vans don't move. The FBI LEGAT from our Mexico City embassy sent an agent to the last known coordinates in Monterrey. He saw four vans parked inside a chain link fence at an industrial complex. They're probably waiting for the last two before doing anything, so we still might have time."

Jack felt guilty unloading on his boss, but he had no choice. This case was too important, had him on edge. As Gordon stared at his notes, Jack decided he should be more cautious. "Boss, with your permission, I want Pablo to tell Luis the final two vans are ready for pickup here in Chicago, as you had us do with the first two. Hopefully, once they have all six, they'll reveal what they are up to."

Gordon met his gaze, as if reaching a truce over the misunderstanding. "I have confidence in what you're doing, Jack. Notify them, but be sure the tracking devices are working, so we know where they are."

"Right." There was that word again, straight from Pablo's mouth. Jack was obviously spending too much time with his informant. Jack went back to his desk, aware his supervisor did not grasp how the tracking system worked, and that worried him. He sincerely hoped he would not have to rely on Gordon for back up in a dangerous situation, which was surely around the corner.

WITH JACK TELLING HIM what to say, Pablo arranged over the telephone for Luis to send two drivers and the balance owed to Interstate Vans the next Wednesday. To his delight, this gave Jack a final weekend on the *Day Dreamer* in Pentwater. Ten o'clock Friday night, he entered southern Michigan from Indiana, believing he had covered all contingencies in the case. Winston was snoring happily in the backseat.

Jack slipped in a CD of an artist whose harmonica playing sounded like water rushing over rocks, perfect music to keep him company. He got started late because he made a brief stop at his former lieutenant's retirement party where he shook his hand, ate a plate of spaghetti, then headed home.

One advantage to the late hour, there were few cars traveling north to the beaches. His cruise set at seventy-three, Jack tapped fingers to the music on the wheel, jumping when his cell phone vibrated on his belt. He grabbed it, the LED showing a 703 area code, for northern Virginia. Was Eva calling? He turned off the music and answered.

"Sir, this is the duty agent at the FBI tech lab. We are showing movement on one of your Sprinter vans in Chicago, the ones supposed to be parked at Interstate Van Conversions. I thought I better notify you."

His mind going a hundred miles an hour, Jack touched his brakes, disengaged his cruise. The vans were ready for pickup, but Luis's people were not supposed to come until Wednesday. Jack wondered if Pablo was indeed pulling an after-hours stunt.

"Where is the van now?" Jack looked for a place to turn around on the highway.

"Sir, it just entered Interstate 55 near Kedzie Avenue, headed in a southwesterly direction."

The route would take it to Mexico. Jack struggled for composure. "We'll try to catch it. I'm in my personal car right now, but I gotta call for backup, so I have to hang up."

The duty agent was cool, as though used to quick action in a crisis. "Give me the number you need to contact, I'll call it, patch you through. I can remain on the line and keep you posted as to the van's whereabouts."

Jack swung through a median cut labeled "for authorized vehicles only." Stones spinning under his tires, he entered the I-94 southbound lane and, racing back to Chicago, waited for the duty agent to get Ricky Vasquez on the line.

"Jack, I'm at my niece's birthday party. What's so urgent?"

"We have a huge problem." Jack briefed him, asked Ricky to call the other CPD officers on the task force. "Make a bee-line for that van; it's possible Luis's people came early and stole one."

The duty agent interjected, "Your van just turned off I-55. It's northbound on Cicero Avenue."

To Jack, that was a good sign. "Sounds like a circuitous route. Let's hope it's some kids on a joy ride."

The duty agent stayed with Jack and kept Ricky, who was already speeding toward the van and calling their officers, on the line. If this resolved soon, Jack could make another turnaround and head once again for his boat. He really wanted to get her snug before October, but that might have to wait. Jack just knew before the night was over, Gordon would order him back to the border.

His instincts were partially correct. His dreams for a weekend at Pentwater were dashed. An hour later, Jack drove his personal car with Winston sleeping in the back seat—a canine unit of a different sort—to join three other task force cars near the Ford City shopping center. There was the tall, white conversion van parked near the main entrance. Nobody was in it.

After Jack thanked the FBI duty agent for vectoring them to the van and ended the call, he and his group gathered around Ricky's undercover car. It was late, nearly midnight, but each of them was determined to spend the rest of their Friday night to discover who stole that van.

Jack and Winston left his personal car and got into the undercover car driven by police officer Dennis Reed, who everyone called Charts. That way he would have radio contact with the other officers. Jack figured Dennis got his nickname because he liked to sail.

He said, "It's gonna be a long one, Charts." Jack wrestled with how this happened. Security at Interstate Vans was tight. Only Pablo, Jack, and Ricky had keys to the doors. As he watched and waited, anger seeped in, anger that he wanted to take out on Pablo. Must be his informant *was* on the take, pretending to cooperate, while working side deals.

What he saw twenty minutes later shattered most of Jack's distrust against Pablo.

Charts whistled, "Would you look at that!"

Two black youths, wearing baggy pants, football jerseys, and one with a backward baseball cap, sauntered out to the van, unlocked it with the key and got in.

Jack keyed his microphone. "Ricky, these guys have keys. Do you have yours?"

Ricky's voice came back, "Affirmative."

"Let's see where they go. We can get a marked unit to make a traffic stop."

Not long after leaving the mall, the pair circled the block, came to a stop next to a convenience store on south Ashland Avenue. In the parking lot light, Jack saw them get out of the van, and scope all around them, as if looking for heat. The youth with the ball cap waited a second outside the full-length glass door before following his friend inside. Were these two on Luis's payroll, testing if police were watching the vans?

Over the radio, Jack told his officers, "Don't make any hasty moves."

Within minutes, both youths ran out the door, jumped in the van and sped south bound. "Stay with them," Jack called.

Just as he said this, the CPD radio in Charts' car broadcast a robbery of the convenience store. About to give their location to the dispatcher, Jack decided against it, he'd have too much explaining about the van. Unsure of the identity of the two young men, Charts and Jack stayed a car length behind.

The van pulled into a convenience store on 95th Street near Halstead, after circling the block twice. Jack wasted no time. Rather than notify dispatch and reveal his undercover case, he keyed his mic, "Ricky, here's our chance to steal back the van. Bring me the keys."

Charts quietly edged to park on a side street. As Jack exited, Charts handed him a portable radio. Ricky drove by, slowing enough to throw Jack a set of keys. In seconds, Beretta in hand, Jack started the van and pulled out of the lot, heading east toward the Dan Ryan expressway.

He did not get far when Ricky's voice squawked on the portable, "Both guys are looking for their ride. They're running toward the alley. We'll cover both ends to trap them."

Over the portable radio, Jack's words came in a rush, "I'm parking the van. Charts! Come pick me up."

Jack swerved over to the side of the road, slammed the gear into park, and climbed out just as Charts pulled in front of him. He locked the van and jumped in the front. Charts cranked a u-turn, headed back to the action as the dispatcher broadcast descriptions of the suspects in the latest robbery.

Jack had a plan. He and his partners watched the culprits run through alleys, walk down side streets until they got to the corner of 87th and Halstead streets, where they sat on a bench at a bus stop. It was too late to catch a bus, so Jack helped them out—he got on his radio and arranged for a ride.

While these two confused thieves panted on the bench, several blue-and-white squad cars without flashing lights descended on the bus stop. On their common channel, Jack told the arriving throng that Charts, who saw the two leave the scene of both robberies, would meet them at District headquarters to make an ID.

By three that morning, Jack and Ricky returned the van to Interstate, locked it inside the building and replaced the lock, which was cut from the fence gate. Jack and Winston went home exhausted, no longer interested in driving to Pentwater.

TWENTY FOUR

When Terry had met Luis in Venezuela, the Hezbollah commander promised that, when the time was right, Terry and his five recruits would each receive one of the Sprinter vans. He looked forward to it then, but steering the new Dodge van onto I-40 leaving Memphis, Terry felt a little uncomfortable driving such a luxurious vehicle.

While he did not live the typical destitute life of a graduate student, he had plenty of money for gas, food, and clothing, Luis *had* instructed him not to live lavishly. Still, moving this van to its next strategic location was part of Luis's plan; he might as well enjoy the ride, and the clear October morning. On the radio, he found a soft music station, one that complemented his need to think over his final assignment for today.

Yesterday, when he and four of the five recruits took delivery of the vans in Memphis, one of the Mexican drivers told Terry his van's transmission was stuck in second gear. At first, unsure if he should ignore it, Terry decided it was best to get it fixed right away and not risk a total breakdown on the ride back to Chicago. He found a Dodge dealership in Memphis. That van was now working great, but he was a whole day behind schedule to deliver the sixth van.

Partly, it was Stan's fault, now waiting for him in Lexington, Kentucky, because he insisted he could not get to Memphis in time. Anger stirring in his stomach, Terry hoped using Stan was not a terrible mistake. Terry selected the name Stan for Ishmael, his last recruit from Boston, using it on private communications with Luis over the prepaid cell phones. Terry's first choice in Boston—Felix—transferred to George Mason University before he finalized his role.

Glad he had not chosen Stan on his own, Terry made sure not to speed or change lanes quickly. The summer before, Luis had met Stan's father at a training camp in Syria, so any blame for Stan's ineptitude rested with the Hezbollah commander.

While he craved anonymity on the highway, Terry did allow himself one trapping of the wealthy. He ate a breakfast east of Nashville fit for a sultan. Pancakes were light and feathery, the scrambled eggs creamy. When he saw a man next to him eating bacon, contempt for pork eaters almost tempted him to spit in the man's food, but an inner voice warned him not to.

Five hours later, he sat with Stan in an Ethiopian restaurant famous for grilled lamb. Lexington was the perfect place to complete this last step for his planned attacks. With horse farms set amidst rolling hills lined with white fences, it was pure Americana, and few, if any, of its citizens would ever guess such a covert meeting was happening in their midst.

Moreover, it was a halfway point between Memphis and Boston, so—dealing with Stan's balking about the drive to Memphis, Terry decided yesterday to meet in Lexington. At least Stan had shown up, and that was a good thing. Terry timed the meeting so as not to interfere with his required times of prayer, and now he sipped water, a nice refreshment after the long trip.

The city boasted another advantage: The University of Kentucky had a thriving international student body, so a student of Saudi descent meeting with one from Syria would not attract undue notice.

A waiter set down baskets of pita bread and hummus, and Terry tasted these right away. The spread was delicious, with just the right tinge of lemon. Moments later, the waiter hurried over with two steaming bowls of lentil soup. Terry plunged in with a spoon. He whispered to Stan, his tablemate, "Eat first, then we'll talk."

After Terry scooped up the last of his soup, he talked in a code, of sorts, in case someone nearby was listening. "Are you going to the games on Sundays?"

Stan blinked at Terry, with eyes that looked like he just woke up from a deep sleep, then he nodded.

"That is good. Other fans will be used to seeing you there."

Irritated at Stan for not getting to Memphis yesterday and for not answering him now, Terry began to wonder what really went on in his brain. He formed a test. "You remember when to go to the last game?"

When he blinked again, Terry grew impatient. "Well?"

Stan spoke in such heavily accented English, Terry found it hard to understand him. "What is your problem, Ishmael?"

The sound of his given name coaxed Stan to life. "English is difficult for me to understand and speak. It is what my father wants and I do everything he asks. I owe him my life. Tell me when I go to this last game."

"Sunday, October 28. You will get two tickets."

Stan nodded. "Will you contact me before that day so I know what to bring?"

Terry sensed the waiter approaching. He lifted a finger, signaling Stan not to speak. Without studying the bill too closely, Terry plunked a couple twenty-dollar bills onto a black tray, and the waiter hustled away. When he returned with his change, Terry carefully followed instructions to blend in, and left a fifteen percent tip.

"Come on Stan. Let's walk outside."

The two students picked up identical backpacks and textbooks they carried for cover. The books were a loophole a smart investigator could trip him on; because of Stan's incompetence, he had no time to check if this University used the same ones. The chance anyone would check was small, so he walked out into the azure-blue day feeling more confident in Stan, who correctly took Terry's backpack, leaving Terry to take his. Things would turn out well. After all, this mission was from Allah.

On the sidewalk, Terry motioned to the backpack Stan slung over his shoulder. "Memorize what I say."

His recruit blinked those enormous, lazy eyes, and Terry felt a shudder blaze through him, his confidence eroding. It was too late to get anyone else now.

"The keys are inside. As promised, the van has two propane tanks. If asked, you need two for extensive wilderness camping; you cook and heat with the propane. Everything will go according to instructions I gave last time we talked."

The way Stan's eyes did not meet Terry's was disconcerting. Was he listening with his heart and mind or simply with his ears? "On what day and time will you act?"

Stan's reply of noon, October 28, was correct. Terry stopped at the corner, where he would part with this unlikely recruit. The two men would not see each other again until they got to the place where all martyrs went in paradise. Terry was certain he would be there, but he wasn't sure about Stan.

Terry lowered his voice, and put his hand over his mouth as if yawning. "In the backpack is a cell phone. Use it for *no* other reason than to call me if there is a problem you cannot solve. On October 28, be alert for anyone trailing you. If you are followed, do not go to your target until the very last moment. Do you comprehend this?"

Stan shook Terry's hand, as a good American did when departing. His eyes, those half-open black ones, looked sleepy again, almost as if he was on some kind of medication. Would he even make it to the twenty-eighth?

During the taxi ride to the airport to fly back to Memphis and get his own van, Stan's parting words burned in Terry's mind. *A man of honor keeps his word no matter the cost.* Something annoyed him, perhaps the flat, emotionless way Stan said them and not the words themselves. Terry did not question what he was going to do. For a cause greater than he, if Allah wanted him to sacrifice his life, so it would be. Stan, on the other hand, did not seem committed.

Terry paid for the taxi and entered the Lexington airport, thinking of Pat, a recruit from Washington, D.C., who received her van in Memphis. An international student at Catholic University, where her uncle once studied to be a priest, Pat's cover was perfect and she was a most ambitious agent, having been abused as a child at the hands of a neighborhood priest in her native Philippines. A Muslim convert, Pat believed, as did Terry, that the western world would only be fit to live in after every person converted to Islam.

If only Terry could believe that Stan, who he hoped was not an informer, would perform as well as Pat. He lugged his backpack forward in line at the ticket counter, another thought burning in his brain: *Better to die a martyr than be confined in an American jail cell.*

THOUGH JACK WORKED in the same city as Abu Tarim, he never met an international student called Terry, Hezbollah's cell leader in America. Still, the call Jack received at his Chicago office deepened lines on his forehead, ate at his stomach worse than a whole pot of coffee would. He half-walked, half-ran down the hall; his mind operated more clearly when he was moving. Key thing was to make Gordon understand—and act—without Jack losing the job he loved, so much so that he was still single because of it.

Time served a purpose—being married to Melissa would have been disastrous. With what he just found out, he would have to work night and day to eliminate the danger, which he now realized Melissa could never accept.

His boss was on the phone, so Jack rehearsed a speech he hated to give. No way he'd grovel, even though Gordon was adept at protecting his back. Finally, Gordon hung up and Jack strode in before he could make another call.

"Boss, we need to talk. Things down south are beginning to pop."

Gordon looked up. "I don't like the way that sounds. What do you mean, pop?"

His teeth clenched, Jack began with the bare minimum. "Head-quarters says the alarm on the tracking receiver was switched off. Don't ask how or why, someone in Washington messed up, and no one's taking the blame."

He had to ignore the shocked look on his boss's face or he'd never get through this. "Our six vans slipped from Mexico into Texas with no one noticing they were on the move. When the FBI techs discovered the alarm switch was off, they reviewed the memory. The first three vans entered at the Laredo border crossing. One good thing," Jack tried to sound upbeat, "the transmitters indicate nothing was added to the hidden compartments when they crossed the border."

Gordon's lean face was etched with worry. "Where are they now?"

Things were too serious and Jack wanted to give the details, without interruption. "They waited near Laredo, while the other three vans crossed. Border inspectors discovered nothing amiss." He swallowed, looked down at his shoes, without noticing how scuffed they were. "While in Laredo, all six vans were loaded with some kind of cargo, and then they headed to Memphis."

Gordon was out of his chair and pacing in a semicircle behind his desk. "I *knew* it would get screwed up. We will never find them." He pounded a fist in his open palm. "I'll end up transferred to New York City. Of course, *you* work for the Chicago Police Department and can never be transferred."

Jack could not believe it, but he laughed. "When Chicago coppers mess up, they're sent to work with the FBI. So, my attitude is, go ahead and hurt me."

Oblivious to Jack's barb, Gordon paced and cursed. Jack plunged ahead. "The FBI located one van near the campus of Southern Methodist University in Dallas. Late yesterday, Dallas FBI got a sneak-and-peek search warrant. Before the ink was dry, techs from Virginia flew there and found that van now carried two twenty-pound propane tanks."

Gordon slowly found his seat. "And?"

Jack nodded. "The techs replaced them with identical tanks of identical weight. Last night, FBI explosives experts dismantled the tanks removed from the Dallas van. Guess what they found?"

Gordon opened his mouth to reply, but Jack told him, "Those tanks have a small bladder with only enough propane, less than a pound, to pass a lighting test. The rest of the space is filled with plastic explosives."

On his feet again, Gordon glared at Jack as if this disaster was his fault. "How did they get bombs into the vans without us knowing it? You said ICE found nothing when they entered Texas."

Jack decided to stand, too; looking his boss in the eye felt less like he was in the hot seat. "But the sensors worked, that's why we do know it. ICE now thinks the terrorists smuggled the tanks under the border, through a tunnel somewhere near Laredo, and then placed them into the vans. Our techs examined the tracking memory and found weight was added, probably in Laredo."

He shoved his hands in his pockets. "There is more. These vans, if parked in the right spot will explode like IED's. They each have the potential to kill hundreds of people. I don't even want to think about how many people could get hurt."

His face gone pale, Gordon seemed to grasp the magnitude of a problem that Jack had grappled with for the past few minutes. "Do we know where the other five vans are so we can disarm them, too?"

There was no easy way to tell Gordon. "In the dismantled bomb, they found a timing device set to detonate at 11:00 in the morning on Sunday, October 28. We have three weeks to find the rest, which I think we can do. One may be harder to find."

With both hands, Gordon slammed his desk. "What about that one?"

Angry, too, Jack sucked in a breath. "The tech lab is tracking five vans around the country and should have no problem disarming them."

"What about the other *one*?"

Jack had never seen anything go so wrong on a case, with such potentially disastrous consequences. "In Memphis, the satellite alerted. By the time they got agents to that van, the tracking device quit working. I hate to say it, but no one knows where it is."

Gordon could barely speak. "We'll have to start a nationwide search."

His stomach in his throat, Jack edged toward the door. "I'm going to call my contact at the FBI tech lab. You could coordinate with your boss and FBI Headquarters. Agents in Dallas are trying to learn who was driving the van they neutralized."

Jack gestured roughly with his hands. "We know this much. The Dallas van is now a dummy. Another is near Tampa. Two are being tracked into Tennessee, and one went to Washington, D.C. That makes five, which FBI agents are surveilling as we talk, and no doubt will try to disarm ASAP."

Gordon grabbed his suit jacket. "Three weeks to find a missing van armed with enough explosives to kill hundreds, maybe thousands of people. I'm going to brief my boss."

Jack stepped out of Gordon's way. "Remember, we were first notified by someone at FBI Headquarters to watch Interstate Vans. Maybe you could talk to their super-secret source, learn more about the terrorists and the missing van."

Gordon shot back over his shoulder. "Good idea. Since there doesn't appear to be one in Chicago, there's a limit to what we can do here."

Jack got moving himself. He ran the VIN through a national database that tracked vehicles involved in accidents. This search revealed nothing to help. Jack kept at it, vowing to neither eat nor sleep until he uncovered one piece of hard evidence.

A call to his Virginia technician went unanswered. Undeterred, Jack put the VIN through Daimler-Chrysler's warranty system. Bingo! The missing van had warranty work done in Memphis. That was no surprise, since that was where it was last tracked. He desperately hoped to find something they could use, a description of the driver, license number, anything.

Gordon appeared in front of Jack's desk. "Well?"

Not wanting to be premature, he shook his head, and his boss stalked to his office and slammed the door. Next, Jack made a pretext call to the Memphis Dodge dealership. "I am from Interstate Van Conversions, trying to follow up on one of our vans that you worked on right after we delivered it to a customer. We're doing a quality control check to figure out if we did something wrong on our end."

The friendly man checked the computer. "Mr. McKenna, we did warranty work, but I was not the one who signed it in."

Jack stopped taking notes. "Oh?"

"It says here the person bringing it for service was M. Mouse, his address, 3703 Main Street, Orlando, Florida."

Most likely a phony name and address, Jack wanted to grill the guy, but since he had not identified himself as the police, he felt limited in what to ask. "Can you describe the work that was done?"

A keyboard clicking, he said, "Let me see." Silence, then, "We honored the manufacturer's warranty and replaced a faulty sending unit."

A new sending unit was simply not enough to tell Jack how that might affect the tracking unit. "Thanks—like I said, I wanted to make sure my guys hadn't messed it up."

"It says here, the transmission was stuck in second gear. Seems the speed sensor was defective, so the transmission did not know when to shift. This is the same device that locks your door when you get up to a certain speed."

A noise made Jack look up. It was Gordon again, a questioning look on his face. Jack held up a hand for him to wait. "So that isn't—"

"Hold on, another note says there was an electrical short, possibly from some after-market work. The customer has not returned, so I guess we got it fixed."

Jack thanked him and told his boss, "The FBI techs installed the tracking device to the speed sensor, and they must've caused a short. By fixing it, the dealership managed to disable the tracking transmitter."

His lips a strange shade of blue, Gordon looked like his air supply cut off. "That van is out in some city, a traveling time bomb."

He left to find refuge in his office. A million questions swirled in Jack's mind. This thing was big, bigger than he, the task force, or the whole justice system. How to find one van, its license plate no doubt changed by now, which could be hidden, put on a ferry, parked in a tunnel, or at a school?

He knew God saw it and the driver. Soon as he thought this, he got an idea. He had meant to ask Gordon, who fled so quickly, it rattled Jack. He pushed away from his desk, determined to make Gordon tell him about that original source who linked Interstate Vans to terrorism, because he or she might just hold the key to the armed and missing van.

TWENTY FIVE

The following Monday, Kat sat in the passenger seat of the station's Jeep SUV while Ian drove. She looked into the side mirror, her eyes locking onto a blue sedan following so closely on their rear bumper, it would ram them if Ian suddenly stopped. Was it her imagination or was the driver, a man with slicked-back hair, following them?

She reached over, tapped his arm. "Someone's right on our bumper. Be careful."

Ian's hands gripped the steering wheel. Traffic in the express lanes of the Dan Ryan Expressway was heavy, but his lips flashed a brilliant smile. "Watch this." Without warning, he cut into the left hand lane, giving rise to honking horns.

Kat's head snapped forward. "Ian, what are you doing? Trying to get us killed?"

Ian turned serious. "After I filmed your piece in front of the church and while you interviewed the church secretary about her thousand-dollar tow bill that blue sedan was parked across the street."

She could hardly believe it. "The one tailgating us?"

"The driver watched you go in and come out of the church."

Bolts of fear shot through her. Kat's eyes flew to the side mirror. "Where is he?"

Just then, she looked out the window and down onto the driver of the blue car. The driver wore shades and it was a cloudy day. "Ian," she hissed, "He's right next to us. Slow down, I want his license number."

Kat held her small notebook, slid the pencil from the spiral. The driver refused to cooperate. When Ian slowed, he did too. When Ian sped up, he played copycat. She reached into her bag, pulled out a prepaid phone. She called Jack, left a message for him to call right away. On a whim, she punched in some numbers.

"Who are you calling, Kat? The police?"

"Sort of," she muttered.

Relieved Eva answered, as Kat talked, she kept her eyes on the sedan beside her window. She hoped to get info about Zorn, but with Eva, an indirect approach was better.

Before Kat could say a word about the ominous blue car, the agent sighed, "Kat, among other things, I am still investigating the issues surrounding your tape. It is confidential, and I can't tell you more. You'll have to trust me."

Kat did trust Eva, so she'd have to be satisfied with that for now. "Okay. I'd like to ask you about something else. It's about the JFK assassination."

"I've got two minutes. Go."

"Last night, I was reading about the October 1962 missile crisis with Cuba. It seems there are newly declassified documents. I was wondering if you will help me understand the national security implications."

"I can, but not for currently classified information."

Kat lowered her voice, "Eva, Senator Zorn was the FBI Agent who received evidence of a second gun purchased at Klein's and sent to Dallas. He covered it up. I called Senator Arlen Specter's office to ask whether he still believes a lone bullet crashed through Kennedy and seriously injured Governor Connally, only to exit in pristine condition. I left messages, but no one called back. You just left the Senate, any ideas about who I can ask next?"

Eva said nothing about Zorn, just a vague, "I was assigned to the Intelligence Committee. Specter is on Judiciary. I may have a contact. Kat, have you gone on the web site lately?"

She noticed Eva did not say *CamelotConnection.com* aloud. "Yes. I got information about the daughters of the pilot killed on Elliot's plane. And Eva, someone is following us, has been all day. That's what I called to tell you. If I get the license number, I'd like to query it on the site tonight."

Eva replied, "That is fine, but since it's happening in Chicago be sure to let Jack know about that car. Kat, I need you to make a request, if you can, at three o'clock today, about anything, even if you don't get the license plate."

Kat agreed and hung up. As Ian glanced her way, Kat pointed out the windshield, toward the gridlock ahead of them. "Forget what you heard and drive."

Eva's words swirling in her brain, Kat maintained a vigil out the window. More serious than any game she played in her life, she *had* to see that license number. Just then Ian jerked the SUV to the right, and her notebook flew off her lap to the floor. He was trying to thread his way into a gap the size of a compact car.

"Kat, hold on. I'm trying to get behind the jerk."

She pressed her feet to the floor. "Quick, help me memorize the number."

"Here," he pulled a pen from his front pocket, tossed it to her. Kat wrote the plate number on her palm.

"Did you get it?"

"Yes! It's from Indiana."

As if hearing their conversation, the blue car swerved to the far left. Ian smiled brightly. "Perfect, Buddy. We'll see you later."

With that, Ian pulled into the local lanes, leaving their would-be follower stuck out in the express lanes. "He won't be able to catch us now Kat. We'll get off before the lanes merge again. Does he work for the tow truck operator, do you think?"

"I wish I knew." Glad for a juicy tidbit to enter into *Camelot,* Kat could not help but wonder what Senator Zorn was really after by having her followed.

BACK AT THE STATION, while entering the license number into *Camelot,* Kat fumed about first being spied upon and then followed, which was more than any person should have to endure. She got busy working on a story for the evening newscast. Of course, Kat would not reveal anything to hurt her case, and while most viewers would never experience what was happening to her, there were plenty of people who had their identities stolen, their credit ruined, or who were stalked over the internet.

After she wrote it up and her news director approved it, Kat had a quick minute to brush her hair, touch up her lipstick. Okay, a deep breath and she was ready. Her eyes like laser beams into the camera lens, Kat steadied her nerves, a volatile mix of anger and stress, all because of a nameless power who was beyond her ability to control, yet continued to hound her. Folks needed to be on the lookout for those who could invade their lives, and hide behind the internet.

The script was rolling on the teleprompter, but she knew it by heart. "Why are we so modest when changing clothes, but then so careless about sharing our most personal information with total strangers? As I dug into new information about the JFK assassination for a special broadcast that will air this fall upon the anniversary of his death, I found something disturbing. Data brokers collect and store private information about you, about me, which anyone with a credit card can buy for a mere fifteen dollars."

Images of credit cards and credit reports shared the split screen with Kat. "Even some governments, the ones we expect to protect us, sell our driver's license photos to private companies for as little as a penny apiece. Just think, when you register to vote or buy a house, that information can be sold."

Her time was fleeting. Kat talked even faster. "The other day, I covered a story about a man convicted of loan fraud. Do you know where this felon got the social security number? He simply copied it from another man sitting next to him who was applying for in-store credit. Yes, it is that easy. So guard your personal information as if it is as precious as your life."

The producer held up his finger. She had one minute left. "I call our campaign to help you, BE SMART, and have put together seven important ways to protect yourself. We have time for only three. First: Block your outgoing cell phone number, and make sure your landline phone number is unlisted. A criminal or stalker can use internet 're-verse look up' and obtain your home address."

She took a quick breath. "Second: Expect trouble. Whenever you are asked for information, consider ways to keep it private. And third: Secure your passwords, using a jumble of letters and numbers and change them often."

Her seven bullet points flashed on the split screen as she finished her report, "Electronic technology is like a giant vacuum cleaner, sucking our personal info from credit card purchases, careless communications and then selling it for pennies. These hints are posted on our station's website. Now, back to Randy for the latest on the city's boil water order."

Kat felt exhausted. She wanted nothing more than to go home to a cup of tea and a good soak. She only wished she would hear from Jack first.

AFTER TALKING WITH KAT, Jack's head began to spin. She told him she had done a TV special for the evening news about invasion of privacy on the internet and implied she was getting closer to revealing what *CamelotConnection* and its unknown client—namely Zorn—had done to her. He'd taken no time off over the weekend, simply crashing at his desk for a couple of hours. Tonight, he rubbed his sore neck.

Between searching for the missing bomb-laden van, and checking the plates on the blue car that followed Kat, Jack saw so many sinister possibilities. The car was licensed to Louis H. Bultema and according to the Indiana State Police, that name belonged to a fellow who died five years ago.

Jack even began questioning how much the FBI knew about Luis's order for the six vans. In response to Jack's dogged questioning, Gordon admitted a "highly placed source" gave the initial tip about Interstate Van Conversions, and claimed the intel was passed down the chain and ultimately given to Jack.

As hard as Jack pressed Gordon for more, he got nothing. It made no sense. Sure, he did a good job at the task force, but why hadn't an FBI agent claimed the case as his? The truth hit Jack, and it hurt. Someone wanted a cop from the task force, who would be reluctant to ask too many questions about the identity of Bureau informants.

Without knowing all of Kat's leads on her Chicago corruption case, or all she had pieced together of Big John's theories, he had figured out that the transcripts were sent to her by that website *after* their meeting in Pentwater. What did it mean? The tap certainly recorded his conversation with her about the Kennedy assassination and the second gun. Yet, he had to wonder if someone tapped her phones to get to him and his terrorist bomb case. After all, her calls were re-routed to Kazakhstan. Maybe it was some terrorist training camp.

These unresolved issues led him to lunch with Lenny Moses. After devouring a huge order of fries and two dogs apiece, they threw the greasy sacks into Barney's trashcan. Jack hopped into Lenny's Explorer; it still had the magnetic telephone company sign on the door.

Lenny got the heat going to cut the chill. "Okay Jack, what super-secret project do we have planned for this afternoon?"

The eager way Lenny said it behind those thick glasses made Jack laugh, and it felt good. "You've been reading too many mystery novels."

So far, he had not told Lenny what they were going to do. "Remember the device you found on Kat's phone?"

Lenny nodded, and Jack licked celery salt from his lips, almost wishing for another hot dog. "We're driving over to a place on Ogden Avenue, and I want you to see if there's a similar one on their phones."

"You're not kidding are you?"

"Nope. Will you do it?"

The man sighed, but said, "You got it."

Jack gave him directions to the alley behind Interstate Van Conversions, where Lenny donned his hardhat and Jack followed, checking behind him as they walked down the alley, a certain unease settling in his bones. Lenny located a green utility box, took out a tool resembling a circular key and opened the door to the box. Jack stood a foot away, checking the alley and watching over his shoulder.

Careful not to touch anything, Lenny pointed. "This is where the phone wires from most of the buildings on this block intersect and where we will most likely find something, if there is anything."

To Jack, that box was organized confusion. Rows and rows of electrical junctions and thin spaghetti-like wires came out from behind the terminals, made a connection and disappeared again.

Lenny loosened a few bolts, moved aside a panel. "Here's a no-no."

Jack leaned in, and Lenny's finger directed his gaze to another device. "This is exactly like the forwarding device on the lady's phone. Man, how do you know where to find these things?"

Jack blew out his breath, stunned by the find. It took him some time to admit, "Lenny, it was a hunch."

Because his case was active, Jack could not reveal anything more to Lenny about Interstate Van Conversions. He took some risk even bringing his friend in on this.

"I want outta here, but need to check something first." Lenny connected his butt set, began dialing numbers. He made notes on a pad, then gestured to a tag. "I think a phone company technician put that here, but after what I saw on the lady's wires, I know this is not a phone company installation."

"Why is that?"

He handed Jack his note. "I dialed the number where the tag is attached. Someone answered, 'Interstate Van Conversions.' But, get this," Lenny's solid face was serious, "it's diverting to the same international country code and city code where Kat's phone was diverted. I recall that was Kazakhstan."

Jack's mind shifting into overdrive, he faced the ugly facts. Whoever did this was listening to Pablo's calls, *and* to Jack's calls to Ricky at Interstate from the FBI office phones. Worse, someone in Kazakhstan was monitoring his sensitive calls. His mind scrambled. Had he used the Interstate Van phones to call federal agents Eva Montanna or Griff Topping?

Though a cold wind whipped about them in the alley, sweat broke under Jack's arms, on his forehead. He wiped off his face with the back of his hand, and then he remembered. He made all calls to Eva and Griff from his cell or the FBI phones.

Momentarily relieved, the calm didn't last long—a new fury welled within him. Jack now understood how Kat felt about someone eavesdropping on her calls, because now he felt it, too. He yearned to talk to her, find out how she was handling things, but there was no time.

Lenny stared, waiting for Jack's reaction. When he got none, he asked, "What do you want me to do with this thing?"

Jack's brain was at war with itself. If the FBI had a court-ordered tap on Interstate's phone, he as the lead investigator would know about it. Reasonably certain the FBI was not tapping her phone; he wondered if the National Security Agency was behind it. Jack quickly discarded the notion. NSA certainly had more sophisticated equipment than this.

He wasn't sure he was doing the right thing, but it was his case, and he had control over the evidence. "Lenny, remove it carefully, protecting any fingerprints. I'll secure it and see what reaction we get to its disappearance."

TWENTY SIX

Kat's request on *CamelotConnection.com* was about seventeen hours old, so Eva arrived at Main Justice that morning looking forward to what she would find. Her anticipation eclipsed any weariness she felt at getting little sleep last night. She bypassed the security gauntlet at Main Justice, greeting Obi, the guard she had gotten to know. Smiling, he waved her through.

Eva unlocked the door to the fourth-floor office, recalling the awful dream that had disturbed her sleep. Lee Harvey Oswald and a Cuban spy were laughing about plans to kill President Kennedy. Eva watched it all, heard it all, as if they were on television, where she could not reach them to stop their wicked scheme.

Then, a loud bang woke her. She sat up in bed, and hearing only Scott breathing next to her, she threw on a robe and went to check the children. Little Marty slept in his crib like an angel, in the same room as Andy. She kissed her sons and went to Kaley's room, where she picked up blankets wadded on the floor.

After covering and kissing her daughter, too, Eva went downstairs to find all the locks secure. No sign of anything wrong, she turned on the backyard light, but hesitated going outside in the middle of the night. Hand on the doorknob, she felt something against her leg and stifled a scream. She flipped on the hall light and waited for her heart rate to return to normal. It was just Zak, the family cat. Man, was she jumpy. Eva picked him up in her arms before shutting off all the lights.

Zak, who usually slept on their bed, must have followed her downstairs. Back in the master bedroom, she dumped the cat at the foot of the bed, tossed her robe on a chair. Sleep never hers again, her mind fixated on what Kat asked her about Kennedy and the car following her. To Eva, it seemed there was a connection.

Not wanting to wake Scott, she gave up on sleep, slipped back into her robe and went to their shared office downstairs. There she found the culprit that had awakened her. Her "outstanding employee" plaque had crashed to the floor. Without bothering to hang it, Eva began to make notes. She worked until she heard the alarm ring and Scott start to make coffee.

Now, at her office desk, Eva put down her commuter mug and keys, slid the note pad out of her laptop bag and read what she had written in the wee hours of the night. After Kat's call, she reached Jack, who informed her that Kat strongly hinted she was ready to expose Senator Zorn as the culprit listening in on her.

Eva looked at her list of evidence against him. Kat aired a story implying he was involved in security leaks. After her transfer to Chicago, transcripts of Kat's telephone calls and copies of other personal records were mailed to her by *CamelotConnection.com*. Kat staged a fake call about an incriminating tape on a certain Senator and, conveniently, Zorn's aide showed up at Union Station to watch the exchange.

What brought it all together was Kat telling her yesterday that Zorn was the FBI agent who tried to bury evidence of a possible second gun to kill President Kennedy. Eva would liked to have known sooner, but didn't tell that to Kat. No way she wanted Kat to find out about the task force or the wiretap on *CamelotConnection*. If a U.S. Senator was involved in illegal activity, she had no problem going after him.

What burned her insides like hot sauce was the constitutional issue—the Executive branch investigating the Legislative branch. Serving ten months on the Hill let her see just how touchy Congress was about perceived threats to the balance of power.

She had worked on her list the rest of the night, all the while devising a way to catch Zorn without leaving any doubt he was involved. Of course, maybe he was clean and Kat had jumped to the wrong conclusion. Anxious to see if any new evidence showed up, she walked straight to the tech room, past the sign, *Court Ordered Personnel Only.*

As supervisor of the task force, her name was on the court-approved wiretaps, which were being monitored 24/7 behind the door. Besides, Eva's magnetic access card opened the door. Inside, Griff hunched over a computer screen as Earl fidgeted with a printer that seemed jammed.

The door banged shut, and Griff rolled back in his chair. "Hope you brought eggs and bacon. I never want to see another potato chip or sweet roll."

Earl grunted in agreement, "A long twelve hours, but profitable, right Topping?"

Griff drank something from a mug, probably the muddy end of hours-old coffee. Eva offered to make a fresh pot. Griff waved her away. "Nah, I'm off java for life, or at least until tonight. Get ready for your briefing because, in five minutes, it's eight o'clock and I am out of here whether Sal shows up or not."

Eva pulled a pen from her pants pocket, "Kat was supposed to make a request yesterday about three o'clock. Was there activity on her Camelot account?"

Griff stood, and with one arm leaned on the back of the chair, using the other hand to cover a yawn. "Last night, we hit the jackpot, not that I play the slots, but here's the deal. Earl monitored Camelot while I caught up on our activity log."

When Griff yawned again, Eva poked his arm. "Cut it out. I got no sleep either." She struggled to stifle a yawn herself. Her eyelids heavy, she needed fresh coffee, and soon. "What happened with the transaction?"

Griff pointed to the computer. "We watched Kat's request funnel through Kazakhstan. From her bank account that Camelot uses to get paid, they extracted thirteen hundred dollars. That money was transferred to an account in the Bahamas—Nassau to be exact."

Eva's mind grew alert. "Give me a list of the account and routing numbers. I'll get with our contact at NSA. They can monitor funds going by wire transfer to that account."

Earl handed her something. "That's what I was printing when you came in. The stupid machine was out of paper."

She perused the numbers. With Kat's increasing frustration over the lack of progress, it would be difficult to keep a lid on this boiling story. Then, an idea popped into her mind.

"Kat gave me a copy of an invoice with her transcripts, the one she thinks Senator Zorn requested. Earl, if you match that transaction in Camelot's accounts, we might find his account number, and use it to study other requests made under his number."

As Sal burst in the door with sacks of food, Griff seemed to understand just where Eva was heading. "And, we just might find out if a U.S. Senator named Lars Zorn violated any laws."

Sal looked crushed, "You guys made the case without me."

No one laughed as Eva said, "No, but we may be getting nearer the truth. Griff your trip to Almaty next Monday may provide even more answers. I hope you also learn why Harding postponed your trip by another two weeks. That makes me suspicious."

Griff flashed a smile beneath his moustache. "That's okay. By staying on this wire day and night, I got to study the email traffic for Camelot. Now I'll have a better idea what to look for."

Sal thrust a wrapped breakfast burrito in Griff's hands. "Yeah. You better get over there and back before their cold weather sets in. I hear it's nothing like ours."

THREE DAYS LATER, things around his office were so tense, with Gordon biting his head off every five minutes, that Jack decided to take the weekend to winterize his boat in Pentwater. A week had passed and they were no closer to finding the missing van. He hoped the change of scene would give him a clearer picture of what he should do next. Along the drive, with Winston in the front seat looking out the windows, dramatic red and gold leaves perked his spirits.

Earlier in the week, after leaving Interstate Vans with the listening device, Jack phoned Kat. He was still waiting to hear if she was going to drive up and meet him for breakfast tomorrow. The wait came hard, so tonight he walked alone to Abbey's Roost, where he enjoyed a tasty burger. In this town, where he had gotten to know Kat, he missed her company. He hoped she decided to come, but he was reluctant to call again. On the way back to his boat after supper, he noticed her cottage was dark, so he supposed she wasn't coming.

As he walked, the more sinister problem of the missing van haunted him. He was one cop, in one city of thousands all over the country. What made him think he could find it? With Ricky's help, they stepped up surveillance of Pablo after work hours, but caught him doing nothing wrong.

With Winston snoring, Jack propped on a pillow in the berth, a book on military history unread, and replayed the whole incident of the missing van. October 28 was only two weeks away! They would have to tell the nation. So far, they alerted all police agencies, but the FBI Director did not want to cause public panic.

There was some encouraging news. Various FBI agents had located the five vans. All were in the possession of foreign college students, at large city universities. As with that first van discovered near Dallas, agents kept these other four under constant surveillance until they removed and replaced the bombs with unarmed propane tanks. No one was surprised that each of the five contained the same timing devices, all set to detonate at noon eastern, eleven o'clock central time, on October 28.

Jack tried to think what those cities—Boston, Dallas, Nashville, Tampa and Washington, D.C.—had in common. No closer to an answer, Jack threw down his book, startling his dog. "Okay, fella, time for your walk."

Under millions of stars, Jack lifted heavenward his fears that, in the biggest investigation of his career, he would fail to stop what looked like one errant bomb, meant to explode with the other five, now disabled.

Higher-ups at the Bureau did not want to arrest the five students for fear they wouldn't talk, deciding that surveillance might be the better way to dislodge clues about the sixth van. The idea was to arrest them all on the 28th.

Jack told Gordon he favored picking up one of the students and trying to flip him. One of the five might talk in the face of life behind bars. The air cold, answers elusive, he decided to turn in. Waves gently rocking the boat, he washed his face in the little galley and was about to turn off his cell when it rang. It was Kat, and even though he was tired, he answered.

She seemed sensitive to the late hour. "I just got in. Want to meet for breakfast?"

He did—at Abbey's—and Kat agreed to eight o'clock. In no mood to talk further, he said goodnight and closed his phone, realizing he probably sounded gruff. Suddenly, he was too wound up to sleep. Maybe he could take Big John, who loved football as much as Jack did baseball, to Soldier Field to see the Bears play. He erupted from his berth, turned on a light and seized his wallet from his pants pocket.

Winston snapped to attention, as if he needed to protect them both, but he settled back down. In dim light, Jack dug through a stack of business cards and receipts, but could not find the Bears season football schedule. He gave up and turned out the light.

Winston was back snoring, but not Jack. Adrenaline pumped through his veins. Breakfast with Kat should be interesting. Recently, she said she wanted to ask him something important. With her that could be anything.

WHILE SOME OF THE NATION'S most secret business happened at night in corridors of power, this clandestine meeting was neither at the White House nor Capitol Hill, but in Flip Harding's office on K Street. When Wilt Kangas asked to meet, he insisted on a late hour, when all staff had gone home. Intrigued, Flip agreed, even bowed out of a rotary dinner, knowing Wilt reached out only when it was urgent.

The marble clock on Harding's credenza rang at half-past eleven. The two spymasters drank a pot of coffee Flip brewed and talked of recent events in Cuba, until from out of nowhere Kangas banged the conference table with his fist, wiping off coffee that splashed on his hand.

"Today, Senator Zorn introduced a bill to cut back on our funding, overturn the Patriot Act." His voice became sharp. "He wants to be President and won't vote to raise taxes; so American security suffers."

Flip leaned back in his chair, examined the man who demanded to see him, practically in the middle of the night. Never had he seen Kangas this rattled. Something major was eating him. Maybe Flip could wriggle it out of the spymaster.

"Political football, the kind Zorn plays, has been going on for years. Congress hides new taxes by raising fees, so that the media can't point to any one member who hiked taxes. Take this summer. I went camping with my wife and paid exorbitant fees in the federal parks."

Kangas drummed the fingers of his left hand on the table. "I could care less about your parks. Last time we talked, I told you that I would never bring up the Bay of Pigs. I changed my mind."

Harding listened, more than ready to discern where the conversation was going. Soon Kangas shared what was weighing on his mind.

"Under Kennedy, anti-Castro exiles were killed because our government pulled back air cover. Well, that ill-fated invasion led the Russians to think we were weak, which led to Khrushchev assembling Soviet ICBM's in Cuba. Our U-2 spy planes confirmed it. Do you know how close we came to the brink of nuclear war?"

Truth was, Harding was too young to remember the crisis itself, but his mind retained everything he ever read on it. At the Agency, he was the Cuban specialist. "Yes. Those missiles could have hit all our big cities except out west. After one of our U-2 planes was shot down photographing what Khrushchev was doing in Cuba, we schoolkids had our heads under our desks for thirteen days."

Too worked up to care if his cup was full or not, Kangas pounded the table again, spilling more coffee. "It was about politics then, and is today."

"Do you equate what is going on in Cuba today with what happened in the sixties under Kennedy?"

Kangas exploded from his chair, a wild look in his eyes, as if secrets he bottled up for years were about to spring from Pandora's Box. "Yes! You of all people know I spent my entire life trying to protect our country. But, this is not about *me*; it is about the future of *freedom*."

He paced the room and Flip, trying to keep the pacing tiger from attacking *him*, spoke calmly. "Wilt, sit down. Tell me how I can help."

Kangas appeared tormented. Still, he sat and looked Flip straight in the eye. "We have a problem, and it's due to your greed."

Flip objected, but Wilt stopped him. "This time you bit off more than you can chew. You supply the Bureau with Intel, and are paid well for it. Why couldn't you be satisfied with that?"

Blindsided by Wilt's accusations, Flip grew defensive. "I don't have the foggiest idea what you're talking about."

"Simply put, like Kennedy, your reign over Camelot has come to an end. If you asked I could have warned you that, anytime you get into industrial espionage, you're going to get into trouble."

Now Flip jumped to his feet. "What exactly are you hinting at, Wilt?"

"Hint my eye. Remember you sent people to cover the meeting Kat Kowicki had at Union Station with one of her sources about a certain senator?"

Flip never told Kangas about that operation and willed himself not to blink; thereby depriving Kangas of any satisfaction that he had something on him. Zorn had requested that *Camelot* send people to see if the female reporter had dirt on him.

The quieter Flip remained, the more Wilt talked. "Don't think you are the only ones listening these days. We, too, are extremely interested in what Zorn is doing. After all, he is a U.S. Senator on the Intel Committee and he is running for President. National security is at stake. You should never have started selling your services to politicians or media moguls. Both can hurt you. Apparently Zorn didn't trust you to get the tape because he sent his staffer to observe."

Flip deflected the criticism with some dirt of his own. "I'm sure the Senator would be unhappy to learn the CIA is spying on him."

Kangas chuckled, the closest he ever came to laughing. "Good point. It might ensure our continued funding at that." He dropped the grin from his face. "Flip, I'm sorry if your young man who snatched the tape was injured. My people said he struggled courageously with the homeless man who stole the tape from him."

A smug look spread across Wilt's face, but Flip knew he wasn't done. Years in the spy business taught him that silence would prompt him to continue. Finally, it did, but not before the DDI leaned close and lowered his voice to a whisper, even though there was no one else in the room.

"You and your client need to know that Kat Kowicki is on to you both. She suspects Zorn paid to have her phones tapped. As far as any tape her source claimed to have, it was a ruse. Our homeless guy got a worn cassette of singing vegetables, some kid's video called Veggie Tales."

So, the reporter was good at using subterfuge. Flip made a mental note to call Senator Zorn when Wilt left and arrange to meet right away.

A spent fury, Kangas still was not through. "Listen to me now. It all resulted from your carelessness. Apparently, your people at Camelot mailed Kowicki the results of work you did for Zorn. The answer to her request went elsewhere."

It took Flip a few seconds to digest the magnitude of the problem. Senator Zorn *never* told him the transcripts failed to show up. His pulse raced. Such a mistake had disaster written all over it. As if Kangas enjoyed stringing him along, he perched so close, Flip saw his bloodshot eyes.

"Harding, what you don't know, is that Kowicki has her teeth into President Kennedy's assassination. We and the Bureau made mistakes in that investigation, many of which have long been covered up or, shall I say, *deflected* by volumes and volumes of irrelevant data. Worse, she formed a tight alliance with a Chicago detective, who is working a terrorism case."

Flip could not believe it, but a word escaped, "So?"

Kangas stared with those red eyes. "So? Guess where the detective got the tip to investigate Interstate Vans? From intel *you* sold the Bureau. If he figures out your involvement, and compares notes with the reporter, they will blow you out of the water, and soil the Agency and the Bureau."

Flip had heard enough to know he had a serious situation on his hands. He had to find a way to stop Kowicki from ruining what took him a lifetime to build. Kangas was the only one who could help him.

He cleared his throat. "Our support of your mission is worth more than you pay us. And," Harding's voice was barely audible, "the work we do in the private sector gives us both intelligence that we could never get before, even with Grand Jury subpoenas."

Wilt crossed his legs and arms. "I'm listening."

"Congress would have raked you over the coals at that hearing this summer if it wasn't for me. Are you forgetting a man by the name of General Raul San Felipe, who—"

Kangas looked irritated, "Leave him out of it."

Flip just might reserve that for later, if it came to it. "All right, take those indictments against the oil executives. The info that Justice used from people inside their companies they got from us."

He held up a second finger. "The Brits broke up a terrorist sleeper cell in London last week using our evidence. Don't sell us out too quickly."

Wilt Kangas wiped his brow. "It's a cancer."

This time, Flip slapped the table. "That is just what I have been saying. Terrorism is a micro-biotic disease. It hides, then strikes. We never know for sure who it will destroy next."

Wilt's body slumped inward as if he had no sleep for days. "I'm not talking about terrorism."

Flip studied the former spy's face. "What do mean, Wilt?"

Wilt stared at his hands spread out on the table. "Found out yesterday. I start chemo next week."

Flip didn't know what to say. Wilt, now silent, surveyed the room, finally spoke. "Never mind the details. I am not going down without a fight. Know this—my people are watching her. I am not going to let a snip of a reporter muddy the Agency. And, I am not going to allow Hezbollah and their terrorist allies to carve a deeper foothold into the Americas."

He pointed at Flip's chest, almost poking him. "By that, I mean Venezuela, Nicaragua, and Cuba. Specific intelligence is classified."

Flip listened, never taking notes, so if subpoenaed; he would have nothing to turn over except his memory, which was always a fluid thing. He returned to a subject Kangas had earlier refused to discuss. "General San Felipe is finally talking, is he?"

Instead of looking rattled that Flip possessed classified information, Wilt took it in stride. Flip's people had transported San Felipe out of Cuba. The regime agreed to allow him into Venezuela for cancer surgery. The General was smuggled out of Venezuela, then into the U.S. through a clandestine tunnel on the Mexican border. Where he was now, only Kangas and the CIA director knew.

Wilt eased his large body from the chair. "You understand my meaning. Hezbollah is planning a big strike. Only they're smarter than Khrushchev ever was. They are not assembling missiles above ground in Cuba. Seems the General's son, Luis, converted to Islam and is running Hezbollah's Latin American squad."

Flip knew all about Luis's quest for an Islamic world. He rose and leaned against the conference table. "Where is the General now?"

Kangas's skin glowed, as if he was already in a faraway place. Flip did not think of that place as heaven, because he did not believe in any afterlife. Wilt lifted his chin. "The general is getting the best medical attention and being questioned round the clock. Not only will we find out what the Cubans have been doing with the Iranians, I plan to question him personally about Lee Harvey Oswald and the Kennedy assassination."

They were in a new fight, one that was much more serious than old grudges, and when they shook hands, the professional competition that plagued them for years vanished forever. Wilt left, and Flip realized one positive thing. Wilt had enough dirt on Zorn to ensure the CIA got all the support it needed from the Senate Intelligence Committee, which meant Kangas would have plenty of money for Flip and his company.

TWENTY SEVEN

To sounds of honking geese, Kat welcomed morning with a cup of tea on her Pentwater porch, where she had gone mostly to see Jack. Chicago days were empty without seeing or speaking to him, so when he invited her to breakfast she jumped at the chance. This morning, she brushed her hair until it shone and pushed it from her face with a new black hairband. Today, she wanted Jack to notice her.

All she wanted was time alone with him, even in a crowded restaurant, where she could look into his blue eyes and confide what was in her heart. Dressed in black jeans, and woolen sweater to which she fastened a gold pin her mother gave her, Kat scrutinized her image in a floor-length mirror. Since the man in the blue car followed her, she began wearing black from head to toe. When Ian commented how elegant she looked, black was now her color, and she banished the bright pinks and greens in her life to the far end of the closet.

Elliot, now strong enough to get on an airplane again, was in Washington, attending to his recently-acquired stations. Yet, he was kind to call last night, so her evening at the cottage was not a complete loss after Jack hung up on her so hastily. On the way to the restaurant, the breeze blew through her sweater, giving her a chill, so she ran back for her jacket, and zipped it up to her neck.

For some reason, whitecaps on Pentwater Lake disturbed her soul. The anger she once felt here for Elliot was replaced by a lingering sadness, intensified by falling leaves and empty trees around the shoreline. There was no laughter of children carrying sand shovels to cheer her. Only a howling wind kept her company, and even though a new dawn lifted back the four corners of the night, the grayness nearly suffocated her.

Her whole body prickled with a desire to cry, to put her head on Jack's shoulder and feel his comfort. The haughty call of a seagull caused Kat to look up, see what caused the fuss. Apparently nothing, as he lofted away on an air current, leaving her a solitary figure, feeling alone. She drew the jacket tighter and hurried to the restaurant.

The place was crowded all right; but warm. She waited for a clean table in the back. Kat ordered tea, rehearsing how to question Jack about her eavesdroppers. After a time, Jack seemed to be a no-show. She swallowed a lump in her throat at being stood up, and pulled out her notebook on the JFK assassination to review her notes.

If he ever arrived, there was a fresh angle she wanted to tell him about. She had ordered a refill on her tea when Jack finally appeared, seriously out of breath, and all apologies. "Winston cut his paw this morning. He bled all over the boat, so I tried to patch it up. I wanted to call, but I had left my cell on the boat."

"I hope he is okay. Do you need to cancel?" She held her breath.

As Jack pulled out a chair to sit on, Kat released her breath ever so slowly. The server brought her tea, and he ordered coffee and two bagels.

Kat wanted a toasted bagel with cream cheese. "On the side, and not an onion bagel. Do you have raisin?"

They did. Jack started telling her how he took Winston to the vet when his cell phone rang. He picked it up, and without answering it, turned off the ringer. "Sorry."

"I thought you left your cell on the boat."

Jack grinned sheepishly. "I did, but when I took Winston back, I grabbed it."

"I'll tell you something, if you share something in return."

Jack smiled, and her heart felt tossed to one side. "Anything in particular you want to know?"

"Maybe. In January 2006, German television aired a documentary made by a German filmmaker, Wilfried Huismann with Gus Russo. Guess who they point to as culprits in John Kennedy's death?"

She caught Jack looking at his cell phone. "Hmm?"

Kat felt like leaving. Instead, she repeated her information. "You really are someplace else."

Their bagels arrived, which distracted him as he spread a thick layer of strawberry jam on a piece. "I love this stuff. All right, who shot Kennedy? I read in Dad's memo that the New Orleans mafia figured in highly."

Kat tried to camouflage her irritation at his cavalier attitude. He reminded Kat of her mother, how even when she was physically in Kat's presence, she was rarely there mentally.

"Your dad had reams of notes on the mafia, especially Carlos Marcello, the chieftain in New Orleans. Oswald's uncle had a connection to him. I think we should put the mobsters aside. Everyone knew Bobby Kennedy was after them. It makes no sense to risk getting caught for murdering the President. They were all in the U.S. and subject to prosecution. These filmmakers offer a whole different slant."

Jack started on his second bagel. "You think it was Vice-President Johnson?"

Engrossed in her story, Kat forgot to eat. "Some researchers think he had the most to gain from JFK's death—the Presidency. However, Big John does not think so and neither did this documentary. They uncovered never-before-seen records from the Mexican government. You know, Oswald visited both the Soviet and Cuban Embassies in Mexico City a few weeks before the assassination."

"So, it's the Russians. I always thought so."

Kat took a quick bite of the bagel, turned to the next page in her notebook. "Jack, right after the assassination, our government re-leased a photo of a man they claimed was Oswald, only the photo is a different man. Two allegations point to someone other than the Soviets."

He looked in her eyes. "I've used up all my guesses."

Certain she now had his complete attention she sprung it on him. "Cuba."

Jack simply stared. "Fidel Castro was behind this?"

Kat returned his look. His eyes *were* as stunning as she remem-bered them. "I don't know if he personally ordered the killing, but the reports I read reveal the documentary aired interviews with former Cuban agents who said the assassination was an operation of Cuban Secret Service G-2. Johnson was afraid if he pursued it, after the Bay of Pigs and Cuban Missile Crisis, we'd be in World War III."

"If that's all your evidence, it's pretty thin—at least to my cop's mind.

Kat turned a page, and pointed to something she wrote. "Reports claim a Cuban intelligence officer flew on a private plane the same day Kennedy was shot, November 22, 1963."

"Flew where?" Without waiting for her reply, Jack picked up his phone.

"To Dallas." She narrowed her eyes. "There's more, but I don't think I'll tell you. It's your turn."

He flipped open the phone. "Kat, I'm sorry. I have a message from Eva. Let me listen; it could be important."

She reread her notes about the German documentary, which she had not been able to view, because no U.S. networks had aired it and to her knowledge it was not yet in English. Maybe Elliot would, or—even better—maybe he would let her do her *own* documentary. Suddenly Kat heard Eva's voice on Jack's voice mail, and strained to listen. She did not catch all, but heard her ask if Jack knew of a connection between Harding & Associates and Kazakhstan.

Kat wondered if it involved her phone tap and watched Jack's reaction. He closed the phone, connected it to his belt. "I can call back later."

"Jack, tell me the truth. Do you know any more about my phones?"

His face told a lot; but his lips were in a tight line. "I wish I had something to share, but this phone call from Eva tells me she's working on it."

Ah ha! What Kat had managed to hear gave her a new lead. As soon as she left, she would get on her laptop and dig into Harding & Associates. "Jack, make your phone call. I have things to do, too. Are you free later?"

NOT WANTING TO DELAY CALLING EVA, Jack strode back to the boat, cell phone in hand. Winston was sleeping, not only on Jack's bed, but also across his pillow. Jack punched redial. This time she failed to answer, so he left a message. He quietly left the boat, walked to the Pentwater Township Library at the north edge of town, a few blocks east of the main drag.

During breakfast with Kat, he kept thinking of the Chicago Bears game on Sunday, October 28. Now he used a library computer to get onto the Bears' web site, and what he found made his face fall. What he suspected was true—while agents in five cities would be monitoring the five vans—the Bears were not in Chicago that day.

They were playing the Buccaneers at Tampa, so he couldn't take Big John to a game after all. Most likely that day, he'd be checking out, along with other Chicago coppers, public venues for the missing van.

Jack stretched out his legs, browsed the NFL's site, and quickly found the on-line schedule for the Tennessee Titans. Sure enough, they played the Baltimore Ravens in Nashville. His mind alive, he could not scroll down the schedules fast enough. The Cleveland Browns were playing the Cowboys at Dallas, the Patriots were hosting the New York Jets at Boston, and the Eagles were up against the Redskins at Washington, D.C.

This could be it! Five vans would be in cities where NFL teams played home games, the last Sunday in October. It made sense. At eleven forty-five on the east coast, ten forty-five in the central time zone, parking lots would be crammed with fans cooking burgers and hot dogs.

What better arrangement than an RV small enough to park in a standard-sized space, amidst thousands of revelers enjoying beer and brats, and loaded with enough explosives to destroy the cars and people around it?

Should he call Gordon and tell him what he found out, or do more investigating? Either way, there was still a missing van. A phone call would not solve that problem. He decided to check his emails.

KAT WAS ON AN EXCURSION of her own to the Pentwater library. Laptop computer in hand, she swung open the door and looked for an out-of-the-way place to access the wireless. She blinked, could not believe her eyes. There was Jack, sitting at a public computer terminal. Would he turn his head and spot her?

She really wanted to do her research privately and that way control what she told him. Fortunately, he was preoccupied with whatever he was doing, so she waved to the librarian and picked a soft chair by the windows at the far end. On a search engine, she entered "Camelot, Kennedy assassination" and waited.

After discarding many prompts as irrelevant, Kat stumbled on a paper written by one Philip Harding given at a 2002 convention on Kennedy's death, entitled, "The Beginning and End of Camelot." Her eyes zoomed to the bottom of the article and her heart began to race as she read Philip Harding, the article's author, was a former CIA employee, and expert on John Fitzgerald Kennedy.

He operated a global security company called Harding & Associates in Washington, D.C., the very company Eva mentioned. What it had to do with Kazakhstan, she did not know. Kat chewed the end of her pencil, connecting in her mind what she overheard. It *had* to be more than a coincidence. Philip Harding's company must also run *CamelotConnection.com.*

Stymied about what else she could do on that now, she scanned a couple articles about witnesses who heard shots fired, not from behind the President as the Warren Commission claimed, but from the grassy knoll, which was in front of President Kennedy. One caught her eye as unusual.

Eva had encouraged Kat to submit requests to *Camelot*, so this time she asked about a witness to JFK's murder, Deputy Sheriff Roger Dean Craig. What he saw and what happened to him after he gave testimony was unbelievable. It proved there was another shooter!

Kat wanted to know more about the man, because it made Zorn's failure to take action on Big John's records more than negligent. Not only did Zorn keep the whole nation from knowing what really happened to President Kennedy, now he wanted to be President himself. Eager to call Eva and let her know what she discovered, Kat decided to wait until she got in her car. On her *Camelot* account, she typed in $500.00 to spend on Deputy Craig and hit enter. The screen said, *your request is being processed.*

Within the next few days, she would receive documents. Next, Kat sent an email to Eva, asking her to call her new prepaid cell phone. Then, she powered off and prepared to leave the library in case her cell rang.

Where was Jack? No longer at the computer, he must have left without her seeing him. As she stood up, she noticed he was outside, talking on his cell phone. On a sheet from her reporter's notebook, Kat scribbled, *Meet at the State Park in thirty minutes by the pier?*

His back to her, she quietly walked up behind, and was about to hand him the note when she heard him say, "Eva, I did not tell Kat that Zorn's aide Ingrid Swanson is involved."

Kat froze. He was talking with Eva about her. She should give him the note and get in her car, but a burning curiosity kept her ears listening, her feet from moving. What else might she learn?

Jack seemed to have no idea she was there. "I agree you need to finish your investigation. If she finds out, Eva, there is no telling how she will run with the story."

Kat cringed inside. Jack considered her a relentless reporter with no thoughts of others. She might be proving him right, but she could not stop listening.

"I don't like the idea of her being followed, and living in the condo with someone creeping in the basement, tapping into her phone."

Wow! Jack was concerned for her safety, maybe even thought she was in danger. Of course, she did not hear Eva's reply. Her conscience finally drove her to slip back inside the door, where she counted to ten before walking out.

"Jack, I didn't realize you were here!"

She crumpled the note into her jeans pocket. "I've had a good day doing research. "Meet me at the pier in thirty minutes and I'll tell you about it."

In no time, she was in her car, when she really wanted to go back inside, turn on her computer and track down Ingrid Swanson. Maybe she was the blonde woman taking pictures at the coffee shop at Union

Station. But that would give Jack a chance to do to her what she just did to him: pop in, read over her shoulder, and discover she was on to what he was trying to keep from her.

With what she learned today, she was not going to let him or Eva stop her. If the ICE agent did call back, Kat would insist Eva confide what she knew. If she refused, Kat would go to Elliot and expose Zorn as a sneak and a fraud. The American public would rise up against his abuse of power and throw him out of office, as Eva said. Forget a criminal indictment; Kat was convinced she had enough on Zorn right now to expose him.

Kat tore out of the parking lot, tires spinning on the pavement, she was that mad. Jack ran toward her, cell phone in hand. The sight made her giggle and slow down. She rolled down the window. "See you in thirty minutes?"

Jack reached her window, breathing sharply. "Kat, I can't get there that fast. I have to check on Winston, call my boss, and see about something else."

He seemed to be stalling, covering up "something else." Curiosity trumped her anger, so she relented. "Okay, you name the time."

Jack checked his watch. "It's three now. About four, we could have an early dinner, and go to the pier if the wind dies down."

Kat studied Jack's face to see if he really wanted to spend time with her. After what she overheard him tell Eva, she was unsure if she trusted him. She saw no deceit there, so she bobbed her head in agreement. "I'll pick something up and meet you at the marina." With that, she drove off, her tires burning just the tiniest bit of rubber, and her mind building a wall around her heart.

TWENTY EIGHT

Faced with a dilemma, Kat drove around Pentwater, blowing off steam and wondering what to do. Here she had a sizzling revelation about Ingrid, Senator Zorn's aide, which was proof positive he broke eavesdropping laws to smear Kat's character. Should she wait for Eva or go public? She heard it said sunshine was the best disinfectant.

The question was how to let in light without ruining the chance for a conviction. Kat had seen over-anxious reporters do just that. Yet, if she waited, time might be on the Senator's side. After all, he was obviously on to her, and he'd had a couple months to cover his tracks. Before she and Jack got together for dinner, she had an hour, a whole sixty minutes in which to calm down, hone her own strategy.

She called Sydney on her cell and found her shopping with her niece, whose mother had finally agreed to let Sydney be guardian until Nikki graduated from high school. It seemed she was unwilling to let go of her husband, even though he went back to prison.

Sydney shared how Nikki's grades in school soared this term. "We're at the bookstore, buying a book about Thomas Jefferson for her American history project."

"Give her my best."

Kat hung up, grateful things were turning out so well for Sydney. Five minutes later, she was back at the Pentwater Library, sitting in the same spot waiting for her laptop to access the wireless—only this time Jack was nowhere around.

She entered *Camelot,* requesting all information about Senator Lars Zorn and Ingrid Swanson, for which she was willing to pay two thousand dollars. Once, Kat played the slot machines in Atlantic City, and after winning a small jackpot, she found it hard to stop. On this blustery afternoon in Pentwater, she was just as driven to win, to reveal the truth behind the Senator's quest to ruin her as a reporter. In doing so, there was an added benefit. She just might sink his run for the Presidency.

As she waited for confirmation, the site disappeared from her screen. Assuming it was caused by a technical glitch, Kat re-entered the site, typing in her account number and access code. The screen went completely blank. Her mind flashed back to what Jack told Eva about her condo not being safe. What else did he know?

She found the empty black screen alarming. Unseen people, somewhere out there, not only knew what she was doing, they knew what she knew. Beginning to get scared, Kat shut off her computer, contemplating what it all meant—from her piece about Zorn, which caused her demotion, to Jack's reaching out to her via email, wanting her to help his dad track down who killed Kennedy.

Afterwards, transcripts of her phone calls appeared in her mailroom. The phony meeting at Union Station shook loose Zorn's employee, Ingrid Swanson. Now, when she entered a request about them on *Camelot*, the system crashed. It must be more than a fluke. Her head spinning, Kat decided to ask Jack right out, was she safe living at that condo?

If he asked why, she would tell him about the homeless man who followed her *before* the guy in the blue sedan. He knew about the second one, not the first. Kat sensed danger swirling around her, and looked carefully around the parking lot before running out of the library and hopping into her car.

Heart pounding, she locked the doors. As she turned the key, it dawned on her, the information she entered into *Camelot* came from a conversation she overheard between Eva and Jack. Truth seared her conscience. How could she ever admit to Jack that *she* had listened in on him?

KAT ENDED UP BUYING GRINDERS, roasted eggplant for her and Italian sausage for Jack. Cold, unrelenting wind dashed their plans to eat on a bench along the channel, so they took shelter on her porch, overlooking the water. From the fridge, she got them each a bottle of sparkling black-cherry water.

Kat twisted off the cap. "How is Winston?"

Jack had just bitten into his sandwich, so chewed before answering, "This is great, Kat, thanks. He's sleeping. Poor dog is worn out from his injury."

"He'll bounce back." Her stomach in knots, Kat set down her sandwich. "Jack, I have a confession to make. I did not know I was going to do this when I saw you at the library. I hope I have not messed things up for you."

When he gave her his attention, he had a way of absorbing Kat with one look and she could not stand his scrutiny just now. She grabbed her water bottle, started to tear the paper wrapper into pieces.

He was perceptive. "I sense I'm not going to approve, but let's have it. You bought a boat twice as big as mine."

The light touch might have helped if she was not so convinced she'd made a tremendous blunder. Kat bit at her bottom lip. "It's not funny."

The way he stared made her unable to say she overheard his conversation and searched on-line about Ingrid. She changed tactics. "I requested information on Camelot about deputy sheriff Roger Dean Craig."

A quizzical look flashed across his face. "You mentioned him before. So?"

"Remember when we met with your Dad recently? I promised to let him know of new leads and haven't called him."

Jack reached over, took her hand in his. "You're upset over nothing. Big John trusts you on the assassination story."

When he touched her, Kat felt like she never wanted him to take his hand away. This should not be; Jack was still aching over his breakup with Melissa. Besides, he made it clear he wanted to be friends, nothing more.

She slowly pulled away her hand and went back to clutching the water bottle. "It's a little more complicated, okay? After Kennedy was assassinated, Roger Craig's life was a mess, all because he told the authorities that minutes after Kennedy was shot, he saw Lee Harvey Oswald run west down Elm Street from the Texas School Book Depository and get into a light-green station wagon that pulled up alongside him. The Warren Commission claimed Oswald escaped on a bus."

"Kat, I am no expert, but a lot of people saw things that neither the Warren Commission nor the House Committee were able to resolve."

The label torn off, she rolled it in her fingers. "Lots of witnesses who heard shots from the grassy knoll were never interviewed by the Warren Commission. Other witnesses saw a man run from the depository and get into the Rambler station wagon. However, Deputy Craig testified before the Commission. Right after he went on talk shows telling his views, he was shot with a shotgun, maybe self-inflicted. I read about it in the *Dallas Morning News* archives."

Jack's voice was calm. "When did the deputy die?"

"1975. If what he and the others saw was true, it is solid evidence at least one other person besides Oswald was involved, the man driving the car he got into. When the House Committee released its report in 1978, it concluded there were not just three shots as the Warren Commission said, but a fourth one. The Committee found there was a conspiracy to kill the president but, unfortunately, did *not* go to the next step and tell America who or why."

Jack's gaze was steady. "The House report was almost thirty years ago. What significance does it have today?"

With both hands, Kat pulled off her hair band. "Six months before Deputy Craig was shot dead, he was shot in the shoulder when he opened his door. Other assassination witnesses have died under suspicious circumstances. Don't you see, I thought Senator Zorn was tapping my phone, ordering transcripts because he wanted to destroy my career."

"Now you think it's not him?"

Kat released her hair, allowed it to fall around her shoulders. "Jacko me boy," she said with an Irish lilt, "I went back to the library today."

His trusting face melted her resolve. She *couldn't* tell him about Ingrid and Zorn, so she fudged. "That is when it hit me. This harassment started after you asked me to help your dad on JFK. This is bigger than any aspersion I cast on the Senator. Someone is alive who knows what happened to the President and wants to stop me from finding out the truth. There is no statute of limitations for murder. Someone could still be tried."

Just saying this made her feel sick, but Jack winced as if he had bitten his tongue. He leaned forward. "You have always struck me as rational, and not a conspiracy junkie. I see the strain this has had on you, Kat. I talked with Eva today, and she told me to tell you that she is closer to the truth of your phone tap. We need you to hang on a bit longer. I told her I am uncomfortable with you staying at the condo."

There, he told her just what she heard him say to Eva. Kat gave him a chance to explain by saying, "Me, too."

When he stayed mum, she tried another idea. "I might check into a hotel for a few days, closer to the station. If, by then, you do not solve this, once Elliot knows, he will come down on you and Eva like a Mack truck in overdrive. Believe me, I know him. I only wish Eva returned my call today."

Jack shrugged. "When we hung up, she was heading somewhere with her family. Maybe that's why she gave me a message to pass along."

"I hope your message is not too late." To Kat's ears, she sounded bitter. "What I mean is—" Unwanted tears kept her from finishing. A rare occurrence, Kat was clueless how to handle them. She certainly did not want Jack to think she was faking it for sympathy.

As Kat blinked them back, a thought assailed her—if only someone really cared. Since Elliot's crash, she talked with her mother only a few times. Sydney was raising Nikki, as she should be. Jack was, well, Jack was independent and unavailable. Still, he was here on her porch, and seemed interested in her.

Yet, if she admitted she listened in, and then used what she heard, he would think her no better than a nut, or worse, someone not to be trusted. Jack's folded arms told her that her display of vulnerability had failed to move him. From sheer force of habit, the hardened part of Kat that had developed from being on her own since she was four years old won out. She would not tell Jack what she did, not ever.

She whisked up the remnants of his sandwich. "Let me warm this for you. It's gone cold with all my rambling. You're right. Eva is right. I'll wait and we'll both see what happens."

As she got up to go inside, Jack stood up and blocked her way. He took the sandwich in the wrapping, set it down on the table. For a minute, Kat had a strong impression he wanted to comfort her, maybe hold her, but then just as suddenly, he dropped his arms. Her vivid imagination must have fooled her again.

"Kat, I ah, enjoy our times together. You are a good friend."

That clinched it. To him, they were friends. Better than nothing, she supposed.

"Thanks. I feel that way, too."

A sheepish grin etched over his handsome face and Kat felt weak at the knees. She must feel more for him than she realized. It would crush her to reveal how she felt, only to have him repeat they were simply friends. She'd be in the cold again, just like from Laurel. Kat loved her mother, and look where that got her—being raised at a boarding school. Jack was talking.

She pretended to have heard. "Oh?"

He nodded. "Yes, Winston needs to go out on the leash. I mean it, Kat. If you need anything let me know."

He was leaving. She had to say something. "Are you driving back to Chicago, tomorrow?"

"Yes, after church."

"What time?"

For some reason, Jack looked at his watch. "I'll probably leave after I give directions to the Marina to get out my boat and shrink-wrap her for the winter. I plan to go to the early service, just up the street at the Methodist church, which starts at nine thirty."

He took a small step toward the door, and then turned back. "Would you like to come with me? A man is speaking who just returned from a trip to Cuba."

The German filmmakers pointed a finger at Cuba for killing Kennedy. It would be interesting to talk with someone who had been there. Before she said so to Jack, she thought a minute. Going to church was not her thing. Back in school, she went to chapel, but this was different. She could always get his name and call him on the telephone.

"I don't know—I have to close up things here before I head back."

She looked around the kitchen, her eyes lighting on Jack's half-eaten sandwich, giving her a lonely feeling. "My mother hired a company to clean, but there are things I need to pack. I can be ready in time." Kat noted him watching her. "You and Winston could follow me back to Chicago."

His face lit up. "I would like that. We'll stop at Michigan City for lunch."

Less than two seconds later, Jack was gone, leaving Kat alone with her troubled mind and heart.

TWENTY NINE

While the Sunday-evening crew reported the news, Kat huddled at her desk, recalling the drive from Pentwater. All the way back to Chicago, she relished the sight of Jack in her rearview mirror. They stopped for soup and a slice of apple pie. Winston slept the entire time in Jack's car, making Kat wonder if the vet, who, it turned out, was the same surly man she had encountered on the beach that long-ago day in July, had drugged the poor animal.

As she waited for her laptop to power on, Kat recalled the way Jack's face perked up when he took a bite of pie, slathered with melting vanilla ice cream. Besides being a terrific cop, Jack McKenna was a real human being, and she felt more connected to him than anyone, except Elliot.

At lunch, it seemed they were forging a bond, with a chance at something deeper. If only they could do fun things and not always concentrate on work. On the Skyway Bridge, Kat peeked in her mirror and there was Jack. Later, when he waved, she felt a thrill in her heart.

Now, the computer stalled on its startup page. Kat shut off the power, and rebooted it. Her life was not cooperating any more than her computer. On the way back to the city—she dared not call Chicago home—Jack saluted one last time, but when she exited at Stony Island, he went on toward the Dan Ryan Expressway. Apparently no longer concerned for her, hours had passed and Jack had not called. Kat was still not sure if she should check into a hotel and wanted his opinion.

Reality smarted, like a slap across the face. Jack saw her as a colleague, working on a story for his dad. There was no earthly reason why he should be interested in her. To begin with, she was not right for him. Big John hinted that Melissa was not, either. Maybe she realized the same thing Kat saw, she could not live up to Jack's ideals in life.

Yesterday, when she overheard him talking to Eva about Ingrid Swanson, which for reasons of his own he did not share with her, Kat used the information to do more digging on her *CamelotConnection* account. Last evening on her porch, about to admit it all to Jack, the weight of her deception stifled her.

More than anything, Kat wanted some clue what *Camelot* did with her request about Lars and Ingrid. At the library, her account went blank. Now at the station, she again entered her account number and access code. What happened next pushed out all thoughts of Jack.

Log-in error occurred. Please re-enter correct account number and access code. Kat quickly typed it in again. Twice more, she received the same error message. The final response was upsetting. *Access Refused. Account Closed.*

A cold chill grabbed her and a voice in her head told her she was reckless to tinker with someone like Senator Zorn. By seeking information about him, another user of *Camelot,* she had stirred up a hornet's nest. She suspected the closing of her account would not be the only fallout.

There was only one thing to do. She would tell everything to Elliot, who should be back from D.C. by now. It was easier to convince him to see things her way and she had to tell someone. When she found him home, relief flooded her. Without confiding the reason, she arranged to meet him at his place in an hour. Kat hung up, surprised to see her fingers actually shaking.

The temperature below fifty degrees, her thin jacket provided no barrier to the cold. She blasted on the heat in her car, directing warm air on her toes, which were freezing in canvas sneakers. Washington never seemed this cold in October, another reason to move back there. At their building, she cautioned herself to be careful what she told Elliot.

Involuntarily, her foot nudged the brake. After all, if her goal was to shine in Chicago so that she could return to D.C., her whole plan would backfire if Elliot thought she was still after Zorn and she'd end up reporting the news in Lexington. Not that she had anything against Kentucky, but news there did not affect the lives of most Americans.

Resolved to tell only what was necessary to garner Elliot's help, Kat swiped her security card, and the garage door opened. The large metal door shut behind her, its clattering sounds putting her on edge. Not seeing another person in the garage, she grabbed her laptop case, used the remote to lock the doors, and ran to the elevator.

At the top floor, the door slid open to a quiet hallway, its serene beauty a total contrast to the cold, gray garage from which she just fled. Watercolor paintings of crews sailing on Lake Michigan decorated the walls and hurricane sconces cast a golden glow. Kat knocked on the solid wood door. Several locks clicked open, and Elliot was pleased to see her, even pecked her cheek. She returned the gesture and, without realizing it, glanced once more over her shoulder.

Elliot's condominium was one of only three on the top floor, and in the expansive living room he sat on a leather sofa made for him in Italy. "My dear, rest a moment. You look all in. Before she left, Maggie fixed sandwiches and hot cocoa. Help yourself."

Kat liked Elliot's housekeeper, Maggie, who made the most delicious cucumber and cheese sandwiches. To please him, she poured two steaming cups of cocoa, gave him one, and took a bite of the sandwich.

He watched her over the rim of his cup. "What is so urgent it could not wait until tomorrow?"

When he put the cup onto the saucer, the clinking noise made her body jump. Elliot must have seen her involuntary shudder, because his tone became gentle, "Kat, never mind the lateness. I have nothing more important than listening to you."

He made her feel so comfortable and loved at that moment, she confided it all—how the strain she was under these past weeks, of knowing someone was spying on her, drove her to a decision she now regretted. Just saying Jack's name, her cheeks grew warm, and a confesson—about how she eavesdropped on him and then took advantage of the information—spilled out.

"When I heard Ingrid Swanson's name, it was like a guide wire within me snapped. If she is in league with Lars Zorn to wreck my life, I have to stop them. Jack is working on finding out who bugged my telephone, but I took things into my own hands."

Elliot's elbows rested on his knees, his hands folded under his chin. "I believe you did such a thing. In your interview of Senator Zorn on Capital Hill, I saw your resolve to expose him for a fraud. This concerns me for you, Mary Katherine. You believe I was angry that you aired Zorn's obscene gesture. In fact, you had every right to do so. His reaction to a legitimate investigative question was news, and it should have been broadcast."

Kat stared as if he just said he was giving her a million dollars. She could not believe it; Elliot approved of her story about Senator Zorn. "I wish you had told me that before," she managed to say.

He dropped his hands. "I didn't have the chance. You wouldn't talk to me, answer my calls. I was on my way to see you in Pentwater when my plane crashed. Even after all that, I sensed you were not ready to hear it. I'd like to know why you consider your actions yesterday to be wrong. Maybe this time we can correct it together."

Emotions surged within her. Kat wiped her eyes, which were for the second time this weekend filled with tears. Just as she did so, her prepaid cell phone rang. Should she answer it? It might be Jack, or even Eva—not many people had this number. She said hello and heard a *click* in her ear.

The interruption helped redirect her attention away from feelings onto what she wanted to show Elliot. After gathering her wits, Kat slid her laptop from its case. "I'd like to say more, but," she stopped, looking around the spacious room, "is it safe? I mean, you know what they are doing to my phones."

Elliot stood, stretched his legs, and sat next to her on the sofa. "I missed my workout today and feel stiff. Technicians from the station routinely come by and sweep my place for bugs and taps. They did two days ago."

Kat glanced toward the door. "Would you have mine checked? If you find anything, I am out of here and going to a hotel."

"Before you moved in, I had it checked. Be sure, Kat, I look after you very carefully."

"That was before my calls were spied on, right? It should be done again."

"Let's see about the website first."

Kat opened her computer and told Elliot what happened when she tried to access *Camelot* earlier. He grew pensive. "We'll change your locks tomorrow, if that makes you feel better."

It did, and Kat told him so. From his desk, Elliot retrieved a pad and pen, and Kat called, "It's up now. Let me show you what happened. I seriously debated whether to get into this with you, so promise not to overreact."

He was back at her side. "I will promise no such thing."

Three times Kat typed in her account number and access code and each time, it indicated an error. On the fourth try, her screen showed the dreaded message, *"Access denied. Account closed."*

Elliot gripped his pen. "What was your request when you got shut down?"

"I asked for background information on Senator Zorn and Ingrid Swanson. Five minutes later, I was shut out." Kat pushed out her bottom lip. "Ask for something unrelated on your account and see what happens."

Elliot scratched out a few notes, and then looked at her squarely. "I never told you this. At a Press Club luncheon in Washington, the Deputy Attorney General was talking about cyber crime, I met a man at my table who handed me a card. He was in the intelligence community and owned a company that provided security for corporations like mine."

Kat was impatient for Elliot to enter a request. "What's his name?"

His eyes closed, as if he was conjuring up the past. "He told me about the website, invited me to use their services. I wish I recalled his name. My lawyer assured me a former CIA-type ran it." Elliot was silent until his eyes flew open. "I think the name was Hardy or Harding."

He walked out to the window and Kat joined him, both looking out toward the darkness that was Lake Michigan with car lights streaming below on Lake Shore Drive. His voice was so quiet. "I do not understand what this group's tie is to Senator Zorn, or why they are spying on you."

Kat drew in a breath. Did Elliot have a link to these people in ways she did not understand? She gently probed those still waters. "Want to test your account?"

His immediate answer gave her courage to continue. "Kat, I do. Ask for information about me, my televisions stations. I have wondered how much Camelot releases on one of its own clients."

She forced out her bottom lip again. "It depends how important the client is. Remember, someone asked for a tap on my phone, and got it."

"And you think that someone was Senator Zorn?"

Renewed resentment at her enemy electrified her. "I have evidence he is involved. I set up a sting. I had my friend Mary call me on the condo phone, offer to give me a videotape about an unnamed Senator. Zorn's aide, Ingrid Swanson, the one I just told you about, watched the meeting at Union Station, where some kid stole our tape and ran off with it."

"The fact she works for Senator Zorn does not mean she was involved. We need corroboration before running it as a news story."

Kat looked straight in Elliot's eyes. "I know what happened to me when I took him on in June. He got me transferred here. Anyway, I am determined to make a go of it in Chicago. I have Camelot's web site on screen. Do you want to give me your account number or do you want to type it?"

When he said, "Neither," Kat felt deflated. Elliot sat by his desk in front of the windows overlooking Lake Michigan. The vast darkness over the lake acted as a mirror and, in those windows, Kat watched the reflection of the man who was like a father to her as he contemplated the next step.

She laid a hand on his shoulder. "Thanks for asking me here tonight. I needed help with this."

Elliot patted her hand. "Enter the inquiry on my computer, just in case."

"If Zorn comes after me, a television reporter, just think what he does to people without the power of the media behind them."

Elliot concentrated on what he was typing, so did not react. To fill the silence, Kat talked on. "If a reporter inquires about Camelot's wealthy or influential clients, they either claim they have no information, or close their account, like mine."

Suddenly it hit her. She grabbed Elliot's elbow and shook it without thinking. On the screen, a dozen dots appeared where he was typing his access code. He erased these and started over.

"I came across two new Cuban connections to the JFK assassination. Put in one of their names."

"Who are they?"

"One is a Cuban General, alleged to have instructed Oswald and given him funds to carry out sabotage against the United States. He publicly denies any involvement. I also found a web site put out by the Cuban underground, which implies General Raul San Felipe, once held prisoner by the communist regime in Cuba, is now talking about Cuba's role in recruiting Lee Harvey Oswald at the suggestion of the Russians."

Elliot turned on his chair. "Talking from Cuba, I doubt it. Kat, I had not heard about the Russians connecting Oswald to the Cubans. What is your source?"

Kat retrieved her file from the sofa and showed Elliot the results of her search on the web. "It was aired in a documentary by Wilfried Huismann and Gus Russo. They had a source inside Cuba, who saw the reference to the 1962 KGB message about Oswald."

"What was that message, exactly?"

"Allegedly, Vladimir Kryuchkov, a future KGB chief, sent a telegram to the head of Cuban intelligence about Oswald on July 18, 1962, about one month after he returned to the U.S. from Russia. It said the Cubans should take a look at him."

Elliot traced some of her notes with his finger. "I always thought it was suspicious for a pro-Marxist to suddenly get disillusioned with the Soviet Union and come back to America."

Kat agreed. "And bring a Russian wife and baby daughter. What better way to infiltrate vibrant Russian exile groups and spy on them for Moscow?"

Elliot typed in General San Felipe's name. "I'll ask for his background and his present whereabouts."

Both watched for confirmation, but after nearly three minutes, the screen went blank. "Elliot, that's what it did prior to closing me out."

He re-entered the account number and code, getting the same reply she had yesterday. *Access denied. Account closed.* Elliot's face was unreadable. "They must have a filter on the system to detect subjects and people that are protected. You are on to something with the Kennedy assassination, Kat." He closed his computer. "Keep digging. I trust you have the beginnings of an explosive new special."

She could hardly contain her excitement. "Start signing up advertising, because I don't think it will take long."

Elliot had something else in mind. "Go downstairs, get all your files. I want them in my safe. And, get your toothbrush while you're at it. Until we get your place swept and locks changed, I want you to stay in the guest bedroom. You're not safe down there."

Kat felt a surge of relief at not having to find a hotel tonight, and also at the depth of his concern—but mostly, at no longer being alone.

THIRTY

Midnight came and went in the air with no fanfare. FBI agent Griff Topping raised the window shade on the plane uncertain of what he'd see. Only darkness welcomed him. There were no lights, except the green one pulsing at the end of the wing. It seemed the wide-bodied airliner had plunged from blackness into nothingness.

He was finally on his way to Almaty, Kazakhstan, and would arrive in the wee hours of Monday morning. The flight from Dulles was smooth, with no seatmates poking him about possible terrorists. In Amsterdam he boarded this KLM wide body, which boasted passengers in every seat save one behind Griff. Though it wasn't too noisy on board, sleep proved elusive. He pushed the shade down and plucked from his pocket a card from Dawn.

In it was a photo of her and her teenage son posing by the Blue Angels at Pensacola Naval Air Station. Griff admired more than Dawn's black braid, draped over her shoulder, or almond-shaped eyes. She was a beautiful person, who cared deeply for her son, especially after the death of her husband, a Navy pilot. He wished Dawn lived in Virginia, but never said so. Her son was still in high school, and she had a great job.

If he would not transfer for Dawn, no way he was moving to Kazakhstan. Of course, his buddy who worked for Harding thought he was ready for such a move. A smile in his heart, Griff put the picture and card, a funny one with a pink flamingo wearing huge sunglasses, back in his pocket. He stepped into the aisle and freshened up in the lavatory.

Back in his seat a few minutes later, Griff watched a man reeking of alcohol stagger past to the washroom. Thankful he was not sitting next to him, Griff's mind leapt to what Harding & Associates were up to in Kazakhstan, forgetting the man until he passed by going up the aisle. This time Griff detected the sweet aroma of marijuana.

If this were an American plane, he'd report a smoking violation to the first officer. This being a Dutch aircraft, he found himself unable to act, and feeling a bit uncomfortable at having left behind the safety of American soil to travel overseas.

Despite misgivings about landing in a foreign country, as the plane descended, he yearned to explore a place he had never been. From a friend at the State Department, he received tips on the former Soviet satellite: drink bottled water, avoid raw foods, and don't get into any taxi at the Almaty airport. Reportedly, ruffians had driven visitors to the countryside, pretended to be out of fuel, and demanded cash in exchange for a ride back to town. No problem there; someone from Harding & Associates was picking him up.

He hoped whoever met him at three-thirty this morning would know where he could grab a sandwich. A city of over one million people, there were plenty of western-style restaurants near the embassies, but not much on the outskirts by the airport. Upon landing, he stood in the aisle, along with hordes of people. An elderly Korean man pointed to his right arm, which was in a sling. Griff recalled reading that Joseph Stalin, the brutal Soviet dictator responsible for millions of deaths, forced North Koreans to work in Kazakhstan.

Griff bowed his head slightly. "May I help you?"

Taller than he, Griff simply followed the man's finger to a bag tied with red string and heaved it down. He snatched his backpack, slung it over his shoulder; his only other luggage a computer case containing his laptop, electric adapter and extra socks. Griff packed light for his "fact-finding mission" with Harding & Associates, which only he and Eva knew had covert implications.

At Customs, Griff got stuck behind the inebriated passenger. With a shaking finger, the man kept gesturing at Griff, saying something in Russian. A tough-looking security officer must have surmised they traveled together, because he searched Griff's backpack before calling over his boss. The supervisor's neck, bulging under his white shirt, suggested he was a former weight lifter. He ordered Griff to turn on his electric shaver and laptop, which Griff was happy to do, proving they were not being used to smuggle in contraband.

After assuring the surly official he would take his shaver and computer back to the United States when he left in two days, they allowed him through a set of glass doors to the free world. In the waiting area, a slight man with gelled-back hair and wearing a black leather jacket, held a sign in front of him with the lettering, "Harding for Mr. Griff".

Computer case in his left hand, Griff stuck out his right. "You with Harding and Associates?"

When he spoke, the man's lips barely moved, but Griff learned one thing right off; his accent was definitely Russian. "With Harding. You Griff?"

"You bet right on that."

The man's brow drew together. "You Griff, yes?"

Griff quit the funny business. "I am. Who are you?"

"Sergei Yushenko. Follow me."

As Griff walked to the exit, the warning flashed in his mind about not leaving in cars with strangers. He took one look at the unlit parking lot, and stopped in the doorway, taking advantage of light from behind him. He tapped Sergei's arm, eased his passport from his jacket pocket and flipped it open. "I was told *you* would show identification."

Sergei, his front tooth pure gold, reached for the passport. Griff pulled it back, pointed to Sergei. "No, you show me.

It took some doing, but finally Sergei pulled a laminated card from his pants pocket. It was two-sided, one in Cyrillic alphabet, and Griff had no idea what it said. On the other, Sergei's name was in English under Harding & Associates, his job title assistant to the security director. The phone number and address appeared correct. With no photo, the business card made Griff uneasy. He thought better of demanding to see a Kazakh driver's license and followed Sergei to the car, which turned out to be a van.

As Sergei started the van, Griff repeated the name and address of his hotel a few times. Sergei's reply, "Da," Russian for yes, told Griff he should go to the right place. It was embarrassing, how his stomach growled sounding like a tuba, but Sergei didn't seem to notice as he ran a red light. Griff gripped the side arm, and heard a rustling sound in his jacket pocket. He reached in, and found an energy bar he forgot Sal had tossed him at Dulles.

"Thanks, Sal," he mumbled, as he tore open the wrapper.

Just then, Sergei hit the brakes. The bar flew to the floor. As he leaned down for it, two hands gripped tightly around Griff's neck.

He snapped back. Everything went black. A hood, something, was draped over his head. With no chance to fathom who did such a thing, his claustrophobia reared its ugly head, and Griff fought against outright panic. "What's going on?"

In reply, Sergei jammed to a stop. Griff tried ripping off the hood; someone held it down. He pulled on the door handle. It refused to budge. He groaned, at the mercy of robbers, just as he'd been warned. Seconds later, his car door flew open. His attackers must have disabled Sergei, too, because the man seemed to have disappeared. Yanked from the vehicle by one arm, Griff swung with the other, hitting something hard, maybe a man's upper arm. If only he knew how many held him captive!

With force, they wrenched his right arm behind his back. Bolts of electricity shot up his neck. Griff lashed out with his left, jabbed at air. He tried again to pull off the hood, began kicking. Held fast by both arms, Griff felt someone cuff his wrists behind him.

Pushed back inside, Griff resisted, and with every muscle of his body, wanted to run. His heart was pumping hard, sending blood where he needed it. Adrenaline rushing through him, he prepared to lunge out the door, until a punch landed on the right side of his jaw. Intense pain staggered him long enough for the kidnappers to bind his feet.

Griff arched his body, yelling, "Sergei!" No answer. "Take my money!"

Another blow to the head, and Griff was out. When he came to, he had no idea where he was, or how long they had driven, ten seconds or ten minutes. Dragged from the van with his feet bumping over something like large stones, his jaw and arms ached.

Griff defied an urge to shout, and with his senses alert to danger, he listened. Were those footsteps on gravel? He had to think—how many feet were there? He counted, *crunch, crunch*. Okay one pair meant one man.

If he dove at whoever was holding him, he could knock him down. Hood on, handcuffed at both ends, that was impossible. Maybe if he relented, pretended to be unconscious, they would be caught off guard and he could gain an advantage.

Hauled up over two steps, he thought a door opened. A few more feet and he got dumped. When a door closed, no one spoke or told Griff what they wanted. He felt or at least imagined his wallet was in the back pocket of his khakis. Course, his money might be long gone. Just when Griff was certain he was alone, strong hands pulled him along the floor. Cold metal on his right wrist, someone was touching his handcuffs. Sure enough, he heard the snap. He must be secured to something sturdy, a pole maybe; it didn't matter what, he had no way to straighten his stiff arms. He held his breath. When nothing happened, he was relieved not to be punched again.

One set of steps moved away. Griff breathed out, very easy like, and jerked his arms toward his back. They moved less than an inch. Held fast, he could not budge it, whatever "it" was. His heart not thumping so fast—he was getting used to the hood over his head—Griff forced himself to think about who had him and why.

However, his mind grasped nothing other than *Eva knows I am here in Almaty.* This thought prompted another. He was supposed to call her when he checked into his room. How many hours behind was Virginia? *Think man!*

Oh, right, ten hours. That meant if it was five o'clock in the morning in Almaty—his brain dropped this thread to listen to a sound he thought he heard, which came to nothing. Griff turned his mind to Eva waiting for his call, and remembered—it was seven in the evening for Eva. If enough time passed and he failed to get in touch, he counted on her to sound the alarm. His mind working more clearly now, like an engine with sufficient oil, there *was* something he could do.

Griff put his panic where it needed to be—in God's hands. Surely, he saw him in this forsaken place, wherever he was. Trusting God did not come naturally for Griff. Handcuffed and alone, what else could he do? Something close to peace descended upon him, and he went to sleep, even though he was hungry and thirsty and felt searing pain in more than one place.

SOMETHING STARTLED GRIFF AWAKE. His eyes opened, but it did not matter, his world was still black. Each time he breathed, rough fabric pressed against his nostrils. Every muscle in his arms and legs screamed out, longing to move. He was cold, his jaw throbbed, and his bladder was about to burst. Griff's stomach was so empty it felt hollow.

While he felt the weight of his watch on his arm, Griff had no way to see it. *What was that?* Footsteps were coming nearer. In another instant, the hood was snatched from his head! Griff sucked in air. His eyes flew open, but the lights were so bright he could not see.

Eyes adjusting, he saw he was within a chain link enclosure inside a warehouse-like room filled with crates, barrels, and equipment. Weakened, but definitely not defeated, he would fight his way out of the fence, out of the room. Regular running at the park kept his legs and lungs strong. If they removed the cuffs holding his legs, he would kick with all his strength.

He doubted Eva would bring in the authorities, yet. Questions about Griff's presence or missing status would alert the wrong people. An amazing thing was happening. He felt cuffs slide off his wrists.

While who was releasing them was a mystery, he had read of angels. Could it be one helped him now?

His ankles were free! When Griff tried to stand, his knees crumbled. Two unexplained hands lifted him to his feet. When Griff swung around, he faced an old man who, a good five inches shorter, bone-thin and face unshaven, was definitely not Sergei. One thrust to his skinny stomach, Griff could take this old buzzard, no problem.

He did not get the chance. In perfect English, which Griff recognized as flavored with an Irish brogue, the man held up his hands. "Sorry to trouble ye laddie. I am told a great mistake was made."

The way he stepped on his "r" gave Griff the idea he had left Ireland recently. He soon found he was wrong on that, and other things.

The old man shook his head, clucked his tongue. "I'm the watchman here. A real shame it is."

Griff stretched his back, found his voice. "What's your name? Who do you work for?"

The little man danced back a couple of steps. Like a magician pulling a rabbit from a hat, he produced a towel and a bar of soap. "They call me Tristan. Follow me, laddie and have a wash-up, while I make ye some tea."

Tea in this dump? The man must be insane. Griff grabbed the towel and decided to humor the old gent. He seemed kindly enough. Besides, if he had water, there might be a bathroom, which Griff desperately needed. He followed him through a door, to a small room with a cot, a little stove, and a sink. Tristan pointed to a curtain.

"I'll leave you to it behind there, and put the kettle on. A hot cuppa will put you right."

Griff wondered what horrible trick awaited him on the other side of the dirty fabric, but somehow he trusted Tristan, a strange fellow in a foreign land. Over tea, he might discover who kidnapped him. Behind the curtain, to Griff's profound relief, were facilities, and even if rudimentary, he was never so thankful for a hole in the ground. Icy cold water splashed on his face helped refresh him.

In minutes, he felt more like the old Griff, the federal agent who faced danger and lived to tell about it. Blood was flowing in his fingers and toes. Back on the other side of the curtain, he found a steaming mug of tea with two biscuits on a plate. Not this ravenous since he got over the flu last winter, Griff realized he took for granted small things in life, like drinking fresh water, living in safety, and buying whatever food he wanted at the corner market.

Griff took the mug and sipped some, trusting his "host" had not put anything strange into it. The tea tasted wonderful, though back home he detested the brew.

"Tristan, you seem harmless, and I am not going to take out my anger on you. I need answers, need 'em now. Let's start with who you work for."

Tristan urged him to eat a biscuit, and like a good Irishman, launched into a long tale of leaving Belfast, lost ships at sea, a Korean War bride, and making his home in Almaty since his wife's family was here.

It might have been the blow to his head, but Griff had difficulty following the ramblings. "That's a mouthful, Tristan. Answer me, where am I?"

"Want more tea, Mr. Topping?"

"How did you find out my name?"

"Sergei Yushenko told me, when he gave me the key to unlock ye."

Griff started to fume. He wanted out of this warehouse, wherever it was. "Tristan," he pointed beyond the chain link fence, "If I walk out that door, what will I find?"

"A grand day, Mr. Topping, a grand day." Tristan poured more tea from the kettle into the cup Griff still held. "Drink up, laddie. Aren't ye glad to be alive?"

"Of course, I am, but that doesn't change the fact Sergei must answer for what he did to me. Where is he?"

Tristan turned the burner on under the water. He crooked his finger, for Griff to lean down so he could whisper something in his ear. Almost silently, he said, "There's listening devices," and gestured with his eyes to the ceiling. "This is Harding's. Don't ye make trouble for me, an old pensioner."

Griff gave Tristan his cup. "I'm to see Mr. Harding's assistant, a Mr. Meijer, who is expecting me."

Just then, two men dressed from neck to toe in navy-blue, including berets and heavy boots, sauntered in. If they were with Harding & Associates, Griff figured they had to be armed. Every muscle in his body tensed. What a predicament. He was a visitor to a former Soviet Republic and on the property of an international security firm. The men stood by the door, arms locked across their chests, as if guarding the entrance to a king's tomb.

If Harding treated all his potential employees so harshly, and if his company was involved in illegal tactics, Griff would bring down the full force of American law upon their heads. Those were two big ifs, but for now, Griff sought to uncover equally strong evidence to make the case.

A tall, brawny guard motioned with a snap of his head for Griff to come with him. Griff took a last look at Tristan, who seemed to tremble at his leaving. As Griff said goodbye, he thought ol' Tristan actually winked at him. The fellow then danced away on his nimble feet.

THIRTY ONE

With the bulldozer of a security guard leading the way, Griff took one glimpse at his surroundings and knew that any idea for a fast getaway was ridiculous. An eight-foot high wall snaked around him on both sides. It would take some doing to scale that brick monster with his bare hands. A second armed guard followed so close behind, he drove Griff into some prickly bushes growing alongside, scraping his arm.

This trip was so bizarre, he prepared himself for the next test concocted by Harding to see if Griff was man enough for the security company. He hoped that's what was going on, because he faced serious trouble if Harding's sources knew Griff was investigating him undercover. The path abruptly ended. At the three-story brick building, Griff envisioned going inside, eager to tear into Harding, a coward at best, hiding behind electronic equipment and spying on citizens. But, if he was not here, Griff would find another way to settle the score.

The lead guard swiped a card to open a steel door, and Griff was hustled down a bright hallway, fluorescent lights burning his eyes. A fan of spy movies, at this moment he felt smack-dab in the middle of some cold-war flick. If only he had his Glock, which at home he always carried. With no firepower, he had to rely on his wits and slowly returning strength.

Another thirty feet, another steel door, but this time the second guard swiped a card, and Griff walked into a large room, where behind a glass enclosure a man with no beret studied a wall of video monitors. Hands pushed Griff toward a magnetometer, then a vacuum-sealed device. He hated the closet-like thing that smelled for explosives. Similar ones in federal buildings in D.C. brought on his claustrophobia every time. In seconds, he burst out the open doors, breathing deeply.

There was a metal gate, where Mr. Heavy punched in a code, reminding Griff of turnstiles separating commuters from the D.C. Metro, only he had no way to control this with his card key. Down a ghastly-yellow corridor, Griff tried to memorize his steps, but lost track. Outside a door with keypad, guard number two, seeming even bolder now, punched in numbers, shoved Griff inside. Could this windowless room be his new prison cell with its one table, and two chairs?

A deep voice from behind boomed, "Mr. Topping, You may sit."

The Russian accent, though slight, drew Griff to pivot slowly where he looked into the eyes of a man also six-foot-one, his full head of brown hair turning silver. He handed Griff his passport, which he quickly stowed in his pocket.

With no pretense at shaking Griff's hand, the man tented his own. "I do not say welcome to Harding and Associates, but will save the niceties for after you rest in our guest room."

Griff balled his fist, sizing up his latest adversary. His Russian accent barely discernable, as if he spent years in the West, perhaps he was a former Soviet diplomat. He seemed the right age. Dressed in a suit, starched shirt, and blue tie, in appearance he was many levels above the guards. No doubt, he would prove to be slick, very slick indeed.

Disgust rumbled in his belly, though Griff struggled to regain self-control. It was impossible to fight his way out of this situation. "You obviously know who I am. After my kidnapping, I awake to find an old man serving me tea on Harding property. Do I thank you for my release or condemn you for my capture?"

A pleased look on his unyielding face, the man said, "I am Dmitri Federov."

Griff did not have to dig far into his memory for that name to come rushing back.

"Ah, I see you remember, Agent Topping. A clever fellow like you keeps track of such things."

Disgust swiftly became boiling anger, a steam engine ready to blow. Dmitri Federov, former KGB spy, would be sorry for this. Yes, he would! In seconds, Griff began plotting the perfect payback. "*You* are connected to Harding and Associates?"

Federov held up an enormous hand, nearly the size of a bear's paw. "All will be revealed, after you rest. You will find new accommodations more to your liking."

Dmitri narrowed his eyes, the light above casting a dangerous glow to them. They were glassy, devil eyes. "You are smart, Topping, and will not mention to Mr. Harding what is between you and me. You see, I have not forgotten it was you who played tough with my son when you arrested him in a cabin in the Virginia woods."

He stepped over to Griff, thumped him hard on the back. "The look on your face, when you heard my name, makes it worthwhile. When Harding told me you were coming to Kazakhstan to work with me, I could not resist playing this little trick on you. In fact, I delayed your trip so I could see to your arrival personally."

Ah, so it was Federov himself who changed the schedule. Eva had been right to be suspicious. What the Russian did next was tantamount to declaring war. He laughed. Intense rage burned within Griff, but he struggled to contain it. Outgunned and outmanned, Griff knew this was not the time to seek revenge. Rather, a gentle reminder might let Federov know he could not get away with such a dangerous "trick."

"Dmitri, I haven't left the FBI yet."

Dmitri was not worried. "Your father was FBI, yes?"

What did that have to do with anything? Federov probably had a secret means of reading Griff's personnel file, even if it was illegal. Still, Griff would admit nothing to this former Russian spy. Instead of being some strange test of his mettle, this whole thing, Griff now realized, was a setup by Federov. "Why do you ask?"

"I am former KGB, as was my father before me. He taught me many things, including once a lie is told, it stays a lie. Take your Lee Harvey Oswald for example. My father met with him in Moscow on July 8, 1961, the same day he received his passport back from your American Embassy. How do I know? My father made a secret report, which never went into the files. You wonder why I tell you this?"

Federov began to walk toward the door. "Topping, you and I are on the same side now, fighting extremists. We are no longer cold-war warriors, seeking to topple competing governments. What you observe at our complex will amaze you. Then, you will see where your future lies."

Griff approached the man, keeping his ears and eyes open, remembering what Sal once told him about Federov. After a long history with KGB, he defected to the U.S., until the Soviet Union's collapse convinced him to return to Russia. Since then he had made lots of money in the international oil-and-gas trade.

During a recent criminal case that Griff and Sal had worked on together, Sal got a cryptic call from Federov to meet. When Sal brought what he learned to Bureau higher-ups, the Director confiscated Sal's notes, as if his meeting with Federov never happened.

The way Federov mentioned Oswald telegraphed to Griff that the Russian had inside info about the Kennedy assassination. If Griff stayed vigilant, he might pick up something to bring back to the FBI. He accompanied Federov back through the maze, to an elegant building more like a hunting lodge. His new room was pleasant, with large bed, sitting area, and private bath, but Griff sensed it was just another means to keep him off guard. Sure enough, in moments, he fought back a yawn battling for release.

A crooked smile on his face, Federov handed Griff a card key to get in and out of his room. "This does not work on any other doors. Here you will remain until I send for you. Soon, lunch will be provided."

When Federov left, Griff took out his wallet, counted his money. It was all there. He found Dawn's photo, pressed her face to his lips. When he got home from Kazakhstan, he was definitely going to see her; Dawn had asked what he was doing for Thanksgiving.

After a nap and wash, a plate of grilled beef with rice was brought to him. Though hungry, Griff ate the food without tasting it, his mind consumed with outwitting Federov.

GRIFF HAD JUST SET KNIFE and fork on his plate when he heard a sharp knock. There was Dmitri, on the other side of the open door, holding a basket of fruit. "Our apples are legendary."

He declined to take it. "No thanks."

Federov pushed his way into the room, set the basket on a small table. "Topping, it's a peace offering. Take one and I will, too. Then we begin our tour."

Unsure what Federov was up to, Griff picked up a piece of fruit, vowing not to eat it. Apple in hand, he sauntered toward the door. The sooner he got things going, the sooner he could leave. "Ready if you are."

A well-practiced smile was fixed on the Russian's face. "We both have enemies who mean to harm us. You have Al Qaeda and Hezbollah, and we have the Chechens. It is best we work together. The KGB knew Mr. Philip Harding by his reputation as a former CIA agent. When he recruited many of us to Harding and Associates, I learned his true genius."

Unwilling to reveal a thing, Griff crossed his arms and glared.

Dmitri did not seem offended by the icy stare. "This was a Soviet communications station during the Cold War. Harding convinced the Kazakh government to sign a long-term lease. True to his word, the people he employs help the local economy."

Outdoors, the sight of the high walls topped with razor wire dampened Griff's momentary sense of freedom. Thoughts of walking away from the compound vanished. Armed guards were everywhere, outside his room, the lodge, and around the grounds. Griff breathed in deeply, aware of something less obvious. Federov's behavior suggested Harding & Associates' activities just might be illegal.

As he walked, Federov ate his apple, core and all, and then waved at large satellite dishes, posted like sentries and aimed at the sky. "You see, the place came with equipment Harding needed."

Tight security at the complex proved Harding was nervous about extremists, some of whom chose violence in the name of Islam. So far, Griff saw only what was on the surface and kicked his brain into high gear, reckoning that this massive electronic spy-palace might stamp out things besides terrorism.

In virtual silence, befitting the wealth of surveillance around them, the two men strode down a cobblestone path winding between two stucco buildings, its windows nestled high under the eaves. Griff had no secret means to read the Russian's mind, nor did he know what danger lurked just beyond the cross street they were approaching.

At this corner, Federov quit walking. "Twenty years ago, the CIA tried to find out what the Soviets were doing here. Today, we are a multinational but private effort to combat terrorism."

Like a sponge, Griff tried memorizing what he saw and heard. "Harding realized two things. First, intelligence gathering is very expensive."

Federov did not have to tell him that. Griff felt the squeeze in his paycheck; Congress was always tinkering to cut costs.

Dmitri was talking, still not moving. "Secondly, with intense oversight by politicians and ever-present media, it is better to purchase intelligence than maintain an infrastructure to gather your own. What you see here is the result."

A sudden burst of pride lit in Dmitri's eyes and Griff made a mental note. This high-tech facility was impressive, even if his introduction to it was hostile. About to ask Federov what his role was, Dmitri offered the information: "With trained linguists, I gather electronic intelligence from Russian-speaking countries."

As Federov continued boasting, Griff understood why they stayed rooted at the corner as well as the reason for the Russian's pride. "We work from the building on your immediate left. Our Russian team wears navy-colored shirts and slacks, with gray canvas belts. Like a huge vacuum sweeper, we suck from the worldwide electronic super-highway phone conversations, email traffic, and financial data."

Griff quickly figured there must be other teams. Would Federov admit as much? "So, you monitor Russia, the 'Stans, and other countries where Russian is spoken?"

Dmitri ignored the question. "Our computers and analysts filter out valuable intelligence and transcribe it. The dollar value varies. Harding and Associates sells the information to whichever country has a use for it."

Or is willing to pay the most, Griff thought but left unsaid. "Aren't you competing with the Russian government's own agency that gathers signal intelligence?"

When he replied, "That is an excellent question and I will tell you," it seemed that Dmitri treated Griff as a future partner on Harding's team, although he did not address his question directly. "The building on the right is the first of two English-speaking sectors and receives all British signal traffic. Former American intelligence and law enforcement officers work there. It is the operation you will supervise."

At last, he discovered how Harding saw him fitting in. Griff played along. "When do I meet Philip Harding?"

The Russian batted the air with his massive paw. "Harding is detained in the U.S. on urgent business for your government. He is leaving you entirely to me."

That did not sit well with Griff, who was hoping to connect Harding more explicitly to the activities of *Camelot,* and prove others besides Federov were involved in illegal espionage. This idea he filed away as Federov was telling him something he should remember. "Americans on the English-speaking team receive and analyze phone calls to and from the UK. While that intelligence may be sold to the Brits, the government at Ten Downing Street can honestly say they are not violating the privacy of any Brits."

Federov's laugh was genuine. "That's because, if it is happening, it is being done by Americans. Everybody on your team wears gray with navy belts."

Each week, for many years Griff called his grandmother in Cornwall, England. The thought of former FBI or CIA agents listening to his conversations enraged him, but he swallowed his rage until he could use it, later.

They walked now, Dmitri pointing to a second building whose occupants spoke English. "Former British intelligence types listen there and analyze signal traffic to and from the U.S. They wear khaki uniforms with black belts. Who do you think Harding sells this data to?"

Though it was repugnant to him, Griff acted as if such conduct was acceptable. "I imagine to my government, which gives it plausible deniability that U.S. agents are violating any U.S. citizens' civil rights, because to hear you tell it, they're not."

Dmitri slapped Griff on the back. "Harding was right; Griff, you are the man for this job. There are huge profits for everybody. Some governments pay rewards and a percentage of monies recovered. So if our American team finds a business that skims money and hides it offshore, Harding sells the info to the IRS, then gets—"

"I know," Griff interrupted, "we call it moiety, a percentage of the recovery."

The truth shocked him. If the Americans were not listening to his phone call to Grandma on its way to England, then the Brits could listen as he dialed out from Virginia. Of course, he and Grandma were no threat to national security. Still, the principle was the same, and Griff felt numb.

Despite Federov calling him Griff instead of Topping, he stayed on his guard. Cold rain started to fall and, with no umbrella, he hoped the heavens did not open up. Meanwhile, his host was bragging up Harding & Associates. "Same thing for currency recovered from drug traffickers who move money around the globe. Best of all, at year's end, we supervisors get a hefty bonus based on the percentage."

Apparently anointed the presumptive leader of the team spying on Brits, Griff probed, "What kind of money are we looking at Dmitri?"

"Your salary depends on what you negotiate with Harding, but last year, each team leader received a two-hundred-thousand dollar bonus. Mine went straight to my Swiss account. Flip has a special deal with Swiss banks. Everything is done by direct deposit to our numbered accounts."

A small man with olive complexion, wearing a green outfit with beige belt, passed by, and nodded toward Dmitri, who grunted.

"Who was that?" Griff wanted to know.

"Spanish speaking team covers South America and Spain. We do not get to know each other. Harding does not permit fraternizing among the teams, but it does occur. There's not much else for foreigners who speak no Russian or Kazakh."

The street ended at a chain link fence decorated with razor wire. The only way in or out was by a locked gate. Griff's eyes searched beyond it and settled on a large building surrounded by the same fencing. Two men wearing denim sat on a bench, smoking cigarettes, perhaps Americans. "What goes on in that building?"

Dmitri cut him off, "You have no need to know."

Undeterred, Griff wiped raindrops from his face. "No, Dmitri," he stressed the Russian's first name, "if I am to be in charge of your British sector I think I do. Otherwise, it's a no-go, buddy."

Dmitri squared his shoulders. "It is a special division of Harding."

Still unsatisfied, Griff pressed, "That does what?"

Rain began to fall in earnest, and Dmitri picked up the pace away from the protected building. "I suppose you will find out. Flip Harding gives a separate service to private industry throughout the world. Data brokers, they do security consulting, personal protection of executives, and industrial espionage. They operate signal intelligence in there. Flip keeps us from knowing much about that side. Those Americans do not mix with us. I am told they make *lots* of money."

As Griff and his new "friend" headed back to Dmitri's office, heavy rain pelted them. He sensed that winter was about to sneak in hail and ice any moment. Good thing his jacket, if thin, was rain-repellant. He should have listened to Sal about the harsh weather here. They ducked as they ran, and rested under an eave.

With the rain, Dmitri's flow of information was more fluid than ever. "With advances in technology, we know almost everything that happens around the world. When our fathers were in the trade, they had to rely on informers and wiretaps."

Dmitri stopped talking long enough for a sideways glance at Griff. "That is why we Russians first thought Oswald was spying for your Naval Intelligence. The KGB suspected he was one of several sailors and marines sent to Russia posing as defectors." Dmitri's grin was wicked. "Due to a source inside Naval Intelligence, my father knew they were coming."

Griff never knew U.S. Naval Intelligence sent "defectors" to Russia. What was Federov getting at? He kept his own counsel and listened.

Dmitri was not done sharing secrets. Must be there were no hidden listening devices, or maybe there were and this was all part of Dmitri's plan to get his voice on tape. Griff did wonder why there was no guard at this entry.

"My father co-opted Oswald, convinced him of the evils of U.S. policy. He sent him back to the U.S. as a Russian agent. Did you know Oswald worked at a U-2 base in Japan?"

To Griff's shrug, Federov said, "He was very uncontrollable. KGB turned Oswald over to Cuban intelligence, which could not control him either, but they did find a way to use him, too. The FBI used him to infiltrate activist groups. No doubt, your government destroyed much of his file, as did the KGB. What was left and released when the wall came down was nothing but innocent surveillance."

How much did the Bureau know of what Federov was telling him? Probably Hoover learned much of it before he died in 1972. Griff decided to ask something innocuous, see how Dmitri took his lack of interest in Oswald. "What about Tristan? I don't like Harding taking advantage of someone like him. The building must be fiercely cold in winter and he lives in poverty. Riches haven't flowed his way, have they?"

The Russian swiped his card key. "Do not concern yourself with Mr. Tristan. He lives the way he wants to. He has money enough to move."

"You mean he chooses to and you are not requiring him to live in that building?"

Federov merely nodded as if the subject was closed.

Griff pressed on. "Why?"

"Who understands the hearts of men when they are atoning for past wrong."

"I find it hard to believe Tristan did something so wrong. He is kind."

In dismissal of Griff's questions, Federov opened the door. "Tonight, I have arranged for you to be taken to one of Almaty's finest restaurants. Your host is a man on our staff, whose idea it was that Mr. Harding hire you. He worked with you in the past and gives nothing but praise about your skills and tenacity. I guess I proved that today."

Ignoring the snide remark about his capture, Griff was curious who in Almaty knew him personally. "Who might that be?"

Federov lifted his lips ever so slightly, "I enjoy surprises."

THIRTY TWO

Perched on the bed after his tour with Federov, Griff felt less like a prisoner than when he first arrived. He considered what to tell Eva when she asked what he thought of his Russian host. His answer would not be a simple one. Informative about intelligence sharing, Federov was cagey about that "secret" building and, at heart, was still Griff's enemy.

He stared at the uneaten peace apple, making a pledge to go beyond resentment of Federov, to do all he could to shut down this rogue operation. Sure, aggressive techniques were unavoidable in this era of imminent terror strikes; however, intelligence must be gathered legally or the West would descend into chaos.

Anxious to call Eva while his memory was fresh, with listening devices all around, Griff figured it would be imprudent to use his cell phone. He made a mental record of what Federov told him, which on the flight back home he would start writing down.

Then there was his so-called "supporter." Besides Griff's retired friend back home, he knew no one here who might recommend him for a job in Kazakhstan. Now, he was about to have dinner with the person. Simply put, it was absurd and Griff prepared for another mind game.

Thoughts of his colleagues being involved in this gritty enterprise forced Griff to set aside prejudice against Kat Kowicki. Her phones no doubt tapped by this super-secret operation, in the future, he'd go easier on her, if there were a next time.

When the phone rang, he answered carefully, realizing it too was probably tapped, "Hello," was all he said.

"Laddie, it's good to hear your voice."

Surprised at the strong British accent, Griff immediately thought of his grandmother's friends in Cornwall. None of them, including Grandma, knew he was here. He drew a blank, said nothing in return, surmising it was one of Federov's traps. What the caller said next hinted Griff might have found a friend.

"It's Miles Brewster. Welcome to Kazakhstan."

Griff placed the name and voice as a British MI-5 agent that he worked with some years back. They lost touch, although last summer Griff left a message for Miles, and never heard back. "Miles, your being here is a surprise."

"Guess so. Even my own people do not know. Grab your appetite and let's go. I am waiting out front."

Griff looked around the room and decided to bring his laptop. "I'll be right out."

What was Brewster doing here? Maybe he was on special assignment in Central Asia. Along with Eva, Griff met the British agent in London when they worked a case that traced funds to terrorists. Together with MI-5, the British equivalent of the FBI, they captured the commander of a Middle Eastern terrorist group.

Twenty minutes later, after small talk about Miles's parents and Griff's grandmother back in England, Griff loaded his plate with salad, fruit, and grilled meats to compete with any of Washington's finer restaurants. The time at the buffet helped Griff mask the shock at seeing a British intelligence agent he admired who was linked, not only to Harding, but also to Federov. His respect of Miles was so solid, he began to consider the possibility that what went on at the compound was legitimate, and the bug on Kat's phone was an aberration.

At the table, Brewster stirred his tea; there were only a few cucumbers and tomatoes on his plate. "Your appetite hasn't changed since we took that nice little cruise aboard the USS Constellation together. You must admit though, your food looks better than what the U.S. Navy served us."

Griff removed a linen napkin from around his silverware. "You look as fit as you did then, but no pipe in your pocket I see. Looking together for that trawler in the Indian Ocean was a great coup for our countries, though I hated being stuck below its decks."

Miles absent-mindedly reached for his phantom pipe. "I quit smoking as a concession to get my wife to move here. The Crescent, I think, was the name of that trawler. I still have a scar from the tussle we had with those fierce fighters. Your Navy medics didn't worry about leaving one on me."

Brewster drank some tea. "I'll never forget Eva dangling from a chopper and dropping onto the Crescent's deck. How is she?"

Forced to do something else he despised, in his undercover role, Griff deceived Miles and kept from him that Eva was spearheading his insertion into Kazakhstan. "We both work for our respective agencies, so I don't see her much. She has a new little boy, Marty, named after her grandfather."

Griff motioned to a waiter passing with a coffee carafe, pointed to his empty cup. He was not going to be stuck drinking tea a second time on this trip. The cup filled and waiter gone, Griff changed the subject. "Federov claimed you recommended me, but did not admit your involvement. Am I the right guy to be working for this outfit?"

Miles ate a slice of cucumber, wiped his mouth with a napkin. "Yes. Philip Harding and I worked together when he was CIA. When he approached me about Kazakhstan, I was reluctant to leave MI-5, but the package he offered was irresistible. I think you'll find it to be as well."

Griff tried the grilled lamb. The pump primed, he was not about to impede Miles, so let him continue. "While Harding was pleased at your coming on board, Federov objected. Seems you arrested his son and he is convinced you roughed him up. Harding asked me about it. I told him, if Griff arrested Federov Jr., he most certainly deserved it."

Miles stopped talking, allowing the waiter to serve him more tea. "Harding relies on me a great deal. You are the one he wants to supervise the non-American English program. You know what that means?"

Griff chewed on, wanting to hear it from Miles. The Brit leaned a bit closer, so did Griff, to hear his lowered voice over sounds of clinking tableware from other diners.

"You would be protecting my homeland, while I protect yours. The way it has worked for centuries is the way it works here. Our enemies always gathered intelligence on our countries. Now, with terrorist groups infiltrating our societies, we have to infiltrate their schemes for killing our citizens. This is one way to do it without violating our laws. Our governments purchase information, just as they purchase janitorial services. I don't need to tell you it's a whole new game."

It sounded right, but Griff felt uneasy. In one of the biggest terrorist busts for both countries, Griff and Miles had put their lives on the line, working side-by-side. Yet, in this part of the globe, where the rule of law tended to be the size of your bank account, could Griff trust Miles? Maybe the Brit had sold out his ethical side to pad retirement.

"I don't know. There is the issue of legality. To me, the ends do not justify the means."

Miles forged ahead with a hard sell, leaving his skimpy salad uneaten. "I am not at liberty to tell you how many terror plots my British staff already thwarted in the U.S. Even I do not know how many attempts your American team stopped in Britain. I do know we saved countless lives. Most of these are secret but, to me, each life is precious."

Griff could not argue with lives saved. Still, he felt a need to dig deeper. "That building at the far end of the complex, where a team collects data and intelligence for private businesses, what goes on there? You and I have served to benefit people, citizens of our countries. Are you comfortable working for a firm selling information to non-governmental types? Are you certain what they do with it?"

Even though Miles now peered through narrowed eyes, he held Griff's steadily. "If I knew more about that division, I might not approve. Flip insists the two sides not mingle information, or staff. I know it is a cash cow for him. Businesses pay big bucks for intelligence, which our governments don't have budgets for."

The way his lips pressed into a thin line, it seemed the former British Intelligence officer wanted to say more. Mindful of unfriendly eyes and ears all around, Griff pushed to see what he could uncover. "Back a few years, your appetite was healthy as mine was. Don't you like the food here, Miles?"

Griff hoped Miles would catch on he was referring to Harding's enterprise. Never dropping his eyes from Griff's he seemed to. "I did think I would find more British food, fish and chips and all that."

Unsure where to go next, Griff punted. "How about you give me a ride back to the airport and we can stop for something you like instead?"

Miles grasped his hand so firmly; Griff knew he found the chink in Harding's armor. That simple touch went a long way to restoring Griff's belief in Miles, and in why he had come to Kazakhstan in the first place—to find the truth no matter the cost.

UNABLE TO SLEEP during the flight from Kazakhstan to Amsterdam, Griff typed cryptic notes into his laptop, to be assembled into a detailed report later. The meal with Miles on the way to the Almaty airport was like their time together years earlier, sprinkled with the same camaraderie.

Griff had posed a challenge. "Miles, if I convince you there is a more sinister side to Harding and Associates, would you return to MI-5?"

Miles reached for his non-existent pipe, needing to think it over. Griff grew more persuasive. On the plane now, he stopped typing and made no written reference to the hypothetical he shared with Miles. Based on what happened to Kat, he had told him, "What if Harding's private sector actually taps phones of their influential clients' perceived enemies or competitors?"

The Brit's eyes flashed, offended by the suggestion. "That is not happening."

Griff did not give in. At the end, Miles conceded it "might" be possible Harding was involved in things he knew nothing about, and was open to returning to MI-5. The critical factor being if, within a month, Griff did not report for a job in Kazakhstan, then Miles would understand he had no confidence in Harding. To Griff, it seemed that Miles could not hide his relief at the thought of returning to British government service.

THIRTY THREE

Glad to be back in northern Virginia, Griff crammed between two other agents for Eva's Wednesday morning briefing, of which he was the star witness. Despite a throbbing headache and less than two hours of sleep, he began with a flourish, leaving out his kidnapping escapade. "Governments, even ours, pay Harding and Associates to spy on domestic groups by monitoring their international calls."

Behind new gold-rimmed glasses, IRS Agent Earl Simmons turned to stare at Griff. Eva snatched a legal pad and, with one swipe of her arm, moved away empty foam cups. "Are these calls being diverted to international locations?"

Griff massaged his temples, "You would not believe the scope of the enterprise there in Kazakhstan. Nobody dares talk about what goes on in one particular building. It's huge, completely fenced, with only one way in or out. I never got inside. Sal, you remember Dmitri Federov."

Sal lifted his chin. "Yeah, former KGB spy I met with, only the Bureau says I never did. What about him?"

"He runs the operation collecting info in Russian-speaking countries and is in deep, using his espionage tricks in the private sector."

After Griff explained what he had seen, the others just stared at him, as though in shock. "From Schiphol airport in Amsterdam, I called Philip Harding and told him I needed two weeks to think about his offer of two hundred thousand dollars per year, plus housing, expenses, and annual bonuses that could equal that salary."

Together, Sal whistled and Eva sighed. "We have to brief Alexia Kyros. If what you say is true, Griff, and I believe you, we may be dealing with crimes against American citizens and, just possibly—" she paused, tapped her pen on the legal pad, "the Constitutional crisis I was hoping to avoid."

Eva picked up her telephone and reached the office of the Deputy Attorney General, who supervised the task force. In moments, Dean Shepherd came on the line. Eva took a deep breath, and began slowly.

"Sir, I am calling about the matter General Kyros approved for us to work on, and need to meet with her as soon as possible."

She explained that the agents were in her office. "We have uncovered illegal wire taps, offshore bank accounts, violation of the privacy of our citizenry," she nodded; no doubt, the DAG was asking her to explain. "Sir, a clandestine operation of retired and former government investigators and agents gather intelligence, sometimes by illegal means, and sell it to our government and others. Time is of the essence."

A thundercloud passed over Eva's blue eyes. She looked at Griff as she said slowly, as if to reveal the absurdity of what she was about to say, "You mean the Attorney General is too busy to be informed of this violation before the media find out?"

Eva's face grew deep red. "No, sir, I do *not* suggest my agents would leak this to the press. I believe something this explosive could get out." She paused, "Okay, tomorrow, at five-thirty."

Griff wrote down, *where*?

"Yes, sir, at the Attorney General's office, and I will bring two of my staff, plus Jack McKenna, a Chicago police officer assigned to the FBI Terrorism Task Force who has knowledge pertinent to this case."

Griff hated one-sided conversations and wished Eva would put Shepherd on the speakerphone. Of course, he was blasting her, so Griff understood why she did not. Eva was the boss, and with that came grief she might not want to pass down to her team. Keep them all pumped up was her motto.

She stayed silent for a moment. "No, I have not briefed anyone else. You and I agreed it should be closely held."

Griff crumpled up breakfast sandwich wrappers. Eva drew her brows together and put a finger to her lips. Admonished, he sat down and silently listened. Not one to keep still, he ached to get moving against Harding and Federov.

"We will see you then, sir."

Eva ended the call and looked at Griff. "The meeting's been moved up to five-thirty today. No Chicago police officer; we are ordered to keep this in the federal family."

It was Griff's turn to whistle, remembering what happened when his partner Sal came up against Dmitri Federov last time. "Do I have to attend this grilling? How about Sal, he was the first one to get Federov's call."

"I want you and Earl. The Attorney General may get into the tax implications. Sal will review the Camelot traffic since your trip. I'll call

Sonya and have her come in early to help him. I want to step up the pace. And guys," Eva looked over her team, "tell no one about this, and I mean no one."

JACK HAD SPENT the last few days running down his idea that football games might be the target of the terrorists. Not only did he contact his counterpart in Dallas, where the first van was disabled, he stayed up late Monday night typing a long report to give to his boss on Tuesday morning. Only Gordon was at high-level meetings with his superiors and Jack hadn't yet talked with him.

This Wednesday morning, with a pot of coffee already wreaking havoc in his stomach, Jack checked his mail slot and found a classified report from the Boston terrorism task force. It came in over the secure system. The title made him freeze in place. *"Subject: Interstate Van Conversions; Possible Terror Activity."*

Something serious must be happening with the vans. Marked "Top Secret," only six field offices and Headquarters got a copy, Jack's eyes consumed it. He was surprised when the opening line not only furnished Luis's complete name, it also confirmed his worst fears. *It is believed the Luis who ordered six Dodge Sprinter vans, is one Luis San Felipe, a Cuban, now living in Venezuela, and a key figure in the Venezuelan branch of the radical Islamic group Hezbollah.*

Jack already knew five of the six were located, found to have been equipped with plastic-explosive bombs disguised as propane tanks, and neutralized, so he read further down the page.

One van arrived in Boston. Boston JTTF conducted extensive surveillance, and found this van in the custody of Ishmael Jama'a, who is a Syrian national enrolled at Boston University. Unemployed, he lives in an apartment complex, home of many international students. Seen driving the subject van to and from classes and a local mosque, he uses the name Stan.

Jack's eyes rushed to find the conclusion. *The Chicago JTTF is requested to determine from its original source any information about the ultimate target for the disabled Boston bomb."*

As if it singed his hand, Jack dropped the thing, offended by the author's simplicity. Didn't that agent know if Chicago JTTF had access to the original source, they would have already supplied the target? It reminded him that Gordon said he would ask Headquarters to contact their source, but never told Jack what he found out. Perhaps his weekend brainstorm would provide the targets—cities hosting NFL games that matched the vans' locations.

He quickly read two more reports, from Tampa and Nashville. In both, FBI terrorism task forces were watching the vans, each in the custody of foreign students. Unlike Boston and Nashville, the one in Tampa was a female from Panama.

Jack blew out his breath. Hezbollah made incredible inroads not only into South America, but within America as well. In five days, they had to find that missing van!

In seconds, Jack grabbed his report about his new theory and started keying in more info, detailing what the vans looked like, white, camper-types, and tall enough for a person to stand inside, making them easy to spot in a parking lot. For each, he supplied the VIN and to what he had already written, he now asked each city to see if the temporary plates had been replaced, and the vehicles re-registered in the new states.

He was typing fast, but his fingers could not keep up with his brain. Jack made many corrections. Finally, his report contained the most up-to-date information and he raced over to Gordon's office hoping he was in. Jack needed his initials before he sent the message out to each of the five cities, and the other ten cities hosting home games on October 28.

"Boss, each of the five vans is still in the possession of foreign students going to universities."

Gordon was on the phone, but hung up after he saw Jack. "Any leads on the missing one?"

"None, but I thought of a possible way to narrow our search."

Gordon stared at Jack. "Well?"

Blood pounded in Jack's ears; he just might have cracked the plot. "Five vans found by the FBI in five cities, which all have home games on the last Sunday of October."

His boss responded with a blank look, so Jack helped him to see his point. "You know—football games. The dismantled bombs were set to go off at noon out east and eleven o'clock in Dallas and Nashville. Imagine these vans parked at tailgating events."

Jack said no more. Gordon turned into a man of action, bolting out of his seat and reaching for his suit coat. "I want your report ASAP. I'm telling my boss."

He was through the door before Jack could catch him. "Here, I have one for your signature."

Gordon grabbed it, kept going. "Great work McKenna. Great work."

USHERED INTO THE ATTORNEY GENERAL'S conference room, Eva took in the elegant décor, dark-stained wood, and painting of George Washington. Before her Presidential appointment to head the Justice Department, Alexia Kyros was U.S. Attorney in Northern Virginia and created Eva's Virginia task force, which resulted in the two women getting to know and respect each other.

In the stately room, Eva felt the gravity of the moment. Her friend and mentor once recommended Eva for management. Now as AG, Alexia oversaw the entire Department, where she ensured that federal prosecutions were just. Earl and Griff stood with their hands at their sides, looking awestruck at being in this inner sanctum of justice.

Moments later, Alexia arrived wearing a beige suit and pearl necklace. In gray slacks and blazer, Eva felt outclassed, but wardrobes had no bearing on what she was about to share with the Attorney General. Eva collected her thoughts as she and the agents took seats around the massive mahogany table, Alexia at its head.

She nodded to Eva. "Agent Montanna, I read your report detailing how Harding and Associates use former law enforcement and intelligence agents to gather intelligence on individuals from various countries, including the U.S. I understand there is something new. Be succinct. I have a White House meeting in twenty minutes."

All heads turning toward her, Eva seemed unperturbed by the reserve in Alexia's tone, and handed the AG a manila folder marked "Classified." Alexia slid out a multi-page report.

Arms folded on the table, Eva began. "Griff Topping, the FBI agent on our task force, just returned from an undercover visit to Almaty, Kazakhstan, which Harding and Associates believed was to recruit him to leave the Bureau in order to run part of their operations. I'd like him to summarize."

Alexia also knew Griff from his work on many federal cases on the Northern Virginia task force. She nodded for him to proceed.

Griff cleared his throat. "Philip Harding is formerly Assistant Deputy Director of Intelligence at the CIA, founder of Harding and Associates. His company, CamelotConnection, uses a secured web site through which a small cadre of privileged clients submit requests, and receive, via express air parcels, their product. An efficient scheme, it attracts little attention. Top executives spirit the proceeds into foreign banks."

His silence was Eva's cue to explain legal and political aspects of their investigation. "The court-ordered wiretap on the Camelot web site reveals six Senators and more in Congress use it, some legitimately, others not so. That includes Committee Chairs in both the Senate and House. Ranking members with any influence have accounts, as do large corporations and media bigwigs."

Alexia tapped Eva's summary report. "You contend several foreign governments use Camelot to spy on opponents and perceived enemies."

"That is why we," with her hands, Eva included Earl and Griff, "asked for this meeting today. The repercussions are staggering."

Not one to run from political fall-out, Alexia's normally placid face bore a look of pain. It had not been easy for Eva to hear what Griff reported, but she had come to terms with the next step.

Alexia now asked something to which Eva had no answer, yet. "Do we have evidence to prosecute for unlawful eavesdropping or a civil rights violation?"

Eva shared the Catch-22. "Harding and many of his staff were formerly CIA and much of their information is sold to the CIA. If indicted, their defense attorneys would subpoena classified records. The Agency, citing national security, would refuse to comply, and we'd be forced to dismiss the cases."

She turned to Earl. "IRS agent Earl Simmons is working on possible income tax violations. Harding has carved out a complicated system. It seems even the FBI paid him to provide the Bureau with information, which ultimately led to prosecutions of defendants. The problem is some of those convictions were based on illegally obtained evidence."

Alexia lips formed a red line and Eva knew what she was thinking before she asked, "How many convictions will we lose when we disclose illegally obtained evidence? The numbers could be staggering, *if* there is any way to find out how many cases are involved."

Griff addressed her question. "Madam General, in casual conversations with colleagues at the Bureau, they tell me intelligence they get from Harding's group is so good, arrest and conviction statistics are way up. It may not be as bad as we think. FBI Headquarters feeds the information to field offices, referring to it as a 'confidential source,' and the agents do develop their own probable cause to make arrests."

Obviously shaken by the news, Alexia asked Eva, "Who else knows of this?"

Not daring to look at her watch, sure that the allotted twenty minutes was about to expire, Eva said, "Deputy Shepherd and our task force. The question is, how many government officials know the information they are paying for is the fruit of the poisonous tree? I am sure the FBI does not; they believe they are dealing with informants."

Alexia tasked the DAG with a mission. "Dean, have our legal counsel research the Patriot Act, for any leeway to use this kind of information against terrorism. Our national security is at stake, which is different from using improper evidence to catch white-collar criminals. I have gone before Congress and the nation, lauding successes in keeping them safe. It is untenable we may have violated their rights to protect them. This could frighten the American public, and that we will not do needlessly. No one outside this group will know of our discussion. Is that clear?"

As the four others around the table agreed to secrecy, Alexia stood, and so did they all. "We meet again on Friday. Keep Dean posted as to what you learn on the wiretap. Meanwhile, we need to close this Camelot operation down without violating the Constitution."

"Oh!" Eva nearly forgot. She pulled a document from a thick file and handed it to Alexia, already on her way out. "It's an application for a wiretap for Philip Harding's office and home phones. Mr. Shepherd has signed and we need your signature."

The room was quiet for some minutes as Alexia read the summary page. Eva handed her a pen, and to her relief, the AG scrawled her signature on the last page. "If this fellow is as smart as you say he is, I doubt we will get anything incriminating. As you requested, my approval is for two weeks only."

While Eva got her order, she had been an agent long enough to sense this might prove to be her trickiest case yet. She wished to avoid having to testify before the Senate Intelligence Committee and become another witness skewered on the point of a political sword. Griff and Earl followed her to the elevators, silently, as if reading her mood.

Eva lived her life, made her career, by being honest in the face of trouble, and she was not about to change now. If only she could confide her worry to Scott, but that would be cheating. Tonight, when she got home, she would ask him to pray for her. Eva had no doubt he would, without asking why.

THIRTY FOUR

Wednesday evening crept up on Kat. She'd spent a chaotic day with Ian trying to find and interview FBI agents retired from the Chicago office. She filmed their reactions to claims that the mafia put out a contract to kill President Kennedy in Chicago at Soldier's Field during the 1963 annual college all-star football game.

When Ian suggested they get dinner together, Kat turned him down. "I'm bone tired and will just pull an apple and glass of milk from the fridge."

Ian laughed. "Well, I'm still on duty anyway."

It was starting to drizzle, so he hailed a cab for her and then drove off in the live truck. The taxi speeding north on Michigan Avenue, Kat stared out a window smudged with raindrops, and turned her mind to Zorn's tapping of her phone.

The deadline Kat gave Eva and Jack was fast approaching, but she had mixed feelings. While it was light enough to see other drivers, their eyes glued to the cars ahead of them, she found their racing along an apt metaphor for her life and the revenge she once wanted against Zorn. As much as she hated to admit it, it seemed that her desire to hurt him was not so intense.

Along Lake Shore Drive, she glimpsed Lake Michigan, and examined the why. Sure, time had passed, but that never stopped her from holding a grudge before. No, it was something else she felt. What it was eluded her. She did know that never again could she admire the beauty of the lake without a chilling reminder of Elliot's crash into those waters.

Before his accident, Kat never thought about her goal for living, except to be the best television reporter, and achieve fame for her major stories, as Laurel had. Then, meeting Jack, questions about her future multiplied in number and intensity. None of her past relationships were that serious; she had never been in love.

The taxi entered the circular drive and she wondered, *Am I in love with Jack?* Without plans for the evening, Kat stepped from the cab, in no particular hurry. She passed the door attendant and headed straight for her mailbox. Letters in her hands, and computer bag over her shoulder, she snapped out of her reverie when the attendant said, "Ms. Kowicki, your phones should be working again. I saw the repairman leave your condo."

Kat spun around so fast, she felt dizzy. "What did you say?"

He turned to face her. "This afternoon, they fixed your phones."

Puzzled, she said the obvious, "There is nothing wrong with my phones. I didn't authorize anyone to fix anything."

"Well, I saw him." The attendant turned away to help an elderly woman coming in with an armful of packages.

Alone in the elevator, myriad questions ran through her mind. Did Elliot have someone sweep her place today? True to his word, he had the locks changed, but she was certain that he would have mentioned it if anything else was going to be done in there.

Kat's hand trembled even putting the key in the lock. She was half-scared to turn it, afraid she might startle someone snooping inside. Who or what would she find? She pushed the door open slowly, expecting to see a mess. When Kat flipped on lights, nothing was askew. Tentatively, her eyes swept the living room, and rested on the ugly lamp, which she never would have purchased.

The lamp! Each day she had turned on the wall switch controlling it and its twin. Now with the news of a stealth phone technician, that hideous beast seemed an old friend whom you could count on in the worst of times, all because of FBI Agent Griff Topping. When he checked out the phone wires in the basement, it was his idea to install that lamp and another equally bulky one in her study.

Kat had watched as he and Jack installed the lamps containing hidden video cameras. Griff promised it was a perfect way to tell if anyone entered her home without her permission. Her fingers still shaky, she leaned over to inspect the lamp made of glued seashells. Jack and the agent had plugged the lamp into an outlet controlled by a wall switch, unscrewed the light bulb, and instructed Kat to throw the switch "on," when she left her condominium, so it could photograph any activity in the room.

This evening, she intended to find out if Agent Topping's idea worked. Jack had been distracted lately, so instead of calling him, she went to the safety of the lobby, and with her throwaway cell phone, called Ian. When it came to technical knowledge, he was a genius; his nose was always in the latest computer gadgets. Ian had told her that he once applied for a federal job, but for some reason landed in television broadcasting.

Careful not to reveal her suspicions, Kat stressed it was urgent. Bless his heart; Ian came right over. Single like her, he had no family commitments to entangle him after he got off work. She met him just outside her condominium door, in the hallway. He arrived in his work gear, green rain slicker, jeans, and a wider smile than when he left her a while ago.

Ian's windblown hair stood up straight from his scalp, but he was ready to help. "At your service. What's up?"

She nearly laughed at his comical appearance, and his presence calmed her battered nerves. Kat spoke in a hushed voice, "Someone has been in my place. I think they installed listening devices, because not one drawer is disturbed."

Ian raised his eyebrows, and Kat led him to the lamp in the living room. In total silence, she removed the shade, turned the lamp upside down, pulled off the felt pad and showed him how the base unscrewed. Inside it, they found a tiny digital video recorder and pinhole lens.

Ian looked in wonder, his lips mouthing, "Wow!" He whispered in her ear, "Turn on the radio to mask our voices. I saw that in a movie once."

Kat selected a CD to play in her portable player. To an old Beatles tune, Ian explained quietly, "This motion detector is wired to the recorder, so when the lamp senses movement in the room, it turns on and records for a set amount of time. That must be why they told you to turn on the switch when you left the room. Otherwise it would record you drinking coffee and mundane stuff, and use up all its memory."

Griff had explained some of it to her, but somewhat technically challenged, Kat forgot exactly how it worked. She pulled on Ian's sleeve as a signal for him to bring it with him and follow her outside the entry door. In the hallway, she gaped over Ian's shoulder at the gadget. "Do you think it recorded the telephone guy?"

Ian turned it over. "This is too cool. I've never seen anything like it." He found the playback switch. The three-inch screen flickered to life, showing the inside of her living area and closed entrance door.

Although they were in the hall, Kat whispered, "Back it up some more."

When he did, they saw a man walk to the door, his back to the camera. "We need to rewind it," Ian said and hit the button. "That's him leaving your place."

She felt icy cold, her mind heavy with worry. "No one has been inside my condo except me, certainly no man, in case you wondered."

"I hear you, Kat. What kind of bizarre story we working on here?"

Kat's stomach flipped, as if she had just dropped a hundred feet on some carnival ride. Oblivious to her emotions, Ian rewound it while in the play mode. Kat saw the video reversing and suddenly a man walking backwards from the study and out the entry door.

"Stop it there," she cried. "Can you see his face? Who is that creep?"

Ian switched to play. Instantly, the same man, wearing a hard hat, entered her condominium and walked in. He stopped for an instant and then went right to her study, as if he knew where to go. She studied the tiny screen. "It looks like he has on an ID badge. Can you read it?"

"Not really."

"The lamp in my study has another one of these recorders."

Instead of moving, Ian turned to stare at her. "What secret things are you into that you have two hidden cameras? Are you working for the CIA or NSA?"

Ian's question made Kat laugh despite her fear, and that helped dissolve tension she felt in her neck, her shoulders. She doubled her fist, slugged his shoulder. "No, I am not working for the National Security Agency. Sometime I may tell you the true reason. Until then, you have to promise you won't tell anyone, not even Elliot Tucker."

During the next half hour, with Ian's help, Kat disassembled the other lamp. In the second video, the technician searched through her desk, even her wastebasket, but took nothing. Watching him remove the faceplate from the receptacle on the wall near the floor, her heart pounded so hard within her, she felt it would leap from her chest.

Ian shut off this second camera, walked over to the same receptacle. With a screwdriver, he removed the faceplate, pulled the outlet from the wall and unscrewed some wires. With Kat trailing him, he did the same thing to outlets in the living room, and one in the bedroom. Neither of them said one word until Ian was finished.

"Okay, it should be safe to talk. The fake phone guy replaced your electric receptacles with these small transmitters. Even though they still work as wall plugs, every word you said in here would be transmitted to a receiver and recorded somewhere nearby."

She should have followed her instincts to move out of the condo. New locks weren't the answer after all. Now, in her living room, she felt exposed, uncovered from head to toe. If it had not been for that attendant casually mentioning her phones being fixed, she would have never discovered an invader was in her house, planting transmitters.

On wobbly legs, Kat dropped to the sofa. "At least I found out right away. Ian, what should we do?"

He stood there, hitting his palm with the screwdriver. "Call Elliot? We do work for him, after all, and he's got to know people in the right places."

"I suppose so." Her mind seemed frozen in place.

Ian sprinted toward the door. "I have an idea. You could stay here, or come with me to get an adaptor from the truck."

Kat practically jumped off the sofa. Together, they went outside to the truck, where Ian got his equipment. Rain poured from the night sky, an open faucet. Thirty minutes later, faces toweled off, Ian and Kat studied the burglar on the larger screen of her laptop computer, Ian having copied the data from the recorder memory card into it.

Hair a mess, and jaw hanging open, the sight of Ian made Kat laugh, but her friend stared so intently at the screen, he did not seem to hear. "Looks like he's a real telephone company employee, after all, or at least he's doing a good impression of one. See the logo on his ID tag. You need to call the company."

Kat made up her mind what to do. Once she did, her will replaced fear. She now had an iron determination to prevent this scheming and spying from hurting the lives of other innocent Americans. "No, I have another way of handling this. Thanks for your help. When I expose it all, you can be the photographer, if you want."

Resolve must have showed on her face, because he wrote down his home number. "Whatever is going on Kat, give me a shout. I'll be right here with you."

She memorized his number, handed him back the slip. Ian reassembled the two lamps, and put electrical tape on the exposed wires in each receptacle. He promised to buy new ones and install them tomorrow. Three transmitters now in her hand, she walked Ian to her door, where he fidgeted for a minute. "Kat, if you need a place to stay, my mom is alone 'cause my Dad's on a fishing trip."

Touched by his concern, Kat had other ideas. "I am calling a detective friend about this."

"Be sure to change the locks if you mean to stay here."

Not thinking of that proved her mind was not as clear as it should be. "Maybe I'll call from the lobby and stay there until he comes."

Down in the lobby, Ian waited while she called Jack. It was amazing, but this time he answered. "Jack, if you could stop by. I've had a visit from a burglar."

"You're kidding."

Kat raised her voice. "No, I am not. Someone in my building saw a man leave my condo today, claiming he fixed my phones. My phones work fine, except for that one little problem you know about."

"Big John and I are playing a game of checkers, but he will understand if I need to help a lady in distress. Besides, he's winning. If it's okay, I want to see if my friend Lenny, who found your tap in the basement will meet me there. Where are you calling from?"

Not wanting anyone else to come, Kat hesitated. Still, if Jack needed Lenny, she could not say no. "I'll meet you both in the lobby."

"Is a guard or anyone there with you?"

Kat smiled at Ian. "Yes, a friend from work stopped by."

"Good. Have her stay with you until I get there. Is there a chance you can stay with her tonight?"

Inwardly, Kat chuckled. Jack assumed she had a woman friend over. Once she deceived him, not again. "Ian shoots my specials. He offered to let me stay with his mother tonight."

She held her breath. How would Jack respond? He said nothing at first, and then, "I'll be right over."

Kat hung up, gracing Ian with a smile. "You can go now if you want. He's on his way."

Ian's youthful face was tense. "Are you sure?"

She assured him she was, so he walked out to the truck looking as if Kat had taken away all his fun. That was unfortunate, but she really did not want him around when Jack watched the video. Mainly because this would be the first time she had seen Jack since they got back from Pentwater, and there was so much to tell him. She only hoped Lenny would leave before Jack did.

LATER THAT NIGHT, Kat sat curled in a chair closely observing Jack and Lenny huddle over the recording device inside the now-dismantled lamps. Earlier, when she peered over Jack's shoulder, it upset him. "A little space would be nice," he hinted, so, eager to please, she perched on her chair, but continued watching from a distance.

Lenny wiped his brow and they kept tinkering. She could not resist leaning in to see what was taking them so long, but Jack warned, "This is confidential technical equipment."

At his caustic tone, which she rarely heard him use before, she stalked off to a different chair, completely out of his eyesight. Arms crossed, Kat decided *not* to tell him that she had already seen the video recordings with Ian. Thirty minutes before, when Jack arrived with Lenny, he'd not asked one word about Ian, which was okay. She was not trying to cause trouble. It was odd Jack never seemed to think of her as someone who ever had a date. Not that he ever asked either.

Remarkably, Lenny might have thought he was whispering, but his voice carried to her waiting ears. "I recognize Ken Kirby. He worked with me at the phone company. Now he does contract work like me. You probably can't see his ID tag, the picture's too small."

Kat heard Jack's reply, too. "We need to keep that memory card and put in a new one."

As if no longer interested in what they were doing, Kat pretended to doze off. After they reassembled her lamps, Jack was about to walk Lenny to the door when Kat uncurled from the chair and headed them off in her foyer.

"Well, guys, do you know who broke into my place?"

Lenny hid behind his big glasses, content to let Jack do the talking. "Kat, we won't know for sure until we see the images on a larger screen."

Kat began to do a slow burn. Jack McKenna, seemingly so honest and a gentleman, was once again withholding information from her. She turned to Lenny. "You might know him; he works for your phone company."

Lenny shrugged so hard, his glasses slipped down his nose. Kat tried a new strategy on Jack. "Maybe you could tell me more if you saw the larger image now."

She stepped over to her computer and opened it. "Before I called you to come over, I downloaded the memory card. On my enlargement, you can almost decipher the man's ID tag."

Within seconds, the man's image popped up on the screen and Kat froze the picture. "See, his name is Ken Kirby." She glared at Jack. "What do you intend to do about his breaking and entering into my home, let alone invading my privacy."

Lenny and Jack looked alternately from the screen to each other in apparent disbelief that Kat already knew what Lenny whispered to Jack minutes earlier.

Rising tension and Jack's failure to respond caused Kat to snap, and her mouth gushed freely, "If you two geniuses investigated thoroughly, you'd discover Kirby installed three transmitters, all of which Ian helped me remove from the electric outlets."

Jack shoved hands into jeans pockets, looking sheepish and very uncomfortable. "I have to find out who he works for. With this evidence, we have the upper—"

Without thinking, Kat cut him off. "How much time will that take?"

"Well, it's hard to—"

Again, Kat jumped in, this time at Lenny. "No doubt, you heard of Amber Alerts, where they flash on TV a picture of a missing child, so every viewer can help locate the child. Well, if by five tomorrow, you guys haven't reported some major progress, I'm going on TV with a Kat Alert, and your Kirby is going to be revealed to Chicago for the criminal he is."

Heat rushed to her face. She did not want to be so angry, but Jack just stood there, mute. Kat sought to soften her stance, without taking back her promise. "I may be a TV reporter and not a federal agent or cop, but if you or the FBI don't take what I have already figured out seriously, I must go public, for the safety of others."

Lenny ducked his head, as if dodging flying arrows, and made for the door. Jack escorted Lenny out into the hall. "Thanks, but for now, forget everything you saw and heard here tonight. I'll get back to you later."

Jack returned inside, but not very far. Kat's heart was bursting to wipe the hurt from his eyes. He did not let her; he built another wall, a higher one meant to protect his professional dignity. "Kat, I promise to work quickly. You have to promise not to interfere or act prematurely. If only I could tell you what is on my plate right now, but I can't. If you don't feel safe here anymore, maybe you should move."

With that, Jack turned on his heel toward the elevator. Pride welled in her heart, the kind that said she was right and he was wrong, the kind that prevented her from calling after him, going to him. She stood by her door, listening. The elevator bell rang. The doors closed, leaving Kat to realize that she and her impulsive mouth just lost the best friend she ever had.

THIRTY FIVE

After Jack left her standing at the door, Kat locked it, but that once-reassuring act now did nothing to make her feel secure. It took her all of three minutes for her to realize she was either going to stay with Ian's mother or find out if Elliot was home. She threw a few essentials into a pink canvas bag and then stuffed Big John's file of research and her laptop computer into a small rolling suitcase. The thing was heavy, but she intended to pull it behind her from now on, wherever she went.

She rang Elliot. His line was busy, which meant he was home. Kat kept on several lights, locking the door behind her. A short elevator ride to the top, she knocked at his gilded door, feeling more like a refugee than she did when she flew to Chicago from Washington. Kat flirted with the idea of going to Pentwater but, driving alone so far at night seemed foolish. Instead, she pressed Elliot's doorbell.

Elliot's housekeeper, Maggie opened the door, held a finger to her lips. Her hair was sculpted into white waves, reminding Kat of rolling whitecaps on Lake Michigan.

"Meester Elliot," she whispered, "he is on a call from London. It is your mother, but don't tell him I said this to you. My son is downstairs to pick me up. I must go now."

Kat promised. She liked Maggie, a refugee from Hungary, not just because she was a great cook, but also because they'd become friends. Maggie had been with Elliot since Kat was a teenager. As Kat slipped into the living room, Elliot thrust the phone into her hands. She pretended not to know it was Laurel, saying simply, "Mary Katherine."

In reply, her mother shared some astonishing news. "Kat, dear, I land Saturday at O'Hare."

Kat probed for all the details, her heart twisted with emotions. One moment, she was crushed, finding her place broken into and Jack stalking off, and the next, she was floating on air. Kat could not remember looking forward to seeing her mother with such anticipation. Laurel decided to stay with Kat, so booking into a hotel was unnecessary.

It was curious her mother should visit now when the world was swirling around her. A fraction of Kat's brain, the part that distrusted her mother, told her Elliot was responsible for her mother's sudden appearance. He always was adept at orchestrating her arrival for big events like Kat's graduation from high school and college, as well as her twenty-fifth birthday party.

Another part of her heart, the larger part that longed for love from her mother, rejected the cynical idea. After all, Laurel said she wanted to spend time with her daughter, and she acted upset just now when Kat told her about Ken Kirby. Elliot fumed about the break-in and insisted she stay in his guest room until her mother arrived.

By Friday morning, Kat woke refreshed and ate oatmeal with Elliot. To prepare for her mom's arrival, she drove to a health food store where she bought fresh fruit, veggies, ready-made lentil and minestrone soups and pita bread. She also stocked up on yogurt and several kinds of tea she thought Laurel might like. They could eat out often, but still, Kat wanted her to be comfortable.

As a treat, Kat felt giddy selecting a few extras. Back at her place, the locks changed again, Kat nestled goat-milk soap, peppermint oil for relaxation and a loofah into a gift bag tied with a pretty ribbon. She set the welcome gift in the spare bedroom, ready for Laurel to open and feel how much her daughter cared for her, despite years of distance.

Fresh sheets on the beds, Kat grabbed a cold water bottle from the fridge, letting her mind go neutral for a change. Maybe she had time to review her final research for the special on the JFK Assassination. To be ready to air it in a little more than a month, before the anniversary on November 22, they were shooting some of it in two days. Kat had taken video in Dallas and Ian had photographed the retired FBI agents in Chicago.

Jack had no idea how close she was to exposing the truth. He had not called, nor had she permitted herself to call him. Something had changed in their relationship. This summer, they talked nearly every day, and Kat grew used to asking for his ideas about decisions, listening to what went on with Winston and his dad.

Such memories stirred deep feelings for him. Loneliness creeping into her heart, Kat acted on impulse and called his house. If he answered and seemed aloof, she could always pretend she had called for his dad. After all, she wanted to tell him of her latest discovery about the Cuban general. Also, through a source in Mexico, she gained permission to look at official records from 1963, including Oswald's visit to the country.

Jack's answering machine came on. Kat tried to sound upbeat, asking either father or son to call back. About to hang up, she added, "Jack, my mom is—"

The memory must have been full because a dial tone buzzed in her ear. Kat clicked off the prepaid cell. Her shoulders heaved with a sigh. With one last look at her timeline for the documentary, she closed that program and clicked over to pay her bills online. If she took care of them now, one less thing would divert her when Laurel arrived later. Kat so wanted her mom's undivided attention.

On her bank's homepage, she typed in her user name and password, having selected new ones when she opened her checking and savings account in Chicago. Kat paid bills for her charge card, rent, and student loan. She still owed twenty thousand on her loan and that, with interest, would take more years to pay than she felt like counting.

Kat logged off the checking account, and for no real reason, opened her savings account, knowing she had three thousand dollars in it. Wait a minute! She blinked; she must not be seeing right. No way did she have that much money in her account, not now, not in ten years. Blue numbers against the white screen made her head spin. She must be going crazy. Her balance showed, not $3,000.00, but $103,006.22. Impossible!

As fast as her fingers could move, Kat scrolled down, clicked on "Account Activity." Yesterday, a deposit went into Kat's bank account for $50,000.00. Another deposit went in today for the same amount. It must be a huge mistake.

A sinister idea occurred to her tired mind. Was it a payoff of some kind, and, if so, from whom? Kat guzzled her water, searching her mind. She heard of defendants paying hush money, but the criminal cases she worked on—wait—Kat was covering the city corruption case. Beasley, the Public Works Supervisor, kept a double set of books and had several secret accounts.

What would he have to gain by paying her off? The State's Attorney filed fraud charges last week, and Kat possessed no new threatening information to convict him. This must be another dirty trick by Senator Zorn; a payoff for the supposed tape she had of his illegal activity. Since he bugged her phone, and she had transcripts proving he did that, he hired people to bug her apartment looking for the real proof she had on him. This extraordinary amount of money suggested that somehow, Zorn must have found out that she and Jack had caught Ken Kirby.

What Jack was doing about that, besides keeping secrets from her, she did not know. How could they ever get past the distrust? She knew that he, a Chicago cop working on federal cases, had an oath to keep. The next thought brought a tinge of sadness. It was becoming clearer that Jack held her profession against her; felt she was untrustworthy. If she told him about this money in her account, he would do nothing about it.

Yet, she had to do *something*. This latest act proved it was bigger in scope than Zorn was. He was crafty, but it was improbable he would risk his public career by brazenly depositing a bribe in her account, which was easily traceable to its source. Maybe this money stemmed from her planned documentary about the Kennedy assassination. The Cuban general, Raul San Felipe, was still alive, that much she had found out. What did he want her to do, keep quiet about proof of the second gun used to kill President Kennedy?

When she and Elliot entered the general's name on *Camelot,* while they were never able to access anything, the people behind the search engine could have traced the request, knowing what she and Elliot discovered. If so, did he receive money as well? Maybe Big John did, too, and that was why Jack was being secretive and distant.

If the money was a bribe, it was criminal, and she *should* tell Jack. Then her mind switched gears, convincing her to wait until her mother arrived. Kat was so confused, but finally she decided that Laurel had been a reporter for over twenty-five years and would have some idea what Kat should do about a possible bribe not to report on a story.

Despite these thoughts assailing her, Kat realized that every second the hush money stayed in her account she was part of some terrible cover-up. No, she could not wait to do something about this bribery, pay-off, whatever it was.

Kat remembered her third account, the one she set up to pay for *Camelot* requests, and for which they had her password. With the push of a couple buttons, she transferred the entire $8,447.29 into her savings, leaving the third account at zero. Initially, she felt better; *Camelot* had no password for her savings account. Then her heart sunk. How could she be so naïve? The people at *Camelot* knew where she banked. It would be easy for them to deposit money even if they did not know the exact number. Besides that company, only she and Elliot knew where she banked.

In the morning, she would call the bank and demand to know who made the deposits. If they refused to tell her, or claimed they did not know, she would move her meager sums to another bank, leaving the dirty money alone until she discovered the truth. For evidence, Kat printed out the page showing the deposits.

Thankfully, Elliot answered her call; he was still up. After telling him she had new ideas for the Kennedy documentary, he invited her upstairs to talk it over. Twenty minutes later, wheeling her suitcase of evidence behind her, Kat found him planning a surprise party to celebrate Laurel's return after being overseas the past two years.

Thoughts of assassination evaporated as the two of them created an invitation list of who's who in Chicago, and a few friends from Washington. Happy at the thought of Laurel coming home, she confessed, "I never guessed your sending me back here would lead to our reunion."

That seemed to please Elliot, and for a while, the idea of being with family eclipsed concern over money burning up her bank account, with Kat even offering to call the caterer.

With the back of his hand, Elliot covered a yawn. "I am sorry, but it's been a long day. Are you staying in the guest room tonight?"

The thought of the payoff in her bank account came roaring back, giving her the creeps. "I'd like to." She thought to tell Elliot about it, but instead he asked how her script was coming for the special on John Kennedy. "Sure you want to hear about it yet tonight?"

"Yes. I'll put up my feet."

She told him about Deputy Sheriff Craig's testimony of Lee Harvey Oswald running from the back of the Texas Book Depository and getting into a Nash Rambler station wagon. "I found records of other witnesses who saw something similar, and spoke several times with Elaine Greenburg, a researcher who used to work for the CIA. She emailed me a copy of the Warren Commission Document, number 5, which the Warren Commission omitted from its twenty-six volumes. She—"

Elliot interrupted, "How did Greenburg get it then? Did she remove CIA records? I won't air anything illegally obtained."

At his hostile reaction, Kat chuckled. How could she have ever thought he was behind the phone tap? Elliot Tucker was the original Mr. Clean, earning his money the hard and legal way. "Nothing like that. A different researcher discovered number 5 in documents housed at the National Archives, and Elaine got a copy. Anyway, it reveals an FBI report of an interview on the day after the assassination containing the eyewitness account of Marvin Robinson. He was driving west on Elm Street at the time of the assassination."

On a piece of paper she took from Elliot's desk, Kat sketched out the streets running along Dealey Plaza. "Kennedy's motorcade was traveling north on Houston Street, and made a sharp, some say it was ninety-degrees, left turn onto Elm Street, which is where the President was shot. After the shooting, I don't know how many minutes later, Robinson approached the Book Depository. Just like Deputy Craig, he saw a light-colored Nash station wagon pull to a stop in front of the Book Depository. Then, a white male walked down the grassy incline from the building and got into the station wagon that drove off."

"Did Robinson ever identify Oswald as that man?"

Kat wrote this down. "That is a good question. I'll try to find out. It seems to me the Warren Commission ignored any witness who failed to support Oswald as the lone gunman."

A strained look on his face, Elliot picked up her drawing. "On November 22, 1963, I was in my office at a LaSalle Street brokerage firm. When I heard the news, I was shattered to think something so brutal could happen in America. After Jack Ruby shot the assassin, my mind closed that chapter, and I paid no attention to the Warren investigation. In our special, I want to tie up loose ends. Let's interview your German filmmakers if we can."

Caught up in Elliot's enthusiasm, Kat remembered another witness who saw a man get into a Nash Rambler. "Elliot, this witness said the Nash was driven by a dark-complected man. And the white man he saw get into the car was stocky and wore a hat, sport coat, and glasses, which is not like the slender Oswald. Of course, Oswald allegedly went back to his room where he had time to change clothes."

"I want to read the newest assassination books. Can you make me a list?"

She nodded. "Here's something else. Deputy Craig witnessed Oswald in the police captain's office after his arrest. It seems not a single officer took notes or recorded what Oswald said in those interrogations. I find that negligent and highly questionable."

He slapped his knees, grunting as he stood. "I agree, however, it's time for my green tea. I'm eating and drinking healthier these days." Elliot walked into the kitchen and turned on the electric teakettle. "Let me tell you what things were like in the mid-sixties, before the advent of crime shows. Americans were different then, believed in the government. Even most in the media swallowed the official reports."

Kat wondered what she would have done if she had been a reporter in Dallas covering the story. In the photographs of Oswald's shooting in the basement of Police Headquarters, she had not seen any women reporters. Most likely, she would have been typing pool reports.

The kettle whistled and she got out two ceramic mugs. "I'll fix the tea. You should rest."

He obliged and, when she returned to the living room, Elliot was staring at her hand drawn map. Kat gave him a cup, leaving hers to cool on a coaster. She sat next to him on the sofa. "I combed the records detailing the covert aspects of Oswald's life. You probably know he was discharged from the Marines after serving more than three years, but the way he achieved it and how he got into Russia led Big John McKenna to believe Oswald was already working for our side, maybe Naval Intelligence."

Elliot arched a brow, looking surprised. "Why?"

As she tried to compress all she learned, Kat rifled through her memory as if turning back the pages of a history book. Too tired to retrieve the file from her carry-on bag, she winged it. "I talked to a source who worked for the U.S. Naval Intelligence back then. He confirmed Big John's theory. During the Cold War, some claim Naval Intelligence actively recruited soldiers to fake defections to the Soviet Union. Oswald was stationed in Japan at a U.S. airbase that tracked the secret U-2 spy plane."

Elliot interrupted. "Kat, from what I remember, he was thrown in the brig for fighting and basically washed out."

Kat shook her head. "There is much more to Oswald. Not only did he have prolonged absences from his unit, he arrived in Russia speaking the language quite proficiently."

She told him how Oswald got a passport in short order, lied to the Marines about needing to take care of his mother, and stayed with her about one day before sailing to the USSR. "Someone in authority had to know the true reason. Oswald was supposedly poor, yet he traveled across the globe and had an Intourist visa, which was like having an expensive stateroom on a cruise ship. Who do you think paid for that?"

Elliot sipped his tea, seemed lost in thought. "You raise valid questions. Get me a book on this background as you've outlined it."

Kat did not have to think too hard. "That would be *Crossfire: The Plot That Killed Kennedy*, by Jim Marrs. While Oliver Stone relied on his book to make the JFK movie, when I read it, I didn't agree with all of his conclusions; neither did Big John. Want to come with me to get it from my study?"

"Sure. The problem with our documentary is going to be narrowing down what we want to say. Will you interview John McKenna on air?"

"I plan to."

"Then I want to invite him to Laurel's party, along with his son. That should give me a chance to meet them both."

Unsure that was a good idea, Kat tried talking Elliot out of it. He insisted, so Kat offered to make those calls herself. Elliot interrupted her thoughts of Jack with an unusual subject. "Since I was saved from the air crash, I have been attending the same church my pilot Mark went to."

Suddenly, his voice broke—no doubt over the death of a good friend. Kat stood up, rubbed his right shoulder. "Elliot, it was an accident. I hope you are not still blaming yourself for his death."

He wiped at his eyes. "No, I turned my grief over to God, who determines the length of our days. I actually read that in the Bible."

Elliot was reading the Bible. It took a minute to absorb the news, but, given his miraculous survival and recovery, she guessed it was not strange.

"Kat, I feel responsible for helping his family, so I do what I can. Not deserving it, I have found incredible peace in God, whom I never knew. Something you said about deceiving Jack, that you were sorry, made me think you might want to join me Sunday."

A protest sprang from her lips, "Elliot, I am thankful you are alive and did not die in that crash. With so much evil around us, I have a hard time believing there is a God. Look what happened to Mark."

Tears in his eyes, Elliot patted her hand. "I felt the same way once. To me, God has become real. That is faith I guess, and is why I ask you to think about your life and its meaning before it is too late for you."

While she had no understanding of his faith, the warmth of Elliot's voice made her feel special, and she had to find a way of letting him know. Kat had not seen much of him lately; she'd been busy chasing Jack and unnamed assassins. With the eyes of her heart, though, she saw Elliot was a changed man. Before she could tell him so, he was on his feet, walking to the door.

"We'll get your book. As far as Sunday, it would make me happy if you came to church. Before the crash, I was a proud, ambitious man, caring about you and Laurel, but no one else. I did not mind collecting a few enemies and I am still making amends."

"You are?"

Elliot unbolted his entry door. "Last week, I settled a lawsuit with a professor who slandered me."

She walked out ahead of him and, locking the doors behind them, Elliot told her something she would think about later in his guest room, when she had trouble falling asleep. "Kat, I am no longer willing to spend whatever time I have left on earth fighting folks in court. If you give it a chance, your life, too, may never be the same."

Did he mean her life would change because her mother was coming tomorrow? Laurel's arrival was more reason not to go church. She explained this to Elliot, hoping he would drop the subject. His face held such anticipation that she could not let him down.

"By next Sunday, Mom should be settled in. I will go with you then."

As if the Queen had just knighted him, Elliot's face beamed, filling Kat with joy. Still, when it came to organized religion, it might be smarter not to give in. She had seen little evidence of a loving God, only misery and pain. A not-so-small voice in her head chided her, *wasn't Elliot saved from a terrible crash?* Kat pushed the thought away as she would a strand of hair in her eyes. Elliot was lucky, very lucky.

THIRTY SIX

For Jack, something had to give. With his days and nights consumed with finding the explosives-laden van, he couldn't focus on Kat's problems. He wanted to help, but he didn't have the time. And that's where things turned ugly.

On his way to pick up Ricky Vasquez, he turned on the car radio, looking for some tunes to block Kat and her eavesdropping issue from his mind. Tense enough already, he turned it right back off when a newsbreak came on about a twenty-car wreck on the Kennedy Expressway. He popped a stick of red licorice in his mouth, trying to forget what Kat did the night she called him to her condominium to investigate the break-in. Not only did she keep vital evidence from him, she nearly took his head off.

Kat was complex. Still adjusting from his break-up with Melissa, he had no appetite for another rocky relationship. He appreciated that Kat was helping his father. For that, he owed her. If there was a conspiracy behind Kennedy's death, which hadn't been brought to light in all these years, then it should be. The records Big John found of a second Mannlicher-Carcano rifle were compelling evidence of a second assassin. If that gun truly was the murder weapon, Jack wanted Kat to verify it while Dad was still living.

There was something else to ferret out. If the electronic surveillance of Kat resulted from Dad's records that he turned over to her, then he had a duty to look after her welfare. Was it Zorn, as she thought, or someone else? That someone in Kazakhstan was recording her calls—suggested something bigger, a conspiracy with international scope.

Like most good cops, Jack didn't buy into the existence of unsolved conspiracies like the general public was prone to do. Seasoned investigators knew that someone usually talked. But with what Kat had brought to light, he started to think it might be possible that in 1963—at the height of the Cold War—an international conspiracy was behind the murder of an American President on the streets of Dallas.

He pulled into Ricky's driveway and idled the engine. Where was Ricky? It looked like no one was home. Jack wanted to tap the horn for Ricky to get a move on. If they missed Kirby tonight, that would mean another day with no good news for Kat, and he was starting to think she was cracking under the strain. And he had to solve this now, so he could focus all his attention on the terror case.

What he felt for Kat was more than friendship, but beyond that he refused to go. With all the pots boiling, he had to prioritize, and right now that meant keeping in touch with the FBI task forces in the five cities. They were monitoring the vans and the student drivers, and nothing seemed extraordinary. Fact was—they all gave him credit for his idea of the football stadiums being the most logical target.

FBI in Boston reported that Stan kept to the same daily routine. They searched his trash, found no clues. Jack and his boss had talked it over that morning over coffee. It was very possible these five students would drive to different cities on Sunday and detonate their bombs at zoos or shopping malls. So the brass at the top had ordered no arrests until the time the disassembled bombs were set to explode. That way the FBI could prove the bombs' intended targets.

The waiting was getting on everyone's nerves, especially Jack's. It was all so frustrating he sounded a short burst on the car's horn. "Come on Ricky," he muttered.

The missing van could be in any other city where NFL teams were playing on October 28, from Oakland to New York—and a bunch of cities in between. Jack had notified all of them to be on the lookout. He gnawed another piece of licorice, calculating how impossible it would be to find one vehicle in all those cities.

Ricky flew out of his house, zipping his jacket. "Sorry, I got stuck in a jam up on the Kennedy."

The one Jack had heard about on the radio no doubt. Instead of giving him grief, he handed Ricky a licorice stick, and twenty-five minutes later the two detectives parked on North Lakewood Avenue waiting for Mr. Kirby, the intruder caught on video, to arrive home. With Lenny's help, Jack had determined Kirby, a former phone company technician, was the man in Kat's condo who installed three audio transmitters which sent every word she spoke to a recording device somewhere in her building. Jack had these devices safely in his computer bag in the back seat.

While they waited, Ricky asked for more candy. "Think our guy figured out we're on to him?"

Jack grunted, "I hope not," and tore into a new bag; it looked like it was going to be a long night. "I sat on his house yesterday. He should be home any time."

In this neighborhood of three-story walkups, Jack expected Lenny's former colleague to roll down the street, and park parallel on either side; there were no separate driveways. Over the years, this part of Jack's job became routine. Snatch 'em unexpectedly and give 'em less time to create a plausible story. You never knew, though, if a suspect would pull out a gun and try to escape. He saw that plenty of times, too.

Time dragged on. It got darker; streetlights came on. He and Ricky finished a whole pack of licorice while they discussed every angle of the terrorism plot they were working on together.

Jack adjusted his seat to get more comfortable. "I think the missing van will show up in either the eastern or central time zones because those were the only two zones set on the dismantled bombs."

Ricky checked his watch. "Where is this guy? I guess you're right. It makes no sense for a bomb to go off at nine in the morning in Seattle or Oakland. Stadium lots would be empty."

Restless, Jack shifted in his seat. "Maybe Kirby made plans for the evening and we'll—whoa—over there!"

Headlights of a car parking maybe a hundred-fifty feet behind them shone in Jack's rearview mirror. "That's him."

He nudged Ricky's leg with his foot, cueing him to get ready. Kirby got out and started walking toward his house. In an instant, Jack and Ricky bolted from the Chevy and approached the same man in Kat's video—only this close he appeared much older, his face lined from smoking. Cigarette smoke clung heavy on his clothes, even outdoors.

With two men rushing him, Kirby came to a dead stop on the sidewalk and glanced around for an escape. Jack walked up, badge out, and snapped it back in his pocket before Kirby knew what was happening. "Detective Jack McKenna; this is my partner, Detective Vasquez."

Ricky flashed his badge, as well. Kirby held his palms open, friendly, and grinned at the detectives. "What's this all about?"

"You're under arrest for multiple charges. Put your hands on top of your head."

When Kirby complied, Ricky stepped behind him and placed his own hands on top of Kirby's. Jack pulled open the suspect's jacket, looking for a weapon, finding none. Ricky took Kirby's hands from his head and slid them behind his back, into handcuffs. As they moved

Kirby to the rear seat of Jack's car, he asked to go into his house and tell his wife.

Jack snapped,"It doesn't work that way, Ken. You'll get a chance to make a phone call after we're through booking you."

He got behind the wheel and drove to the 20th District Headquarters. Ricky sat directly behind Jack, watching the prisoner and making sure he did nothing funny. As they escorted Kirby into the station the man shook so violently that Jack thought he might confess without much bother.

He was wrong. It took an hour to process and fingerprint Ken, and the whole time the man said nothing, except to ask for a smoke, which Jack refused. After a while, in the drab interrogation room, with no ashtray, Jack sensed Kirby softening by the trauma of his arrest and no smokes. The prisoner sat across from him, his eyes bloodshot as if vessels had burst.

Maybe it was time for Jack to really squeeze him. "I notice you haven't asked us why we arrested you. Think maybe that's because you knew this day would come sometime?"

Kirby kept his mouth shut, so Jack began probing in earnest. "You probably realize we haven't asked you any questions, either. Nor, did we warn you about your rights to keep silent." Jack lightly tapped the table with the flat of his hand. "That's because we don't need you to say anything to help us convict you."

The man stared straight ahead, occasionally blinking those red eyes at Jack, who was just getting wound up. "Two days ago when you unlawfully entered Katherine Kowicki's condo, you left something behind."

Knowing it could grease a confession, Jack pulled the transmitter from his computer bag and plunked it where the prisoner got a good look at it. Now Kirby flinched. His denials, however, could not have been firmer. "I don't know the woman you're talkin' about."

Jack scraped his chair along the floor until he was three inches from Kirby, who continued to protest, but this time his voice had a tremor, like a taut string about to break. "Never been in her condo, and never saw that thing over there."

Ricky leaned against the gray wall, arms crossed, watching Jack straddle the chair, sitting backwards, with his arms folded across the chair's back.

Jack leaned closer to Kirby, now invading his personal space. "Look Ken, I'd rather you say nothing to me, or maybe 'lock me up, I have nothing to say.' Because if you sit here and lie to me, you embarrass yourself, and I have no confidence in your story. Later, if you decide to testify against the people who hired you to commit this burglary, I first have to tell the judge, jury, and the attorneys about the lies you're telling me tonight."

Jack slid off the chair and perched against the edge of the table. "We see you as a low-level helper, hired by someone else to install," Jack picked up what Kirby left behind, "this bug in the lady's place. We want you to tell us who hired you to do it."

He stopped for a second to watch Ken's eyes, but not long enough for him to answer.

"Now, I know you're trying to figure in your head how much evidence we got, if you left any prints on the bug, and how many years you're facing. Let me help you. We are charging you with burglary, that's a good beginning, right, Detective Vasquez?"

In a flash, Ricky was in a chair right next to the detainee, whose eyes flickered around the room like a dying light bulb. "That's right, Detective McKenna. Ken should know we're on a federal task force. If he doesn't tell us who hired him, then we'll charge him with a bunch of other crimes like illegal eavesdropping and violation of civil rights in Federal court, where the sentences are pretty stiff."

Where Ricky left off, Jack picked up, and Ken's head bobbed in a circle. "You're probably looking at a good twenty-five years if the state and federal sentences run consecutively, plus the lady will probably sue you. Your family will lose the family home. While you're doing time in the pen, your wife will have to live with relatives."

Kirby shifted his chair, twisting his thin body as if uncomfortable. Jack walked over to the laptop computer that he had set up on the other end of the table. "Oh, I forgot to answer one of the questions you haven't asked yet: Do we have enough evidence to convince a jury? Let me show you this, see what you think."

Jack adjusted the computer screen so that Kirby had full view of the show. There was no mistake about who was walking around in Kat's condo and wearing a phone company ID photo tag. After showing him a quick view of the incriminating pictures, Jack turned off and closed the computer.

"Here's the way Detective Vasquez and I see it. If you tell us who hired you, we will press the Assistant U.S. Attorney to come up with a plea deal, maybe get you probation instead of hard years in prison." Jack let sink in what he was offering, "Or, you protect your bosses with silence. That way *you* face all the charges and do all the time. Would the guy who hired you take heat to protect you? You decide."

Jack stood and picked up his computer and the bug. "Detective Vasquez and I are going to get us a cup of nice, hot coffee. You sit here and think about your future. You want us to bring you back a cup?"

Kirby shook his head and dropped his eyes, saying nothing to either of them.

IN THE 20ᵀᴴ DISTRICT LUNCHROOM, Jack poured two coffees; put a buck in the honor can. Ricky sipped coffee before launching into a speech about Kat, which Jack found a tad awkward. "I've seen Kat Kowicki on the news. She is a feisty reporter. Not hard to look at, either. Seriously Jack, do reporters make enough money to live in the high rent district where you found the transmitter?"

The thought of Kat, pointing at him in her hallway, was enough for Jack to throw up a roadblock. "I don't really know her well enough to even guess about her finances. I'd say her mother has money."

Ricky studied Jack for a moment, "I hope Kirby talks, because I'm curious to know why someone bugged her condo. Do you suppose it's one of those love triangles?"

The very idea of it caused Jack to think back to what Kat said about a relationship gone sour, with the anchor named Randy. The name Ian popped into his mind—the guy she said was over there helping her. When Jack arrived, he had already gone. Really, he knew very little about Kat's social life. "I suspect it's related to a story she's doing."

Of course, Jack said nothing about the JFK angle or his dad's evidence. Ricky finished his coffee and tossed the foam cup in the trash. "Ready?"

He looked so eager to get back to questioning Kirby that Jack hated to douse the flames. "Give him a few more minutes to stew about life behind bars. Tell me what's new with Pablo."

Ricky bought another coffee, his two quarters clanging in the can. "He's a little too quiet for my liking."

"Think he knows the whereabouts of the missing van?"

Ricky shrugged, and Jack decided it was time to see how Kirby was holding up. With Ricky a step behind, Jack sauntered in, finding their man sitting pretty much as they left him, only his head had collapsed on his folded arms.

Jack sat across from him, and read the Miranda rights. "We don't have much time left. What is it going to be, help us or go to prison big time?"

Kirby lifted his head a few inches from the desk, a mournful expression on his face. "Buddy Smith, a retired ATF agent first hired me. We freelance for an operation outside the country. Buddy calls the guy he works for Flip, but I never met anyone besides Buddy."

Jack wanted to give Ricky a high-five but he kept his composure, leaned close enough to see gray and red whiskers on Ken's chin. Getting the names was only the beginning. "Why is Buddy or this Flip targeting Ms. Kowicki?"

Ken was biting his lip. "I never know who or why. I am just told to put bugs in homes or to tap the phones and where to divert the calls."

There was more to it, Jack knew. For the next hour, he and Ricky took a signed statement from Ken Kirby, who not only installed the first phone tap and the transmitter in Kat's condo, he also installed the phone tap at Interstate Van Conversions, plus seven additional ones around Chicago and northern Indiana. His confession in writing, they booked him and began the process for someone to get him out on bond in the morning.

In the hallway, Kirby wrung his hands, shuffled his feet. "You know, if Buddy Smith or the Flip guy find out about my arrest, they will be none too happy."

Jack tried to assure him. "There won't be much chance of publicity, the way Detective Vasquez and I have it planned."

He did not explain to Ken that all too many times arrestees such as Ken just got swallowed up by the system. Sometimes even convicted murderers were released, their paperwork lost. Kirby's arrest was a small blip on the radar of the Chicago justice system, but it could be huge for advancing the case against the eavesdroppers. The question was, how long could Jack keep his arrest from Kat?

That was no simple question and one to which Jack had no easy answer. He had something else in mind for tonight that did not involve tangling with Kat. He and Ricky talked it over and decided with Kirby's confession Jack should send the Interstate Van's electronic device to Griff Topping for FBI fingerprint analysis. That just might lead them to the identity of Kirby's mysterious "Flip."

Jack forged another plan in his mind. First thing in the morning, he'd show Ken's statement to Gordon. There was no way Jack was going after a retired ATF agent without sanction by higher-ups. Anxious to uncover the full extent of the bugging conspiracy, which he and Ricky had dubbed "The Gold Coast Caper," he was not crazy enough to take on a hornet's nest single handedly.

EVA MONTANNA AWOKE EARLY the next morning, and anxious to see if any new evidence developed overnight, she sped along I-66 an hour before the HOV restrictions began. In her office, sitting behind a surplus desk on a surplus chair, she waited impatiently for Earl to finish doctoring his coffee. Each day she approached her office, she wondered what others at Main Justice thought of the unmarked door with its sophisticated lock and alarm system. Alexia Kyros had demanded that no one except Deputy Shepherd and Eva's agents know of their presence or purpose.

"Earl, how much sugar are you going to put in that cup?"

She didn't hear his answer. Her mind drifted to the remnants of the recurring dream that had awakened her at 3:00 a.m. for the past two nights. Lost in Bern, Switzerland, she roamed all over a building complex, even driving her car up and down a set of steps. Now, to keep alert, she guzzled her fourth, and by no means last, cup of coffee. She liked it full-strength, and had little patience for those who weakened it with additives.

Even though her dream bordered on the bizarre, she had experiences in the past where, no matter how hard she studied physical evidence, her dreams provided insights into cases she was working on. Rarely were they obvious clues, so she kept mulling over the meaning of the current dream. Yesterday, while driving to the office at four in the morning, she recalled that *Camelot* executives had numbered Swiss bank accounts. So, the first thing after arriving at work, she'd asked Earl, who was on the night shift, to comb his mind, his files, to find some connection to Switzerland.

"Eva?"

There was Earl, standing in front of her, holding his thermal coffee cup in one hand and a load of documents cradled in his other arm. He was all smiles. "Your idea was brilliant. I forgot about the conference I attended last year in Switzerland. At a session about Internet fraud, I met a guy named Claus who works for the Swiss government, Police Liaison Office."

He carefully dumped the stack on the edge of her desk. "You want to know how we can pay this new informant?"

The IRS agent wedged his cup in between the stack. "Before you say there's no way to do that, let me tell you that he's an invaluable source for this case and future ones. Remember when taps on Philip Harding's phones and the Camelot web site revealed debits from customer accounts into bank accounts in Switzerland?"

Eva grabbed her ever-ready legal pad, started taking notes. "Go on."

Earl removed his glasses, rubbed his eyes. "A long night. Anyway, how this came together is amazing. I gave Harding's account name and password to Claus, who confirmed that not only does Harding have a very active account at a Swiss bank, so do most Harding and Associates employees."

He put his glasses back on and frowned. "He claims he's not permitted to tell more."

Eva leaned back in her chair, wondering what was next. Surely, Earl did not want to pay anyone for such minimal information. He could not be ignorant of U.S. laws prohibiting bribes to officials in sovereign states, and Claus was such an official. On a previous case they'd come up against a federal judge who didn't believe one of Earl's affidavits. Aware how that criticism had stung the agent, Eva proceeded gently. "We cannot do what you're thinking of."

Animated, Earl waved his cup in front of him. "Wait for the rest of the story." Eva nodded for him to continue. "Okay, Claus is not his real name. It's how he wants it, but I have his full name written up in here." Earl tapped his folder. "Anyway, Claus called me last night on some kind of prepaid phone."

"Yes?"

"I was monitoring Harding's personal wire and did not want to be distracted. Claus stressed it was urgent. He has experience in Fedpol—their Federal Office of Police—and is familiar with Swiss banks and banking laws. Eva, he is retiring and going to work for a private company that consults with Xenon Bank in Switzerland, which handles *all* interbank fund transfers."

Earl was onto something, and Eva's pulse began to race. "If Claus helps us obtain evidence against our Mr. Harding, what does he want in return?"

The IRS agent, who made a career of tracking finances, slid forward and spoke quietly, "You won't believe how brazen he is. Claus wants a percentage of whatever money he helps us recover from Harding's criminal conduct."

Before Eva could object, Earl selected a folder from the large stack. "I told him we would have a hard time paying him money if he insisted on keeping his identity a secret."

The agent snapped his fingers. "He's agreed to become our confidential informant. I am to fingerprint and photograph him in Bern. Then we'll find out, once he's retired from government service, if he can provide anything of substance. I filled out the forms to make him an informant and just need to process him in Bern."

Still skeptical, Eva took the folder from Earl. "Before we send you off to Switzerland, did he give you a precise idea what he might provide us?"

"When I tried to pin him down, he was evasive; kept saying Swiss laws are strict. Before I hung up, he hinted he could do something. I say Claus is smart enough to realize, no help, no moiety."

Eva's phone rang. "Earl, I'll lock this folder in my safe for now. We'll talk later."

She answered a call from Jack McKenna, trying to find Griff. He told her, "We arrested Ken Kirby, a retired phone guy who installed some audio-transmitters in Kat's apartment."

"Is he connected to the transcripts she received in the mail?"

Jack's reply was swift. "My supervisor approved a search warrant for the retired ATF agent who hired him. We're going up the chain. That's why I need Griff."

"He went home to get some sleep after pulling an all-nighter. Can I help?"

"If you could pass it along, I'm about to execute that warrant."

Eva told Jack where to send the device he wanted tested and hung up, relieved that Jack had not asked about their investigation of Senator Zorn and Harding & Associates. A professional never would and nothing he'd done so far led her to believe he was anything but professional. She looked at her notes, thinking what an asset Jack would be to her team, if only he lived near D.C. But it was unlikely she could lure him away from Chicago where he was a second generation Chicago cop. Loathe to wake Griff, she dialed his number. Sleep was a luxury they couldn't afford right now.

THIRTY SEVEN

Laurel slept away most of Sunday and Monday after her long flight. Today Kat took the day off. At the Field Museum, mother and daughter enjoyed ancient Egyptian pottery together. It was a perfect setting, not too intimidating after such a long separation, yet it provoked a lively discussion. Laurel liked the fossil exhibit, while Kat could not stop staring at two wild-eyed stuffed lions, known as the man-eaters of Tsavo, which had supposedly killed scores of people many years ago in Africa.

Laurel unbuttoned the olive-colored trench coat she always wore on newscasts and fanned her face with a museum brochure. "Whew, I was not prepared for this heat. Kat, are you determined to get home, or do we have time for a ride to Grant Park? I would love to see the fountain. It's been ages."

Kat had not visited the beautiful Buckingham Fountain since one spring night when she and her classmates strolled from the Hilton Hotel, in tuxedos and prom gowns, to watch its marvelous display. Her smile to Laurel, the woman she once called Mommy, was genuine. "Let's do."

Laurel tapped the cab driver on the shoulder. "Buckingham Fountain, please."

The cabbie, who had told them he was a refugee from Afghanistan, shot out in front of a tour bus barreling down Lake Shore Drive. Kat squeezed her eyes shut, waiting for the inevitable sound of crashing metal. When nothing dramatic happened, she opened them and looked at her mother, who until a few days before, she had not seen in more than two years.

Her face was serene. Laurel's eyes gazed past Kat toward Lake Michigan. "When Elliot was in the hospital, after the plane crash, I told you he would survive."

The cab jerked suddenly to a stop, slamming both women forward, striking hard against their seat belts. A space opened twenty feet ahead, the driver jumped on the gas and, without warning, careened toward the curb.

Laurel tossed a twenty-dollar bill at the driver and elbowed Kat, "Get out quick, before he kills us."

No sooner were the two women safe on the sidewalk than the cabbie pulled away, nearly crashing into a woman wheeling a stroller.

Laurel slipped her arm through Kat's and the two women laughed as they walked toward the fountain. "I doubt he ever took driver's ed. How could such a creature get a license to operate a taxicab?"

Being this close to her mother was a lifelong dream that Kat never really expected to come true. She vowed to savor this moment for the rest of her days and felt a twinge of regret for the way she had greeted her mother at the airport a couple days before. The first words out of Kat's mouth were, "How nice of you to come see me, Laurel."

Laurel's eyes showed the hurt that Kat's cool remark had inflicted. But her mother didn't criticize her for not calling her Mother. She simply enveloped her daughter in an enormous hug and whispered in her ear, "I am so proud of you."

On the ride to the condo, Laurel had squeezed Kat's hand and told Kat of her travels. Then yesterday afternoon, over lentil soup and toasted pita bread, Laurel opened up in surprising ways. "I would have come months ago, but I was following a story I absolutely could not leave. An influenza outbreak ravaged an orphanage and, because of the caste system in India, the head mistress could not get medicine. I worked with a church group to help them get antibiotics."

When her mother described the tremendous needs of those abandoned children—how after the outbreak, no one would go near the place to bring food or fresh water; how Laurel called in favor after favor to bring in equipment to dig a well, plant a garden and fruit trees—Kat cried in her mother's arms. The chasm between them bridged, this wonderful afternoon was their new start on the future.

The whole world seemed right for a change, and Kat walked happily beside her mother up to the fountain. "In the cab, before we were nearly turned into roadkill, you said you knew Elliot was going to survive. At the time, you implied it wasn't because of what his doctor told you, and I wondered what you meant."

Before them, sparkling water mingled with brilliant rays from the sun, casting tiny rainbows that floated away. It was cooler here, so Laurel buttoned up her coat, and Kat zipped her fawn-colored jacket up to her chin. She spotted a bench away from the water spray and nudged her mom in that direction. "You can tell me about it while we sit. There's something else I want to talk over with you."

Minutes later, drinking in the warmth of the sun, Laurel took Kat back to a day last July, to the tiny Indian village, two weeks after the bacterial epidemic had done the worst damage. "Two girls died, one in my arms. Kat, she was four, too young to fight."

For the first time, Kat noticed more than a few gray hairs sprinkled throughout her mother's chestnut hair—evidence that experience must have taken quite a toll because Laurel was a woman Kat thought would never age.

Laurel dabbed her eyes with her palm. "A missionary from Australia, Marlene Boyle, has dedicated her entire life to this oasis for abused, unwanted children. Her face contains few wrinkles, even though she is close to seventy. When I complained about the conditions that I believe led to the death of these children, she said something so odd. Marlene believed that God, who formed them in their mother's wombs and planned the full length of their days, wanted two rosebuds for his Heavenly garden. At first I found her answer flippant, as if she had no regard for the grief I felt."

In Laurel's honey-colored eyes Kat saw something she hadn't seen there before, profound wisdom born from seeing the ravages of evil all over the world.

"Mom, it sounds so hard for you. To think you were going through all this when I ran away to Pentwater, feeling miffed because Elliot transferred me. I understand now why I rarely heard from you."

Sorrow did not leave Laurel's eyes, yet they held something special for Kat. "I should have called more often, but I was stuck in a bleak place. Fortunately, we are together now." Kat squeezed her mother's hand, "Ready to head home?"

Laurel had more to tell. "Marlene came by the house where I was staying and brought me a Bible. I will never forget her handwritten note encouraging me to read the one verse she marked. It was just two words—'Jesus wept.' I wanted to know more. One night, by the light of an oil lamp, I read about Jesus's life and really grasped for the first time—his miraculous birth, the way he healed the sick and demonstrated forgiveness, and his death on a cross."

Her mother drew both of Kat's hands in to hers. "That was the night before Elliot's crash. In the wee hours, before dawn, something broke in me. It is hard to put into words, but I was convinced I needed to know Jesus. I am not sure why I did it, Mary Katherine, but I knelt on the straw mat, closed my eyes and told God I needed him. I told him something else, too, that I was sorry for neglecting you."

Kat pulled back her hands. "You didn't *neglect* me."

Laurel's voice was so soft Kat had to lean close to hear. "Yes, I did, in many ways. Your mother put herself, her career before you. In that house in India, I saw myself as God did, bereft and in need of a savior. Such peace came over me, knowing he forgave all the wrongs and hurts I committed. When I went to sleep that night, I dreamed you and I were in Pentwater, you were running from Lake Michigan toward me, and as I hugged you, I heard Elliot say, 'I lived long enough to see you two together at last.'"

Fascinated, Kat wanted to know what happened next. A faraway look came into her mom's eyes. "My dream ended and I woke up with a powerful sense you and I would be reconciled. The next day, I learned Elliot was in the hospital. Somehow, God spoke to my heart and I had a clear sense Elliot *would* live to see us together. That afternoon, I was supposed to fly home, but the flight to London was canceled due to terrorist threats."

Kat's heart filled to overflowing, she now knew there was a spiritual dimension to life she'd never found because she'd never looked for it. All she managed to say was, "At the time, I was surprised you didn't get on another flight, do whatever you could to come back and see Elliott."

Laurel agreed. "By the time I could get out, Elliot had regained consciousness, but I learned that Marlene was deathly ill. I went back to nurse her, to keep her alive."

Until now, Kat had no idea what had been going on in her mother's life, or anything of her grief, her despair. It was almost too much to bear, sitting on a bench in Grant Park, with young kids running around and a baby crying some distance behind them. She felt chilly and wanted to get home, make tea.

Kat had always seen Laurel as independent, a woman who always relied on her own strength, and she wanted to be what her mother was. But now, with all Laurel had said, Kat began to wonder what her mother's transformation would mean for her.

BACK IN KAT'S LIVING ROOM, they warmed themselves with mugs of hot tea. Laurel, appearing more rested since her arrival, set her teacup on an end table, next to the ugly lamp. "The JFK special you are doing sounds intriguing. I know better than to ask, but how did you find this new evidence?"

Kat was not about to keep confidential sources from her mom. "I was contacted by a Chicago police detective who I met long ago, at a school dance."

Laurel's painted eyebrows came together, spoiling her relaxed look. "Don't remind me how many years ago that was. I missed it because I was on assignment in Bosnia."

"I know." Kat reached over, rubbed her hand. "I'd like to tell you about Jack. He is a few years older than I am, but he went to the prom as his cousin's date. She was in my class." Thoughts of Jack and his blue-blue eyes warmed her more than tea ever could. Her mind veered from JFK to wondering what Jack was doing.

"Kat?"

Her mom was staring at her, brows raised and a tender smile on her lips. Kat waved her hand in front of her face nervously. "In my special on Kennedy, you'll meet Jack's father. Right after the assassination, he helped seize the records for the purchase of Oswald's gun, along with a record showing a second, identical gun was purchased from the same supplier in Chicago, which the authorities back then ignored. He's a retired Chicago detective who everyone calls Big John. He had a mild stroke on the same day as Elliot's plane crash."

Ever perceptive, Laurel crossed her legs and leaned back on a red silk pillow. "So, you and Jack both had to deal with almost losing someone close to you, just as you were getting to know each other."

Kat felt her cheeks grow hot, but she smiled brightly. "We're just friends, Mom. Anyway, Big John accumulated lots of evidence and has some excellent theories of what happened. I'll tell you more as we get into preparing a script. I'm so glad you'll be working on this with me. I want to learn a lot from you."

Laurel looked teasingly at Kat. "Does this prom date have a last name?"

In answer, Kat strolled to the kitchen, took hummus and celery sticks out of the fridge and put some on a plate for each of them, taking time to find her equilibrium. Jack had not called in days. She felt, rather than heard, steps behind her on the tile.

Laurel snuck up behind and reached around her to snatch a plate. "This looks delicious, just what we need to tide us over until dinner with Elliot."

Kat crunched a stalk before saying, "His name's Jack McKenna."

"Elliot said you're spending time with Jack. What are his particulars?"

Baffled as to how to reply, Kat didn't.

Laurel pointed at her with a piece of celery. "Come on, you can't play coy with me. You know what I mean. Is he available, and worth having?"

Laurel sounded like she was after a story of her own. How to describe Jack, when he'd left her heart in knots? "Mom, he has a boxer dog named Winston and is the nicest man I have known." Kat's mind stumbled to find the words, "He, um, got left at the altar earlier this year."

A cloud crossed over her mom's face. "Be careful. Those kind can be quite needy."

At that, Kat had to laugh. "You don't know Jack. If he's needy, he hides it well."

Uncomfortable with her mom in interview mode, Kat changed the subject. "When Elliot agreed to let me create this special, I was thrilled. It's my first complete piece. The more I probed into the official story, the more Elliot and I realized there are those in authority who want to keep a lid on the truth. Many of the same fears that infected the 1963 investigation still exist today."

"Are you referring to the tap on your phone?"

Instinctively, Kat lowered her voice. "Yes. I first believed Senator Zorn wanted to silence me. Now, I think it is possible that former, maybe even current, government officials are trying to impede my Kennedy research. You know, Mom, shadowy cover-ups then and now."

Laurel put her dish in the sink. "With all you're facing, I'm glad I got here when I did. Elliot wants us to close the documentary with me interviewing you. I like the idea—do you?"

In spite of her concerns, Kat giggled. "I suggested it. We secured the Armour family library at Lake Forest Academy for the setting. To return *with* you to a place where I spent much of my teenage life without you is more special to me than even doing the program."

Laurel put her hands on Kat's shoulder. "Honey, it's meaningful for me, too."

She hugged her mom, feeling loved and cared for. And for the first time in years, she could love her mother back. In Laurel's next comment, Kat felt her mother's concern for her and keen interest in their joint project. "I wonder how many in your audience will know about the details of President Kennedy's assassination. It happened over forty years ago. We have time now to go over some details of what you are planning."

Kat's mind raced. Where had she put her file? She hadn't given it a thought the entire afternoon. She remembered it was in the suitcase, in her bedroom closet. "Be back in a sec."

To Kat's horror, the file was *not* in her bag. She pulled off the blanket she had thrown over her laptop computer. Her eyes grew wide. It, too, was gone! She ran to the hall closet, her second hiding place, shouting, "My computer is gone. The whole file, too."

Laurel came immediately from the kitchen to help. "Where did you put it last?"

Kat's brain felt trapped in glue. She had to think. Having her mother here was great, but their talks kept her from work. "Last night, I shut it down after checking my emails."

"Where did you put it, Kat? Calm down, we'll find it."

She was anything but calm. "What if Zorn or his cronies broke in here again?"

Before Laurel could react to that, Kat dug her cell phone from her purse. "I'm calling Jack." Oh no, his voice mail clicked on. Should she leave a message? At the sound of the beep, she vacillated, and then said, "Jack, call me right away. It's important."

Meanwhile, she saw her mom opening cabinets and cupboards. "What am I looking for, one of those black computer bags?"

Beside herself, Kat set the phone on the counter. "Yes! Mom, it's the record of the second gun shipped from Klein's Sporting Goods. At least Big John still has a copy."

Someone was after her and the evidence. That someone had to be Zorn, who wrote the letter rejecting Big John's proof of a second gun. A shudder ran up and down her arms, and Kat rubbed out the giant goosebumps.

A loud bang startled her and she jumped, turning to see Laurel shrug her shoulders. "Your cookie sheet on top of the refrigerator slipped out of my hands."

Kat ran back to the bedroom, and lifted up the bedspread. Maybe she put the computer bag and file under her bed.

"Kat," Laurel called, "I think you'd better come back to the kitchen."

Now what? Had she found some new eavesdropping device? Kat dropped the spread and hurried to find Laurel pointing to the oven. "You better look in there."

The way she said it, Kat didn't want to. Slowly, she opened the door, looked inside, but it was all black. "I don't see anything."

Laurel clicked on the light inside the oven. Kat could not believe her eyes. Her computer bag was in the oven!

She rolled her eyes at Laurel, "I forgot. I must have put it here for safekeeping." Kat leaned over and pulled. It was heavy and did not move easily over the rack.

Her mom shut the door while Kat searched her bag. "I hope everything is in here!" In moments, her fingers gripped her laptop, and then the file. Both were safe. Kat let out a deep breath. Her cell phone buzzed on the counter and she grabbed to answer it.

It was Jack, who launched into an apology as soon as she said hello. "Kat, sorry I've been incommunicado lately. It's my work. You sounded stressed on your message."

Kat backpedaled, regained her composure. "My mom is here from India. We're talking about my TV special."

She returned Laurel's wink with a faint smile. Her mom was not supposed to know about Elliot's party. Careful not to give anything away, Kat walked slowly to her bedroom where she whispered, "Elliot is having a surprise celebration Saturday for my Mom. Can you and your dad come? I called to invite you both, but you never called me back."

When her question was met with silence, Kat worried that she might not see Jack again. His reply flooded her with relief.

"I'm sorry Kat, I meant to call, but I'm in the middle of the most serious kind of case." She heard the strain in his voice as he added, "I just had to put my life on hold. I am sure we would both like to come, but Saturday is a few days away. Anything could happen."

It would be wonderful to see him again. "Jack, it's for dinner, so it might give you a chance to forget your case for a bit. Elliot goes all out for these things. The best caterers in town. Bring Big John if you can. Elliot wants to meet him."

Jack hesitated before asking, "Are *you* all right?"

A small sigh forced its way from Kat's lips. "There's so much going on. The surprise party, my mom being here, working with her on the Kennedy special, the wiretapping. Oh, and on top of it all, Elliot invited me to church on Sunday, and I told him I'd go."

His reply was like the old enthusiastic Jack. "Great. Which one?"

"Forest Grove Community Church."

A whistle pierced her ear. "Get ready for a real crowd. That church has over twenty thousand attenders. Say Kat, is the party formal?"

She remembered how fantastic he looked in a tuxedo and was tempted to say "black tie," but then he might not come. "It's casual. See you soon."

"Sure you're all right?" He paused, and added, "I've missed checking in with you."

Was she reading more into that than he meant? Maybe tonight she would find out. "Since you asked, something strange happened to my bank account, and I'd like to tell you about it."

"I sensed something was amiss. Can it wait until your mom's party? I am really swamped, just now."

Kat swallowed her disappointment at having to wait. Yet, he sounded stressed and there was no urgent need to add to it tonight. "Yes. Are you sure you're all right?"

"Just extremely busy. See you Saturday; maybe I'll have news to share with you."

Reluctantly, Kat ended their conversation and went back to Laurel, who was now curled up in the living room reading Kat's JFK file. She looked up and, to Kat's immense relief, asked nothing about Jack. Her mother's instincts had probably told her that Kat wanted privacy to tell Jack something personal. Well, Kat did, but it was going to take more than a phone call to do justice to what was in her heart.

Laurel picked up where they had left off when Kat went on a wild goose chase for her computer. "Many viewers, like you, were not alive in 1963. But nobody who was alive then can forget exactly what they were doing the moment they heard about the President's death."

Kat eased next to her mom on the sofa. "What do you remember?"

"The shock is deeply etched in my mind. I was in the seventh grade. The janitor stuck his head in our room and, choking back tears, said someone shot the President. My teacher cried, all the girls cried, and the boys tried hard not to. I thought the throne of government, which at the time was called Camelot, was empty. Through a crisis of another kind in India, I learned God is on the throne and forever will be."

Kat did not know what to say. Thankfully Laurel filled the awkward silence. "Your piece is not going to be easy. Everything I have read suggests the official investigations were incomplete. President Kennedy rode in the back of the open limousine with the First Lady, and Governor and Mrs. Connelly rode in the jump seats ahead of them. There was a controversy over a last-minute change in the parade route. The Secret Service drove the President right past the Texas School Book Depository where Lee Harvey Oswald was working."

Just then, Kat felt a thrill at being the one to break wide open a mystery that plagued the country for decades. She leafed through her papers, finding the one she wanted. "After it was announced the President was coming to Dallas, Oswald applied for jobs at three different places, all along possible parade routes. He was prepared, no doubt helped by others, in his efforts to be employed and legitimately present along whichever route was selected."

"Where is that in your research? I was not aware of that."

Kat held a copy of *The Oswald File,* a book by British author Michael Eddowes. "All my research is not original. Some of Oswald's job applications are reprinted in here."

She handed the dogeared book to her mother. "Eddowes was a British solicitor who believed a KGB spy named Alek was the assassin. Alek was the name used on papers found in Oswald's things after he died. Believing Alek was an Oswald lookalike who took Oswald's identity, Eddowes worked tirelessly to prove it—even going so far as to have the body exhumed. When it finally was exhumed and confirmed to be Oswald's body, Eddowes must have been crushed. He died a year later. "

Laurel looked through the book Kat handed her, stopping to examine the employment applications. "This looks interesting. After dinner, I'll stretch out and read it cover to cover." She rose. "I suppose now is a good time to freshen up."

Kat grabbed her mom's arm. "Something else happened, just before you came."

Laurel looked deep in her daughter's eyes. "You mean *besides* your phones being tapped and the break-in? What is it honey?"

Kat was moved by her mom's empathy. She swallowed the lump rising in her throat and replied, "One hundred thousand dollars was put into my bank account."

Said like that for the first time out in the open, it sounded like a bombshell. Kat hurried on, "The bank manager refused to tell me anything. Claimed the money went in with no way to trace it. I know that isn't true. They don't care, they're just happy the money is in their bank. I pulled my own money from the bank and went to a new one."

Laurel seemed stunned. "Kat, I had nothing to do with it." She shook her head sadly. "I see you might think with my coming home," her words trailed off, until she took a deep breath. "Money cannot make up for what we've lost. But time and love can."

"Mom, I never for one minute thought you meant to buy my love. I think it's a bribe of another kind."

Kat told her mom about Senator Zorn, even producing the letter, which he wrote when he was with the FBI, rejecting Big John's second weapon theory. She explained how Zorn had kept that second gun order form. Mother and daughter talked it over and decided it was best for Kat to tell everything to Jack and do whatever he suggested about the money.

THIRTY EIGHT

A t three o'clock Sunday morning, while Kat and her mother slept soundly after enjoying the gala surprise party at Elliot's, Terry set up a tripod in his Evanston, Illinois living room on what might be the last day of his life before being transported to martyrdom. On it, he affixed a small video camera and prepared to film his last words. He wrote the script with great care and then changed into a silk shirt and tan slacks. For this event, he must look just right.

Camera on, Terry sat on the small sofa, looking at the camera while telling the whole world why he had to kill others. Righteousness of his cause shone on his face.

I am Abu Tarim. My mother and father have met their eternal reward. They will be proud to know their son did not pursue higher education for riches, but to pronounce judgment on a sick world, a world that oppresses others by its thirst for oil. Hezbollah has helped me see there is only one truth from one religion. Mission Red Moon will show the world that all those who refuse to be one of us will be killed. There is no other way. Allahu Akbar.

Terry walked out of view from the camera lens and shut it off. He looked at his watch. What he expected to happen next should happen in one minute. And it did. His prepaid cell rang once. Shortly a text message appeared on the screen: *It begins.*

Terry carefully erased the message, and replied to an arranged international number by typing in one word: *Ready.*

This same instant message he sent to his five recruits. Mission Red Moon, the holy mission, which he and Luis planned these many months, was ready to commence. All Terry had left to do was to say his prayers, which he did with greater vigor than ever before.

For the next two hours, he sat on his floor reading the Koran, as he learned at the madrassah in Saudi Arabia. When the time for reading concluded, Terry took it, along with his backpacks of contingency supplies, and locked his apartment door, giving no thought to whether any of his neighbors, international students all, would be hurt in the attack he was about to launch.

He passed apartment number three, occupied by two Japanese students. The girls never gave him any trouble, even inviting him over for a meal of rice and grilled tuna. To be polite, he had accepted, but was horrified to be in the same apartment as a statue of Buddha.

Since joining Hezbollah, he came to agree with the Taliban that blowing up the ancient Buddha statue in Afghanistan was the proper way to handle such evil. Feigning a sudden cold, Terry had fled their apartment without tasting any food. He even made himself sneeze on the table.

He hurried down the steps, past apartment number two, where a fellow Saudi lived. Terry went to mosque with him, but finding him too radical for his undercover role, he refused to talk with him again and walked past him without a greeting whenever they met in the hall.

Oblivious to the cold, Terry started his rental car and drove off, fallen leaves littering his windshield. One large leaf was wedged beneath the wiper and he stopped in the road to yank it off. Anger rippled through him. Even a one-second delay could ruin his plans, his mission.

Back in the car, he pressed hard on the accelerator to arrive at his first appointment. Outside the Lebanese restaurant Terry parked the rental in the lot and pulled from his backpack a pair of eyeglasses and leather cap. He put them on and then donned a black leather jacket. He tapped on the window, as instructed, and waved to the pretty, young Arab woman preparing food for the day.

She unlocked the door and Terry asked for his order. "You have my kabobs ready?"

On high heels, she clicked away behind a wooden door, leaving Terry with a bitter disgust at her modern dress. It was not right for an Arab woman to appear so western.

She returned pushing a shopping basket on wheels. "Twelve dozen beef sticks, twelve dozen lamb, all in coolers on ice as you ordered."

Yesterday, he paid cash for all of it, but she handed him a receipt anyway. Terry tried to smile. "I am sure my friends will enjoy them. Did you give me extra marinade to brush on during cooking?"

"That's in the bag. My father gave me some cards for you to place by the food. We appreciate your business."

His pretend smile long gone, Terry took the cards, shoved them into his jacket pocket. "I will certainly try to send customers your way. Goodbye for now."

Goodbye forever, he mocked inwardly. Once his food was stowed in the trunk, he stepped on the gas, staying close to the speed limit so the police would have no reason to stop him. A speeding ticket would not only put him behind schedule, it would provide a verifiable record where he was, at what time.

Back on the Edens Expressway, he drove to the storage facility, his mind reviewing how everything was in place. Excitement coursed through him—his dream was about to be accomplished! One thing remained, and that was to switch this rental car for the Dodge Sprinter van, where his cooker was all ready for its eternal use. Not a single person confronted him at the storage facility, which was perfect—the fewer people who saw him drive the van the better. He chose this location with care; it was en route to his final destination.

Terry threw open the metal door and quickly transferred the coolers full of meat kabobs into the back of the van. After locking the rental car, which had been rented through the end of the week, he hopped into the van and headed for the Northwest Tollway.

Once westbound on the Northwest Tollway, Terry processed his plan for the other five cities, fully confident that each of the six bombs would explode and that their blasts would take the greatest possible number of lives. Luis seemed pleased, telling Terry he would like to use him for greater tasks if he survived this mission. Terry timed it all and was certain he could. He drove to his destination with no fear. Even if he misjudged today he would become a martyr, living on in paradise.

Thirty minutes later, Terry pulled into the parking lot, so early that even those directing traffic paid him little attention. Men stood around with walkie-talkies and coffee cups, chatting with each other. As he trained the five others to do, Terry found a strategic spot to park and quickly slid open the large side-door, struggling to half-roll, half-lift his stainless steel cooker made heavier by two propane tanks filled with plastic explosives.

To cook the kabobs, he set up near his van. Beneath the cooker, there was a "T" fitting in the gas line that joined the two tanks and ran to the burners. Terry opened the valve on one of the tanks and ignited the burners. In no time, he had fresh beef and lamb kabobs grilling in the parking lot. As they began to sear, he readied his sauce.

GORDON HAD DENIED Jack's request to fly to Tampa for the football game and assist the JTTF in surveillance of the van. Disappointed but not defeated, Jack helped his boss coordinate efforts from Chicago's southwest side to find the missing camper.

Using Jack's memo, Gordon sent a general "be on the lookout" message to law enforcement agencies nationwide for a white camper van, stressing it might be in cities hosting NFL games. They cautioned agencies to guard details of the BOLO, so Americans would not be unduly frightened. Homeland Security raised the security level to Orange.

Jack's phone rang, and it was his Tampa counterpart on the line. "Jack, the female from Panama is being careful driving the van."

"Is she at the stadium?" By that, Jack meant Raymond James Field, where the Buccaneers were to play Jack's Bears this afternoon.

"Not yet. She just left her apartment complex. I'll keep you posted."

At his desk, littered with cups half full of stale coffee, Jack gnawed on licorice. His phone rang again. This call was from Headquarters, giving him an update on two other cities. Before the receiver was in the cradle, Gordon appeared, looking like he had not slept all night.

"What did you find out?"

Jack had never seen Gordon look so tense. "The two subjects in Boston and Washington, D.C. got up early and drove their vans to local mosques."

"That's it?"

He nodded. "Don't forget, Boss, these other five vans are harmless. FBI agents replaced the bomb tanks and timers with real propane tanks."

"How do I know that, this time, the satellite worked, and the terrorists didn't switch them back?"

That terrible possibility had occurred to Jack when he was driving home from Elliot's party the night before. One fact gave him comfort. "The JTTF in all the five cities have been watching those five students day and night."

Gordon grunted and stalked off, making it seem like it was Jack's fault the sixth van, the lethal one, could be anywhere, waiting to explode. For a brief time last night, Jack made small talk with Kat and ate cocktail shrimp, tried to be engaging. Even she sensed his distraction. When she mentioned that a whole lot of money showed up in her bank account, Jack thought he was listening. However, at this moment he could not remember what he told her to do about it.

He and Big John met Elliot, who graciously conferred with his dad over the Kennedy assassination. Jack thought Kat's mom was terrific, although they spent just a few minutes talking as she had many others to greet. Finally, the festive atmosphere wearied him. He tugged on Big John's arm and they left.

Of course, he could not sleep and, after walking Winston, jumped in the Chevy and came to the office, where he'd been ever since, agonizing over mental pictures of a live bomb detonating in any one of the NFL cities.

A message from Tampa was relayed from headquarters: The female driving the camper van headed straight for Raymond James Stadium. Instead of going there, she passed the exit! Agents followed her. The woman went north toward Tampa on 589, the Sun Coast Toll Road, and exited onto North Dale Mabry.

His licorice all gone, Jack chewed on the end of a number 2 pencil, the old-fashioned kind. He'd already bitten off the eraser. His stomach was pure acid from the pot of coffee he'd drunk in the last hour.

Suddenly a similar report came from the agent tailing the van in Washington, D.C. Instead of going to FedEx field, where the Redskins were playing the Eagles, that van zigged and zagged in traffic, south on the Capital Beltway like other Sunday drivers, until it veered suddenly onto Braddock Road near Springfield, Virginia.

Jack paced around the office, now plagued with doubts about his theory that the bomb was going to explode in parking lots at NFL home games. His mind acting like a video recorder on rewind, he reviewed every bit of evidence he learned during the investigation.

His phone rang. It was HQ, the duty agent, "The van in Tampa exited off the Dale Mabry."

"Where is she going?"

"The van is now entering a parking lot."

"A parking lot to a college, university, or what?" That seemed improbable. Only the NFL played football games on Sundays.

"I am getting that now, sir."

Jack's insides were a volcano, about to explode. "Quick, Man!"

"Yes, sir, I want to be accurate. Okay, the agents report it is an enormous church. The driver stopped the van, is saying something to parking lot attendants."

"Now what is she doing?"

He was only one cop, but Jack wished like crazy he was in Tampa right now and knew exactly what was going on. Removed from the action, he could only bite down on the pencil and wait, hoping the agent had his act together.

The duty agent came back, "She is driving her white van to the church entrance, parking it under a covered entryway."

A church! What better place to detonate a bomb than at a megachurch on Sunday morning? Jack yelled into the phone, "The vans are all going to churches! Put out the alert. Quick."

Jack threw down the phone. Out of nowhere, he remembered Kat mentioned she was going with Elliot to church this morning. Which one? His mind in overdrive as he ran to Gordon's office, he came up with it. Everyone in Chicago knew Forest Grove Community Church, where roughly twenty thousand people attended church during several services on Sundays. In the Chicago area, there was none bigger.

In his office, Gordon was on the phone. When he saw Jack's face, he asked, "What?"

Jack's words came out in a rush, twisting on his tongue as he battled the mind-numbing fear he would be too late to save Kat, Elliot, and thousands of people who could be hurt, or worse, in a bomb attack. What if he was wrong and it was some other church altogether?

"Gordon, the van in Tampa just pulled under the entrance of a mega-church. The camper in Washington, D.C. didn't go to the football stadium, either."

He could scarcely breathe. "Listen, I think they're headed for large churches where they can kill the maximum number of people."

Gordon dropped the receiver, jumped from his chair. "There's a lot of churches around Chicago!"

Unused to giving orders to superiors, Jack did not waste a second explaining. He talked all the while he was securing the Beretta in his ankle holster. "I'm racing out to Forest Grove. My foolish football theory may have cost lives. Their location has nothing to do with football, and we can't take a chance it's not right here in Chicago."

He pointed to Gordon's phone, checked for his extra ammo clip. "I could be wrong. Have Headquarters notify Homeland Security. They need to put out a nationwide BOLO for our missing van to be at large churches, *now!*"

Gordon picked up the phone as Jack kept talking. "We have less than an hour; there's not a minute to spare. Have Ricky and the others meet me at Forest Grove Community Church, ASAP."

Jack spoke over his shoulder as he thought of something else. "Call the security office at the church, and tell them to look for a tall white Dodge Sprinter van. If they find it, they need to get everyone far away from it."

In seconds, he was out of the building, hoping Gordon would get it all right. On the Eisenhower Expressway, he set his magnetic red strobe light atop the car and headed east to the circle interchange, then north on the Northwest Tollway, siren blaring. Soon he was in the extreme left lane, traveling in excess of ninety miles per hour and dialing his cell phone with one hand.

When Kat's number went to her voicemail, his alert level went way past orange. Obviously, if she was in church, she had it muted. Jack shouted above the wail of the siren. "Kat, there may be a bomb at church. Get everybody out! Avoid a tall Dodge camper van. It may be in there!"

THIRTY NINE

Terry finished cooking his kabobs and pushed his stainless cooker up the entryway to the three stories high Gatheria, a cavernous indoor garden where worshippers met near the coffee shop before and after services at Forest Grove Community Church.

By the door, a woman greeter smiled, but nodded at the cooker. "You can't cook in here with that."

Terry put on his friendly face. "I know." He tapped the flat surface of the cooker. "As part of your international student festival, I am serving Middle Eastern treats and will use the warming plate, that is all. I cooked them outside. Would you like to try some?"

The woman seemed satisfied. She asked the male greeter to open the adjoining door so that Terry could wheel in his cooker. He passed, and the man grabbed his arm. "Our college pastor, Ned Barnes, was here a minute ago asking about you."

At those words, Terry instantly started to perspire. The man's bald head wrinkled as he pointed, "He's by the table under the blue umbrella."

For what reason did Barnes want him? It was true that Terry had befriended one student who went to church here, only to have a cover for his coming and going at the church, while really he was conducting surveillance. Once at a student meeting, he encouraged Barnes to host the festival, but he pulled back from getting involved when the man asked too many questions about Terry's life and schooling. Determined not to allow the ever-curious Barnes to compromise his mission, Terry started to think how he could take him out. At all costs, he would not allow an infidel to stop him.

The watch on his wrist said it was nearly ten-thirty. The second service would be out soon. He intended to share treats with those leaving the service and be in position for the mob accumulating for the eleven o'clock service. Nearby, an Asian student offered little paper cups each holding a tiny egg roll.

Terry loved fried egg rolls and, since his stomach was empty, he thought about eating one. Luis hinted other missions were his, *if* he survived this one. Well, an egg roll should not slow him down. He ate one, and then reached to grab another one when, from the corner of his eye, he saw Barnes turning his way. To maintain total deception, Terry waved.

That did it. Barnes, always inquisitive, came right over. "I saw you out in the parking lot cooking, and now I smell the wonderful results. Your selection will sure be popular."

On this of all mornings, it was nice to be appreciated. Terry handed a kabob to the pastor. "Try one. I marinated it with a sauce, which is a family secret."

The pastor sampled the meat, talked between bites. "This student festival is great. We owe you thanks for suggesting it. You give our church family a chance to become familiar with different cultures, talk with students, and include you in more activities."

He picked up a cocktail napkin from Terry's display and wiped his lips. "Oh, and here's a coincidence. I received a call from a large church in Tampa. Right this minute, they are staging an international student festival, too. I am not sure how their pastor heard of our event, but we agreed that reaching international students is something we want to do every year. Who knows, Terry, maybe you started a movement that will spread nationwide."

The more Barnes talked, the more Terry wanted to flee. What else had he heard? The man seemed undisturbed, eating another one of Terry's kabobs. Dozens of families, old and young, even small children, were mingling around his area. Some reached for the kabobs, complimenting him on the delicious taste.

Barnes tossed a stick in the trashcan. "Terry, meet as many of our people as possible. You'll soon find out what a welcoming family we are."

One thing Terry had learned, people in this church were friendly. They had accepted him with no questions. That made blowing them up all the easier, as it should be. If they insisted on rejecting the one, true religion, there was nothing to do but rid the world of them until only the faithful remained. Hoards of people flocked around his cooker, distracting Terry from his mental high.

He knew some people were leaving the service, while others were arriving. Soon, his bomb would level all of them in one blast. Terry knew he better get out and save himself. His hands were moving the last of the kabobs from the warming tray when an ear-piercing horn resounded throughout the church.

Suddenly, an announcement came from an overhead speaker. "Attention please, this is an emergency. A dangerous situation exists. Everyone leave through the east entrance, immediately! Clear the building. Be orderly, but get out now!"

WITH NO WAY FOR JACK to be sure he was going to the right church, frustration seeped from his skin in a thin layer of sweat. Forest Grove Community Church was *the* largest in the suburbs of Chicago, so it made sense from a security standpoint to rush there now. That Kat and Elliot were there made his heart pound, his foot press harder on the gas.

If he knew for sure that Gordon had alerted them, and if Headquarters had spread the word to other major cities with large churches, he wouldn't feel quite so panicked. Chicago might not be a target, but he could not take the chance. Even though the FBI disabled bombs on five vans, there could be others besides the one they searched for, parked in unsuspecting mega-churches, waiting to kill untold numbers of people. It was mind numbing to live in an age of terror and yet be at the mercy of technology.

Near the church, Ricky's voice squelched over his police radio speaker. "TF-7, are you out there?"

Jack picked up the microphone, squeezed the key. "Yeah, two minutes from the church."

Ricky's voice came back, "About the same. Let's hope we find that van."

Jack yelled above sounds of his siren, "The bomb will go off in minutes. Hurry Ricky. If it's there, the van should stand out in the lot."

"Ten-four. Be careful, Jack."

The radio crackled again. This time it was Gordon's call sign. "TF-1 to TF-7."

Jack swung into church entrance, going against a tide of cars pouring from the parking lots. "Seven here, go ahead."

Gordon sounded as anxious as Jack felt. "I told the church to clear the building. Your instincts are correct. Nashville JTTF called HQ. Their van just turned into a huge church on Old Hickory Boulevard, west of Nolansville Pike."

"I'm at Forest Grove now."

Microphone in hand, he spotted Ricky's car approaching the west side of the church parking lot. Jack screeched past a parking lot attendant who must not have gotten the word. On his radio, Jack heard Ricky shout, "I see it—white camper van, west lot."

Just then Jack saw the unmistakable top of what surely was the sixth and missing van. Adrenaline pumped through his whole body. "Block it from the front. I'll close in from behind."

Amid screams, throngs of people ran around the church to find shelter on the east side of the massive building, all except for one man. Jack spied him going full bore toward the van. Jack and Ricky closed in on him with their cars. He then changed course, ran in the other direction, away from the van.

Despite Jack's instructions to block it, Ricky drove right by the van, past the lone runner in the parking lot and slammed on his brakes. Within seconds, he was out of the car and tackled their man to the ground.

Jack squealed his car to a stop directly behind the van and jumped out. He sped to his trunk, removed a pry bar. With one swift move, Jack drove the point into the edge of the door where he knew the propane tank to be and twisted with great force. Thankfully, the small lock yielded. Jack stared at an empty chasm. He was shocked. Where were the tanks?

Ricky approached the van, dragging the man with him. Jack hollered, "Where are the propane tanks from this van?"

Jack looked at his watch. It was 10:53. Based on the bombs the FBI took apart, in seven minutes this bomb would go off. Was there a mistake? Couldn't be, this guy was running away from the church, toward the van.

Grabbing the front of the man's shirt, Jack shook him. "Is it inside the church?"

Cold steely eyes met his demands; the man must be guilty, he was giving away nothing. Jack released his grip, and snatched a pair of handcuffs from his belt, clamping one side on the man's wrist. The man struggled and strained, but Jack and Ricky both forced him to a nearby light pole, stood him facing it, and grabbed his other arm to handcuff him around it.

Jack and Rick ran full speed to the church while their suspect could only watch from where he was shackled to the pole. Inside the church, Jack was surprised by a three-story high, open area large enough to hold thousands of people at once. In the vestibule, outside of the sanctuary, he spun around, looking everywhere for Kat. Thankfully, he did not see her; she must have gotten out. What a relief.

In fact, he realized most worshippers were gone, just a few still escaping through the exits at the far side of the room. At least they were going in the right direction, and Jack soon saw why. Two off-duty sheriff deputies directed people out that way, and away from the tall camper on the west side.

Jack flashed his badge and asked a deputy, "We checked the van out in the lot. It has no propane tanks in it. The bomb must be inside. We arrested the only man running away from the church. Mid-twenties, dark hair and eyes, he looks Middle Eastern, but I cannot be sure."

His demeanor unruffled, the deputy made a sweeping motion with his arm. "I've checked around, but so far haven't seen anything suspicious."

With his eyes, Jack followed the deputy's arm to several brightly decorated tables, some with food still on them. That's when he saw a huge stainless steel cooking grill. Ricky must have spotted it at the same instant, because they made straight for it. When Jack opened the doors beneath the grill, he sucked in a deep breath.

Rick blurted, "Look at that."

There were *two* twenty-pound propane tanks inside a grill that would never need more than one. "Ricky, grab the other end. This must be our bomb."

As fast as they dared move, Jack and Rick hauled the heavy grill toward the west parking lot, in the opposite direction from all the fleeing people. The deputy held open the door. The clock on the wall now said 10:56. Four minutes before the bomb would explode.

Both men dragged the cooker through the doorway, out into the parking lot until they were steps away from the handcuffed student, and there they stopped, right by his hate-filled face. To concoct such evil, to want to kill innocent men, women, and children—surely he deserved to die with his bomb.

Jack waged a ten-second war in his mind. Contrary to his sense of true justice, he shouted, "Do you want to stay here, or run with us?"

Even though it was a cool fall day, sweat poured down the man's face. His eyes held a look of pure terror. "Please, I will run with you."

Jack inserted the key in the cuff to release Terry from the pole. He clicked the cuff to his own wrist and turned to run. Suddenly, he tripped over the student. Had the man fallen? No, he had thrown himself to the ground. Excruciating pain shot through Jack's left wrist, and his whole body doubled to the pavement, as his prisoner pulled him down.

The man looked up at Jack with eyes of a madman. "We shall die here together. Allahu Akbar."

Trapped, about to be killed by a homicidal bomber, Jack cried aloud, "God, help me!"

Ricky soccer kicked the student in the head and he went limp. Ricky lifted him from the ground. Jack's breath coming in short blasts, suddenly, it was if a hand hauled him up, and then bent him over. Seconds later, Ricky heaved the student over Jack's shoulder, pulling Jack along. "Come on! We might make it if we run like crazy."

Surprised he could even run with a man over his shoulders as a firefighter might, under the weight Jack found strength in his legs and back. Something like hope filled his heart and lungs to go the distance. As he and Ricky got farther from the propane grill, and neared the safety of the church, Jack's lungs felt as though they were about to burst.

Just when he thought they would get outside the periphery of the blast, his prisoner came to and struck Jack in the back with his free hand, kicked at his legs, trying to topple him again. Jack struggled to keep moving, when a massive explosion rocked the parking lot.

Car parts flying everywhere, around Jack's head, his feet, a fireball seared the sky. The force of the concussion propelled all three men through the air. Jack landed hard on the asphalt, the homicide-bomber crashing on top of him. An entire glass wall on the west side of the church's Gatheria was gone. Twisted metal hung from the roof. Jack felt hot pain, and then nothing.

THE DETONATION ROCKED the east side of the church. Thousands of frightened people, ducked down among cars in the east parking lot. Even though they were on the far side away from the explosion, car windows shattered. Kat screamed and stumbled to the ground. Strong arms wrapped around her, protected her. Sobs escaped her lips as she heard Elliot's voice in her ear, "God help us."

He was crying, too. Neither knew what to say. Kat could not stop the tears. Before she fled, she had been standing next to Elliot and Laurel in the Gatheria, uninterested in food. Instead, the minister's message of the lost condition of the world helped her to see herself in a new light. It was when she whispered to Elliot how wrong she had been, and asked him to forgive her, that he told her an astonishing thing. He had meant to surprise her; and had deposited enough funds in her bank account to pay off her school loan and make a down payment on a home.

Kat was reeling from that disclosure when an alarm and loud voice ordered them out of the church. Now, minutes later, she knew terror unlike anything she'd ever felt before, even with Elliot's arms around her. Kat thought of her mom, facing famine, war, and death around the world. Was this why Laurel found God? Her mother was on a cell phone, calling 911.

In the distance, sirens pierced her ears, coming closer. From training or a force beyond her, Kat realized she was probably the only local reporter on the scene. She wiped her eyes and nose and moved back a little from Elliot. Still on the ground, she removed her cell from her purse and, following Laurel's calm example, called the news desk.

"This is Kat Kowicki at Forest Grove Community Church. There has been an enormous explosion. I am with Mr. Tucker and Laurel Eastland. People appear safe, but I have not been out front. Get Ian here, now. I'll prepare a script and be on my cell."

Elliot rose and helped her up. "Quick thinking. Are you all right?"

Kat brushed off her legs. "Wobbly and my legs hurt. Are you?"

He looked at the palms of his hands. "A little bruised, but amazed to be alive."

"Mom, you okay?"

Her eyes wet with tears, Laurel's face was full of scratches. "I think so. Let's see if anyone needs help."

The trio hurried around to the west side of the church. Already, a police officer pushed folks away. Kat flashed her press credentials and assuring him she'd be careful, he let her inside. What she saw twenty feet ahead stung her heart, nearly collapsed her mind. There was Jack lying on the ground, bleeding and handcuffed to a man who appeared lifeless.

Kat flew to his side, kneeled down. She cradled his head in her arms and sobbed, "Jack, Jack," again and again until a paramedic pulled her away.

FORTY

Seven-hundred miles away, agent Eva Montanna and her family went to church early, stopping afterwards for pancakes at a favorite breakfast place, a nice respite for her, away from the rigors of her secret task force, even if it was for only an hour. Sal had bought tickets for her and Griff to attend the international student event at his church he'd told them about, but, with pressure mounting to make a case against *Camelot,* they all skipped it, even Sal. He and Griff were covering the wiretap.

At home, she changed into slacks and a sweater, kissed Scott goodbye, and headed on I-66 for Main Justice. With gospel music on the car radio as a welcome backdrop, her thoughts turned from worship and family to disappointment; the court-ordered taps on Harding's home and office phones turned up nothing illegal or remotely usable in a criminal case against him.

She was nearing the historical town of Falls Church when a news alert broke into the musical program and made her heart stop. Two Chicago detectives had thwarted a large-scale terrorist attack at Forest Grove Community Church, in a Chicago suburb. They went to a live-feed and Eva heard a voice that sounded like Kat Kowicki's say, "Jack McKenna is a hero."

Eva got off at the next exit, desperate to get home and check on her family. She circled back westbound on I-66. Minutes later she found Kaley and Andy working on a puzzle at the kitchen table and relief flooded her. Eva walked into the living room and turned on the television news, knowing that for some people near Chicago, life had changed, and would never be the same.

The only reporter at the scene, Kat's face was smeared with dirt and she had blood spatter on her beige suit, but her voice was strong as she told America, "Chicago detectives Jack McKenna and Ricky Vasquez are credited with saving the lives of thousands of churchgoers, many of whom have minor injuries. Both men are being treated at a hospital, but we have learned their injuries are not life threatening. The bomber, who drove a van rigged with a bomb, is dead, killed by his own blast. His name has not yet been released."

Scott rushed in. "Eva, I thought I heard you come back. I was putting Marty down for his nap." He seemed to grasp that something terrible had happened, and stared at the television with her. "Where was the explosion?"

Eva muted the sound long enough to tell him about the bomb attack, and then turned the news back on. They learned similar vans had gone to churches in five other cities, including the one Sal attended, in Springfield. The intent was to detonate bombs in each city, but unknown to the terrorists the FBI had disabled their bombs beforehand.

What a major feat, yet one bomb had exploded. Scott folded her into his arms and Eva leaned against his chest, absorbing his strength for only a moment before pulling away. "The mastermind who planned this, who tried to kill all these people in six large churches, Scott, I have to find him. With all the work we've done to stop terrorism, I never, ever gave one thought to how vulnerable we are at church."

Eva felt weak at the knees, dropped to the couch. Scott muted the sound and sat next to her, keeping his voice low. "Let's not get excited in front of the kids. They're too young to see us scared."

His hands covered hers. "Listen, I know you've gone after these guys before, and may think you can do it again. But, Eva, you have enough on your plate. Besides, there's a whole nation of FBI agents who no doubt are all over this thing as we sit here in our living room."

Eva appreciated his viewpoint, but she had to make him see hers. "Scott, Detective McKenna came to Washington and helped me on one of my cases. There could be a connection. I have to try to help him, if I can."

Kaley and Andy started arguing about whose turn it was to add a puzzle piece. Scott went to the kitchen to quiet them, but Eva made up her mind. She followed him and kissed her children. In her husband's ear, she whispered, "I'm going to check in with Griff and Sal. I'll be back to make dinner.

True to her word Eva was home in time to chop carrots and celery for chicken soup, the only thing that sounded good to her. There was nothing at the task force office that required her attention and she couldn't get through to Jack. After they ate bowls of hot homemade soup with grilled cheese sandwiches, she tried again to reach Jack at the hospital. The fact that his cell kept going to voice mail was perhaps proof that Scott was right; she should leave this alone. Still, she struggled with it all evening.

Finally, over a cup of hot chocolate Scott had brought her, she said, "I will try Kat's cell phone and, if I can't reach her, I'll forget it as you suggest."

Scott drank his cocoa. "Sounds like a plan. Either way, we need some shuteye. The Secretary called a staff meeting about this new terror threat for seven." He yawned, and Eva stared at her open cell, debating if she should even try Kat. Yet, Scott had agreed, so she pressed speed dial.

Surprisingly, Kat did answer. She was at the hospital, where Eva learned she had gone immediately after reporting what happened. She took the call in Jack's room, but went out into the hall to talk. Kat sounded stressed, "The doctors insist Jack remain here, to be monitored all night. He has a concussion and is sleeping just now."

Eva felt compassion for Kat and Jack. "From what I heard, I'm surprised that's his only injury. I saw your newscast. You could use some attending to yourself."

A sniffle or two told Eva that Kat was showing the wear and tear of the day. "It was awful. I've never been so afraid."

Eva assured Kat that she would be praying, and then asked a favor. "Kat, could I talk to Jack? I want to see if there is anything I can do to follow up on this end."

Kat whispered, "I'll go see and call back."

Minutes later, it was Jack, not Kat, who called Eva. Eager to share what was on his mind, his breath, though, came in short bursts, "I met undercover with Luis San Felipe in the Bahamas. Wait, a nurse is here."

Eva held on, afraid if she hung up, she'd not get him again. "Okay, I'm back. Luis flew on a Venezuelan airplane. FBI Boston confirmed he is Hezbollah, known for using terror to accomplish their ends. Eva," Jack coughed. "Just a sec, I need some water."

A pause, then, "Okay, the diverter I sent to Griff, the one that transferred Interstate Conversion calls to Kazakhstan, did Griff find anything?"

"I'll check, Jack. When I saw him today, he didn't mention it."

Jack's voice started fading away, but she heard, "A Mexican drug smuggler, Manuel Ochoa, set up the meet at Norman's Cay."

Eva thought it best for him to rest and arranged to call him tomorrow morning. In the chair beside her, Scott was asleep, and to sounds of his snoring, the vicious circle of Harding and *Camelot* and drugs and terrorists revolved in her mind. What connected them? She spent a restless night, tossing and turning, trying to figure it out.

FOR EVA, MONDAY MORNING arrived too soon. Frustrated by the lack of answers, she took the three children to the sitter, who agreed to drop Kaley and Andy at school, since Scott had already left for his meeting. Alone in the car, she couldn't drive in the HOV lane, Eva drove into D.C. on the back roads, scheming and planning against America's enemies, both foreign and domestic. By the time she arrived at the office, she was wired for victory. Her entire team must have sensed her ambition. They gathered round, eager for their share in the action.

Eva steadied her voice, about to command the others. "I asked myself all night what links Jack McKenna's bomb case had to Harding's security firm in Kazakhstan. Know what I came up with?"

Griff had his own idea. "I couldn't find any prints on the diverter he sent me."

She held up a hand. "For what I have planned, that won't matter. Listen, the one common denominator is the CIA, namely, Deputy Director Kangas and his former assistant who now runs Harding and Associates. I have the Attorney General's permission for what I am about to do. Sonya, you and Earl go right now and monitor Camelot's website. Griff and Sal, stand by in case I need technical help with the electronic device Jack sent from Interstate Vans."

As Eva waited for CIA Deputy Director Wilt Kangas, to come on the line, Griff warned, "Don't mention anything about Sergei Federov. You might be sorry if you do."

When Kangas came on, he was abrupt. "Ms. Montanna, the AG's office told me to expect your call. How can I help you?"

Eva quickly told him not only what she learned from Jack the night before, but also what she, Griff, and Sal had pieced together in the intervening hours. "We are seeking an arrest warrant for Luis San Felipe, the Hezbollah organizer in Venezuela, responsible for the church bombings this past weekend. I have every reason to believe Luis San Felipe is the son of General Raul San Felipe, with whom I talked earlier this year."

"You what?" Kangas roared.

"Sir, I was the one the General first called asking to be freed from a Cuban prison hospital." She had not told her group of the General, but had no qualms doing so now. "I referred his plea for help to your agency, namely CIA agent Bo Ryder. I was never informed what happened to him."

Kangas seemed to retreat into spook-mode. "Never mind the General. He's no concern of yours."

Eva supposed that was true and, besides, she had other ways of getting the truth about General San Felipe.

Kangas cut to the heart of Eva's request. "You want Luis to show up in the U.S., so you can serve him with a federal warrant."

"Yes, sir." Eva held her breath. If the CIA refused to bring Luis in, they were dead in the water; neither Homeland Security nor Justice had jurisdiction in a foreign country.

"I'll see what I can do." Like a phantom, Kangas was gone.

Their call concluded, Eva summarized for Sal and Griff, who had listened only to her side of the conversation. "We didn't exactly strike out, but didn't hit a home run either. Kangas will see about getting Luis out of Venezuela. Now, I'm going to call Jack McKenna."

The detective was back home now. "It's Eva. Griff and Sal are sitting here in the office. Remember your guy on the island? Can you get a Federal arrest warrant for him, in Chicago?"

Slow to respond, Jack's fatigue was apparent. "First thing tomorrow morning, I'm to meet with the Assistant U.S. Attorney who is putting me before a Grand Jury. We should have the warrant tomorrow night."

A thumbs-up signal for her group, Eva lowered her voice for Jack. "I just got off the phone with someone who will try to ensure he shows up here in the U.S., where he'll be taken into custody."

Jack stammered, as if choosing his words carefully for an un-secure phone. "Ah, you haven't been talking to that company in Kazakhstan, have you?"

Eva speedily changed the subject. "Jack, you deserve recognition. Others claim the title, but you truly are a great American."

She could tell he was uncomfortable with praise when he deflected it. "I was just doing my job. Truthfully, I have been recognized by the one who gave me the idea to go to Forest Grove Church in the first place. Eva, this may not make sense to you, but I believe God has a way of communicating with those who know him. It's up to us to listen and act."

"I understand, more than you know." The thought of having another person on her team who believed and thought as she did was intriguing. "I know you've got a lot to deal with right now, Jack. But, would you consider working with our task force here in Washington? With our cases so intertwined, I believe the Attorney General would approve payment for your temporary assignment here."

Jack's silence made Eva wonder if he was still on the other end. Finally, he replied, giving no answer, "I'll have to think about that."

To Griff's "Well?" Eva forced a smile, and it felt almost foreign, things had been that tense. "You both heard what I told Jack about the warrant. He seems open to joining our team."

Griff stretched his arms above his head, cracking a few knuckles on his hands. "I'm impressed by McKenna. He'd be a real asset. Me, I'm thinking of lunch at the Old Ebbitt Grill. It's just past eleven, so the real crowd won't arrive for thirty minutes. You know it will take Kangas time to contact his people."

Eva picked up her fanny bag where she kept keys and essentials, like her 9mm Glock. "He's going to brief the President. It could take hours before we hear anything."

Already at the door, Griff said something that was no surprise. "Exactly, and I'm not one to wait on an empty stomach."

Sal still looked a bit shellshocked. "To think, the students that Maria and I cooked for wanted to blow us up. She was there, at our church, where they arrested the bomber."

Eva locked the notes she took after talking to Kangas in her desk, pocketed the key. "I know Sal. Scott and I said last night it rekindles those terrifying feelings from 9/11 all over again." A sinister thought came to mind. "Do either one of you think Kangas knew about Harding's illegal activity? Jack suggested someone might use Harding and his people to snatch San Felipe."

Griff's eyes flickered, and Eva thought it probably crossed his mind as well. He clapped Sal on the shoulder. "You need to get out of here for awhile. As far as Kangas, let me put it this way. With the outcry about civil rights violations, I doubt Kangas will risk his career by further associating with Harding. If, and I stress, if he does, and we don't know how the terrorist Luis San Felipe gets to the U.S., I say thanks for an early Christmas gift."

Eva let it be, went to get lunch orders from Earl and Sonya. All through lunch, Griff's off-the-cuff remark lingered in her mind until it ripened into doubt about whether she had been wise to contact Kangas. Still, Alexia Kyros had approved it, so technically Eva was in the clear. She must trust Kangas would use legal means to capture the wanted terrorist, in whatever way was best for the country.

WILT KANGAS WAS NOT ONE to stare at the phone, wondering what to do next. Though his chemo treatments had begun, for a whole five minutes he thought it might be smart to take time away from the CIA to finish them. In his heart, he knew there was no vacation from terror, and being absent from his post would kill him faster than the disease. Before he left Langley, his first call was to Phillip Harding at his Fourteenth Street office.

The phone on the other end continued to ring. Wilt's right hand started shaking and he grabbed it with his left to steady the phone. Flip's phone kept ringing, but Kangas was patient. He had to be, this call was too important to give up on.

Before the church bombing, he seriously mulled over retiring, living out his days at home on the Chesapeake. Luis San Felipe, using his wicked sleeper cell to infiltrate colleges and target churches changed his mind. Not only would he beat this cancer with the best medical help he could find, Wilt would further neutralize one terror cell by removing its head.

At last, a voice mail came on. His message gave no details. "Flip, call on my secure line ASAP."

The Deputy Director hung up that secure phone, put on his suit jacket, prepared to meet with the President and do whatever it took to strangle the foothold Hezbollah was trying to make into the country, a country that he loved almost as much as life.

FORTY ONE

When it came to a certain Russian whose bad deeds seemed to go unpunished, Griff devised his own method. The Attorney General had announced indictments against several of Harding's low-level employees the day before, but the name of the Russian who had tangled with him in Kazakhstan was not on the list, so Griff's mind went to work.

No matter how he tried to argue himself out of it, a plan of action evolved, and he was about to put it in play. Without so much as a cup of coffee or a piece of toast, Griff left home at 5:30 a.m., arriving at the office long before anyone else. The court-ordered wiretaps on Harding's phones had expired, so the agents no longer staffed it around the clock.

From a locked file cabinet, Griff removed a phone-tapping device, the very one Jack shipped to him to analyze. With no fingerprints, it was useless to make the case against Ken Kirby. He was cooperating anyway, so Griff contrived another use for it. The way he saw things, the gadget that once transferred calls from Interstate Conversion Vans to Harding's facility in Almaty, Kazakhstan, was a key piece in what he deemed "sweet" justice.

He removed it from a plastic bag and cleaned off any residue from the fingerprint detection chemicals. Out of his wallet, he slid Dmitri Federov's business card and the home telephone number Griff was to call if he needed Dmitri's help at settling into his new job and residence in Almaty. Next, he moved his knight into play: He programmed the diverting device to forward to Federov's home telephone in Almaty.

Outside, the day was crisp, and the sky was so blue and bright it hurt his eyes. His misgivings not strong enough to stop him, Griff took the steps of the Embassy of Kazakhstan two at a time. Aware he was entering the sovereign territory of Kazakhstan for the first time since his mugging overseas, what happened to him over there had inspired him to dare venture inside today.

In the quiet lobby, he shook off vivid memories of being hooded and handcuffed, and approached the receptionist, a beautiful woman with almond-shaped eyes who reminded him of Dawn. He asked to speak to Gora Sajak, the liaison officer who had arranged for Griff to meet the Ambassador.

His features eerily similar to Sergei, the man who picked Griff up at the Almaty airport, Gora ushered him into the Ambassador's office. "Ambassador Mangistau, this is the FBI agent, Mr. Griffin Topping. He asked to meet with you privately."

Gora discreetly left them before the Ambassador uttered a word. Griff had no fear of being alone with the Ambassador; he made it clear to Gora he wanted no witnesses.

Griff took a step closer but remained standing close to the door, just in case. He would not sit, even if asked to. "Sir, the FBI is concerned for the safety and security of the foreign representatives who live in our nation's capital."

Ambassador Mangistau remained in his high-backed chair. His curt nod was polite, if not a little impatient for Griff to get to his point. Not wanting to spend any more time than necessary in this foreign place, he obliged. Griff stepped forward and placed a wrapped package on the carved-wooden desk.

Griff's cover story veered from the truth in a couple of ways, but he had wrestled with the deception and then firmly decided this was the only way to handle a rogue KGB agent named Dmitri Federov.

"I was contacted by a telephone employee doing repair work near your home. He found this," Griff tapped the package, "connected to your home phone line."

He lowered his voice for effect. "Sir, someone was eavesdropping on your telephone calls, sending your private conversations to be listened to at a number in Almaty, Kazakhstan. Since we have no jurisdiction in your country and no way to determine who installed it here, we refer the matter to you."

Funny how personal attacks make one sit up and notice, but that is exactly what the Ambassador did now. In an instant, he was interested in Griff and his package. He picked it up, turned it over gingerly, as if with respect. "Where are my calls going in Almaty? There may be a legitimate explanation."

Inwardly, Griff noted his English was silky-smooth like Dmitri's. He wondered if the Ambassador knew Federov and his plan would fizzle. Griff gave his prepared answer to the question. "Your phone calls are being transferred to a phone number which we have noted and affixed to the device. I know nothing else, but I am sure you have ways of investigating further."

Seeds of suspicion firmly sown against a man he considered an enemy, Griff turned to leave. Amazingly, the Ambassador stood and hurried around the desk. "Thank you, Agent Topping, for bringing this to my attention. I know how to handle this matter."

Before opening the door, Ambassador Mangistau pumped Griff's hand heartily. Mission fulfilled, the FBI agent wasted no time getting out of there. On the sidewalk, well out of range of security cameras, he stamped his feet to rid them of any remnant of Dmitri Federov.

Mixed feelings swelled in his chest. Doubt banged up against any satisfaction he felt that the Ambassador would find a measure of justice for Federov. Maybe he should have talked to Eva first, but in this case he followed the old axiom that it's easier to seek forgiveness than to ask permission.

Second thoughts behind him, Griff left Federov's fate to the Kazakh government and in his bucar found his way back to Main Justice, where he had an important phone call to make. Greeting Eva and the team, saying not one word about where he had been, Griff placed a call to MI-5. He half expected the London agency to tell him, as they did prior to his trip to Almaty, that Brewster Miles no longer worked for British intelligence.

If Brewster was still in league with Philip Harding, Griff would hang up and forget his old friend. He had clearly warned him the company was verging on the illegal.

He really admired the MI-5 agent, and, to Griff's profound relief, the operator said, "Mr. Miles is not in. I am happy to connect you with his voice mail."

When he heard the smart clip of the Brit's accent on the other end, Griff laughed aloud.

Sal yelled over, "What's so funny Topping?"

"Shush, would you." Griff quickly left his message. "Miles, it's Topping here. Glad to find you home where you belong. Keep an eye on the news for developments of interest to us both, and call when you can."

He walked over to Sal, who pretended to be put off by Griff's telling him to shut up. Griff punched his arm. "Let's get some lunch. I don't know about you, but I'm starved. That Tex-Mex place you like sound good?"

Sal was out of his chair. "Yeah, cheesy enchiladas are just what I need."

Ensconced in a booth with Sal, for once Griff's appetite was a little off. He tried to figure out, maybe never would, if all along Brewster

Miles hadn't been on an inside job of his own at Harding, recommending Griff for the Kazakh job so that the FBI could learn what Brewster had already discovered.

THE NEXT MORNING, at main Justice, Eva turned away from the statue of Lady Justice, where the Attorney General had just addressed a nation uneasy with the turn of events. She felt betrayed by former colleagues and wondered what it meant for her future as an ICE agent. On the elevator with Griff and Sal, none of them said much, which gave her the idea she needed to have a post-op debrief and quick. In the common area of the makeshift office, a stark contrast to the grandeur of the Great Hall, Eva got her team together.

She wanted them in the office, just in case Alexia stopped by. Eva had seen her do that before on major cases but didn't mention this to the agents. Besides, it might be therapeutic to discuss their feelings about the massive arrests of former agents.

"Earl and Sonya, you watched on television what we saw live. Reporters questioned General Kyros on the successful capture of the Hezbollah church bombers and the arrest yesterday of *twenty* former government agents and their accomplices for illegally wire-tapping U.S. citizens. I'd like to know what you all think."

Sal, rarely at a loss for words, said what every agent in that room felt, at one time or another. "Yeah, there is nothing wrong with any of us using good information furnished to us so long as we don't know how it was obtained. In the future, we should be careful not to ask our sources how they got their information."

Hands stuffed in her jacket pockets, Eva offered her thoughts for the group to chew on. "I have a response to what Sal just said, if you can stay with me. None of us wanted to do the work of internal affairs. However, we received information about wrongdoing and we had to follow it to its natural conclusion. I am not happy so many ex-agents apparently violated our laws."

Griff veered back to Sal's comment. "Here's how it went down. We helped McKenna follow up on Kat's complaint about her phone tap. He and the Chicago JTTF discovered a link back to Harding and Associates. That's the first any of us knew our agencies were paying for intelligence, unlawfully obtained."

Eva shook her head. "Sal, I know you feel personally affected because your church was a target, but if we find out information is tainted, the courts say we cannot use fruit from a poisonous tree. So as good as the intelligence was, it would have been unconscionable for us to let it fly, so to speak, and not shut down the tap on Interstate Van Conversions and arrest ATF agent Smith."

Griff interjected, "We might lose some evidence against five would-be bombers, because it stemmed from an unlawful wire tap."

That was a result Eva did not even want to consider.

His face grim, Sal was not retreating. "These terrorists are among us and we have to use all possible avenues to run them to ground before they get us first."

Griff leaned back against one of the desks, folded his arms across his chest. "I keep telling you guys, look at the big picture. McKenna got injured trying to outrun the bomb with that dirtbag Terry on his back. Terry put the whole operation together, his body protected Jack's, and the shrapnel from his own bomb killed him. To me it doesn't matter if the judge throws out the evidence, Terry's already been sentenced by the court of the Supreme."

Agent Haddad, her head nodding and black hair moving around her shoulders like a giant wave, agreed. "Griff is right. That is a just result."

Eva felt everyone but Earl was satisfied with the outcome; his hands were hovering over his computer keyboard, so she asked, "What do you say, Earl?"

His fingers tapping the keys, Earl looked over his shoulder. "Our source helped us locate and freeze Swiss bank accounts in the names of Venezuelan citizens, which were really controlled by Hezbollah in Venezuela, totaling nineteen million. I think it's great the AG will pay Claus ten percent if the Swiss government seizes the funds connected to terrorism and I think they will."

A chorus of "Great!" almost made Eva wait for another time to raise the question she needed answered. "Philip Harding managed to sneak out of the country before the indictments. Is there a way we can seize the twenty-seven-million that our court-ordered taps have traced to his Swiss bank accounts?"

His glasses off, Earl wiped his eyes before turning to face his colleagues. "I did all I could. I mean, I gave all the information I had, Harding's account numbers and passwords, everything to our source, but the Swiss won't touch it because we cannot trace Harding's money to terrorism."

Eva plunked in her chair. "That's a lot of money to let slip through. Harding should pay in some way."

A slight grin played around Earl's thin lips. Eva wondered if he knew something he wasn't sharing. "Come on, out with it Earl."

Earl put his glasses back on and didn't keep them in suspense long. "Claus did hint there may not be much money in Harding's account to help him through the coming years of exile in Kazakhstan. Living on the lam in a foreign country can get expensive. It takes lots of bucks to pay bribes just to remain in the country."

A ringing phone collided with Griff's spontaneous laughter. Eva answered and simply listened. As soon as she hung up, she began issuing orders. "Tidy up around here. The Attorney General is on her way to thank you all for a job well done."

FORTY TWO

A week before, Kat was at Jack's side when he came to, and she refused to take her eyes off him. She had fussed with the nurses, even running down to the gift shop to buy red licorice for him. Ms. Lizzy, Jack's neighbor, once again cared for Winston, but Kat offered to help in any way she could. Though Jack looked tired as he lay there in the drab hospital gown, he tried to act tough and insisted that she and Big John go home because he wanted to sleep, suggesting they return in the morning.

With her nicest dress on and her hair pulled back, Kat rushed to get there by nine that Monday morning, and when she found Jack was a *former* patient, that he checked himself out earlier, she was furious. Later in the evening, she had called him at home, and in a whisper, Big John told her Jack was asleep. He also said the doctor believed that the concussion Jack suffered when the bomb blast knocked him to the ground did not cause serious damage.

Since that time, Kat was reluctant to let her detective out of her sight, even asking Elliot to postpone her taped interview of Big John until she was certain Jack was all right. He was, going back to work at the task force and being lauded as Chicago's hero. Every time Kat thought about how he saved her and so many others, putting his body between the bomb and the people, she almost came unglued.

But this was her big night at Lake Forest Academy. All day, Laurel had helped calm her, sharing stories about how she had handled her first big special. Against a stack of books in the library, Jack looked casual, easy as he often did on his boat in Pentwater, and no one would be the wiser what a man of courage he was.

A funny grin flashed just for her evoked melancholy feelings; it was here, at the Academy, where she first met him. Kat reached within to steady her mind, find the skills for what she was about to do—begin unraveling the Kennedy assassination starting with Big John. Ian motioned he was ready, but was she? Her eyes drifted to the rest of her family for support, but her mom was immersed in a quiet conversation with Elliot, who whispered in her ear. Kat hoped they were not being critical. She forced herself to think positively, and chose to believe instead that they both were proud of her.

She turned her full attention to John McKenna. "All set to be interviewed on camera?"

It was not a live take; this session would get spliced in with other interviews and tapes of the evidence. To Kat, John's skin seemed ruddy, his cheeks almost blotchy, as if his blood pressure was too high. Though he said that he was prepared, Kat motioned the producer to get some bottled water. "Open the door a crack."

Cindy darted away to fulfill the requests. Whenever filming a major story on location, she brought bottled water in compact coolers.

Kat leaned over to Big John, whom she admired nearly as much as his son Jack, but in a much different way. She deferred to him as she might her own father and gave him leeway in selecting the questions he would answer. "Mr. McKenna, why not remove your sweater. Your light blue shirt and tie will look great on camera."

Jack's father slid off his sweater, handing it to Jack. The library was warm, yet Kat kept on her suit jacket and tried to think cool thoughts. She chose to kick off her special in this cozy room at her high school Alma Mater. Fire burning in the fireplace on this November night, a golden glow bounced off the richly paneled mantel where the Armour family had once enjoyed reading. Kat thought the homey feel would draw in viewers, make them stay, watch, believe.

"Miss Kat," he had taken to calling her that name, "ready when you are."

Ian held up two fingers, then one, indicating his camera was filming. John McKenna explained why the Kennedy assassination was important to him. "I was a Chicago Police officer, retiring as a Detective. On the night of November 22, 1963 I was called out to help the FBI locate the owner of Klein's Sporting Goods in Chicago."

Kat jumped in with what she considered the most important question, "You found something in the store's records leading you to believe there was a second shooter. What did you find?"

In their conversations, she had never seen Big John look so serious. He told how the FBI agent wanted his help finding who ordered a 6.5 millimeter Mannlicher-Carcano recovered at the Texas School Depository, and where it was sent. "According to microfilm records at Klein's, the order for the Italian military rifle came in on an order form torn from the February 1963 issue of the *American Rifleman* magazine. The purchaser used the name A. Hidell. Klein's mailed it out on March 20, 1963 to P.O. Box 2915 in Dallas, Texas."

Kat interjected, "Tell our listeners who used the name A. Hidell."

His cheeks rosy-red, John looked right into the camera as if talking directly to the American public in their living rooms. "Lee H. Oswald opened that post office box on October 9, 1962 in the name of A. Hidell. Oswald closed the box on May 14, 1963. He bought that rifle and scope with a money order for $21.45."

Kat led him as a prosecuting attorney might question a friendly witness. "We know Lee Harvey Oswald also used the name, A. J. Hidell, on Fair Play for Cuba leaflets in New Orleans the previous summer, and to purchase the .38 caliber revolver found on him at the time he was arrested. You discovered some other evidence that has never been revealed to the public, right?"

The retired Chicago detective handed Kat a sheet of paper, of which Ian had already filmed a close-up. "That night, I got it in my mind to look through *all* requests that Klein's had for guns in February and March 1963. Assigned to the First District, I covered the Loop and Klein's, so when the FBI contacted me, I consulted my list of businesses and called the owner. We all met at Klein's. Once the Bureau agent found on microfilm the A. Hidell order form with a Mannlicher-Carcano rifle going to Dallas, he was gone, leaving me and the owner to close up."

"But, you stayed, right?"

"Yup, I knew the owner. He and I talked about how crushed we were that a President could be riding down the streets of Dallas, waving, smiling, very much alive, and be gunned down the next minute. He was a hero to many people. I know some were critical about the Bay of Pigs fiasco, which caused Soviet missiles to be pointed right at us from ninety miles away in Cuba."

When Big John drew breath, Kat gently brought him back to the night of November 22 and what he did at Klein's Sporting Goods. "Tell our viewers *exactly* what you found after the FBI agent left."

John cleared his throat and Kat thought it might be better to let him talk as long as he wanted, sensing he needed to get his story out. He had waited years for this moment. She could always edit the tape.

"Here's what I found. There was another gun ordered and sent to an address, a rooming house near where Oswald stayed in Dallas in November 1963. This second order, mailed two days after the first, was for an identical Mannlicher-Carcano, a scope, *and* six-point-five-millimeter ammunition and clips. Oswald never ordered any ammo, but Dallas police found spent six-point-five-millimeter cartridges in the Depository. Anyway, I printed out two copies of that second order, one for the Bureau, one for me. The next morning, I called the FBI duty agent and told him what I found."

Kat asked a question she was sure her viewers would want to know. "Was he glad you found it?"

"I couldn't say. He just asked me to initial and date the copy and deliver it to the FBI's receptionist desk at 536 South Clark Street, just south of the Loop. I sealed it in an envelope and dropped it off to his attention. After Oswald was killed in a Dallas jail the next day, and there was no word at all from that FBI agent who got my records, I took a week's vacation and drove to Dallas myself."

Round beads of sweat formed above John's upper lip. Kat wanted to wipe these away, but she left him alone. The moisture gave Big John an air of believability that makeup would only mask. With a smile and slight nod, she encouraged him to keep telling his story.

"In Dallas, I spoke to the landlady at the address where this second Mannlicher-Carcano was sent. Mrs. Pumphrey, she's gone now, rest her soul, was nearly blind and terribly hard of hearing. I showed her photos of Oswald. She told me she never saw him before the day he was shot on television."

Kat could not help herself. "Did you believe her?"

Big John lowered his eyelids a moment as if this answer required more thought than the others did. Perfect, Kat thought, she hated witnesses who seemed rehearsed.

"I do. The good lady remembered that for two months in 1963, a man with a Spanish accent stayed in her lodgings. His mail came there, as did several packages. A rifle arrived for him, although at that time, before Kennedy was killed, she paid no attention to it. She grew up hunting rabbits and squirrels with her father and she said rifles were no big deal to her."

Kat broke in. "Was the name of the man with the Spanish accent Raul San Felipe?"

Big John ran a hand along his chin, seeming to reach deep into his memory. "No, Miss Kat that was not his name. Mrs. Pumphrey told me her lodger once lived in Cuba. Unbelievable as it may sound, she found an airplane ticket from Cuba to Mexico City, but got fearful after Kennedy died, so when Oswald was killed, too, she threw it away."

He leaned back in the chair, stared into the fire. Kat resisted the urge to prompt him to continue, so she waited, her foot moving to the beat of her heart. This was really going well. As she hoped, Big John returned to her, only this time frustration spilled over in his words.

"She tossed out a vital piece of evidence the day before I arrived. I offered to dig through her garbage, but the truck had picked up her trash early that morning. Anyway, back to your question, Klein's sent the second Mannlicher-Carcano to Mrs. Pumphrey's address. It's vital this information is known, because the rifle they found in the Depository was never given a test to see if it had recently been fired. Americans should know the FBI has the information I am telling you, including what I am not telling, like the name of the gun purchaser."

Ah-hah, the moment Kat waited for. "Who within the FBI has this information?"

Big John handed her a report stapled together. When the final documentary aired, a separate cutout of John's letter would fill the screen. "In November of sixty-three, I wrote up this three-page memo, my boss initialed it, and we sent it to Mr. Hoover, along with the microfilm copy of the gun record. Five months later, I got back a nice little letter thanking me for my trouble, and saying my original microfilm would be sent to the Warren Commission."

Kat was on fire now, knowing where Big John was headed. "Did the Warren Commission interview you or ask you for more information?"

Her guest was curt. "No, I never heard a thing from President Johnson's Commission. After the Warren Report was released ten months later, in September 1964, I read it cover to cover." He swiped his chin with his hand. "A few months after that, when the hearing record and all the exhibits were made public, I read those, too."

Big John thrust his finger in front of him, jabbing at an unseen enemy. "I had a personal interest, you see. Not one word was mentioned about my records, the existence of the second rifle, nothing. It was like whatever did not fit the official version, that Oswald was a lone nut, disgruntled-communist crazy, who fired at and killed Kennedy with a single bullet, was ignored."

It was important, she thought, to touch on the single bullet theory for unfamiliar viewers, before moving on. Kat asked the retired detective about it, and as though a veteran reporter himself, John looked in the camera, wanting every American to hear what he had to say. "The official report alleged three shots were fired from the sixth floor window. A young prosecutor on the Warren Commission staff came up with a theory. Your viewers can decide for themselves if I'm right or he's right."

John drank some water, sucked in a deep breath like he really had something to say. "It goes like this. One of the three bullets hit nothing. A second remaining bullet fired from Oswald's gun supposedly coursed through the President's back at the base of the neck without hitting any bony structure, exited his throat at the level of the tie, crashed into Governor Connally's back, shattered his rib, exited his chest, smashed through his wrist, and deflected into his upper left leg."

Kat asked, "Did the third bullet strike Kennedy in the head?"

John nodded solemnly, "Yes, and may be the one that killed him. The real question is who fired it. You see, rather than consider that there was a second shooter, and more bullets flying, this young attorney came up with the theory that Oswald's second shot did all the damage instead of other bullets."

He drew in another breath to last awhile longer, and this time Kat didn't interrupt. "One magic bullet was supposed to have done all that. I say magic because do you know what it looked like after it was allegedly recovered on a stretcher at Parkland Hospital? Pristine, clean as a whistle, not a mark on it. Well, I don't buy that single bullet hogwash for one minute. I do not claim it was an overt coverup, but having enforced our laws for almost forty years, I am saying there were well meaning men who wanted to believe Oswald was the only one who killed Kennedy."

Kat was about to introduce a different angle, but John was not finished. "The wound in the front of Kennedy's throat was most likely a point of entry. Folks should read what the Dallas doctors said about it. To think that a lawyer came up with the idiotic single bullet theory, then went on to become a U.S. Senator and eventually Chairman of the Senate Judiciary Committee."

Kat was anxious to have Big John implicate the one man Kat blamed for hijacking her life, so to get him, a man who spent more than forty years of his life immersed in Kennedy conspiracy theories, back to her intended goal, she gently steered him. "Tell us more about the time when you changed your mind about the existence of a coverup."

His answer got closer to what she wanted, but not quite. "The more I read, and I bought every book written by every researcher until the Congress got involved in the late seventies, the more convinced I became. When the House Select Committee on Assassinations took a fresh look at who killed Kennedy, I sent my memo," he waved it in front of the camera, "one more time to the FBI."

When he stopped talking, Kat found herself wanting to extract words from his closed lips. She had major editing to get just the right kernels to the American public. Kat edged closer, leaned in as she might with a grandfather whose mind was wandering. "Then what happened?"

"I got another letter, basically saying thanks but no thanks."

Kat could wait no longer. "Who signed this letter?"

She held her breath for a good twenty seconds before Big John gave the punch line of his life, of her life. "An agent for the FBI by the name of Lars Zorn."

A smile beamed across Kat's face. She felt the camera lens on her and motioned for Ian to shift it back on John. She was thrilled. Finally she and Big John had exposed Senator Zorn, Presidential hopeful, for his part in one coverup. The second coverup she saved for later. "Is he the same Lars Zorn who is a U.S. Senator, and wants to be President?"

John crossed his arms, as if disgusted by what Zorn did to him and his evidence. "His official website says he worked for the FBI. To me it proves he is the same agent. You requested from the FBI copies of his letter, and my memo. The Bureau wrote you and told you they found zip, nada, nothing in their files. Well, I have a letter signed by Lars Zorn. Go ahead and air it. Let him deny to the American people he ever sent it to me."

Big John's face was too red for a man who recently suffered a stroke. Kat had a few more questions, but she thought it was safer to end on a high note. She reached over, shook his hand. "Thank you so much, Mr. McKenna. You have finally gotten the truth out to the American public."

Ian quit filming, and Kat handed John an ice water. Behind Ian, Kat eyed Jack, who was already coming toward them, along with her mother. She helped John to his feet. "You were great, a perfect lead-in to what my mom and I are going to do next."

FORTY THREE

After a short break for everyone, Laurel sat in the chair Kat vacated, with Kat taking Big John's place. Her mother, never looking down at any papers, held Kat's eyes with her own. Notes in her lap, Kat knew if she hoped to match her mother's poise and skill, she would have to watch and learn. Next, as if every viewer were her friend, Laurel reached out across the camera lens, and Kat watched with awe.

"Attorney and Fox News host Greta Van Susteren called the Kennedy assassination the greatest murder mystery in American history. After your investigation, Kat, what do you conclude?"

Large brown eyes turned to the camera, Kat spoke from her heart. "I want to tell viewers what the greatest murder mystery has in common with the biggest threat to our future. In an exclusive interview, U.S. Senator from Florida Olivia Hernandez told me she thinks the future danger comes from what she calls, 'radical Jihadists who want to wipe the Western world and what it stands for from the earth.'"

Ian filmed Laurel asking her next question. "What do extremists have to do with the Kennedy assassination?"

Kat's mind raced to last week's bomb exploding at Forest Grove Community Church. She looked into Jack's eyes and, for a terrible second, saw again the blood she had wiped from his face. It was unnerving to realize how close she came to losing him.

She swallowed hard, fought for composure. "Back in 1963, our intelligence agencies had information about threats that they never disclosed. I believe, as does John McKenna, that after the President's death some of those same officials covered up these red flags, the warnings of the assassination. Because people in power did not properly control their human assets or interpret intelligence, before and after the assassination, clues were ignored."

"Give an example of what you mean."

Kat looked sideways at Jack, whose smile was so wide, she was instantly at ease with him standing there and scrutinizing her work. If only she could sip water to clear her throat, which felt like it was filled with cotton. Instead, she swallowed, checked the notes in her lap.

"Since the Warren Report was released in 1964, researchers' valiant efforts have resulted in the release of more records. Here is an example of something not made public for years. In the days prior to the assassination, Dallas FBI agent James Hosty was assigned to investigate Oswald. He called at Oswald's home, met with his wife Marina. A few days later, Lee Harvey Oswald arrived at the Dallas FBI and left a note for Hosty. We will never see what he wrote."

Laurel asked, "Why?"

"Hosty was instructed by his supervisor to destroy the note after Oswald was accused of killing the President, so he tore it up and flushed it away. The agent wrote a book about his ordeal."

"Ms. Kowicki, does Detective John McKenna's evidence solve this great American mystery?"

She had discussed with Laurel how best to answer this question, while protecting national security. Kat bit down on the inside of her cheek, then wished she hadn't. Determined to edit out the fragile gesture, it was time to speak the truth.

"Our CIA had a secret program to assassinate Fidel Castro using the mafia. Recently, a German filmmaker put together a documentary, which surprisingly coincides with my theory that the Cuban government somehow discovered these secret plans and, through Oswald and other Cuban agents, got to Kennedy first. I go a step further. The evidence that Detective McKenna found proves a second gunman used a gun identical in model and make and ammunition to what Oswald allegedly used."

"So, who was this second shooter?"

With Laurel pulling words from her mouth, Kat was not sure she really liked being the "star witness" for her documentary. Thoughts of the phone taps, hidden transmitter in her apartment, and greasy man who followed her made her heart flutter. What kind of trouble would rain down on her with what she had to say next?

Hesitating, she glanced at Elliot, whose eyes and set mouth prodded her to go forward. Just this morning, he whispered he was behind her, was praying for her. His support gave Kat strength beyond her, and she found the words.

"Oswald may have pulled the trigger, but he was a patsy."

Kat took some time to educate the viewers about the accused assassin. A troubled military record, his leaving for Russia only to come back again, and allegedly trying to infiltrate pro-Cuban groups, made it easy to conclude he was the lone nut case who shot Kennedy. But Kat and Big John were convinced that, by the time Oswald left the

USSR in 1962, he was working as a double agent. In July 1962, the KGB tipped Cuba off to Oswald and in the fall of 1963, Oswald traveled to Mexico City, where he met his contact at the Cuban Embassy, who paid him roughly $6,000.00.

"To answer your question," Kat said, "the second shooter fired from the grassy knoll. So many witnesses heard shots from there, some even described seeing an unknown person who flashed an ID and claimed he was an agent. Well, he may have been an agent, just not one of ours. In my opinion, the second shooter was a Cuban intelligence officer, the same man who lived at Mrs. Pumphrey's boarding house."

Laurel added some information of her own. "More than one witness gave statements to researchers and others that confirmed a man fitting Oswald's description ran from the Depository and got into a station wagon driven by a man with a dark complexion. This adds credence to McKenna's theory there was more than one man who fired a shot. What else can you tell us about this man from the grassy knoll?"

To get everything in, yet retain the viewers' interest, Kat decided to quickly summarize and move to the second coverup. "That fateful night in November 1963, a small plane flew from Red Bird Field near Dallas. I believe it carried back to Cuba the man who shot Kennedy from the grassy knoll, the Cuban intelligence officer. It was logical for Dallas police and Secret Service to point to Oswald as the killer because the ammo they found matched his rifle."

She paused, selecting the right words. "I see it like this. If the second shooter used the same gun, the same ammo, then flew with his rifle back to Cuba, it never would be found, would it?"

Laurel brought in something Kat had nearly forgotten. "A film taken by Abraham Zapruder from the grassy knoll has been studied for years. It shows a frame-by-frame reaction by the President. His head seems to lurch backwards."

"Yes!" Kat nodded fiercely. "The motion clearly indicates a lethal shot from the front. Not only that, but Dallas police officer Tom G. Tilson Jr. saw a man slipping and sliding down the embankment on the north side of Elm Street, on the back side of the train tracks, and putting an object in the rear seat of a car and speeding away. Tilson and his daughter, who was with him, followed the car and got the license number, which he gave to the Dallas PD homicide division. When nothing resulted from his evidence, Officer Tilson contacted the House Select Committee on Assassinations in 1978. Tilson told the committee investigators that the man was conspicuous because he was the only person running away right after the shots."

Her throat parched, Kat motioned for Ian to quit filming. She reached for her water bottle and sipped. To Laurel, she whispered, "How is it going?"

"Great, but we have to tie in what the two countries gained by Kennedy's death."

"Okay. I'm ready."

With the camera once again running, Kat continued as if there was no break. In the final product, there wouldn't be. She told how during the Cuban Missile Crisis, the Soviets insisted they would remove the missiles only if Kennedy promised never to invade Cuba. "So, basically, they managed to secure a Communist country, a Soviet satellite, ninety miles off our shore. If they could neutralize Kennedy, who was a nemesis to both Khrushchev and Castro, Cuba is safe. President Johnson, who got us deeper in Vietnam, gave the Soviets free reign for their true target, making inroads into the Caribbean and South America. As we sit here talking, something as devious is happening today."

Laurel appeared interested, crossed her legs. "How so?"

Kat segued to the current coverup, the one that had targeted her. "Remember the church bombing a week ago?"

Her mother was adept at identifying with those in their homes who would watch the documentary, to be aired next week. "It was terrifying. I am sure every one watching agrees it is a miracle only the terrorist was killed."

My sources," Kat refused to glance at Jack for fear he would not approve, "won't admit it, but they don't deny it either, that the FBI's original information about the terrorists was discovered as the result of an illegal wiretap. I admit that freelance contractors who sell information to our agencies can be responsible for saving lives. The problem is they obtain this intelligence through means the government is forbidden to use."

Laurel's hazel eyes searched her daughter's, conveying that she felt as tense as Kat did; there was so much at stake. "By making this public, isn't our security being compromised?"

Kat had thought long and hard about such a result, and told the viewers so. "I hope Americans will see that, if the right intelligence had been acted upon, Oswald might have been arrested before the killing took place. We can't undo history, but we can hope to create a better future."

Laurel turned her head slightly toward Big John, who sat beyond Kat out of camera range, in one of the soft library chairs. "Detective McKenna discovered part of the truth, yet no one listened to him. All these years later, you find yourself in the same position, Ms. Kowicki."

"I am. Recently, I uncovered evidence of a conspiracy involving a shadow government. The Attorney General called a news conference announcing the arrest of former government employees who profited from snooping and eavesdropping on people only after we notified the Justice Department that we were filming this special."

Laurel gently led Kat through the ordeal of an illegal listening device on her telephone. "Someone actually ordered transcripts of your calls?"

The pain real and showing on her features, Kat struggled to place her harassment into the larger story. "I was victimized by overzealous people who once worked for the federal government. I still don't know who was after me, individuals, our government, or a politician who paid the same private contractors used by our government."

Laurel's voice reached a pitch that had a searing quality. "You realize some will claim this whole story is your personal vendetta."

Kat fired back her answer to such a charge. "First, I was contacted by Mr. McKenna before I ever knew about a tap on my phone. My research into John Kennedy's assassination may have resulted in the eavesdropping on my phones, but I can't be sure. Second, I am confident our persistence did result in these federal indictments."

Laurel set up what was coming next. "Kat, after you suspected there was a listening device on your telephone and you notified authorities, they wanted you to keep it in place, to try to catch who put it there, right?"

It seemed long ago, but her feelings were no less acute. "Yes."

Her mother continued. "But you didn't sit and wait for them to act. That is because you suspected a certain U.S. Senator, with whom you'd had a public run-in, was involved in having your phone tapped. We will show a tape, while you explain what happened as you waited for government agents to conduct their investigation."

Kat launched into her narration as if the tape Jack took at Union Station was running as it would be for viewers, with her words voiced over it. Kat had seen it so many times she knew it by heart. "I had confidence in Agent Eva Montanna's task force, having witnessed before their work on complicated cases, but I felt I had to help them catch the persons doing this to me."

Kat explained how she and her friend wanted to see if whoever was listening showed up to get an incriminating tape of a U.S. Senator. "As you see on the screen, an attractive woman is watching the meeting. Now," Kat gestured as though pointing to the video, "a young man with spiked hair is stealing the fake videotape from our table."

Kat watched her mom's eyes darken as she asked, "Were you able to identify the blonde woman who not only watched, but also photographed your meeting with your friend?"

"She is Ingrid Swanson, the Chief of Staff for Senator Zorn."

As she said it, Kat felt her life's purpose converge with her life's ambition to report the news. "I think Senator Zorn tapped my phone for his own nefarious reason. Maybe it was because he felt I would hurt his chances to become President, or maybe because John McKenna shared with me a letter signed by then-FBI Agent Zorn, who covered up the FBI's mistakes back in the 1960s."

Laurel asked a final explosive question. "When you asked Senator Zorn to comment on his letter to Mr. McKenna, what did he say?"

Kat glared into the camera for maximum effect. "Nothing. He refused to even issue a statement."

FORTY FOUR

Bile pushing up his throat, Philip Harding switched off the news, broadcast via satellite. He was angry at having to make a hasty departure from his plush Fourteenth Street office suite and his expensive house in Virginia. The former Soviet communications station leased by Harding & Associates was now his home, and he spent his days in Kazakhstan, behind a Soviet-era desk, surrounded by chain link fences and sophisticated alarm systems.

After the church-bombing arrests, Flip instructed retired ATF agent Buddy Smith to retrieve the bug at Interstate Van Conversions. In a panic, Buddy called back. His phone company contractor, Ken Kirby, now claimed the device was gone. Even more suspicious, Kirby refused to accept any new assignments.

All that night, misgiving turned to action. It was time for Flip Harding to make a surprise inspection trip to Kazakhstan. Within hours he had fled the U.S. aboard a chartered jet for a remote country bordering the northwest corner of China.

That was three days ago. From what he just saw on the news, he left none too soon. Many of the former CIA agents and federal agents that had worked for him were indicted and arrested. If he continued to play smart, putting money into the right hands, he could stay in Kazakhstan another ten years. His lease on this property, which he had paid in full, lasted that long.

An enormous amount of money went to certain Kazakh officials, who assured Flip that his permanent residency status was about to be approved. He had yet to see the papers, so he wondered if some nameless official would haul him off in the middle of the night for some "technical violation" in his newly adopted country.

One thing, which was no small thing, gave him hope, the staggering sum now secured in his Swiss bank account. Not a greedy man, Flip was proud he made use of the intricate Swiss system by gathering funds from subscribers to his *CamelotConnection* web site and depositing them into his private account.

In fact, a quick exit from the U.S. was possible because he generously paid the firm leasing him the private jet and pilots. Since he arrived in Almaty, a city where modern plumbing, shopping malls, and refrigerators stocked with gourmet foods were uncommon, a simple fact galled him. Kazakhstan was not Virginia, and extremely cold weather, which he was certain was only days away, caused his bones to start aching.

To ensure the greatest possible future comfort for him and his unhappy wife, he navigated to the Xenon Bank's home page and typed in his essential information. Quickly, he confirmed his checking account, from where he would pay his numerous contacts, had a nice balance of $217,647.03. Nowhere near what he had squirreled away in his primary account, he toggled there next and looked in horror. It was zero!

No, it could not be. There was supposed to be more than 27 million dollars in that account! In this part of the world, a few hundred thousand dollars was chump change. At this rate, he'd be living in a two-room apartment over some mechanic's garage using an outhouse.

His heart beat as fast as his fingers could fly over the keys to check the account activity. It must be a technical glitch. He held his breath. His hope destroyed, the balance still said zero.

Flip, who always had been master of his universe, scrolled to the screen showing his last payments, and stared in disbelief. There he saw a transfer from his primary account, bearing his own password. A single electronic transaction authorized a 27.4 million-dollar transfer, his life's savings, to the International Red Cross, with a note it was a "contribution."

He had no use for the Red Cross. Never in his life had he given them so much as one dollar. This alleged shift of his personal wealth must have occurred somewhere over central Asia, while he was sleeping in his leased jet. Flip sunk back into his chair, deflated, defeated. Someone had trumped him. The 27-million-dollar question burning in his brain was, who?

IN ONE OF THOSE hard-to-figure twists in life, where the sun seems to shine on the wicked when they least deserve it, Flip did not have long to mourn the loss of his money. Before noon, the call came in on his private line, a man reaching out to him from a place in Virginia, who got right to the essence of his call.

"Flip, I may be the last person you want to hear from, but Justice has a warrant for a terrorist, a Hezbollah leader. You and your covert connections are the only ones who can slip into Venezuela and retrieve him. Don't say no."

How dare he call and demand Flip do anything? The man must be insane.

Flip ignored the warning. "You forget. The Department of Justice is the reason I am hiding in a third-world country. Have you been to Kazakhstan lately? Let me remind you, it's no picnic at Rock Creek Park. Now, you want me to risk even this safe haven. Because of Alexia Kyros, I lost millions. All the money I scraped together at Xenon Bank of Switzerland is gone, gone to the International Red Cross, who thanks me for my donation of twenty-seven million."

He was warming up, had much more to say. "If that isn't bad enough, as I was arriving here, my Russian team-leader, whom you know from years ago, was declared persona non-grata and expelled from Kazakhstan. There appears no reason other than possible U.S. intervention."

The man on the other end seemed unconcerned about Flip's losses. "You owe me."

Flip rejected all such threats. "Kangas, take a hike. You should watch out, or someone like Senator Zorn will sponsor an amendment to stop the CIA from gathering overseas intelligence. Congress hasn't done it yet, so I still have a chance to make my money back through my European connections."

Kangas cut in. "Zorn is out. Seems he realized his relationship with you tainted him. He no longer wants to be President; will make it public by week's end. Don't fret over your precious money. As soon as you deliver our fugitive from Venezuela, a courier is on his way to Almaty, bringing cash to you. Ten million should help you remember you are first and foremost an American."

Spit worked its way out of Flip's mouth. "Don't lecture me on my loyalty. I started Harding and Associates because of the terrorists' attacks on 9/11. My worst nightmare is there will be another international conspiracy to kill an American President; just as the Cubans, with Russia's help, did to John F. Kennedy. I need access to the General to find out how to find his son. Luis is who you want me to snatch, right?"

That silenced Kangas, and Flip felt momentary satisfaction that he was one step ahead of the old spook.

Only at length did Kangas confide, "This is so classified, I don't want it traced back to me. The General is on a small island in the Great Lakes, with its own landing strip, under twenty-four-hour guard at our safe house. You give me a list of questions, and I'll have our people ask him. I would not hold out too much hope he can help.

The General was in prison in Cuba, so he didn't have much contact with his son."

"Oh, they had contact all right. Why do you think the former revolutionary wanted out of prison? To save the world from his son's bombs or so I heard it. Anyway, you have my word, Kangas, and you know that means something."

When Kangas started talking faster, Flip heard not fear, but urgency. "Yes, I do. We won't let the General know why we're asking. You should have your answers by this afternoon. No delays, Flip, none. I already lost time tracking you down. I want Luis San Felipe in our custody by week's end. It is imperative the terrorists who call themselves Hezbollah learn America is a formidable opponent. Send your questions via this line."

Flip prepared to end the call, feeling better than he had all morning. Ten million here, another million next week, and by the end of the year, he'd land right back where he started from.

BACK IN WASHINGTON D.C., Griff had no resolution. One call was interesting, but incomplete. He arrived in the office before eight, and Brewster's voice rang in his ear on a cell phone message. "Topping, it's Brewster. As you said, I am back where I belong. When are you coming to England to visit your grandmother? We need to talk."

One down and one to go, Griff went to find Eva and see if Kangas had given her any news about Luis San Felipe, the terrorist commander behind the church bombings.

At her desk, she gave him a worried look. "No, Griff, there has been no word and that's what troubles me. If he is not arrested, and soon, San Felipe, and his whole organization will take it as a sign of weakness on our part."

Sal came up behind him and added, "Yeah, from here we can't do much. Jack McKenna went to Luis in the Bahamas. How do you suppose he got him to travel outside his compound in Venezuela?"

On his own, Griff had thought about that plenty. He rubbed his chin, feeling the stubble. Too distracted by the need to find Luis, he hadn't shaved since yesterday. "He won't leave the security of his compound, not now, not without a very good reason."

The way Eva looked at him, and in her upbeat way said, "I hope you're not thinking what I think you are," gave him the impression what he had in mind might be possible, like it had been when the two of them went after the terrorist commander in the Indian Ocean.

Griff lifted his chin, an impish grin on his face. "Don't say no until you've heard me out. I've never been to Venezuela."

She held up her hand. "Griff, I can't let you do it."

He clenched his teeth. This time around, she was not going to be easily convinced. "Eva, just listen. There are DEA pilot-informants who fly in and out of Venezuela picking up loads of cocaine. Sal and I could fly down on one of those planes, kidnap Luis, get him to a landing strip, and take him out with the next load of drugs."

Sal slapped his fist into his palm. "Yeah, let's get him, Griff."

Equally enthused, Eva shot them down with a word, "No!"

FORTY FIVE

It was Kat's idea to come here, high above the windy streets of Chicago. She wanted the lights of the city to enthrall, to entice Jack away from constant thoughts of work. Yet, the festive atmosphere of The Signature atop the John Hancock Center, located in the heart of the Magnificent Mile, did not do what she intended. Even the fact they could look out over Lake Michigan failed to capture Jack's attention.

Kat wet her lips, feeling a bit foolish that her plans went so awry. She searched for a way to reach him, for his eyes to look into hers with some emotion. "Jack, are you sure you're feeling up to dinner? After all, you are really still recovering."

She was concerned about the purplish bruise on his cheek and around his left eye that had turned a sickly yellow. The orange light from the wall sconces behind him played off his blond hair and gave his cheeks a flushed appearance. When Jack got home from the hospital, Kat had offered to bring food by, not any she cooked, for preparing haute cuisine was not her specialty. On the sly, Big John called yesterday, suggesting Jack could use a night out. Since the church bombing, he told Kat, Jack had done nothing except work.

As a waiter in a starched white shirt and black slacks brought their drinks, diet coke with lime for Jack and raspberry water for her, Jack seemed more distracted than usual. Kat stared at the menu, recalling how negatively Jack had reacted to the luxury of her mom's home in Pentwater. Maybe the steep prices at this restaurant upset him. How she wished she had chosen a pizza place in his neighborhood.

Kat leaned toward him. "The pastry chef makes wonderful pumpkin pie. Elliot loves to order that, and the northern pike." She pointed to an entrée she thought he might like. "It comes seared, topped with jumbo lumps of crab meat."

His blue eyes kind, Jack smiled at last. "Quit trying so hard. It all looks good. Dinner is on me, so treat yourself royally."

Kat swallowed. If she had known Jack was buying, she definitely would have suggested pizza. "I thought we'd go Dutch treat, like always."

His eyes sparkled. "Tonight's not like always."

Their waiter returned. As Jack ordered for both of them, Kat sat stunned. "We'll start with a warm shrimp appetizer, to share, and then the Signature blue cheese salad. For dinner, my lady will have wild king salmon and I'll try the seared pike."

The waiter wrote nothing down. "Very good, sir. May I bring coffee?"

Before Kat could decline, Jack answered, "I will, no cream. She wants herbal tea," Jack smiled and his guess of, "peppermint, if you have it," pleased Kat to no end.

"Certainly, sir."

More than impressed, Kat realized her fears had been for nothing. He was just being quiet, studying the menu and, best of all, thinking of her. She reached over to touch his hand. "Well done. You ordered exactly what I wanted."

Was it her imagination or did his smile get bigger after her praise? She decided not to mention she did not care for shrimp; Jack could eat it all. When his hand cradled hers a moment, her heart soared higher than the ninety-five stories of the Hancock.

When she rushed to his side in the church parking lot, Kat had never been so afraid in her life. Tonight, she nurtured happiness in her heart and felt complete joy. Another second, his hand was gone, wrapped around his glass as he sipped his cola. The warmth of his skin remained; her cheeks flamed. She hoped with the low lighting, Jack would not be able to see them.

She need not have worried, he was checking out the skyline. "Look at that view. I grew up in Chicago and, until tonight, never set foot up here. Thanks for the idea, Kat."

He sounded glad to be with her. A small giggle forced its way from her lips, which she kept wetting to keep her nerves at bay. "I used to come here with Elliot, for special times when my mom was out of the country. On my sixteenth birthday, he asked the chef to bake me a chocolate cake, which even had little sparklers. I'll never forget what he told me that night."

Kat turned to look out the window, vividly remembering Elliot's encouragement to her all those years ago. "He said, 'See the city? You can own it, Kat, plus the whole world, and I'll help you get it.'"

She sought Jack's eyes, and a serious look flashed in them. He set down his glass. "Yet, Elliot brought you back here, against your will it seems. That first time we talked, you implied you wanted nothing to do with Chicago. How do you feel now?"

Just then, her cell phone whirled against her waistband. She had muted the phone, but not turned it off, just in case. Her LED screen said "private," which could mean it was Laurel or Elliot. She had been trying to reach both with no success.

"Jack, this might be my mom. Do you mind?" His, "Not at all," gave Kat permission to flip open the phone.

Laurel was all apologies for not calling sooner. "Elliot and I are, well, we're in Vienna."

As hard as she tried, Kat could not keep down her voice. "Vienna, as in Virginia?"

The diners at the next table gaped at her, frowning because Kat disturbed their meal.

Laurel gushed, "Congratulate us, honey. Elliot and I are in Vienna, Austria, to celebrate our marriage."

Intense feelings assailed her, rendering Kat speechless. Her mother was once again pushing Kat from her life. She wanted to throw down the telephone, run to the ladies' room.

When Jack touched her hand, it felt like he burned her. "Kat is everything all right?"

A hard lump in her throat threatened to block out any words at all, but she said, "They're married."

A question mark planted itself on Jack's face, but he kept his hand on hers, which gave her a measure of courage. "Mom, Jack and I are having dinner on the top of the Hancock building. I wish you had invited me to your wedding, but I hope you both will be very happy."

Her mother's clear laugh was beautiful. "I can't believe this is happening. One minute Elliot and I are debriefing your documentary and the next he asks me to marry him. Kat, I *am* inviting you, and Jack. We're still just getting the paperwork together. Next Saturday, we will be married at Saint Stephen's Cathedral. Will you come?"

How could she even think Laurel had rejected her after how close they had become? This time she whispered, tears pricking her eyes, "I'll ask Jack. Of course, I would not miss your marriage to Elliot. Tell him I'll come."

Her mother sounded relieved. "Wonderful. I want you for my maid of honor. Find something pink to wear, if you can. My suit is simple ivory silk, but I plan to carry an armful of pink roses. Elliot booked us separate suites and there is one for each of you when you arrive."

As the waiter arrived with the appetizer, Kat promised her mom to check on flights as soon as possible and call back with the details. Before she hung up, Jack had eaten all but one shrimp. Kat silently closed her phone, pointing to the lone piece still on the plate. "You eat it. I'm suddenly not hungry."

Jack reached over, took her fork and stabbed the grilled appetizer. "Nonsense, and waste this good food? If your mom is married, I'm happy for her. She's living her life and I am sure she wants you to live yours."

He handed her the shrimp to eat, which she did. Strange how Jack convinced her to do things she did not want to do, but when she did them, things turned out better than she thought. With a hint of garlic butter, the shrimp was delicious.

"They're not married."

"Oh? I thought you said they were."

Kat felt silly, always jumping to conclusions. If only she could learn *not* to act on impulse. A sigh escaped her dry lips. "I know. I misunderstood. They are making the arrangements, and the wedding is next Saturday. You are invited, too. Can you come?"

"I don't see why not. Where is it going to be—Forest Grove Church? The chapel was untouched."

At that comment Jack's expression changed and he seemed to withdraw. She imagined just mentioning the church took him back to the bomb explosion and his narrow escape. Suddenly, Kat understood why Elliot and Laurel were making plans to be married. She vividly recalled crouching on the asphalt, holding Jack's head, and reflected that life was precious, too precious to waste chasing after a Pulitzer prize or some other notoriety.

A smile quivered on her lips. "Somehow I think they are looking for a safer place to exchange their vows—it will be at St. Stephen's Cathedral."

He looked perplexed. "I don't know that church. Is it in Wilmette?"

Kat could hide her glee no longer. "No, it's in Vienna, Austria. Are you cleared to travel that far? Elliot has reserved us each a suite at the Ritz."

The ubiquitous waiter set a salad in front of them, sprinkled with pancetta and blue cheese. Kat wondered if Jack would fly to Austria; it would be fun to tour Vienna together. Jack gave no answer. Instead, he cut into the iceberg lettuce wedge, scraping his knife on the plate. At the screeching sound, she shuddered, and ate a crumble of blue cheese.

Jack was sampling his salad. "This bacon is good. By the way, I talked to Eva Montanna recently."

"You heard from her again?"

"Eva called to ask for my help on a new case."

He kept eating, and kept Kat in suspense. She toyed with her salad, trying not to worry about Jack going after terrorists again.

"Kat—" he set down his knife, balancing it on the edge of the plate. What Jack said next shocked her almost as much as Laurel's sudden news. "She wants me to join their task force in Washington."

Kat's fork slipped from her hands onto the carpet. Instantly, the waiter returned with a fresh one. Kat drew in a breath, and let it out slowly. "What did you say?"

He shrugged. "I haven't decided, not yet."

It was now or never, Kat told herself; she had nothing to lose. "Jack, I have to tell you something that I've been trying to say ever since last Sunday. If you don't care to hear it, so be it. I know how Elliot and my mom feel. After I almost got blown away, too—" for courage, she sipped some hot tea that just arrived, "I do not want to wait to live my life, get married, and have children."

Jack looked stonily into her eyes. "Did you and Randy get back together?"

He looked away, back to the city lights below. If she were going to marry Randy, which she wasn't, she sensed Jack would be sad about it. His reaction gave her hope, prompted her next step. "Jack, look at me."

When his eyes locked onto hers, she said as tenderly as she felt, "It's not Randy I love. It's you."

A light shone in his eyes and he grinned from ear to ear. "Kat, for weeks, I've been fighting my feelings for you. Not just because of my broken engagement with Melissa," he drank some coffee, as if he also had to bolster his nerve to speak. "You and I are alike in many ways, but we're different, and I don't mean just our jobs. You always told me you wanted nothing more than to go back to Washington."

Emotions flooded her mind. Jack was saying he cared for her. "Yes, but now you're the one who's thinking about going to D.C., not me. If there's a chance for me with you, I don't care if I live in Chicago, Washington—or Pentwater."

The waiter appeared at the exact wrong time, forcing Kat to hold back her feelings in the exchange of half-eaten salads for their dinners. The scent of citrus and grilled fish lingered in the air, but Kat only picked at her food. If only there was a way to keep the waiter from appearing every minute with more water and coffee. When he filled their glasses, she took matters in her own hands. "Thank you. We're fine for now." Her severe look said *please leave us alone.*

"Very good, my lady." He turned on his heel and headed back to the kitchen.

"Thank heavens. He's out of our hair for awhile."

Jack ate all the lump crabmeat topping his fish. "You've brought up the very subject I'd like to talk about."

Fork in hand, Kat stared at Jack. "Our waiter?"

His smile was playful. "Not in a million years. What I mean is Heaven. After you and I came so close to death—and we did, Kat, there is no denying it—I started to wonder: Do you care where you will be when that day does come?"

His entire spirit reached for her and Kat was intimidated by the power of it. Jack had a way of exuding such assurance in life; she wanted to be like him. More than that, she wanted to bring him happiness for the rest of her life. But could she, would he let her?

She sensed that her answer would determine if Jack wanted to be with her. The lights of Chicago shimmering below, Kat chose her words carefully. "I think I understand what you are asking me."

Her mouth was dry from nervousness, but still she didn't dare to ruin the moment by stopping to take a drink. "Not too long ago, Elliot tried to explain to me what happened to him just before his crash. As his plane was going down, he called out to God to save his pilot, Mark. For some reason, Elliot was saved instead, and he is convinced it was because God was giving him another chance to make his life right."

Jack's slight nod showed he was listening, but he let her continue. "Elliot knows I wasn't ready to lose him, either. He's like a father to me. Jack, something weird happened that I've never told anyone except Elliott and Laurel. After the crash, I called my mom to tell her, and she told me she had prayed and she *knew* Elliot was going to survive. A little later, there was a doctor in Elliott's room, not the same doctor who told me Elliott needed an MRI. This one's name was Doctor Semeion, and he assured me that Elliot would not need an MRI, because Elliott was healed." Kat leaned forward so that no one but Jack could hear. "The hospital has no record of Doctor Semeion. When the attendant came right after to take Elliott away for his MRI, they checked him again and all his vital signs were normal. He was somehow cured."

"I wonder if you met an angel."

Goosebumps rippled up and down her arms. How could Kat explain what the power, the miracles meant to her when she did not understand it all herself? First, Elliot survived a plane crash and then a homicidal maniac. The first time she ever went to church, at Forest Grove, her life, too, was spared; and there had to be some very important reason.

Jack's blue eyes were inquisitive, no warm; oh, they were so blue and inviting. With her own, Kat sought to convey the profound feelings she had for him, which went well beyond gratitude for his heroic act. Something, a desire to be true, released within her, and words poured forth, words that might change her life forever. "Until coming back here to Chicago, I actually believed I had almost everything I dreamed of except for one thing. I wanted the fame my mom achieved with her career. Only, I had no moral compass."

She dropped her eyes. "One by one, the things I once held dear have fallen away."

"I'm thankful you did come to Chicago." Jack slipped a strong hand over hers, the warmth of it so real.

Was it a touch of friendship or something more? Kat dared not move even a finger for fear that deadlines, uncaught criminals, or some unforeseen urgent matter would wreck this moment, and she would never find it with him again. While it might not make sense tonight, she had to tell him what else was in her heart.

"Jack," her smile was more of a tremble, "I know there is a powerful force beyond me. Elliot told me how after the crash and before he awoke in the hospital, Jesus came to him, *spoke* to him. I won't pretend I know what I need to know, but my life is empty spiritually, and I want to fill it with the truth. At Forest Grove, I got a good look at my shallow character, but I also got a glimpse into the holiness of God that I never knew."

Kat blinked, moistening her eyes. A quick swallow helped her release the few words she had yet to say, "I was hoping we could build a life together, but I guess you're not ready if, as you say, you're struggling with your feelings for me."

She wanted to ask why, but she stopped talking to give Jack time to think. She had already revealed too much. If he was going to reject her, let him be done with it. Kat would go to Austria and convince Elliot to give her another chance in Washington, where she would pick up the pieces of her life, knowing God had something else in store for her.

Jack picked up where she left off. "Kat, I made a mistake with Melissa. I wanted to be sure my love for you is returned. It's important our love is grounded by a common faith. Too many couples break up when they believe only in themselves. Kat, I—"

His cell phone rang; he must have forgotten to place it on mute. He looked at the screen. "This is Eva."

Her dread that the spell would be broken was realized. He took the call, leaving Kat hanging on his every word, only to be disappointed. This time she could not hear Eva's voice, and all Jack said was, "Okay, sure," then, "I'll be there."

When he hung up, Kat blurted, "What's it all about? Where do you have to go?"

Jack secured his phone in its case. "I guess I won't be flying to Austria with you."

Her heart buckled and she waited, just knowing worse news was coming.

Jack lowered his voice. "I'm off to Washington to debrief a major terrorist. In here, I can't say more." He grabbed her hand again. "Before we were interrupted—and Kat, I *had* to take that call—I was about to say, I am a Chicago cop through and through. I may go to Washington temporarily, but I cannot imagine living there for keeps. Could you be happy here?"

Did he mean it? There was a chance for them. Her voice trembled with the intensity that filled her heart and soul. "Please forget what I said back in May. I was a different person. The glamour of Washington has worn off. We can thank Senator Zorn for that." She squeezed his hand. "Our dinner is cold, but I don't care. I want you to know Jack, that I can only be happy where you are."

"You can give up covering national politics, be content broadcasting the news of the Chicago River turning green on St. Patrick's Day?"

Kat was learning to laugh at his jokes. "Funny, how I used to hate green. Now, it's practically my favorite color."

Jack was not finished. "And you can face nights alone when I am undercover, maybe getting shot at?"

She pulled on his arm, "Jack, I know I can. But can *you* believe that?"

That question seemed to startle him. "Let's get the bill. I want out of here."

Crushed, Kat wondered what she said wrong this time. She was always blundering with her impetuousness. A minute later, they got onto the elevator and the doors closed. Alone, Jack pulled her into his arms, kissed her lightly on the lips.

She loved that kiss, but loved even more what he whispered in her ear. "Mary Katherine, I was so afraid I would not make it in time to save your life. You and I are meant to be together, for always."

EPILOGUE

Their target was plucked from Venezuela without Griff ever setting foot in the South American country. He would never know exactly how Luis San Felipe was snatched or who it was that grabbed him. Once in the U.S. San Felipe was brought to the Alexandria City Jail, where U.S. Marshals agreed to lodge him in Virginia.

Griff wanted this terrorist punished for plotting to kill thousands of Americans. He had to be arraigned in Chicago, but first it was up to Griff and Jack McKenna to interrogate him in Alexandria about the church bombing. At Reagan National Airport, Jack's plane was late and Griff waited in view of a television monitor for him to arrive.

He wasn't watching the news, though. Griff was grumbling to himself about how the sudden arrest of Luis had interfered with his plans to fly to Florida to see Dawn for Thanksgiving. In many ways, it was a big letdown—his personal life on hold again because of work. Still, he and Jack were both single, so they didn't leave wives and children alone to eat turkey without them.

When he wrapped this up, Griff planned to take a week's vacation, first going to London to catch up with Brewster Miles at MI-5, eat fish and chips, and see the sights—Tower of London, Buckingham Palace, the whole works. Then he was taking the train to Cornwall to visit his grandmother. The last time he was there, she was using a cane and seemed frail, her life ebbing away.

Winter was coming early, the forecast said so, but that didn't mean it had to be a cold and lonely season in his life. Grandma Topping was a large part of who he was, and he was bringing his tape recorder along to record her stories of World War II. He recently talked to Eva about her Grandpa Marty's stories about the Dutch resistance, and the two of them planned to write it all down. A magazine on military history he read on the plane to Kazakhstan had given him the idea.

A long forty minutes later, passengers spilled into the arrival area. Griff recognized the Chicago detective, offered a friendly wave. In moments, they exchanged handshakes and greetings.

Jack hoisted a carry-on bag over his shoulder. "This is it. I travel light."

Griff laughed. "A man after my own heart. In this heavy snow, I'm surprised your flight even landed. If we get moving, maybe we can beat the twelve inches being forecast."

"I think I'm glad you're driving. Hey, I appreciate your wanting my help to interrogate Luis. My guess is he'll recognize me from my undercover meet in Norman's Cay, and realize our case against him is rock solid."

They were about to leave the arrival area when a television above their heads broadcast a special alert. Both men stopped to listen.

"A suspected mastermind of the church bombing has been arrested in the United States for plotting to blow up six churches nationwide. There is no official reaction from the White House, and the Justice Department is refusing to say how Luis San Felipe, linked to Hezbollah, happens to be in the country. He left Cuba years ago for Venezuela. Both foreign governments deny any knowledge of San Felipe or the bombing."

Griff had an idea how Luis got out. "My guess is the CIA extracted our man from Venezuela, maybe even with Philip Harding's help."

What Jack said next surprised Griff, gave him something to think about, not only on the treacherous drive to the jail, but also in the weeks and months to come. "I know one thing. After seeing Kat's piece on what my dad knew about the Kennedy Assassination, there's no question in my mind that Cuba was more deeply involved in JFK's death than our government let on to the public. But casting the blame on Oswald and calling him a nut case who acted alone probably saved us from all-out war with the Soviets."

They started for the exit, and as automatic glass doors opened, a blast of icy snow pelted their faces. Jack tightened his collar around his neck. "Griff, I have to ask, how involved do you think the Cuban regime is in this latest act of terror? I don't think it's any accident San Felipe grew up in Cuba and now resides in Venezuela. Both regimes are sworn enemies of our country."

Griff tented his hands to protect his eyes from the stinging snow and both men hustled to the car in silence, eager to get out of the cold wind. The last time Griff strode beside Jack it was in Chicago, where they were jumped after finding the diverter on Kat's phone, the night Griff lost his expensive equipment. Though it seemed that the CIA was behind the Union Station caper, Griff hadn't a clue who mugged him and Jack.

He opened the locks, stowed Jack's gear in the trunk. Inside the car, it took a while to get the temperature comfortable. "Jack, you and I are going to get a chance to give Luis the grilling of a lifetime. Maybe God will smile on our nation one more time and Luis will realize his evil plans have come to an end."

Jack directed the heat vent to his face. "On Norman's Cay, I sensed he was up to something more than running drugs. We thought we devised sufficient precautions to protect the public while getting as far as we could into his organization. I don't have to tell you how close we were to a lot more dead than just one terrorist."

Traffic was barely moving in the snow. Griff turned the radio on. "Maybe there's more news about the man we're going to visit in jail."

They caught nothing but a bunch of commercials, so he turned down the sound. Jack was just asking about Eva and the rest of the team when Griff heard a name that caused him to ramp up the volume again.

The reporter was saying, "Dmitri Federov, you were once with the KGB, then made a name for yourself brokering lucrative oil and gas deals between the U.S. and Russia. You say you are ready to tell the truth of what happened with the Kennedy assassination. Why come forward after all these years?"

Jack started to talk about Luis San Felipe, but Griff hushed him. "This man I want to hear."

Federov's answer surprised even Griff, who until moments ago wanted to see Federov destroyed for what he did in Kazakhstan.

"It is time for the truth, the whole truth, to be told. The other day, I saw a news special by an American reporter, Kat Kowicki. Her conclusions were so close that I felt it was my duty to confirm she was right. The Cuban regime did receive Oswald's name from Russian KGB and was only too happy to encourage him to kill the President."

"Mr. Federov, did Oswald act alone?"

The Russian's voice boomed over the radio. "No, he did not."

"Will you identify the other shooter or shooters?"

Federov cleared his throat. "I do so in my book, which comes out in January. Let us wait for that, please. I can tell you that Cuba had a matching rifle, just like the retired Chicago Detective said. All the reports of a plane flying from Cuba into Dallas and back again are true."

"Aren't you afraid, Mr. Federov, of retribution from your former colleagues?"

"No, I do not fear for myself. Your country owes a great deal to the freedom of the press and I want to see it stay that way."

Griff switched off the radio. Out of the corner of his eye, he saw Jack's head leaning against the headrest. He had not even told Eva what Federov put him through when he flew into Almaty. With Federov praising Kat's documentary even if it was to sell his pending book, he felt it appropriate to tell Jack of his ordeal.

"Jack, I have a story to tell you and would like your opinion on what, if anything, I should do."

Jack listened to Griff's tale all the way to the Alexandria City Jail, where in moments the two would meet with the Hezbollah terrorist. Griff felt enormous relief sharing how Federov held him hostage, and how he sought justice by letting the Kazakh Ambassador think that Federov was tapping his telephone, which resulted in Federov's ejection from that country.

Griff kept the bucar idling for warmth. "Now hearing him laud Kat, when the company he worked for was behind tapping her phones, makes me think he is not so bad after all. Do you believe I was right to use deception to find justice?"

In the dim afternoon light, snow dancing across the windshield, Jack seemed thoughtful. "There is no doubt Federov broke the law. The company he worked for, Harding, or Camelot, or whatever, caused mountains of grief for a woman I hold dear. I think you were right. If suddenly he has found a conscience, God may have used your actions to help bring it about. Like in the Old Testament, when Israelite spies hid their identities to avoid capture, and a woman named Rahab lied to protect them."

Griff killed the motor, took his keys and both men got out of the car. This was not the first time he'd been told God used him for some greater purpose, but it seemed hard to believe. "You've got a point there. At least now Kat has another credible source backing up not only her story, but your father's as well. I'd like to see his reaction to Federov's interview."

Jack laughed and nearly fell on snow accumulating on the pavement under his feet. Stepping more carefully, he raised his voice so that Griff could hear. "Not just my dad. I cannot wait to call Kat and tell her that she absolutely nailed what she calls the Camelot Conspiracy. Oh, and Griff, I've asked Kat to marry me. We'd like you to be in the wedding party come spring."

Griff opened the outer door to the jail, holding it for Jack to go through. Marveling at the streetwise Chicago cop who, at the end of the day, relied on God for ultimate justice, he grinned, slapped him on on the back and said, "I'll be there."

As he prepared to confront the hate that some men harbored for those who did not believe as they did, Griff surely hoped Jack was right and that the season of reckoning for Federov, San Felipe—and so many other enemies who never seemed to stop coming—really was at hand.

WHEN THE THICK SNOW FELL, Eva ran out in the yard, scooped up balls of snow and tossed them with Scott and the children. Their snowball fight lasted until their daughter Kaley dropped to the ground to make a snow angel, something Eva taught her to do when she was little. It was great fun making new memories with her family.

This morning's drive into the city turned out to be a slippery mess and gave Eva one giant headache. The special task force had disassembled and each of its members was back at their own agency. At her desk at ICE headquarters, Eva got to work on her new mission. She was the liaison agent with Congress to enact legislation to secure the U.S. borders against illegal immigrants and terrorists. While not as exciting as some things she had done, it was just as important.

A phone call had surprised her. It was Alexia Kyros, the Attorney General, telling Eva to expect to hear from Wilt Kangas at the CIA. That was all she said. Eva went back to her computer, but two minutes later her phone rang and when an efficient-sounding female announced, "Please hold for Mr. Kangas," Eva wondered what new crisis was about to unfold.

"Good morning, Eva."

Despite his informality, she could not help but recall how abrupt he was in their previous conversation. Kangas was a man accustomed to people deferring to him, so her reply was respectful. "Same to you, Sir."

"Eva, I want to thank you for your stellar handling of the plea for help by our Cuban General. Less experienced agents might have dismissed his call as a prank, but your quick referral to Bo Ryder was the right thing to do. We at the Agency have you to thank."

She felt her face flush warm. "I think I did what anyone else on the Committee would have done. At the time, the General seemed so desperate, I could not ignore him."

Eva expected him to say good-bye, but Kangas seemed happy to continue. "No, Eva, you did much more. Bo assures me this is your nature. You and I both know some agents would have tried to parlay the call into a promotion."

Not one for accolades, Eva pondered what was behind the Deputy Director's effusive compliments. She did not wait long to find out.

"I called you today for two reasons. First, someone else wants to thank you personally, and my secretary will connect you to him."

Her heart skipped a beat. Was it the President? Was she going to be tapped for another special task force? Eva reigned in her mind; she was getting ahead of herself. Kangas was still talking.

"Secondly, only the very best public servants rise to the top. You are one of these, one of our patriots. You are in a special class."

He stopped, so Eva slipped in a thank you, thinking now he would transfer her call. She was wrong. In fact, she heard him take in a big breath.

"Agent Montanna, you are aware that each year the President issues pardons. Sometimes it is done without much attention. I've just spoken with the President and he will be issuing one for a man, who like you, is a patriot."

Where was Kangas going with this? Eva put down her coffee cup with a feeling that whoever was on the end of this particular Presidential pardon, she was not going to like it. It could not be the President was going to pardon General San Felipe's son. That was too awful to contemplate.

"Although you and your task force gathered sufficient evidence against Philip Harding, tomorrow he will receive a full preemptive pardon, before he is ever indicted. I don't intend to discuss with you the merits of your case or the pardon, other than to say, that you would not be speaking to your next caller, but for the invaluable assistance we've received from Philip Harding."

Eva was speechless, but in retrospect, she should not have been surprised. When she said nothing, Kangas asked, "Do you have any questions?"

Not about to argue with a man of Kangas's importance, Eva walked a fine line of telling him off and respecting the Constitution, which she held dear. "Sir, we agents focus on enforcing our laws. You and the President have a broader mission. I understand that gathering intelligence in an age of terror is not black and white. Sir, permit me to say I only hope that if I make a major blunder in carrying out my duties, the President will be as kind to me as he has been to your colleague."

Kangas seemed to take her remarks in stride. "Thank you, Eva. I appreciate your understanding. Stay on the line for your next call."

Before Eva could figure out why Kangas sought to soften her up, his secretary said, "One moment Agent Montanna."

Without even an audible click, suddenly she heard, "Hello Mrs. Montanna?"

"Yes, this is Eva." It took a moment to register. His was a voice from her past. Was it possible? How wonderful! This time his voice was stronger, yet the accent was the same.

"I am not permitted to tell you my new name. But 'dis is the same man who called you from the hospital in Cuba."

Tears pricked her eyes and a smile lit Eva's face. "I am so happy to hear from you again. I hope things are better for you now."

He breathed a short laugh into the phone. "Mrs. Montanna, I am slowly gaining back my strength. I cannot say where, but I will live in your country, where the climate is like where I lived before. Also, I have a sadness, but you are not to blame."

Eva was quick to listen. "Is there something I can do for you?"

He told her, "I heard you worked on the case against my son. You know, I did all I could for him before the Cuban regime imprisoned me. His mother and I did not raise him to turn out as he did. I am so sorry."

Eva felt a lump catch in her throat. He was imprisoned for turning his back on communism, for wanting democracy on the tiny island. That he was kept alive all these years was miraculous. She'd like to meet him one day, but that might compromise his security. "Sir, you are safe now. You need not apologize to me."

She heard his soft, "Thank you so much for taking my call that day. Now I will live the rest of my days a free man. May God bless you."

"He already has, Sir, by your freedom and this phone call."

Silence, then she heard him say, "Yes. There is something I must tell you, something I did not tell the man who just connected me to you, something that makes me feel trapped."

Eva's heart skipped a beat. Did he know of a pending terror attack, one the FBI had not stopped? She asked carefully, "How can I help?"

"Hear me first, then decide. On September 7, 1963, Fidel Castro told a reporter a warning that was printed in all major U.S. newspapers. I am afraid that what he said caused a violent act."

That was two months before Kennedy was assassinated. She had to know more. "What did Castro say?"

"Because of possible attempts on his life, he said, 'United States leaders should think if they're aiding terrorist plans to eliminate Cuban leaders, they themselves will not be safe.'"

Castro said that? Eva had never heard of it before. "Are you suggesting his statement may have incited Oswald or others to kill President Kennedy?"

The General's sigh was lengthy. "I have always thought those words were a code, a call for Oswald and his team to act. Only God knows how this has haunted me."

Before Eva could reply, there was a click and General San Felipe was gone. She gripped the telephone receiver in her hand for some time, thinking of all that had happened, and what she should do with the incredible revelation she just heard. Suddenly her mind turned to, of all things, snow. When it fell yesterday, the world around her became a lovely white. Everything in her life seemed fresh and new. Last night over cups of cocoa, she told Scott she had finally put behind her the ache from fellow agents gone bad.

And then this morning, when she went outside to snatch the newspaper from the driveway before it got all wet, she saw her white world was vanishing. Where snow had lain in big clumps, patches of brown grass poked through, and dirty muck from passing cars marred the once spectacular beauty.

When Kangas called to say Harding was getting a pardon, her heart sunk within her, only to be lifted talking with the General, except now she was perplexed about what to do. Both men were being freed, in different ways. The General would live with the pain of a wayward son and a past that could not be mended. Harding would have the stain of needing a Presidential pardon.

If she learned anything from the past few months, she should not let days of black slush overwhelm the good in her life, not even the sizzling truth she just learned. While San Felipe said it was his opinion the words were codes, Eva knew all too well terrorists used reporters to broadcast taped messages to their followers to begin their attacks, including 9/11.

She had precious gifts of her family and faith. No matter how tough her job got, how many acts of violence she thwarted or not, they were real. On a whim, she slid her cell from her waistband and punched in a number.

Scott answered, kept his voice low, just for her. "Eva, I'm on my way to a meeting with the Secretary about China's hacking into our Defense Department strategic planning system."

Eva respected Scott's work schedule, but just now she had something more urgent in mind. "Okay, don't talk just listen. We need to go on vacation, with the kids, and Scott, I want to go where there is snow, lots of heavenly white snow!"

A Note from the Authors: On Fact and Fiction

We write fiction to entertain. We also like to conduct research and include historical facts to enlighten as it fits the story. In *The Camelot Conspiracy*, we include many historical facts about the assassination of President John F. Kennedy, but we also have added fictive elements for the sake of the story line. So that readers won't be confused about the facts of the Kennedy assassination, we provide the following disclaimer for history's sake:

The element of the second Mannlicher-Carcano rifle and ammunition found by fictional character Big John McKenna is for entertainment and to show how the assassination could have been accomplished. All references to that evidence, including the fictional Senator Lars Zorn's involvement while an FBI agent, are invented.

U.S. Senator Arlen Specter, R-PA, was a Philadelphia prosecuting attorney on loan to the Warren Commission in 1964 and the reputed author of the single bullet theory. The reports of witnesses who claimed sightings near Dealey Plaza in Dallas are taken from the historical record, as are the testimony of Deputy Sheriff Roger Dean Craig and other police officers who reported seeing Lee Harvey Oswald getting into a station wagon, and Dallas police officer Tom G. Tilson, Jr., who saw a man running with an object and getting into a car on the back side of the train tracks behind the grassy knoll. FBI Agent James Hosty, who has written a book about his experience with Oswald, is a recognized historical figure. The facts about Oswald, including his military record and his contact with Soviet and Cuban embassies in Mexico is factual. The reference to a Cuban official on a private plane from Mexico to Dallas at the time of the assassination is taken from the research record.

While the creation of the Cuban General Raul San Felipe and his terrorist son, Luis, was for your entertainment, the German documentary is real. We found references to it as we were looking for more evidence to substantiate the theory of Big John and Kat that the Cuban regime was behind.John F. Kennedy's death. Wilfried Huismann's documentary is entitled, "Rendezvous with Death," and, to our knowledge, as of this writing is not available in the United States.

The Sixth Floor Museum, located at the old Texas School Book Depository in Dallas is a treasure trove of information about the assassination, and we highly recommend a tour. The books mentioned by Kat are all worth reading as are many others on the subject, too numerous to mention here.

—Diane and David Munson

ABOUT THE AUTHORS

Diane Munson has been an attorney for more than twenty years. She served the U.S. Department of Justice as an Assistant U.S. Attorney in Washington, D.C., where as a Federal Prosecutor she brought indictments, tried criminal cases, and argued appeals. Earlier, she served the Reagan Administration, appointed by Attorney General Edwin Meese, as Deputy Administrator of the Office of Juvenile Justice and Delinquency Prevention. She worked with the Justice Department, the U.S. Congress, and the White House on major policy and legal issues.

More recently she has been in a solo general practice specializing in mediation and representing children and parents in cases of neglect and abuse.

David Munson served as a Special Agent with the Naval Investigative Service, U.S. Customs, and U.S. Drug Enforcement Administration over a 27-year career. During his career he conducted many investigations and often assumed undercover roles. He infiltrated international drug smuggling organizations. In this role he traveled with drug dealers, met their suppliers in foreign countries, helped fly their drugs to the U.S., then feigned surprise when shipments were seized by law enforcement. Later his true identity was revealed when he testified against the group members in court.

While assigned to DEA headquarters in Washington, D.C., David served two years as a Congressional Fellow on the Senate Permanent Subcommittee on Investigations.

As they travel to research and cloister to write, they thank the Lord for the blessings of faith and family. David and Diane Munson are collaborating on their next novel.

www.DianeAndDavidMunson.com

Facing Justice

First in the Justice series, Diane and David Munson draw on their true-life experiences in this suspense novel about Special Agent Eva Montanna, whose twin sister died at the Pentagon on 9/11. Eva dedicates her career to avenge her death while investigating Emile Jubayl, a member of Eva's church and CEO of Helpers International, who is accused of using his aid organization to funnel money to El Samoud, head of the Armed Revolutionary Cause, and successor to Al Qaeda. Family relationships are tested in this fast-paced, true-to-life legal thriller about the men and women who are racing to defuse the ticking time bomb of international terrorism.

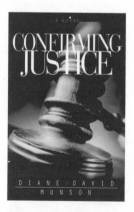

ISBN-13: 978-1932902495
352 pages, trade paper
Fiction / Mystery and Suspense
12.99

Confirming Justice

All eyes are focused on Federal judge Dwight Pendergast, rumored to be in line for nomination to the Supreme Court, who is presiding over a bribery case involving the son of a cabinet secretary. When the key prosecution witness disappears, FBI agent Griff Topping is brought in to find him. In a race against time, the agent risks everything to save the case while opponents of the nomination attempt to expose deeply held family secrets concerning the judge. Soon the world is watching as events unfold that threaten the powerful position and those who covet it.

Confirming Justice is the second in the Justice Series by Diane and David Munson. Featuring a mix of plot twists, legal intrigue and fast-paced suspense, Confirming Justice is sure to be a popular and satisfying read for those wanting a realistic portrayal of what can go on behind the scenes at the center of power.

ISBN-13: 978-1932902594
352 pages, trade paper
Fiction / Mystery and Suspense
12.99